MOONLIGHT SEDUCTION

Cami glanced up through her lashes to steal a peek at the imposing stranger coming toward her. Her heart began to beat faster. He was tall and bold, dressed all in black except for his ruffled white shirt and the gold embroidery sparkling on his vest. She was struck by the dark gleam of his eyes.

Victoine Navar! . . . Cami mumbled her way through the formalities. All through their small talk, she could feel Black Vic's smoldering eyes on her—eying her charms, scheming, planning her seduction, she surmised. The thoughts brought a hot flush to her face and shoulders and even more heat beneath her shimmering gown.

"Mademoiselle, your aunt has given her permission." Vic offered Cami a low bow, then a winning smile. "May I have this dance?"

"Oui, monsieur," Cami murmured, trembling with a mixture of terror and excitement.

She all but swooned when he took her hand. At close range, he was even more handsome. Just looking at him made her want to turn and flee. His slightest touch electrified her. His low, husky voice caressed her. With power and grace he led her confidently through each step of the dance, making her feel totally dependent, a virtual captive of his masculine spell. But the more entranced she became, the harder she fought the attraction. No man should be allowed to do this!

Although permission for one dance was all Fiona had given, Vic refused to give up his claim on Cami, monopolizing her for the entire evening. It seemed that the cooler her demeanor, the more fascinated Vic became.

Cami, meanwhile, found it increasingly difficult to keep her icy distance. As the evening wore on, she became more and more aware of her partner's amorous intentions. His loving approach began slowly. A bit more pressure on her gloved fingers, a casual touch to her cheek, a whispered endearment now and again. Then, during one intermission, he enticed her out onto the balcony.

He sidled close and slipped his hand around her waist. Cami caught her breath, frozen with fearful uncertainty. She stood rigidly still as she felt his arm surround her. Very gently, he forced her to turn toward him. He said nothing, just stared down at her—his face was solemn, almost tense, and his dark eyes gleamed with an unsettling emotion.

One minute Cami was standing before him and the next his lips were on hers. The kiss lasted only a moment, but its imprint was scorched into her soul.

"You needn't be shy with me," he whispered. "I will take good care of you, *ma chère*." His words were a heartfelt promise. "Come with me and you will be loved—no, adored."

This was it—the moment she had always been waiting for . . .

Becky
Lee Weyrich
Whispers In Time

PINNACLE BOOKS
WINDSOR PUBLISHING CORP.

PINNACLE BOOKS

are published by

Windsor Publishing Corp.
475 Park Avenue South
New York, NY 10016

First Printing: March, 1993

Printed in the United States of America

To my sister, Sara,
who, after all these years, is still
the only other member of the Bacardi Club.
Enough said!

Author's Note

VANISHED!

Although *Whispers in Time* is wholly a work of fiction, the fabric of this story is based on the eerie and inexplicable fact that people vanish off the face of the earth every day, never to be seen or heard from again. What happens to these mysteriously missing beings?

A four-year-old boy, separated from his mother at a busy mall, disappears without a trace. Kidnapping? An elderly couple on vacation stops at a motel for the night and are never seen again. Murder? A Navy pilot on a routine mission flies into the Bermuda Triangle, but not out of it. Plane crash? A farmer walks into his field, but fails to come home to supper. Abduction by a UFO?

What really happened to these people? Can we account for their disappearances logically or did they all simply *vanish into thin air*, perhaps into another time?

Vanishings, a volume of Time-Life Books Library of Curious and Unusual Facts, has this to say on the subject: "The possibility of being made to vanish, to lose one's very self, taps such deep human fears that, in ages past, people blamed the devil or other dark forces for unexplained disappearances . . . In the United States alone, about one million people are added to the missing persons rolls each year . . . Their disappearances often occur without visible motive, defy every rational explanation, and thwart even the most diligent investigator."

In his fascinating work, *Great Southern Mysteries*, E. Randall Floyd writes: "Each year, thousands of Americans vanish into oblivion without a trace . . . Of the estimated ten million Americans who are reported missing each year, about 95 percent eventually return or are accounted for within a few days. Five percent vanish forever."

Here are a few among the mysteriously missing:

Charles and Catherine Romer, on their way home from Miami to New York, vanished along with their car from a motel on Highway 17 in Brunswick, Georgia, on the night of April 8, 1980, leaving all their luggage in their room.

Orion Williamson, farmer, vanished from his field in full view of his wife, his children, and two neighbors passing in a buggy in Selma, Alabama, July 1854.

Martha Tuberville, Mistress of Peckatone, vanished one stormy night in 1788 from a road near her husband's Virginia plantation, along with her coach, horses, and coachman. Never a trace was found.

Colonel Percy Harrison Fawcett, from the Brazilian jungle in 1925.

Captain Benjamin Briggs, his family, and the crew from the *Mary Celeste*, in the North Atlantic, December of 1872.

Socialite Dorothy Arnold, from a busy New York City street on a bright afternoon in December 1910.

D. B. Cooper, airline pirate, from a Boeing 727 over Oregon, November 1971.

Judge Joseph Force Crater, from the theater district of New York, the evening of August 4, 1930.

Cadet Richard Cox from the Academy grounds at West Point, January 14, 1950.

Michael Rockefeller, from the waters off New Guinea, November 1961.

Paul Redfern, aviator, enroute to South America after taking off from the beach of Sea Island, Georgia, on August 25, 1927.

Soon two others will vanish:

Detective Captain Frank Longpre, from a street in New Orleans on the evening after Mardi Gras, Wednesday, March 4, 1992.

Psychic Carol Marlowe of North Carolina, from that same New Orleans street on that same post-Carnival night.

This pair can be counted among the five percent who *vanish forever!*

Becky Lee Weyrich
Unicorn Dune
St. Simons Island, Georgia
July 18, 1992

9

Prologue

A lone egret swooped low over the bayou, a silent ghost sailing through fog as thick as unginned cotton. The shadowy swamp was still—*too still*—as the wary Cajun fisherman poled his pirogue slowly through icy, death-black waters.

The solitary figure—swarthy and bewhiskered—shivered inside his down vest from something more than the predawn chill. He squinted an eye under one shaggy brow, trying to pierce the impenetrable curtains of mist that cloaked the Louisiana swamp. He coughed nervously, then muttered encouragement to himself, "Sun, she be up soon, yes."

But he wasn't so sure. Years he'd spent in these parts. He knew the twisting waterways back to front. Yet, the eerie silence this morning, the dark cypresses like bearded skeletons closing in on all

11

sides, and the sense of total isolation induced by the muffling fog aroused ingrained superstitions.

Could be the sun had burned out during the night and would never rise again. Or perhaps he had lost his way in the tortured maze of bayous. Had he poled his pirogue to that haunted region where hapless fishermen vanished into oblivion? Gooseflesh pimpled his thick arms at the thought, and a chill iced the length of his spine.

Far off on a fog-shrouded mountaintop in North Carolina, the sweet-sad strains of harp music faded from Carol Marlowe's dreams. With no advance warning, her deep sleep turned shallow and restless. A vague feeling of dread filled her. The unsettling sensations had nothing to do with any danger threatening her snug mountain cabin. The peril instead sought her out from far away. So often her psychic visions began this way . . .

She twisted about and pulled her granny's old Victorian crazy quilt over her face. The riot of brown curls that clung damply to her forehead seemed almost a part of the haphazard pattern of fancy stitching across the bright satin and velvet.

"Go away!" she mumbled in her sleep. "Leave me alone . . . I don't want . . ."

Her troubled words trailed off. She felt like she was smothering in thick, cottony fog. She gasped for breath while goose pimples roughened the smooth, warm flesh of her bare arms. Dark skeletons danced through her mind and a winged ghost swooped down out of the vast, white nothingness. The vision mesmerized her, terrified her, entrapped her.

* * *

Far away in Louisiana, the fisherman pushed on slowly, slicing through the heavy layer of duckweed that carpeted the surface of the still, dark water like green velvet. At every sound, he tensed. The bellow of a bull 'gator off in the distance became a prehistoric scream. The twitter of birds, anticipating the coming of the sun, seemed to his nervous mind the whispers of spirits rising from their watery graves. And the cold wind sighing through the swamp sounded like eerie music from some ghostly harp.

When the bow of his dugout bumped a cypress knee, he all but jumped out of his skin, sure it was some unseen and unspeakably evil hand.

Cursing his own foolishness, he pulled a plug of Red Man out of his patched jeans' pocket and tore off a chaw with his yellowed teeth. Just as the bitter tobacco juice tingled over his tongue, he caught sight of the first ray of sunlight penetrating the fog. He laughed aloud at his fear of moments before. "No more craziness now," he said. "The sun, she up."

His relief was short-lived. Even as he stood watching the sunrise, his pirogue went crazy, twisting and jerking beneath him, throwing him off balance.

"Damn whirlpool!" he yelped, stumbling in the boat and fighting with his pole to pull himself free from the muddy, swirling water.

His struggle was brief but desperate. When he pulled free from the sucking waters, the fisherman sank down in the boat and wiped the sweat from his broad, leathery brow. Reluctantly, he reminded himself that his wife had warned him this was no fit day to go out alone. "The signs tell it so," she

13

had declared. He'd laughed at her—"crazy woman," he'd called her. Then, before leaving in spite of her fears, he'd kissed her roughly, fondled her big cushiony breasts, and given her a love whack on the wide rump.

As much as he enjoyed poking fun, his Maria's chicken bones, tea leaves, and Tarot cards—he reminded himself now—told the truth more often than they lied. Still breathing hard, he stared at the treacherous whirlpool, crossed himself, and muttered a quick prayer of thanks for his salvation.

As he continued watching the rampant water, a large, unidentifiable object shot to the surface, spinning crazily in the dark vortex. At first, he thought it was only a log, but then his eye caught the glint of gold. He squinted and leaned closer, recalling tales of pirates' treasure buried deep in the bayous long ago. Quickly, he made a loop and tossed a rope out into the water. Snagging the thing on his first try, he dragged it toward the pirogue. He secured the end of his lasso under one boot heel, then leaned far over the bow to pull his prize up to the boat. Straining and cursing, he finally got a grip on it. The heavy object—still hidden from view under the dark surface—felt slippery, slimy to the touch, but he refused to give up his hold. His chest ached with his effort but soon he had it ready to heave over the side. With a mighty groan, he put all his strength to the task.

The next instant, as the thing flopped into the bottom of the pirogue, egrets took flight with shrieks of alarm that almost, but not quite, matched the fisherman's scream of terror.

The astonished Cajun fell back in horror, scrambling to the far end of the boat. Eyes wide with fear, he clutched his heart and uttered another hurried prayer—this time an urgent plea for his deliverance from the horrid thing. He wanted it gone. Now! But there was no way he could bring himself to touch it again to toss it back overboard.

Shaking with fear and revulsion, he threw a tarp over the floater, then turned and headed at top poling speed toward New Orleans.

Maria and her signs had not lied.

In the quiet mist of the North Carolina morning Carol Marlowe cried out in alarm. Her fingers dug into the sheets and mattress as her bed seemed to dance and spin about the room. Breathing heavily, she clung to her pillow as if it were a life jacket. She saw a rush of black water, smelled the rank odors of rotting vegetation and stagnant pools.

A moment later, the dizzying whirlpool-motion stopped. She slept on, but fitfully. And soon the vision returned.

Carol's scream this time was so loud that the frosty windowpanes rattled. She balled up her fists and jammed them into her closed eyes as if she could shut out the hideous sight. But it was no use. The thing remained in her mind—dead eyes staring, mouth agape, long hair streaming with wet weeds and slime.

She shot up in bed, wide awake after her nightmare vision—the same one she'd had every night since shortly after Christmas. She was shaking all over. Her face felt hot, her hands and feet cold. The smell of rot lingered in her nostrils. The harp music was back, disturbing, but far better than her recurring, grisly dream.

Carol's head cleared after a moment. The phone was ringing. She understood suddenly that she had been expecting this call. Pulling on her robe, she hurried from the bedroom to the kitchen. Her body tense, her nerves raw-edged, she sensed what was to come even before she put the cold receiver to her ear.

Chapter One

The ghostly harp music had given Carol Marlowe her first clue that something out of the ordinary was brewing. She'd listened to those ethereal strains inside her head for weeks now—a sure sign that her subconscious and her extrasensory perception were working in tandem, about to spring a surprise. She already had a feel for what was coming. The melancholy melody spoke to her of days gone by, tears of grief, and long-lost love. Actually, she found the mental music damn depressing!

Taking all this into account, when she picked up the phone in the pullman kitchen of her mountain house that frosty February morning in 1992, she wasn't surprised to hear the troubled male voice at the other end of the line. She was surprised by her own warm, totally female reaction to that deep, lazy drawl.

"Miz Marlowe? Sorry to bother you so early." The stranger sounded almost defensive. "This is Detective Captain Frank Longpre of the N'Awlins Police Department. I've put off calling you for a good while, but . . . well . . . the point is, I need your help."

The instant he said "New Orleans," a series of visions—like images flashed too quickly on a screen—zapped in and out of Carol's head. She saw again the heavy fog in some watery, marshy place that had been a part of her dreams these past weeks. With a shudder, she visualized a snake coiled to strike. She glimpsed a man and a woman embracing. And through it all, she heard the harp playing and a child crying pitifully.

"How can I help you, Captain Longpre?" She guessed that her clairvoyant powers had prompted this call. She knew, too, that she could and would use them to help him.

The man hesitated as most people did when they were forced to call a psychic detective as a final resort. They never wanted to admit that they believed in such powers.

"Captain Longpre?" she prompted.

"Yes, ma'am, I'm still here." Again, that sexy, deep voice with its distinct Louisiana drawl. "Can I be real honest with you, Miz Marlowe?"

"Please," she answered.

"I don't see what help anybody can be on this case. I mean, it's like nothing I've ever run up against in all my years on the force. To be right honest with you, ma'am, my boss closed the file on this one last week. But I just can't get it out of my craw. I've got to know what happened."

18

"What do you think happened?"

"I'm not real sure," he admitted. "Could be murder, could be not. And even if it was murder, what then? There'd be no one left to try for the crime. You see, ma'am, this woman's been dead a long time and we don't even know who she was."

"She?" For an instant, the ghastly, staring eyes from Carol's nightmare returned to haunt her.

"Yes, ma'am. A fisherman found her body in a bayou a couple of days after Christmas. I reckon she'd been down in the mud for a right good while. Oddest damned thing! The corpse is preserved—mummified—like—as if she died just a few days ago, but that can't be."

Carol frowned and rubbed at her forehead. A headache was starting. His words were like *déjà vu*. Speeded-up visions came rushing through her mind like a runaway freight train. She was getting a sense of very distant grief, of confusion and hopelessness.

"Captain, just how long do you think this woman's been dead? Months, years, decades?"

He hesitated for several seconds before answering. Finally, Carol heard a long sigh and then, "Ma'am, I'd say *generations* is more likely. No tellin' how long she may have been out there in that swamp."

Now it was Carol's turn to take a deep breath and let it out slowly. The kaleidoscope of visions in her head made her slightly dizzy. She leaned against the kitchen counter for support, then glanced down at the telephone scratch pad. All the while they'd been talking, Carol had been idly doodling the words, "Elysian Fields." What on earth did that mean? she wondered.

"Did you hear me, Miz Marlowe? I said *generations!*"

"I heard, Captain. But what would make you think such a thing?"

"Her clothes, for starters. Now, granted, there were only tatters left. But the boots she was wearing were in pretty fair shape and they go way back. Then there was a necklace still on the corpse that dates to before the war."

"The war?" Carol asked, thinking World War II or possibly even I.

"Yes, ma'am. The War Between the States. Dental work—or lack of it—points to that, too. As for her identity or what happened to her, so far we've come up empty on both counts."

The War Between the States, indeed! Carol thought. She shook her head and her hazel eyes flashed green—always their predominant color when someone angered her. Who did this guy think he was kidding? More than likely the visions and voices she'd been seeing and hearing had nothing to do with this *supposed* detective's *supposed* case. He was just another early-morning crank caller.

"Where did you get my number? How did you find out about me?" Carol demanded.

Always wary of tricksters and people calling simply to poke fun at her, Carol normally asked this question before she went any further. Calls like this were the very reason she had left Cassadaga, Florida, to move to this secluded spot in the mountains of North Carolina. Cassadaga had a reputation as "Clairvoyant City" and fans of the Florida

20

lottery knew it. They had nearly driven her crazy—calling at all hours, offering to split their millions with her if only she'd tell them the lucky numbers in advance. It was impossible to explain to those with avarice in their souls that her precognitive powers could not be used for personal gain. In fact, when she had worked with the police in the past, Carol had refused any payment for her services.

"Well, Captain Longpre, did someone refer you to me or not?"

"Do you know a Jesse Calhoun in Atlanta?" her caller asked.

"Yes, I've worked with Jesse on three cases." Her anger began to cool; Jesse Calhoun was a close friend.

"Yeah, Jesse told me—a missing woman who wandered away from a nursing home, some paintings stolen from a museum, and the murders of all those little children around Atlanta a few years back."

"Then you know Jesse, too." She felt reassured.

"Sure do, ma'am. He and I attended The Citadel together. Wasn't a finer cadet on the place than ole Jesse. We were talking on the phone awhile back and I mentioned this case and the brick wall I was buttin' my head up against. He gave me your number, sang your praises to the skies, and said I should call you if I wanted some help. I have to admit I was right skeptical at the time."

Carol laughed softly. "Why not admit that you still are, Captain?"

"Okay, ma'am, I'll give you that. But if you know a way of solving this one so I can sleep nights, I'll be forever beholden to you. Actually, as I said, the case is pretty much closed, officially. Still, it just keeps gnawing at me. I'd like some answers before I let it go, so I'm taking a couple of weeks off to do some investigating on my own. With your help, I hope."

Silence on Carol's end of the line was Frank Longpre's only response.

"Listen, Miz Marlowe, if you want to call Jesse, check me out, and get back to me, I'll understand."

The harp was playing its sad song again, louder than ever. "No, Captain, I'll take your word for it. Actually, I guess I knew you were going to call."

"How'd you figure that, ma'am?"

"I've been getting signals since right after Christmas, and I just wound up one in a long series of horrendous nightmares starring your Cajun fisherman and his gruesome find. I usually start seeing things right before I receive a call for help. I'll need to come to New Orleans, of course. I can't do this long distance. I'll have to see her."

"I understand that." He sounded vastly relieved. "Let's see . . . this is Wednesday the twenty-sixth. How about I book you on a flight out of Charlotte tomorrow, if that's not too soon for you? We'll put you up at a hotel in the French Quarter. I think you'll like this place. You'll be coming at the best time, too."

"How's that?" Carol asked, distracted by the crying child who was now calling for someone named "Cami."

"Mardi Gras falls on the third of March this year," he answered. "Carnival's in full swing. Of course, it won't be quite the same with all the City Council ruckus over discrimination and Momus and Comus pulling their floats out of the parades. But, shoot, Mardi Gras is still the best free show on Earth. I have an invitation to one of the balls, too, if that sort of thing appeals to you."

Mardi Gras was the furthest thing from Carol's mind right now. However, when the detective mentioned the ball, she got a fleeting glimpse of a woman dancing in the arms of a tall, handsome man. Both of them wore glittering masks, yet Carol could clearly see the look of love in his black eyes. He obviously adored the woman, but Carol sensed, too, that a dark shadow hung over them.

"That would be nice, Captain Longpre. I've never been to Mardi Gras. In fact, this will be my first trip to New Orleans."

"Well, ma'am, you have quite an experience in store. I'll have the airline call you about your flight, and I'll pick you up at the airport myself. It's been good talking to you, and, Miz Marlowe, I sure appreciate your help."

"Hold the thanks until I've done something to deserve it," she answered.

"You *will* be able to, won't you?"

The music and the crying child were now making such a racket in Carol's brain that she could hardly hear what he was saying. "I think so, Captain. I'll certainly do my best."

"Then I'll see you in New Orleans tomorrow, ma'am. 'Bye now."

"Goodbye, Captain Longpre."

The moment Carol hung up the phone, the clamor in her head ceased—a sure sign that these phenomena were linked to the New Orleans case. She sighed with relief, welcoming both the silence and the proof that she wasn't about to set off on a wild goose chase.

She poured a cup of coffee—last night's dregs—and took a sip, her mind racing with seemingly disjointed details. She felt tense and eager to get under way with this case. Somehow, it seemed that something was different this time, more urgent than ever before. She felt almost as if she had some personal stake in this mystery. But that was nonsense, of course. She had no ties to Louisiana; she'd never even been there.

For a time she stood with her back to the kitchen counter, sipping coffee and staring out the window at the bleak but beautiful winter landscape. A light snow was falling, drifting down over the distant mountains. Somehow this morning the view from her windows didn't look quite real. Carol felt removed from the scene, as if she were already far away in Louisiana. She realized she was trembling. Hurrying over to throw a log on last night's embers, she poked the fire up to a roaring blaze.

"That's better," she said, clutching her robe more closely about her and allowing herself an exaggerated, warming shiver.

Thinking back over her conversation with Captain Longpre, Carol decided to call Atlanta, just to be on the safe side and to get some background information on the detective with the sexy voice. She reached for her address book and looked up Jesse Calhoun's number, then dialed it quickly. She was delighted to find him at his desk on the first try. Usually he was a tough man to catch.

"Hey, Carol! How you doin', girl?" Jesse had a voice as southern as a pool of melted butter floating on a cloud of hot grits. He was your standard "good ole boy"—beer-belly, open smile, and a ready if sometimes off-color wit.

"Fine, Jesse. I just got a call from a friend of yours in New Orleans." She was doodling "Elysian Fields" again, wondering what it meant.

"So, ole Frank finally screwed up the nerve to phone you, eh?"

"Reluctantly, I could tell," Carol answered.

"You gonna help him?"

"If I can. It sounds like a strange case, though."

"Downright weird is more like it, honey. I'd have pure nightmares if I turned up a mummified corpse."

Carol laughed in spite of the grisly topic. She couldn't imagine Jesse having nightmares over anything. He was the toughest, most unemotional cop she had ever run across—the kind who could eat jelly doughnuts while observing at an autopsy.

"I'm flying to New Orleans tomorrow to have a look around. I've been picking up vibes already, so I may be able to provide some sort of break in the case."

"Damn right!" Jesse answered. "If you can't, nobody can, Carol. You've got a mind I don't even believe. Shoot, if you ever do get married, your husband better sho'nuff watch his *P*'s and *Q*'s. 'Cause there won't be no way for that poor bastard to keep any secrets from you."

As if to corroborate his left-handed compliment *and* change the subject, Carol asked suddenly, "Jesse Calhoun, is that your *third* jelly doughnut this morning? For shame! And after your doctor told you to watch the cholesterol."

"Thunderation!" Jesse bellowed into the phone. "And just when I was about to sink my teeth into the last of my breakfast. Raspberry, too! My favorite! How'd you do that?"

Carol laughed. "It didn't take any special powers, Jesse. I worked with you long enough to know your morning habits. It's almost ten o'clock, so you've already polished off two of those sweet horrors. And I could have guessed the next one's flavor. You always get one strawberry, one lemon, and your favorite, raspberry, which you save for last. I'm not only psychic, I'm very observant, ole buddy."

"Shit! That ain't fair!" Jesse fussed. "You jokin' around and gettin' me all crawly-fleshed, thinkin' you're readin' my mind or somethin'."

Carol chuckled. "I don't waste my powers on your cholesterol count, my friend. I've got more important ways to use them. But you had better lay off the sweets!"

"Nag! Nag! Nag!" Jesse replied, but Carol could read his true thoughts: *Bitch! Bitch! Bitch!* After last year's Anita Hill-Clarence Thomas hearings, Jesse had abruptly cleaned up his act, too wary of being accused of sexual harassment to use his favorite phrase aloud any longer. At least something constructive had come out of that fiasco, Carol mused.

"So, Jesse, tell me about your friend Frank Longpre. His voice intrigued me."

"Finest cadet ever to graduate from The Citadel."

"He said the same of you."

"Well, hell, who am I to dispute the word of such a sterling fellow? I guess ole Frank must have been second best, in that case."

26

"He's your age?"

"Yep!" A pause, then a long sigh. "We'll both be hittin' the big four-oh pretty soon."

"Let me guess," Carol broke in. "Frank married his beautiful Charleston-belle sweetheart right out of college and took her back to Louisiana where they've raised a passel of pretty little Creoles."

Jesse's bantering tone changed abruptly. "Your psychic powers are slippin', Carol. Frank put in his time in the Army before he married. He said he didn't want his wife to have to move all over Kingdom Come. The minute he got out, though, he and Eileen tied the knot. I was best man at their weddin'."

"What happened to Eileen?" Something in Jesse's tone told Carol that the marriage was no longer intact.

Jesse hesitated and Carol heard a long, slow sigh before he answered her question. "She vanished! Like a goddamn puff of smoke! One reason this present case is probably buggin' the bejesus out of Frank is on account of Eileen's disappearance. It happened just about a year after they married. Never a trace—no body, no murder scene, no ransom demand, no farewell note. She was pregnant at the time, too. Frank's never gotten over it. That was back in 1980, but he's still searchin'. Hell, he's never even had her declared legally dead."

Carol shivered. "How sad! Thanks for telling me, Jesse," she said quietly. "You probably saved Frank some pain and me one of my big-mouthed blunders. God, what a bummer! How has he lived with that all these years?"

"Not well," Jesse answered. "He drank pretty

heavy for a while, just didn't seem to care about anythin' once he realized Eileen was actually gone for good. Then one day, he got out of bed, showered, shaved, and went back to work. Since then, the department's been his whole life. He does tend to get overly wrapped up in his cases, but better that than wrappin' himself around a bottle again."

Carol was receiving new images—all blurred and confused. These had nothing to do with the body from the swamp, she was sure, but centered on Frank and Eileen instead. Nothing clear came through, however. She shook her head sadly, wishing she could give Frank Longpre some clue to his wife's whereabouts.

"I can see why this case has him so unstrung," she said. "Unknown female, dead for a long time, no clues. He must be thinking that it could be his wife."

"Maybe subconsciously," Jesse answered. "But on a conscious level, I'm sure he gave up on findin' any trace of Eileen a long time ago. Don't mention her unless he brings the subject up. Okay?"

"Hey, Jesse, what if I come up with something that could help solve this case, too? Should I tell Frank?"

After a silent pause, she heard Jesse pull in a long breath, then let it out slowly. "I hadn't thought of that. It could happen, couldn't it?"

"I think so," Carol answered. "Just now, when you mentioned Eileen's name, I got a couple of blurred flashes."

"This is a tough call," Jesse said. "We'd all like to know what happened to her, but you've got to understand Frank's state of mind. He's been beatin'

28

himself to death over his wife's disappearance for all these years, feeling guilty as hell. What I'm scared of is you findin' out somethin' real bad and ugly. I don't think Frank could stand that, Carol. He's been right on the edge ever since it happened. I really believe that if he ever found out that Eileen was not only dead, but that she'd suffered before she died, it would finish him off."

Carol felt a cold chill course through her. She sensed that Jesse was right. "That bad, is it?"

"Last time I talked to him, that's the way he seemed. He covers it well with strangers, but I've known him too long . . ."

"So, if I do find out anything, I should keep it to myself?"

"No. Call me. I'll handle it."

"Thanks, Jesse. That takes a load off my mind. I sure don't want to screw things up worse for him."

"Just watch yourself around Frank. Don't ask him any questions about Eileen. And don't even mention her name unless he brings her up."

"You don't have to tell me twice. What do you take me for, Jesse?" Carol snapped, her eyes going green again.

"Sorry. I should have known that you, of all people, would never say anythin' to hurt a nice guy like Frank." Jesse paused and Carol could almost hear the wheels in his mind clicking. "Say, you two might really hit it off, Carol. You're footloose and fancy free now that you broke up with that guy you were engaged to. Ted somethin', wasn't it?"

"Hey, don't remind me! That was too close a call. And, frankly, my friend, I'm not anxious to go through that again anytime soon. I'm sure your

Captain Longpre is a 'sterling fellow,' as you say, but before I fall for another guy, he's going to have to be solid, twenty-four karat gold. I plan to go to New Orleans, do what I can to help, then come right back home to my safe, comfortable, solitary mountaintop."

"Whatever you say, honey. Still, some unlucky guy somewhere is really missin' out on a good deal by not haulin' you off to the altar."

Carol had to laugh. For all his rough talk and tough-guy façade, Jesse Calhoun had the pure and gentle heart of a true romantic.

"I'd better go, Jesse," Carol said reluctantly. She always enjoyed talking to him. "Give my love to Millie and the kids."

"Good luck, honey!"

"Thanks. Sounds like I may need it."

Within the hour, the airline called. Carol would take off from Charlotte the next morning at eleven-fifteen, compliments of the New Orleans Police Department.

"Now, to pack," she told herself.

She didn't know exactly what to take for this time of year in New Orleans. A ball gown, of course, for Mardi Gras. The only problem was she didn't own one.

She brightened. "Yes, I do!"

Suddenly remembering the box of vintage clothes she'd bought for her antiques shop from a Tennessee dealer who'd come through a few weeks ago, Carol went to her closet. Most of it had been pretty shabby fare, with the exception of an elegant green satin ball gown trimmed in gold braid and ribbons. She'd tried it on and found it a perfect fit. Never dreaming she'd have a chance to wear it this soon, she had, nevertheless, kept it in her closet.

"Yes! This should be perfect," she said, holding the gown up in front of her mirror.

Quickly, she chose the rest of her clothes—an assortment of slacks, sweaters, business suits, and one black-sequinned cocktail dress, just in case of emergency. All packed except for the last-minute items like her toothbrush and deodorant, she was left with nothing to do all afternoon but think about the trip and the case and the deep-voiced detective who—she admitted—had aroused more than her curiosity. There was something in that husky, drawling voice that hinted of vulnerability lurking just beneath the surface. Jesse's story of the tragedy in Frank Longpre's life confirmed her initial impression.

Finding herself pacing the cabin, Carol realized the fluttery feeling in the pit of her stomach was pure nerves. She always got the jitters at the outset of one of these unsolved mysteries. But that feeling would soon pass. She loved traveling, meeting new people, and confronting difficult problems. Besides, she felt a tug at her heart every time she heard the phantom harp strings. Whoever this unidentified woman was, Carol felt sure she held the key to unlock the mysteries of the long-lost lady's life and death.

For a time, Carol drifted aimlessly about the cabin, tidying up and checking to make sure she'd packed everything. She glanced out the window and spied a deer nosing around the kitchen door.

"Hey, Bubba!" she called softly.

The buck's head came up and his velvety ears twitched. He knew her voice from many previous visits to the cabin.

Carol went to the door, a coffee can filled with corn in one hand. She scattered some around for her "pets," as she called them. She hadn't owned a dog or cat in years, so she'd adopted the wild things that shared her mountain—deer, rabbits, raccoons. She watched the buck eat for a while, then she went back to the living room and threw another log on the fire.

Restless, she switched on the television, not to watch, but to have some background noise. She felt very alone suddenly. Although she made an effort to concentrate on the movie, it was no use. Her mind wandered. She wished she hadn't thought about pets because that topic soon connected to another, less pleasant subject in her mind. The accident and the beginning of her psychic powers. She was twenty-eight years old, but the painful memories were still as fresh as if that long-ago tragedy had happened only days before.

Carol closed her eyes, not wanting to think about it, but knowing that she couldn't stop herself.

She was once again twelve years old, sleeping in the back seat of the family's roomy Lincoln while her father drove through the night from Palm Beach to his mother's home in Cassadaga to spend Christmas.

"John, don't drive so fast." Carol heard her mother's pleading voice, then a sharp yip from their toy poodle, Truffle, who was nestled in Helen Marlowe's lap.

32

"There aren't any cops on the road this time of night, Helen. Besides, I want to surprise Mama and get there in time for breakfast."

Carol could feel her mother's fear. She tossed and turned on the back seat, trying to get comfortable. It was no use. Finally, she decided to sit up for a while until she felt sleepy again. The moment she did, she looked through the windshield and screamed. Her father swerved off the pavement and slammed on the brakes, cursing all the while.

When the big car came to a full stop, both her parents turned to her—her mother anxious, her father angry. Even Truffle was whimpering.

"What the hell do you mean yelling like that, Carol?" John Marlowe demanded. "You nearly made me wreck the car."

"John, don't fuss at her. She was only having a nightmare, weren't you, honey?" Her mother patted Carol's cheek and stared at her, concerned.

Carol was trembling all over and crying uncontrollably. "No, Mom, it wasn't a nightmare. I saw it! I really truly saw it!"

"What, darling?" Helen Marlowe asked gently.

"A great big truck all black and silver . . . it was coming right for us. We were going to crash."

"There was *no* truck, Carol," her father said firmly. "But we almost crashed, all right. You scared the hell out of me. Now, lie down and go back to sleep. I want both of you to leave the driving to me. Okay? We'll never get to Cassadaga at this rate."

John Marlowe had been right about one thing—they never got to Cassadaga. The black and silver truck Carol had seen in her precognitive vision smashed head-on into the Lincoln less than an hour later, crushing the front of the car, Carol's parents, and poor little Truffle. Since that time, Carol had never owned another pet.

Carol herself had been seriously injured in the accident. She recovered in time, although she experienced excruciating headaches for years afterward. When she was finally released from the hospital, she went to live with her Grandmother Bess in the sleepy little town of Cassadaga near Orlando, where the elderly woman ran a tourist hotel. Bess Marlowe raised Carol, sent her to the University of Florida, and tried to make her understand that the strange powers she developed at the time of her parents' deaths were as natural as living and breathing.

"Why, this very town has a whole colony of gifted people with powers like yours," Granny Bess had told her.

In spite of her grandmother's reassurance, Carol found that friends and acquaintances were far less tolerant of her psychic abilities. They either scoffed or pestered her to perform trivial tricks. So for a long time she tried to pretend that she was as normal as anyone else.

After her grandmother died in 1988, Carol ran the hotel alone for a year. Then she met and almost married a man who literally swept her off her feet with his good looks, charming manners, and fairy tale promises. By the time she realized the painful truth about her lover, she had already sold the hotel, anticipating moving into Ted's condo in Key West. Their breakup put an end to all her dreams. It was then that she escaped to the peace and solitude of her mountaintop retreat, to hide out, lick her wounds, and try to put her life back together.

* * *

Carol roused herself and forcibly shook off the lonely feeling brought on by thoughts of the accident. Going to the kitchen, she heated up the vegetable soup she'd made the day before. She carried her steaming mug back to the living room, determined to concentrate on the old movie and nothing else. That would be the best way to spend a long, snowy afternoon, she decided.

The movie was one of those lush historical melodramas that Hollywood once did so well, but almost never made anymore because of the expense of costumes and settings. It starred an elegantly handsome young Walter Pidgeon as a gentleman gambler opposite an equally young and breathtakingly gorgeous Hedy Lamarr, the plantation owner's daughter. The drama was set somewhere in the Deep South.

Carol stared with envy at Hedy's luxuriously long, raven-black locks. She gave her own short, bouncy curls an impatient tug. Whatever had possessed her last week to cut off all her hair?

She continued watching the flickering black and white images on the screen until she grew drowsy. Gaze fixed on the set, her eyelids grew heavier and heavier. But she remained hypnotized by the scene unfolding before her.

Walter Pidgeon, staring out a window into a storm, was sipping brandy when Hedy Lamarr—ravishingly beautiful in her anger—burst into his room. After a few moments of passionate rage, they turned their passions to better use. Pidgeon coaxed the fiery beauty into his arms. Carol sighed, remembering how it felt to fight like that, then give in to love. She couldn't keep the tears back; she felt that lonely at the moment.

When the hero kissed his darling slowly, thorougly, deeply, it seemed to Carol she could feel his lips on her own. She could taste his brandy in her mouth. She sighed as a wonderful lethargy stole through her body. Her eyes finally closed.

Carol awoke with a start as the sun was coming up the next morning. She opened her eyes and stretched, feeling oddly warm and satisfied. The sweet old movie lingered like afterglow. She experienced a pang of disappointment when she realized that the handsome gambler on the television screen hadn't really held her and kissed her last night. He'd been only a delicious illusion.

"If I could find a guy like that . . ." She shook her head and chuckled at her own foolishness.

A glance at the clock shattered any lingering traces of romance. She had fallen asleep in front of the television and slept right through the night. If she hurried, she would just have time for a quick shower before she dressed to head down the mountain in her jeep. She only hoped traffic between here and Charlotte would be light. She could not miss her flight to New Orleans!

When she dashed into the bathroom to brush her teeth, she stopped for a moment and gazed at herself in the mirror—brown curls tousled, hazel eyes dewy and glittering, cheeks flushed, lips puffy.

"Gad, Carol!" she said to her reflection. "You look like you've been making out in the back of some guy's van."

She licked her dry, kiss-bruised lips and her eyes went wide.

"Brandy!" she said.

The last drink she'd had was over a week ago when she went down the mountain to have dinner one night. And it wasn't brandy! Yet that unmistakable taste lingered on her lips and tongue. She had no idea how to explain any of this; she'd learned from past experience not even to try. Instead, she pushed all thoughts of the movie and its handsome hero from her mind. It was time to set her psychic powers to more serious business than stealing kisses from long-dead movie stars.

Taking one last glance around the cabin, Carol felt odd suddenly, as if she knew she was gazing on her home for the final time. She shook off the odd sensation and headed for the door—for New Orleans and the mysterious unknown that awaited her there.

Chapter Two

New Orleans was, indeed, decked out for Carnival. As her plane taxied in, Carol spotted banners of purple, green, and gold snapping in the breeze. She glanced at the brochure the flight attendant had given her. It stated that Rex, King of Carnival, had established those as the traditional Mardi Gras colors back in 1872—purple for justice, green for faith, and gold for power. Now, here was the proof before her very eyes. She felt her excitement building. She could hardly wait to get off the plane—to smell and taste and feel the Crescent City.

Moments later, in the crush of the reception area, she saw that New Orleans was already one big party in progress. Tourists dashed about, some carrying costumes for the big day. She wondered what she would wear. Most likely, Frank Longpre would keep her far too busy on the case to leave much time for frolic.

Carol's flight had landed in New Orleans a few minutes early thanks to strong tailwinds all the way. She wasn't surprised when she entered the terminal and no one stepped forward to claim her. Maybe Captain Longpre was here, but hadn't seen her in the crush of incoming passengers. Suddenly she wondered how he would recognize her. No one here knew her, she reminded herself. She should have thought to wear a red rose or something.

Checking directional signs, Carol had turned toward the baggage claim area when a hand touched her arm. *"Mademoiselle, s'il vous plait."*

Carol looked around to find a dark, diminutive woman at her elbow. The withered creature was dressed in a rainbow-colored caftan with a scarlet tignon tied about her head. Large, gold hoops tugged at her earlobes and strings of beads and gold chains dangled around her neck and at her thin wrists. She looked as old as time, but her golden eyes gleamed like twin beads of polished amber. A homeless beggar, no doubt, Carol figured, about to fish into her purse for some change.

"Mademoiselle Marlowe," the woman said. It was not a question. She knew who Carol was.

"Yes?"

"It is good you have returned at last."

Carol shook her head as she inched away from the woman, unnerved by her steady, golden gaze. "No, you must have me confused with someone else. I've never been here before."

The oddest feeling crept over Carol. She had the sudden urge to turn and run, yet those twinkling

39

eyes drew her like a magnet. The woman scared her, although there was nothing threatening in her demeanor. Quite the opposite. She smiled at Carol, looking genuinely happy to see her.

"Let me take your hand," the stranger urged.

Before Carol could object, she felt hot, dry flesh pressing hers. With one long-nailed finger, the old lady traced the lines in Carol's palm, muttering in French and nodding her tignoned head all the while.

"It is as I supposed. You are the one. You have come back in the very nick of time."

"In time for what?" Carol was dumbstruck. Who was this crazy old crone?

"In time to do what should have been done long ago. You must go to Elysian Fields. You must set things right. There is little time left."

Carol felt the hair rise on the back of her neck. She backed away. "Please, I don't know who you are. I have to go now. Someone is meeting me."

"There is no need to hurry," the woman said. "He has been delayed—no serious trouble. Simply a flat tire on the big road. I am sorry for his inconvenience, but I needed to talk with you alone before he arrived." Again, she reached for Carol's hand, this time giving it a firm squeeze. "You *must* do what I say!"

"What do you want of me?"

"You know Elysian Fields," the woman declared.

Carol shrugged. "I know the name, that's all. Is it a place?"

The woman nodded. "It is where this all began."

"Where *what* began?"

"You will understand in time. You must go be-

40

fore first light tomorrow to the foot of Barracks Street, beyond the French Market. A ferryman will meet you at the river's edge to take you to Elysian Fields."

"But I can't leave the city," Carol protested. "I have work to do."

"Your work is there, mademoiselle. Do not delay and do not tell anyone of your plans. Not even your man."

Before Carol could ask what she meant by that, the woman pressed a cold object into Carol's palm. She glanced down at it—a coin that looked like old Spanish gold. Or was is simply a Carnival trinket?

"Show this to the ferryman, but to no one else. Do you understand? And tell no one that we met and spoke. If you should be so careless as to involve others, be warned that they will be *wholly* involved."

Carol nodded, speechless. She looked back down at the antique coin. "But, really, I don't think I can . . ."

When she looked up again, the woman had vanished. Carol scanned the crowd, but saw no sign of the bright red headdress. She shrugged and slipped the coin into her purse. Probably, this was just some sort of Carnival prank.

"Miz Marlowe?" She heard a deep male voice calling her name and glanced about. A tall man was shouldering his way toward her through the crowd, his hand raised to catch her attention.

"I'm sorry I'm late," he said, smiling an apology filled with frustration. "Of all days for such a thing to happen, I had a flat right in the middle of the expressway. I hope you haven't been waiting too long. Anyway, welcome to the Big Easy, ma'am."

Carol experienced a moment of total confusion. This, of course, was Captain Longpre. She knew she should tell him immediately about the old woman and explain that his mishap was somehow her fault. But when she tried to form the words, they simply refused to come. The very idea seemed silly. She decided to put the weird old character completely out of her thoughts, at least for the time being. She was here on a case, after all, not to worry over deranged strangers who accosted her out of nowhere, then disappeared like smoke. Maybe she'd imagined the entire confrontation.

Her mind back on business, she took a closer look at Captain Longpre in his three-piece, pin-striped suit. At that moment, she was very glad she'd decided to wear her new purple trapeze dress with high heels. She'd obviously made the right choice when she rejected her jeans, ski jacket, and silver moon-boots for the trip.

She liked Frank Longpre immediately. The detective had a sharp, soldierly bearing that bespoke his years spent at South Carolina's famed military institute. He was tall, athletically built, and handsome in a rather rough-and-tumble way. His manners came straight out of the plantation era. Damned if he didn't almost bow when he spoke her name!

Carol smiled at him and offered her hand. "Captain Longpre, I presume. How did you pick me out in this mob?"

"Well, I could say you just look psychic, but actually, ma'am, Jesse sent me your picture from the Atlanta paper—not a bad likeness for newsprint."

He smiled then, too. Carol felt herself begin to

relax. The warmth in his dark eyes, the black hair with a light frosting of silver at the temples, the slightly crooked nose—no doubt broken playing football by the looks of his physique—all fit together to form a pleasing picture of an easy-to-like guy. They would get on well; she was sure of it.

"Did you have a good flight, Miz Marlowe?" His hand lightly cradled her elbow as he steered her toward the baggage claim area. She could feel a certain electricity radiating from his touch, and the harp music had begun again.

She stopped and turned to him. "Look, call me Carol. Okay? I've found that it's much easier on everybody if we start off on a casual basis."

"Fine by me," he said with a slow, lazy grin. "We're a right casual bunch down here in N'Awlins. My name's Francis, but my mama was the only one who ever called me that."

"It's ole Frank," Carol replied. "Right?"

He laughed—a good, deep, male sound, but with a nervous edge to its tone. "So, you called Jesse after all, eh? Well, I don't blame you one bit for checking up on me before you come traipsing all the way down here. How is that old son of a . . . ?"

"Jesse's fine. He sends his regards."

"Regards, eh? I wish he'd send me the money he owes me on last year's World Series. The welsher!"

Carol laughed. "My psychic powers tell me you should never bet with a man who's partial to raspberry doughnuts."

Frank sighed and shook his head. "I know it. Me, I'm strictly a lemon man, myself."

Carol gave him a serious, appraising glance. "Somehow, I would have guessed that about you."

Their trivial banter served its purpose. Carol was not fully at ease yet, still shaken by her unnerving conversation with the old woman. As for Frank Longpre, she could feel the tension radiating from him as if he had high-voltage current coursing through his veins. Beneath his calm and casual façade lay a tangled mass of ragged nerves. She had sensed his tenseness over the phone and now it was even more evident. Jesse Calhoun had been right about Frank. Not only had he suffered many years over his wife's disappearance, he was still suffering. But it was more than that. This case was taking its toll for reasons he obviously didn't understand. She would have to go easy with him—as her grand-mother used to say, "gentle him along"—until he felt more comfortable having her around. He obviously viewed her unusual powers with more than casual skepticism.

They spent the ride from the airport into the city talking mostly about "ole Jesse." Frank told stories about their college days, their time in the Army together, then their joint decision to go into police work. Finally, he seemed to run out of conversation. He turned to Carol with a questioning look.

"How about you? What's your background?"

"You have to ask? I'm surprised. I figured you would had run a thorough check on me already."

"I did a surface investigation after talking to Jesse. But I've been too busy to dig very deep. Don't worry, ma'am." He turned and gave her another of his sad-sweet smiles. "This isn't official. I'm just curious. I like to know the people I work with."

Carol received a sudden flash—a picture of

Frank Longpre with his co-workers, then another glimpse of his private life. She saw a bachelor's untidy apartment, a little Christmas tree on a table with no presents underneath, a mailbox with only bills inside, no personal letters. As Jesse had told her, Frank's work was, indeed, his whole life.

"There's not a lot to tell about myself," Carol began. "My parents died when I was young and I was raised by my father's mother in a little town in central Florida. Cassadaga. She owned an old hotel there."

"You mean you actually grew up in a hotel?" He sounded intrigued. "That must have been a right interesting life."

Carol thought about it for a minute. "Well, yes, I guess it really was. I always felt self-conscious about telling people that I wasn't raised normally—I mean, in a regular house in the suburbs with two cars in the garage, a swimming pool out back, and all that. But life at the hotel was fun most of the time. Granny Bess and I were certainly never lonely."

The smile faded from Frank's face when she made that statement. Obviously, she would have to watch what she said around him. She didn't want to add to his pain. Her guess would be that this man had been lonely most of his life.

"Go on," Frank urged. "I want to hear everything."

"Well, there's not too much more to tell. My grandmother died a few years ago. I ran the Flamingo Arms alone for a while. Then when I decided to get married, I sold the old place, thinking I'd soon be moving into my own home."

Frank gave her an odd look. "Jesse didn't tell me you were married."

"I'm not," she replied stiffly. "The plans fell through."

"Sorry," Frank murmured.

"Don't be. It would have been a huge mistake. Funny, my psychic powers give me no help at all where romance is concerned. Too bad! I think I could use some insight into matters of the heart. But then, I'm not sure I'm the marrying kind, and my former fiancé certainly wasn't. I realized that when I found him with his lover."

"Oh!" Frank nodded knowingly. "Another woman."

"Another man," Carol corrected.

She felt Frank stiffen beside her, obviously embarrassed. Carol quickly changed the subject.

"Anyway," she went on, "since I'd already found a buyer for the hotel, I decided to move up to the mountain cabin my parents had used as a vacation getaway, at least until I could decide where I wanted to live permanently. I guess you could say I've become a happy hermit. I love living up there all alone. I plan to stay right there on my mountaintop forever."

"What do you do up there? I mean, your psychic stuff can't keep you busy all the time." He glanced over at her, a quizzical look in his almost-black eyes. "Or does it?"

She laughed softly, picturing Frank imagining her on top of some far-off mountain, curled up in the lotus position, muttering mantras from dawn till dusk.

"No, I don't just hang around my cabin playing

with crystals and mixing foul-smelling potions," Carol said with another chuckle. "Actually, most of the time, Frank, I'm quite normal in spite of what Jesse might have told you. You're right, I had to find something to do. I've always had an interest in antiques; the old hotel was filled with them. So, I decided to open a shop in the village at the foot of my mountain."

He glanced over at her, his dark brows drawn low. "I'm real sorry, ma'am. I was so anxious to get you on out to N'Awlins I never thought about you having any other business to tend to."

Carol brushed aside his apology. "It was no problem really. We get a big tourist rush in the fall—leaf-peepers, you know—but things slow down to a snail's crawl after Christmas. I close for a couple of months after the holidays. That gives me time to tidy up the place, bring my records up to date, and do some buying." She grinned at him. "Sometimes I even manage to sneak a vacation into my schedule."

"If you have a mind to buy some old stuff, this is sure the place for it. I'll take you around to some of the shops," Frank offered. "Anything in particular you're looking for?"

"I specialize in Victorian jewelry. I'm curious to see the necklace you said the woman was wearing."

A dark cloud seemed to descend over Frank's features at her mention of the case.

"You'll see everything soon enough," he replied. "Tell me about these powers of yours. I've never met anyone who could see things or hear things or whatever it is you do."

Here it was! The old skepticism rearing its ugly head. She always had to prove her credentials to these guys. Even Jesse had doubted her in the beginning. She took a deep breath, then plunged in.

"I see *and* hear things, and somehow I just *know* things. Where the powers come from, I can't tell you. My first experience was the night my parents were killed. My mother was afraid that night. I knew it; I felt it. Maybe she was the one who passed her psychic knowledge on to me." Carol paused and shook her head. "I don't know. All I understand is that whatever talent I have is meant to be used helping people. I've never tried and never would, but I know I can't use my powers for evil or for personal gain. At times, I've thought of this gift as a curse, but I guess it really is a blessing."

"But how does it work?" Frank said. "Do you ask yourself questions about something, then get answers out of thin air?"

Carol concentrated hard, trying to think how to explain. "No, it's not like that at all. Visions come to me mostly. For instance, when we were talking on the phone, I saw a number of things that I feel are connected to your case."

"Like what?" Excitement was evident in his voice.

"Fog . . . a swampy area."

"That would be where the corpse was found. What else?"

"A snake." She shivered, remembering.

"What kind?"

"I don't know." She shivered again. "I don't do snakes."

"Anything else?"

"A man and a woman embracing—maybe dancing."

48

"You've actually seen *her?* What did she look like? Could you tell where she was?"

Frank's urgent questions tumbled out in a rush. Carol felt almost as if she were a suspect in his interrogation cell.

"Slow down, Frank. Let me think about it for a minute."

He stayed quiet while she closed her eyes, clasped her hands, and concentrated with all her might.

"Yes, I can see the couple again," Carol said at length. "She has long, blond hair. He's holding her and, yes, they do seem to be dancing. They're at a fancy ball. I can see other couples—blurred figures in the background."

"Her face! Can you see her face?"

Carol shook her head. "No. She's wearing a mask. It's really a lovely thing—made of peacock feathers and shiny stones. She has something around her neck. Maybe the necklace you found? Yes, I see it clearly now. It's a cameo fastened to a green ribbon. The woman carved into the cameo is also wearing a necklace set with a single diamond chip."

Frank asked no further questions. In fact, he lapsed into such a deep silence that Carol could actually feel his gloom, a tangible force in the car.

"Did I say something wrong?" she ventured, disturbed by the sudden strained silence.

"You've just described my wife, Eileen, at the Mardi Gras ball shortly after we were married. The cameo with the diamond was an antique— my wedding gift to her. And I bought that mask for her myself at a little shop on Decatur Street. She was so happy that night. You see, Eileen was from Tennessee and that was her first Mardi Gras ball. Her only Mardi Gras ball," he added under his breath.

"Oh," Carol said, feeling a flush of embarrassment. "I was so sure this had something to do with the case."

"It doesn't." His tone was hard and flat. The silence that followed warned her she had rubbed a sore spot.

Carol wanted to squirm through her seat. She almost wished that Jesse hadn't told her about this great tragedy in Frank's life. Finally, she decided that the best thing to do was try to clear the air.

"Frank, I'm sorry," she said gently. "I know about your wife."

"Jesse, huh?"

"Yes. He told me because he didn't want me to say the wrong thing and upset you. Now I've gone and done it anyway."

He glanced her way and forced a smile. "Hey, don't worry about it. That's all in the past."

Is it, Frank? She wanted so badly to ask the question aloud, but she didn't dare. Somehow she knew that if he would open up to her, she could help ease his pain. Maybe she could even uncover some clues that would lead him to his wife. But there was no way she could force him to talk about Eileen. She would simply have to be patient and concentrate all her energies on the case of the unidentified mummy.

They rode on in silence for a time. Then Frank turned off the expressway and into the French Quarter. Carol almost gasped aloud. It was as if they had driven right into one of her visions of the past. The narrow streets, the quaint buildings, the wrought-iron balconies, and, in the distance, the spires of St. Louis Cathedral.

Frank pulled the car up to the curb outside the Hotel Dalpeche on Chartres Street. It was obviously one of the French Quarter's old private town-houses.

"I live here, in one of the apartments," he explained. "I figured it would be convenient to have you here, too. I hope you don't mind staying at an older place instead of one of the swank hotels over on Canal."

The small hotel delighted Carol, with its quaint wrought-iron balconies, flickering gaslights, and cobbled drive that led to an interior court.

"Every room's furnished with period antiques," Frank said, smiling at her. "Wait till you see the one I picked out for you. It's something special."

"Special how?"

"You'll see," he answered mysteriously. "But right now we'll just drop your bags off at the front desk and head down to Bourbon Street for something to eat, if that's all right with you."

Carol took a deep breath and flattened a palm against her belly. "Has my stomach been growling that loud? I never eat much when I fly."

Frank laughed. "Who does? Those little plastic dishes with the plastic food on them. We'll get you a real meal."

The Hotel Dalpeche was only a few blocks from Bourbon Street. Frank parked his car off the street, checked Carol in, then took her arm and headed back out.

"Don't I even get to see this special room before we go?" she asked.

"Plenty of time for that later. First, we feast!"

As they strolled along the banquette, Carol found the whole Vieux Carré a feast for the senses. Music drifted from the open doors of small, smoky clubs. In the cool twilight air, the moldy, earthy smells of antiquated buildings and the distant river mingled with the delicious aromas of food—blackened red-fish, fresh-baked French bread, and the fragrance of steaming hotdogs as they passed a street vendor.

"Hey, you know what I'd love?" Carol asked.

"Name it!"

"A hotdog with the works."

"Make that two," Frank told the vendor.

All conversation ceased as they wolfed down their spicy, juicy dogs.

"Another?" Frank asked.

Wiping dribbles of mustard from her chin, Carol grinned. "That'll do me for now, thanks."

They wandered on, watching twilight turn to darkness over the old city. In a short while, they arrived at the very heart and soul of New Orleans.

They found Bourbon Street alive with tourists and Carnival revellers—a collection of people who looked like the misfits of the whole world gathered in one raucous spot. Strolling about were couples in fashionable evening clothes, bums in rags, and tourists in tee-shirts advertising their hometowns or their favorite ball clubs.

Flashing neon striped the crowded, cluttered pavement of the roped-off street in rainbow hues, tinting the shop windows with a haze of garish colors. Carol window-shopped, enthralled by all the glittery junk, until she noticed that several of the stores displayed ties depicting a certain portion of the male anatomy in rather shocking detail. She averted her gaze, for fear Frank might catch her staring.

Music blasted them from all sides. Everything from Irish ditties to country to cool jazz and hot rock blared, almost overpowering the cries of pitchmen trying to lure customers in to see assorted exotic shows.

"Well, what do you think?" Frank asked, spreading his arms to indicate the whole expanse of the fabled street of sin.

"I'm overwhelmed," Carol admitted. "I don't suppose we could find a *quiet* place to talk."

"I know the very spot, ma'am. Come on with me."

Frank took Carol's arm. She knew the gesture was simply to keep them from getting separated by the surging mass of humanity; still, it was nice feeling protected. She glanced up. This man was nice, too, she decided.

"Where are we going?" she asked. They had worked their way out of the mad chaos into a darker, quieter block of Bourbon Street.

"Just down there." Frank pointed toward a small building that obviously dated far back in New Orleans's history, judging by its *briquette-entre-poteaux* construction exposed through bare spots in the exterior stucco finish. "Lafitte's Blacksmith Shop. It's dark, it's quiet, and you could drown in the atmosphere. Besides, they have a roaring fire and a piano player named Miss Lilly who'll put you right in the mood."

Carol glanced up at Frank, not certain how to take his last comment. "The mood for what?"

He laughed at her wary tone. "For discussing

business with a cop, of course. What'd you think I meant, ma'am?"

Carol decided to consider that a rhetorical question. She merely smiled in response.

Frank was right; the place was perfect. A dark, intimate atmosphere, with smoky rafters overhead, small tables, candles in wine bottles, and a lady at the piano who played numbers so smooth and mellow that the music might have come straight from the harp inside Carol's head.

"This place really was Jean Lafitte's blacksmith shop," Frank explained once they were seated at a table in a corner near the fireplace. "He and his brothers ran it, although I doubt they shoed many horses here. They were into freebooting, and this was their sales outlet for a time. I've heard many a high stakes poker game went on here, too. One tale says that ole Jean, 'the gentleman smuggler,' actually won a man's wife from him in this very room."

The story both amused and horrified Carol. "I wonder what the lady thought of that. I can't say I'd be pleased at being part of the ante."

"The tale goes that she was delighted," Frank assured her. "Lafitte was quite a ladies' man, while her husband was a low-life—a mean, sadistic bastard. I don't know if she ever married Lafitte, but legend says she went away with him when he left New Orleans for Galveston. She was supposed to have been the great love of his life—a Creole beauty named Nicolette."

A waiter interrupted to ask if they would like to order drinks. Remembering Jesse's story of Frank's drinking problem, Carol looked at her companion

54

uncertainly. He returned a confident stare, then said, "A glass of Fumé Blanc for the lady. I'll have branch water with a twist of lime."

Carol smiled. "How did you guess? Or have you been digging deeper into my personal tastes and habits?"

Frank shrugged. "You look like smoky white wine. Pale skin, hazy eyes. What color *are* they? Brown, gray, green?"

She laughed softly. "You're in trouble if they look green. Everyone tells me my eyes turn green when I'm angry. They're mostly brown, I'd say, but with a touch of gold and gray mixed in."

It was Frank's turn to laugh. "I'll have to see if I can't cross you somewhere along the line. I'm fond of green-eyed beauties."

Carol felt herself blushing. Frank's lazy, Southern charm was making inroads. Jesse had been correct when he predicted they would get on well.

Time to change the subject, she decided. "Tell me about the case. What exactly have you found out about this woman from the swamp?"

"Almost nothing," Frank admitted, shaking his head slowly. "There's just nowhere to start without a positive identification, and she goes way back before fingerprints or social security numbers. There is the necklace, though."

Carol leaned closer, all attention. "Tell me about it."

"It's a gold coin—an old Spanish doubloon. What we call 'pirate gold' around here."

The old woman at the airport flashed back into Carol's thoughts. Even now, she was carrying a similar coin in her purse. She should show it to Frank; she knew she should. But something stopped her.

"Do you think she was murdered, Frank? Is there any sign of foul play?"

Again, he shook his head. "No. My guess would be that she got lost in the swamp and either drowned or died of exposure. But the big question is, what was she doing there in the first place? Why would a woman go in there alone, knowing the dangers?" He looked up at Carol, the candlelight reflecting in his dark eyes. "I'm hoping you can supply me with some answers."

"I hope so, too," Carol answered with a sigh.

Silence stretched on between them for several minutes. Carol toyed with her napkin while Frank adjusted his tie.

Finally, Frank spoke. It seemed to Carol that he had been priming himself to say, "There are some other answers I wish you could give me, too. I know it has nothing to do with the case, but I'd give my soul to find out what happened to my wife." He stared at Carol, a look of such deep pain on his face that she suddenly reached out to touch the back of his hand with her fingertips.

"You know I'll help if I can, Frank. Maybe that mystery is even more important than the identity of the woman from the swamp. After all, even if I do learn who she was and what happened to her, who will be left to care? But with Eileen . . ."

Frank had been staring into Carol's face. At the mention of his wife's name, he looked away.

"If anything comes to you, Carol, anything at all . . ."

"Of course, Frank." A silent alarm went off in

56

Carol's heart. She truly ached to help Frank, but she knew from what Jesse had told her, that she had to be careful with any information she uncovered about Eileen.

Frank's eyes held almost pathetic gratitude. Carol found herself biting her lip to keep from crying. She could feel his pain that deeply.

They talked on for a time, until Frank saw Carol try to hide a yawn behind her hand. "You must be bushed," he said. "Why don't we go get some real food, then I'll take you back to the hotel?"

She waved off his suggestion. "Oh, no! I couldn't eat anything else tonight—travel jitters, I guess. I think I am ready to hit the sack, though. It's been a long day."

The old city was quieter as they strolled back toward the hotel. The farther they got from Bourbon Street, the deeper New Orleans slept. They walked along shoulder-to-shoulder. Once again, Carol felt the pleasure of having a man so near. Very simply, she liked Frank Longpre. They seemed wonderfully comfortable together.

Carol paused at the hotel entrance and closed her eyes for a moment, drinking in all the impressions that were bombarding her mind—her very heart and soul. The harp music played very faintly somewhere off in the distance. The weeping child, she was happy to note, was silent now. She realized suddenly that the keenest sense of all was the warmth of not being alone. Until now, she hadn't realized how hungry for companionship she'd been over the last months. Suddenly, she had a sense of belonging—of needing and being needed. It felt good!

Frank walked her to the door of her room, a first-floor suite that had once been part of the servants' quarters. But the minute he unlocked the door and opened it, Carol realized that no servant had ever enjoyed such opulence. The canopy bed was draped in wine-colored damask. Marble-topped tables held Gone-With-the-Wind-lamps, their pale satin-glass globes decorated with handpainted roses. Oil paintings in antique gilt frames adorned the walls.

One of these paintings in particular caught and held her attention. It was a gloomy portrait of a handsome, dark stranger, yet there seemed something almost familiar about the angular planes and strong lines of his face. She caught her breath, feeling the cold stare of the man as if he were alive within his ornate gold frame. His dark eyes seemed to follow her as she moved about the room. A chill shivered down her spine when her gaze met his head-on. For what seemed a long time she stood before the painting, examining its every detail. In the background, over each shoulder, the artist had painted small scenes. On the right was a miniature depiction of what appeared to be the Battle of New Orleans. To the left was a detailed interior—a music room, perhaps—and two figures, a dark-haired woman seated at a golden harp with a young boy standing beside her, his head resting on her shoulder.

Carol gazed fixedly at the images in the painting until they seemed to come alive. She could almost see the woman's fingers moving on the delicate harp strings, almost hear the sad whisper of the music. She ached to know who they were, when and where they had lived, what had happened to them.

Frank cleared his throat, interrupting her thoughts. "Do you reckon you'll be comfortable here?"

"Oh, yes, Frank! It's a wonderful room." She sighed, her eyes still on the portrait. "I'm sure it will be perfect."

She turned to find him lounging against the doorframe, a lazy smile curving his lips. "I hoped you'd like it."

"Like it? I *love* it!" she assured him. "And the little courtyard outside with the bubbling fountain, why, it's my own private sanctuary."

"Well, if you're all settled, I suppose I'd better go on and let you get some rest. Don't worry about getting up too early. I have a meeting first thing that I couldn't postpone, so I'll pick you up at noon and we can get started. I guess you'll want to see *her* first thing."

As Frank turned to leave, Carol stopped him.

"Thank you, Frank, for everything. It's been a lovely evening." She smiled a bit nervously. "I'll see you tomorrow."

Frank took a step closer and grinned down into her eyes, his own dancing with dark lights. For one breathless moment, Carol thought he meant to kiss her. Then she chided herself for such girlish foolishness. This was business, pure and simple. Besides, Frank would be the first to admit that he was a very married man, even if he hadn't seen his wife in over ten years.

" 'Night, ma'am, and thank you kindly," he said, smiling wistfully. "Sweet dreams now!"

Then he was gone, leaving Carol staring after him into the night. Something odd was happening here. She'd known Frank Longpre for only hours

59

yet it seemed that they had been friends for years . . . *forever!* There was a strange familiarity drawing them together that, even with her psychic powers, she didn't quite understand.

She walked over to the window and pulled the drapes aside to see if she could get a final glimpse of him. What she saw instead gave her a heart-thumping start.

Standing there in the dark courtyard, the old woman in the scarlet tignon stared back at Carol. Carol's heart raced and her palms went sweaty. She blinked. She looked again and the woman was gone.

"Cami . . . Cami . . . Cami," the sad little voice wailed inside Carol's head. *"Come back . . . back to Elysian Fields . . ."*

In that instant, Carol knew that she would be at the foot of Barracks Street the next morning before dawn.

Chapter Three

A heavy mist rolled in off the river that morning. The sorrowful moan of a distant foghorn carried on the thick, chilled air. Carol had dressed in corduroy slacks, a wool sweater, and her fleece-lined trench coat before heading for Barracks Street, but nevertheless her teeth chattered uncontrollably as she stood in the cold on the deserted wharf.

"This is crazy!" she muttered between dental clicks. "What ever possessed me . . ."

Just as she was about to turn and head back to her snug hotel room, she heard the unmistakable sound of oars splashing water. Then a deep, male voice called, "Ah-llo!"

A new kind of chill froze Carol where she stood. Her fear gave way quickly to a thrill of excitement. Anxious anticipation engulfed her. If anyone had asked why, she could never have explained the feeling. She was cold, weary, frightened, yet at the same time some inner part of her welcomed the thought of this bizarre, predawn foray into the unknown. She remembered how Granny Bess used to tell her, "Curiosity will be your downfall, child, sure as anything."

On an intellectual level, Carol fully agreed with her grandmother. But she knew from experience that she lived to satisfy her own curiosity. Once she heard the ferryman's call, she could no more have turned back to the safe sanctuary of her hotel than she could have jumped into the cold, muddy Mississippi to swim to the far bank.

She had done elaborate mental scheming from the time she met the old woman at the airport, thinking she would have to convince Frank that she had personal business to take care of alone this morning. Then Frank himself had provided her with an out. As eager as she was to pursue his case, at the moment she was even more anxious to clear up the mystery of the curious stranger who had given her the gold doubloon and the ferryman who would take her to Elysian Fields. Wherever that was! No way could she turn back now.

"Hello!" she called back. "I'm here."

She heard the boat bump the dock and a moment later a shudder ran through the old boards beneath her feet.

"Be careful, you, mam'zelle." The voice was still disembodied. It drifted to Carol eerily, as ghostly as the foghorn moaning out over the water.

She edged toward the end of the dock, testing every step before she put her full weight on each board. As she moved closer, the man standing below in his pirogue materialized into a dark, indistinct shape. He raised his hand to help her down the ladder.

"You the one. Yes, mam'zelle?"

She was perched halfway down to the small boat when he asked his question. Suddenly, Carol realized he wanted to see the gold coin that she had in her pocket.

"Here," she said, thrusting it toward him.

"*Merci*," he replied, taking the gold piece.

Once Carol was settled on a damp blanket in the bow, he took up his task at the oars. She could feel the surge of water against the thin hull. She clung to the sides, trying not to think of the river, running swift and cold only inches away.

The ferryman remained silent. A hint of dawn lifted one edge of the curtain of night. Against the purple-gray sky, Carol could see that her ferryman was extremely tall and lean with a mad tangle of long, dark hair falling about his stooped shoulders. He sang a wordless song to himself as he plied the oars—a deep, throaty, unmusical dirge.

"Where are you taking me?" Carol asked at length.

"*Champs Elysées*," he answered. "Elysian Fields."

"How far away is this place?" she asked, thinking suddenly of practical considerations. "I have to be back before noon."

He seemed to think about her question for a time before he answered. "Too far, mam'zelle, to be told. Still, not too far to see. Choctaw show you."

"Is that your name? Choctaw?"

He nodded silently.

"My name is Carol Marlowe," she offered, hoping he might open up if she started the conversation.

At this, he gave a negative shake of his head. "Cami," he said simply.

Cami—there was that name again. But who was she? And why did Carol keep hearing the voice in her head, calling Cami to come back? She lost herself in thought, trying to remember the first time she'd heard the pleas of the weeping child. For some time, she forgot where she was, whom she was with as she drifted in her own memories— recalling bits of dreams and visions all mixed with the kaleidoscope of long-ago reality.

When she snapped out of it, the sun was coming up, but still the fog lingered, distorting the world around her. They were no longer on the wide expanses of the river, but gliding slowly through a swamp of tall cypresses and twisted, bearded oaks.

"Where are we?"

"The knowing place," Choctaw answered cryptically.

"The *what*?" Carol wasn't sure she'd heard him correctly.

"Where all things come in time, to be remembered evermore."

"What things?" Carol demanded, weary with the man's riddles.

"You have special powers, mam'zelle. No? You see sometimes into the future. Do you not also see the past?"

"Yes," she said. "Bits of the past—tiny vignettes from time to time."

"You know *all* the past. *Your* past. It is time you confronted it."

Choctaw's words only confused her more. Carol simply shook her head at him.

"Look there, mam'zelle. Look there—to the knowing place—and face what was . . . what could be again."

Carol turned her head to see where he was pointing. Before she saw anything, however, the sun faded, plunging them once more into darkness. She cried out in shock.

"Sh-h-h!" Choctaw cautioned. "Make no sound. Only listen. Only see."

Her heart pounding in her breast, Carol did as her guide commanded. Her emotions were doing furious battle. She wanted to believe that Choctaw and his "knowing place" could somehow allow her to see back in time. But this experience was totally foreign to anything having to do with her psychic powers. The golden-eyed woman, the riddling ferryman, the murky swamp all seemed so strange. She was curious; she was also afraid.

Carol strained her eyes, trying to peer through the shadows. Before light seeped back into the scene, she heard the voices. Men's voices. Angry voices.

"Damn you, Lafitte! This is insane! You bury the booty in the middle of this swamp and how will we ever find it again?"

"Perhaps I don't wish *you* to find it again, Ortez. The swamp seems the best place to keep my wealth out of the hands of my enemies. But maybe I would be wise to do as they say Blackbeard did, eh? Kill those who helped him hide his treasure and bury them with it. How does that strike you, Ortez?"

"No, Boss! Please! This spot, she is fine. You will know, but I will never tell because I am lost like a blind man in the bowels of this dreadful swamp."

"Lost, are you?" Lafitte gave a hearty laugh. "Then perhaps I should leave you here. If you can't find your way out, you can't tell anyone where my treasure is buried."

Carol's skin crawled as she heard the pirate's threats. The very thought of being lost in this swamp made her feel weak and ill with fear. It seemed almost as if she herself were the one being threatened. An image of Frank's mummified corpse floated before her eyes. Was that why Choctaw was showing her this scene between the pirates? Had the woman lost her way in these regions while searching for Lafitte's buried gold?

For an instant, enough light filtered through the thick canopy overhead for Carol to see the men. Jean Lafitte was tall, handsome in a swarthy way, but with more than a touch of cunning in his smile. His companion, Ortez, was a short, barrel-chested man with narrow, scheming eyes all but hidden by his rampant black beard and shaggy brows. Between them on the marshy ground sat an open chest filled with jewels and gold coins like the one she had given to Choctaw. She glanced toward the ferryman. He stood in the stern of the boat—silent and motionless, as if he were carved of darkness.

When Carol looked back the scene had faded. Where the pirates had stood a moment before, she watched a snowy egret spread its wings lazily, then swoop in a graceful arc toward the water.

"Did Lafitte kill Ortez?" she asked Choctaw.

He shook his head. "No murderer, Jean Lafitte," he answered. "Yet the greedy Ortez died here.

Came back for the gold, him." Choctaw paused and gave a deep chuckle. "Swamp got that one for good."

Carol shivered. What did all this have to do with her? She knew little of Jean Lafitte, other than what Frank had told her the night before, and nothing of his treasure.

"In time, understanding will come, mam'zelle," Choctaw whispered.

Was he reading her thoughts? Carol wondered.

As they pushed on slowly through the swamp, Carol trained her eyes ahead, almost fearing what she might see next. Off in the distance, half-shrouded in deep shadows, she thought she saw a house—at least, the shell of a once-great mansion. As they drew nearer, she realized her eyes had not deceived her. The sad, roofless structure sat in ruin at the edge of the bayou. Vines snaked through its paneless windows and climbed its crumbling columns. The once-lovely home looked heart-wrenchingly sad—abused by time and elements, forgotten by civilization.

"Who lived there?" she asked.

"*Still lives,*" corrected the ferryman before he answered her question with a single, sharp word: "Cami!"

Confused, Carol blinked, then looked again. When she did, the place had righted itself. Years of decay had fallen away in the wink of an eye. The mansion was suddenly as lovely as the day it was built, with its pristine columns, wide stairs to the gallery, and perfectly manicured gardens.

"Cami?" she repeated in a whisper.

Just then, she spied a big, robust horseman gallop

up the circular drive. "Cami!" he called out with a boisterous laugh. "Camille Mazaret, you come out here right now! See what Papa has brought you."

The front door flew open and a young girl of perhaps nine or ten scampered out onto the veranda, wide petticoats swaying beneath her yellow dimity skirt to offer a glimpse of ruffled pantalettes and dainty kid slippers. Her perfect, heart-shaped face beamed with joy at the sight of her father. Raven-black sausage curls danced about her shoulders as she hurried down the stairs to greet him.

"Papa!" she cried, hugging his boot before he could dismount. Carol actually experienced the little girl's excitement. "I missed you so. What did you bring me from New Orleans?"

The Creole gentleman leaped from the saddle and swooped his beautiful daughter into his arms. "A kiss first, little lady. Then you get your surprise."

The two stared at each other for a moment—the girl's glittering indigo eyes a paler, more startling blue than those in her father's tanned face. Then quickly she snapped her lids shut and pursed her lips for his kiss.

Carol's heart went icy cold when she heard another voice. "Put her down at once, Edouard!"

Father and daughter turned their heads as one to stare at the cold-faced beauty standing in the open doorway. She was gowned in black as if for mourning, and the pallor of her porcelain skin seemed even paler against the harsh color of her high-necked frock.

"Adele," Edouard Mazaret called to his wife, "what ails you? Of course, my girl must give her papa a kiss to welcome him home."

"She will not!" The woman answered in a deep, fierce tone for all her diminutive size. "Come back inside, Camille, this minute!"

Carol experienced a mingled sense of fear and anger at Adele Mazaret's command. Cami obviously shared those feelings.

"But, *Maman* . . ." the girl tried to protest.

"Do as I say!"

Cami looked to her father. His broad smile had vanished; his eyes had taken on a stormy hue. "Mind your mother, child."

Gently, Edouard lowered his daughter to the ground. But, seeing the tears brimming in Cami's eyes, he caught her shoulder and turned her back toward him. "Your surprise," he whispered, pressing a gold coin on a chain into her hand. "A piece of Lafitte's treasure that I found in the swamp. I had two doubloons done up by a jeweler in New Orleans. You can wear this one around your neck."

"Oh, Papa!" she cried, but he warned her to silence with one finger to his lips and a nod toward her mother.

"Keep it to yourself, my little darling."

At this point in the scene, Carol experienced an odd phenomenon. She was no longer an outsider viewing three strangers from the past. Suddenly, Carol *was* Cami. She was ten years old again and torn, with a child's pain, between her love for her father and her fear of her mother's wrath.

Avoiding Adele Mazaret's scornful gaze, Camille hurried up the front stairs and into the house. Once out of her mother's sight, she went to the parlor window so she could spy from behind the drape to see what would transpire between her parents.

69

Her mother advanced only as far as the head of the stairs, demanding with her stern gaze that her husband come to her. The stiffness of her back, the slight quiver of her shoulders, and the angry jut of her chin were enough to tell Cami that all was not well between her parents. As Edouard climbed the stairs, his head drooped as if he feared what he might read in his wife's eyes.

Cami held her breath and watched as her parents came face to face. Her father had stopped two stairs short of the top so that he and the much shorter Adele stood at eye level. For several moments there was only silence. Then, quicker than Cami could blink, she saw her mother's small hand flash up like an angry bird of prey to strike her husband full across the mouth. Cami—Carol gasped. Edouard's head snapped back, not so much from the force of the blow as from sheer shock at his wife's deliberate action. Cami gave a sharp cry, but it went unnoticed, muffled by the heavy velvet drapes.

A wintry smile curved Edouard's full lips. "Thank you, my dear," he said sarcastically. "And may I say that it is indeed a pleasure to be home again. Now I'll just go on in and give my daughter that kiss."

"You'll do no such thing," Adele shrilled. "I know where you've been, Edouard. You've been with *her*. Lips that have touched that woman's shall never kiss my daughter."

Cami watched the color drain from her father's ruddy face. His eyes flashed dark and threatening. He took the other two steps in one giant stride until he stood beside his wife, towering over her. Catching her upper arms in his strong grip, he leaned down over her and planted his wide mouth firmly over the thin, narrow line of his wife's.

Cami's eyes went wide. She had never seen her parents kiss before. She knew, young as she was, that at some time there had been something between the two of them. She herself was positive proof of that, after all. But for as long as she could recall, her parents had lived apart in separate wings of the big house. Not once had she ever seen her father kiss her mother, nor even touch her hand in passing.

When Edouard finally released his wife, she stumbled away from him, striking out at him with one hand while she wiped furiously at her mouth with the other.

"You terrible . . . horrible . . . miserable . . ."

"*What*, Adele?" he goaded. "What am I? Put a name to it once and for all. Let's have this out between us and be done with it. I'm sick to death of your accusations, your suspicions, your cold contempt. Yes, dammit! I kissed another woman while I was in New Orleans! It was the first kiss I'd had in a very long time."

Shocked by her father's rough actions and rougher words, Cami glanced toward her mother, who looked like she might faint at any moment. But the rise of her father's harsh voice drew Cami's attention immediately back to him.

"Yes, I kissed a woman, and 'that woman,' as you call her, has a name and a heart. Fiona is a real, flesh-and-blood, feeling, giving, loving person." When his wife drew back, ready to strike him again, Edouard caught her arm. "No! You'll hear me out this time, Adele. Lord, how I hate these scenes, but

71

this has to be. You know as well as I do why I go to Fiona. That slap across my face a bit ago was the most intimacy you've shown me since the night our Cami was conceived. I've let you put me off and treat me like I was no better than one of the servants all these years, but, dammit, I'm through with being locked out of your chamber, even though you locked me out of your heart long ago. I mean to change all that, starting right now."

Cami—her heart racing and tears brimming in her eyes—watched as her mother turned to flee. But her father caught his wife in his arms and kissed her again. Then, without another word, Edouard Mazaret scooped up the sobbing, struggling woman and strode inside and up the stairs.

Carol shared Cami's fear and uncertainty. The two were still joined at the soul as Cami started for the stairs to follow her parents. But a huge, gentle-eyed black woman intercepted her.

"No, chile," she whispered, taking the weeping girl to her ample bosom. "You come along with me now. I got somethin' in de kitchen for you— something soft an' sweet an' hot from my oven. Don' you worry yo' pretty head none over yo' ma an' pa. Dey'll be fine."

Carol experienced a physical jolt when woman and child vanished suddenly. It was as if she had been torn out of Cami's body. At that same moment, the fresh paint on the plantation house vanished, too. The swamp closed in again; Elysian Fields fell once more into ruin.

It took Carol several moments to catch her breath. When she could speak again, she demanded of the sphinx-like Choctaw, "What's happening to me?"

"The same as happened to you long, long ago. But you just now seeing it clear."

"What about my papa and . . ." Carol quickly caught herself and corrected her words. "What happened between Edouard and Adele?"

"The same like happens with any man and wife behind closed doors."

"The Mazarets weren't like any man and wife," she said. "Adele hated her husband. But why? Edouard seemed like a gentle man until she pushed him beyond his limits. Imagine not allowing him to kiss his own daughter. Certainly, Cami adored her father."

Choctaw nodded. "You see good, these people, mam'zelle. That Adele, she a queer one—don't want her man, but don't want no other woman to have him neither—not even their own daughter. Bad blood there. Much bad blood!"

Carol shook her head and pulled her coat more closely about her. "I won't even begin to try to understand *how* I'm seeing all this. But can't you tell me at least *why?*"

" 'Cause to prepare you, mam'zelle."

"Prepare me for what?"

"You see, soon now."

"I won't be prepared for anything unless you tell me how all this turned out, Choctaw. What happened to Adele?"

" 'Nother seed M'sieur planted that night, but his wife, she don't want no more baby. When she find out, she go very crazy. She take the buggy out alone in a storm. The levee give way. The buggy gone, the baby gone, Madame Adele, she gone, too, into the river."

"Oh, my God!" Carol groaned. "What happened to Cami and to Edouard?"

"Look just there." Again, Choctaw pointed one long finger into the distance.

Carol turned to see the tall-columned mansion draped in funereal bunting. A servant in formal black, his ebony cheeks streaked with tears, stood on the gallery as if expecting callers to pay their respects.

"Who died?" Carol asked.

As if he heard the question, the weeping black servant on the veranda moaned, "De Massa, he gone! And dat pore li'l chile, what's to become of her?"

The black man turned and went back into the house. Carol followed him, an unseen and uninvited visitor in this house of mourning and despair. Although candles glowed in all the rooms, the place seemed dark and oppressive. The smells of mildew and camphor hung heavy in the humid air. From upstairs came the soft sound of weeping. Carol followed the muffled sound. Fearing what she would find, but knowing she must see for herself, Carol followed the servant into an upstairs chamber. There on the bed lay the body of Edouard Mazaret, looking pale but natural in death.

Carol shifted her gaze to the young woman, gowned in black, who sat with her head bowed, weeping at the bedside. In an eerie flash, she felt herself becoming one with the woman, taking her place to share Camille's soul.

Camille and Carol were several years older than they had been moments before. Sixteen or thereabout.

"Mam'zelle Cami?" the servant whispered. "Please, ma'am, don't cry no mo'. You got to leave right soon fo' Mulgrove. De Pinards, dey be expectin' yo' 'for' nightfall."

"I don't want to go," Cami sobbed. "Elysian Fields is my home. I want to stay here."

"But yo' papa, he done said with his last breath dat yo' to go live with his cousins. Dey sent dere boat. It be waitin' right now fo' you, down to de dock. Ain't nothin' mo' you can do fo' yo' po' papa here, chile."

"No! Papa said I should go to New Orleans, to the woman who wears the other gold doubloon."

The servant made no answer, but leaned over and blew out a candle near the bed. As the flame guttered out, the scene dissolved into a confused rainbow of colors. One minute, Carol felt as if she were tumbling through time and space: in the next she found herself back in the boat, but with the aura of Cami's sadness still strong in her mind and heart. She had not yet fully separated from the grieving young woman.

"Why do you keep doing that?" Carol demanded of Choctaw in a voice filled with frustration. "What happened to Edouard? What's going to happen to Cami? Who is the woman in New Orleans?"

"M'sieur Mazaret died of the bad heart back in 1838. Mam'zelle Camille went to her father's cousins, Morris and Beatrice Pinard, to be raised at Mulgrove Plantation with their own daughter, Lorenna. As for she who wears the other doubloon—in time . . . in time . . ."

Carol waited, but the stoic ferryman said no more.

"And that's all?" she demanded. "End of story?"

She watched him slowly shake his head. "All for me to tell. The end of the story, mam'zelle, I leave to you."

"I don't understand . . ."

Slowly, Choctaw's sinewy arm raised, one gnarled finger pointing again. He uttered a single word: "Mulgrove."

At that moment, the bow of the boat hit the end of a dock. A pair of black hands reached down to grasp Carol's arms and help her up to the landing.

"Ah swan, Mam'zelle Cami, if yo' don' look a fright!" A broad, black face scowled into Carol's. "You wanna give de mistress palpitations? It's nigh onto time fo' de guests to arrive an' here yo' is out fishing like yo' was one of de hands. We best sneak yo' up de servants' stairs aroun' back so Miz Beatrice don' see yo' in dat ol' raggedy frock."

"But wait . . ." Carol tried to protest as the stout black mammy tugged at her.

"Ain't no time to wait," the woman said, rolling her eyes. "You listen good, chile, an' do like Maum Zalee tells you. Otherwise, we gonna both be in some kinda pow'ful trouble. Yo' hear, now?"

Carol looked down at herself and stopped dead in her tracks, her breath catching in her throat. Gone were her slacks and trench coat. As Zalee had said, she was wearing a tattered and dated gown of gray linsey-woolsey with several drooping petticoats underneath. When had she changed? Where were her own clothes?

She glanced back over her shoulder. Choctaw gave her a slight signal that passed for a wave of farewell as he shoved off. Immediately, he was swal-

76

lowed up in shadows, man and boat vanishing before her eyes. Her heart sank. He'd gone away and left her in this mad place.

"Wait!" she cried.

"Ain't no time to wait, chile," the servant insisted. "Yo' jes' come along with Maum Zalee now. Lordie, lordie, how'm ah ever gone git all dem snarls outta yo' hair an' de curls back in it?"

No one they passed as they trudged up the wide lawn seemed the least bit surprised or curious to see Carol Marlowe on the plantation grounds. Zalee smuggled her charge up the narrow servants' stairs, then breathed a great sigh of relief that they hadn't run into Morris or Beatrice Pinard along the way.

"Lordie, lordie!" Zalee breathed, big bosom heaving. "Yo' a caution, honey, an' have been dese past two year since yo' come to Mulgrove. But sometimes ah wonder—is ole Zalee up to de task of keepin' you in tow? You got to give up dese bull-headed, tomboy ways of yours an' set yo' pretty self to findin' a husband. Massa Morris, he tell Miz Beatrice jes' t'other day, 'Cousin Cami, she pick her own husband or ah pick one fo' her.' An', honey, he meant right soon now, ah could tell."

"Never!" Carol actually shrieked the word and stamped her foot at the same time. She felt Cami's seething rage at the mere thought of someone else choosing a husband for her.

Carol realized suddenly that she was feeling a lot of things foreign to her—emotions and sensations. There was deep resentment toward Morris and Beatrice, two people Carol had yet to meet. There was also a kind of daughterly love toward Zalee that Carol knew Cami had never felt for her own mother, Adele. And most pronounced was a hollow, lonely ache in her heart for her dead father. Was there a man in Camille's life, Carol wondered, a man she truly loved? Although Carol concentrated very hard, she could feel nothing in Camille Mazaret's spirit that even approached romantic attachment. Still, she did sense that some shadow of a secret was buried deep in the young woman's heart, something that Carol had yet to comprehend.

During the next two hours, Carol was scrubbed, brushed, curled, powdered, and trussed to within an inch of her life. When, finally, Zalee and her two young assistants finished their work and the smiling mammy pronounced her charge "fit for the ball," Carol turned to look at herself in the full-length mirror. She gasped aloud.

Zalee giggled. "Ah knowed ah could do it! You don' even recognize yo' own self, do you, honey? Ah could tell under all that river mud there was still a beauty lurking—just a matter of scrubbing yo' way down to her."

"A beauty" certainly stared back at Carol from the slightly rippled surface of the old looking glass. A beauty who had been a total stranger until this very day. Carol found herself staring into the brilliant, indigo eyes of Camille Mazaret. Gone was Carol's recently-cut brown hair, replaced by long, curling tresses of night-black. The young woman in the mirror was shorter than Carol had been—more petite in every way. Her face was perfect to the last feature from her well-shaped mouth, elegant little nose, and sooty lashes to the delicately arched eyebrows below the dramatic widow's peak high on her forehead.

As she stared at herself—her *new* self—Camille's thoughts and personality shoved Carol completely out of the picture. Surprise at her image suddenly faded to be replaced by a strong young will, a determination to find love before she took a husband and so outwit her scheming Cousin Morris.

"You ready, Mam'zelle Cami?" Zalee asked.

Camille gave a quick, resigned nod. "As ready as I'll ever be for Cousin Morris's parade of gawking boys."

"Now, you be nice, honey!" Zalee scolded gently. "Maybe de very one will show up at Mulgrove tonight."

Cami laughed—a sound as clear and bright as the tinkle of glass wind chimes in a summer breeze, but there was an edge of fatalism to the sound, too. "I wish I could share your optimism, Zalee." Cami hugged the dear servant, then headed downstairs—head high, back straight, bosom swelled.

Carol had one final, fleeting moment of realizing who she was and the bizarre circumstances she had entered. Then she experienced a moment of severe panic at her predicament. What was she doing here? Why was this happening to her? And Frank! What if he came for her and she had disappeared just like Eileen?

Then familiar harp music floated up from the ballroom below to fill the great house and wipe away any trace of the woman who, such a short time before, had been Carol Marlowe.

No longer did the pitiful little voice have to wail to Cami to come back. Camille Mazaret had returned at last.

Chapter Four

Soft music, crystal chandeliers, the scent of magnolias, eager beaus, and Mademoiselle Camille Mazaret. Everything seemed in perfect tune for the ball that evening at Mulgrove Plantation. Everything, that is, except Cami herself.

Out of step, her mind wandering, Cami muttered an unladylike oath under her breath when her partner stepped on her toes. Her fault, she admitted, still managing to keep the required smile frozen on her face. Only the glassy stare of her bewitching indigo eyes betrayed her boredom, her total frustration with this Creole mating ritual.

For Cami, the whole evening had turned into a dizzying blur of over-eager young males wearing too many smiles and too much pomade, each more determined than the last to convince her what a willing and excellent husband he would make.

Willing, she told herself, to take charge of the vast sugar plantation and the fortune my father left me. *Excellent*, she added, at pretending sole interest in Edouard Mazaret's daughter.

Cami had never tried to fool herself. Having inherited her mother's ebony hair, perfect complexion, and startling eyes, a beauty she might be. Charming she could be, when she chose to use the Mazaret smile and the winning ways handed down to her from her father's side of the family. Still, she knew that her main attraction was an ill-gotten fortune in gold buried somewhere in the swamps of Elysian Fields.

Rumor had it that Jean Lafitte himself had hidden a king's ransom somewhere on the Mazaret plantation back around 1815. The gold doubloon Cami wore about her neck—a single piece from the cache her father had unearthed years ago—bore testimony to the fact that the fabled treasure did, in fact, exist. Now, to the victor would go the spoils—Camille Mazaret as a bride, but more importantly, she mused, Lafitte's long-hidden chests of treasure.

Eagerly and systematically, the plantation families of the parish had sent their sons on this quest, no doubt counting doubloons in their dreams all the while. But so far, no one had captured the key to the gold. That key was Cami's heart.

At the moment, one Gerome Arneau—a head shorter than Cami and far too near-sighted to be graceful on the dance floor—was engaged in trying to win her favor. In the process, he was ruining her best satin slippers with his clumsy, stumbling steps. When finally the dance came to an end, he bowed over Camille's gloved hand, squeezing her fingers too tightly.

"Mademoiselle, how can I tell you the fullness of my heart at this moment?" He squinted up at her, twitching his thin mustache in something that imitated a love-sick smile.

Cami stifled a yawn. The short, round Gerome, she thought, had more fullness of belly than his heart would ever know. She had counted his repeated returns to the buffet during the evening. Five plates he had devoured with gluttonous delight.

When Gerome finally released Cami's hand, she stared down in disgust at her white kid glove. Soiled! Gravy, no doubt, or some of the pungent grease from his slicked-down hair.

She sighed and moved away from the dance floor, hoping she could have a few moments to herself. Glancing about the room only reaffirmed an earlier observation. There wasn't one *real man* at the ball tonight.

All the plantation owners' sons were a year or two younger than she, and still, regrettably, acted their age. At eighteen, Cami was older than most Creole maidens. She should have been long-since wed, but her mother's death in a carriage accident, then her father's untimely passing a few years later, had kept her in mourning when she should have been entering society. Now, the only eligible bachelors left were bashful boys or culls rejected during earlier seasons. Camille Mazaret had never been one to settle for less than her heart desired. From the cradle, she had been taught by her father to demand the same excellence in others that he expected from her.

She could hear his words ringing in her ears still: "Accept only the very best, Cami dear, be it horseflesh or husband. Always remember you're a Mazaret. Demand what you deserve." Then he'd flash that smile of his that could break a heart at fifty paces, chuckle softly, and whisper, "And if they try to pawn off second-best on you, just tell them all to go to the devil!"

Glancing about the ballroom, Cami sighed. If only "second-best" were being offered. But the young men her cousins had invited weren't nearly runner-up material.

She felt almost desperate, as if the whole world were crowding in on her, trying to suffocate her. For months now, her guardians, Cousin Morris and his wife Beatrice, had thrown marital prospects in her path as if they were lavishly strewing rose petals at a wedding—truly their fondest hope for her. Cami, who had stalled for months, knew that her time was running out. Soon her guardians' supply of bachelors of *bonne famille* would be exhausted. It was clear that Morris and Beatrice Pinard meant to have Camille married and off their hands before their own daughter began her first season.

Only this morning Cami had overheard Cousin Beatrice haranguing her husband on the subject. "Our pale little Lorenna simply cannot stand up to such competition. Why, oh, why couldn't our daughter have been blessed with the same ebony tresses as Camille? The same porcelain-like skin and dark-lashed eyes? Poor, poor Lorenna with her freckles and shyness and lackluster hair. We'll be lucky if she isn't forced to cast her corset onto the armoire. Maybe the convent would be best. Oh, the pain of it, to have Camille under our roof at exactly this time! It is almost more than a mother can bear. Find Cousin Camille a husband, Morris. Find her one *now!*"

Having finished her impassioned speech, Cousin Beatrice had taken to her bed with a wine-soaked cloth over her eyes. There she had remained, locked away with her suffering, until shortly before the first guests arrived for what Cami secretly thought of as "the viewing."

Camille only hoped Lorenna hadn't overheard her mother's remarks. The last thing in the world Cami wanted was to compete with her shy, sweet Cousin Lorenna, or anyone else for that matter.

"Being left quite alone would do nicely, thank you!"

Cami was a victim of circumstance, forced by propriety to remain at Mulgrove until she was wed. Before her father's death two years ago, he had begged the Pinards to take in his daughter until she married and could claim her inheritance. Until that time, Elysian Fields, the white-columned mansion on the river and its vast fields of sugarcane, would be held in trust, taken care of by an overseer and three hundred slaves.

"Oh, how I wish I could go home!" Cami said, blinking back an unbidden tear.

To marry and raise her children at Elysian Fields was her fondest dream. But that would not be allowed until she made a choice that would change the course of her life forever. Yet her cousins treated the momentous decision as if it were the simplest thing in the world, as if she were picking a frock for the day or deciding what she'd like for breakfast.

All Cami wanted was to live her own life and choose her own husband. Was it so much to ask? However, the traditional dictates of Creole society stood solidly against her.

"If only Papa had lived," she murmured. But merely wishing never got anyone anywhere.

At that moment of realization, Cami straightened her shoulders and determined to set her own course. She had thought long and hard about leaving Mulgrove, but never seriously until just now.

"Papa would approve," she said with a secret smile.

Politely declining another dancing partner's offer, Cami slipped out of the ballroom. She had had all she could take for one evening. She would hide in the ladies' sitting room for a time, compose herself, and make her plans. There seemed to be no way she could make Cousin Morris and Cousin Beatrice understand her feelings, so escape was the only answer.

As Cami stepped into the hallway, she heard the low rumble of male voices near the front door. "I am sorry, m'sieur," Cousin Morris said in a tone mingling embarrassment with anger. "There has obviously been some mistake."

Curious, Cami peeked around a bronze bust of Socrates to have a better view of the marble-floored entry hall. A giant of a man, his back turned to her, stood beside Cousin Morris. A gust of wind from the open door whipped at the stranger's cloak, revealing evening clothes underneath. A late-arriving guest, she surmised. But who could it be? Of those who had been invited, only René Gireau was missing. Camille knew René and liked him well enough. He was a charming young man with a keen wit and a winning smile. But he was only a boy, not a *real man* like this stranger at the door.

"If there has been a mistake made, I assure you, it is yours, Pinard. Is this not one of your invitations?" The man spoke in a low, rasping voice, then flashed a white card from beneath his black, satin-lined cape.

Morris Pinard nodded, but stood his ground. "It is. But be that as it may, sir," he blustered, "as I said before, your name was not on the guest list. Now, will you leave or shall I have Brutus assist you out?"

Brutus, the Pinards' hulking butler, lurked nearby, ready to carry out his master's orders. Tension sparked the air as the two white men jousted for position and black Brutus awaited his command.

The stranger said nothing further, but the vexed tap-tap of his ebony sword-cane echoed ominously in the stillness. For several moments, it looked as if the confrontation might generate something more serious than hostile words.

A slow, conniving smile crept to Camille's peach-colored lips and a merry blue light danced in her eyes. This was something different. This was something exciting. Suddenly, the evening took on new promise.

Surely, Cami told herself, Cousin Morris's high-handed tactics in trying to force her to wed deserved something in retaliation. Whoever this intri-

86

guing stranger was, he had obviously meant to crash the party. Perhaps she could help him. A novel idea with great possibilities, Cami assured herself silently. Even though she had yet to see the man's face, she liked the overall look of him—big, broad-shouldered, with an arrogant tilt to his dark head and a swagger to his every move.

Quickly, she made up her mind. "I shall do it!" she said softly, gathering her courage.

She stepped out from her hiding place, ready to run to the stranger. She would pretend she had invited him to the party. "A dear, old friend of Papa's," she imagined herself explaining to her shocked Cousin Morris.

However, even as she took her first step, the man turned to leave. An instant before he crossed the threshold, he glanced back over his shoulder as if he sensed someone staring at him.

Camille caught her breath as his gaze fastened on her, pinning her to the spot. Raindrops glistened in the rampant curls of his dark hair. His eyes, too, were as black as a moonless night on the bayou. His rugged features were startlingly bold—a slash of heavy brows, a hooked nose with flaring nostrils, a cunning curl to his lips, and a livid scar down his right cheek. Taken in the whole, his countenance was disturbingly arresting, if not handsome. But most of all, the obsidian glitter of his eyes entranced her.

He stared back with such intensity he seemed to be looking right into her heart and chuckling all the while at her discomfort. With maddeningly lazy appreciation, he let his eyes travel over her, lingering for a delicious and disturbing time at the low-cut ivory lace encasing her firm, high breasts. When his gaze returned to Camille's face, a smile of pure seduction spread over his granite-like features. Her cheeks flamed.

Cami felt utterly foolish. Childish. Her lips parted as if she meant to say something. But what? Even if she could find her tongue, she doubted she'd find words suitable to express her breathless, fluttery feelings at the moment. Deep down inside, a voice warned her that a proper young lady did not converse with such a dark rogue. She tried to turn away, but found herself unable to move. As Cami continued to stare—perfectly mesmerized— he snapped a smart bow in salute, turned, and was gone.

The hallway remained cloaked in silence for several moments after the stranger's departure. Cami was conscious of her own heart beating. Then she heard a deep sigh of relief escape her cousin before he spoke.

"Thank you, Brutus. That will be all."

"Cousin Morris, who was that man?" Cami asked innocently, still trying to catch her breath and calm her racing heart.

Her cousin—a portly Creole planter in his late fifties—cleared his throat loudly and waggled his mustache several times before he answered. "No one!" he snapped. "No one of any consequence, at any rate. *C'est de la communauté.*" He frowned deeply, then added, "Well, perhaps he does not come of common stock, but he has fallen far from his beginnings."

"He wasn't invited tonight?" Cami asked. "But, Cousin Morris, I saw the invitation in his hand."

88

"The dastardly fellow came by that invitation dishonestly," her cousin replied sharply, "probably stole it, if my guess is correct. He thought he'd help himself to a free meal and some of my best wines. Well, I put him in his proper place."

"But who was he? Tell me, please." Cami was not above begging to get her answer.

Cousin Morris eyed her suspiciously. "Why should you care? He is nothing to any of us."

Thinking quickly, Cami employed the unused lie she had invented a short time before. "He looked so much like one of Papa's dearest old friends."

Blanching at her words, Morris answered her in a harsh tone. "Your father was a good and honorable man, Camille Mazaret. I am highly insulted on his behalf that you would even hint that he might have associated with such a scoundrel as Victoine Navar."

Camille hid a smile behind her lacy fan. Her tiny lie might have angered her cousin, but at least it provided her with the information she sought.

Victoine Navar. Intriguing! But who was the man? She still had no idea, but she certainly intended to find out.

Sounding all innocence, Cami asked, "Is his plantation near here?"

Her cousin's scowl deepened. "Forget you ever saw the man. He has no plantation and no reputation. So far as I know, Black Vic hasn't even a soul."

"Real-ly?" Cami drawled.

"You are neglecting your guests, Camille," Cousin Morris reminded her. Pointing to a line of partners waiting to dance with her, he ordered, "Return to the ballroom at once."

"Yes, Cousin Morris." She obeyed dutifully, but all the while her mind was on the mysterious stranger. "Black Vic Navar!" she repeated, smiling at the new sparkle in her eyes as she caught a passing glimpse of herself in one of the hallway mirrors.

Cami smoothed her already-smooth hair, fanned herself rapidly trying to cool her blush, then plunged back into the ballroom. Now that she had decided this would definitely be her last night at Mulgrove, she could make herself endure the rest of the evening.

The line of waiting boys, selected for their bloodlines by her father's second-cousin-twice-removed, seemed endless, as endless as this evening had been. She sighed wearily as she accepted the arm of her next puppy-eager partner. But at least now she had something to occupy her mind as she was dragged about the dance floor. Two things, actually: her planned escape and now this fascinating stranger.

Who exactly was Black Vic? How had he come by his invitation? And would their paths ever cross again? She hoped if that happened, she would find it in herself to act in a more sophisticated manner. How amused he must have been by her silent gaping! Camille shuddered in her partner's arms, remembering the way the man's bold gaze had set her trembling.

One dance blended into the next. Face after face passed before Cami's eyes to be smiled at, then quickly forgotten. Champagne, dessert ices, gossip, and then good-nights.

Finally, it was over!

The last guest had left Mulgrove. The last girlish giggle from her Cousin Lorenna had faded. The musicians were packing up their instruments. Her aunt had already gone to bed, no doubt with another wine-soaked cloth, or perhaps simply the wine. Camille herself, exhausted but excited by her secret plan, had already turned toward the stairs when Cousin Morris called to her.

"I'd like a word with you, my dear." His smile and tone were as cloyingly affectionate and totally insincere as those of the young men she'd been forced to endure all evening and through many long, dull evenings prior to this one.

But no more! she reminded herself.

"Yes, Cousin Morris?" She expected him to tell her the date of the next event on his find-a-husband-for-Camille agenda.

Instead, he gave her a sharp look with his Creole-dark eyes and stated flatly, "It is time you chose, my girl. Your father left your fate entirely in my hands, begging me with his dying breath to see you properly wed. I've done my utmost to honor that request. You have been properly introduced to every suitable young man from this parish and several others. Now, it is up to you. There wasn't a gentleman here tonight who wouldn't jump at the chance to marry you."

Camille's inner voice added with silent sarcasm, *Don't you mean jump at the chance to possess my father's holdings and search for Lafitte's lost treasure?*

"Well, Camille?" her cousin prompted. "Give me a name. Immediately! I mean to set the wheels in motion the first thing in the morning. We'll plan a fall wedding at St. Louis Cathedral. Now, the name of the groom, please."

"*A name! A name!*" His harsh voice echoed in her

head as panic spread through her like wildfire. She hadn't expected him to press the issue this very night.

"Who shall it be, Camille?" he demanded. "Arneau? Dapremont? Gravier? Peyroux? Come, come! Out with it."

"Cousin, please!" Camille begged, thinking quickly. "At least give me the night to consider my choices."

Actually, she'd already thought through the list of names he had suggested. Gerome Arneau was too short, too round, too awkward. Simon Dapremont was too dull. François Gravier was too arrogant. Peyroux? She couldn't even place him. But not one of her cousin's choices suited her tastes. She knew that for sure. How dare he put her on the spot this way?

"You are being unreasonable, Camille."

"Unreasonable?" she cried. She was angry now, too angry to hold her tongue. "This is my whole life we're talking about. I can't simply pick some stranger out of a crowd. What about *love*, Cousin Morris?"

Her question brought a deep, humorless laugh in reply. "Foolish, foolish child! A Creole wife loves God and her children, in that order and exclusively. If she grows to love her husband, it is a rare situation indeed, and not very wise on her part. I've been most patient with you. Your father chose not to arrange your marriage before his untimely passing. He made me promise that I would let you have a hand in choosing, that you would not be forced to wed a man you had never met. But he did say you *must* marry. I am only following his instructions.

92

Elysian Fields needs a new master. You have met the very best young men. Now you have but to make your selection."

Camille, her nerves frayed, responded sharply, "Surely, you must realize that parading this odd assortment of bachelors before me is not what my father had in mind. He told me I should never agree to a marriage that didn't please me."

"Your father spoiled you miserably," Morris countered.

"Yes, he did," Camille agreed. "But be that as it may, he wanted me to *know* the man I marry . . . to *love* the man I marry. Papa never wanted me to settle for anything less than true love."

A sly, spiteful grin stole over her cousin's face. "I suppose your father meant a love as great as he had for your mother?"

A little tear of pain ripped Camille's heart. How mean Cousin Morris could be when he set his mind to it! Everyone knew and still talked of the scandal—her parents' loveless marriage, their horrible rows, Camille's mother ordering her husband out of their chamber, then ranting bitterly of his unfaithfulness after she herself had all but forced him to take a lover.

Edouard Mazaret's mistress was said to grieve for him still. That octoroon beauty had been the one and only great love of his life. Camille's mother, who seemed to have been born terrified of men and who died in the same condition, had allowed her husband access to her chamber only long enough to produce a stillborn son and then, disappointingly, a daughter. Feeling her duty done at that point, Adele Mazaret had put aside her wifely duties for-

93

ever, slowly sinking into self-pity and near-madness. After her husband finally demanded his rights, Adele ran away. Some whispered that her death was no accident, that she actually took her own life and that of her unborn child.

Camille's father, a dashing, gentle, romantic man, had finally succumbed to his need, seeking love outside his home. His enduring liaison with his free woman of color was whispered about in New Orleans and all up through the river plantation country. Their love affair had become legend at his death, when Edouard's beautiful *placée* had sworn on his grave that she would remain faithful to him to her own dying day. Camille had never met the woman, but, through the slave grapevine, she had heard much about her. From her own father's lips she had once heard the woman's name.

"Fiona," she whispered, hanging her head so that her cousin could not see her moist eyes.

"Yes, Fiona," Morris Pinard echoed. "Your mother was a dear woman who did what was expected of her without whimpering about her fate. She married your father as their parents dictated and did her duty by him. Your own husband, like your father, my girl, will likely take a mistress after a time. So you needn't worry about trying to make him love you, before or after your marriage."

Camille's tears dried up in a sudden rush of fury. "What about *me*, Cousin Morris? Maybe I'd like to be loved by my husband. Maybe I could give my husband enough warmth and affection so he wouldn't require the services of another."

The aging Creole, who for many years had kept

his own quadroon *placée*, looked at Camille as if she had suddenly lost her wits. He squinted hard and stroked his pointed beard. "Didn't your mother teach you anything, Camille? Why on earth would any well-brought-up young lady wish such a task upon herself? Outrageous! But you'll learn, my girl, in time. Go to bed now. I'll expect your answer first thing in the morning."

Had Cousin Morris been more attentive, he might have had Cami's answer on the spot. But she didn't mean for him to hear her words. She spoke only to herself as he turned and headed up the stairs.

"Never!" she whispered. "I'll be long gone before morning, *dear* cousin."

Camille stared at Morris Pinard's broad backside as he mounted the stairs. A collection of colorful oaths came to mind. Finally, one small "Damn!" escaped her lips. She had been plotting her escape all evening, but not until this very instant did she realize where she meant to go.

Cami hurried upstairs, turning in at the bedroom she shared with fifteen-year-old Lorenna. The girl was in bed, but not yet asleep.

"Cami, wasn't it a wonderful evening?" Lorenna asked in a sleepy but excited voice.

"Not particularly," the older girl snapped. Then she softened. "I'm sorry, 'Renna. I don't mean to sound peevish. I'm just tired."

"I'd be exhausted, too, if I'd danced as many times as you. You're so lucky, Cami," Lorenna added wistfully.

Camille allowed herself a short laugh. "Lucky?"

"Well, yes. You know what I mean. Your looks,

your personality. Why, all the boys just about go crazy for you."

Not the least trace of envy colored her young cousin's words. For that, at least, Cami was grateful. She sat down on Lorenna's bed and took her hand. "You know, dear girl, you're not so bad yourself."

Now it was Lorenna's turn to laugh. "Me? I've heard what Mama says about me—'skinny, witchy-red hair, eyes like a beagle hound.' And I hate having to plaster my face with cucumbers and clabber every night. The freckles won't come off, Cami. They just won't!"

Camille was impatient to get on with her plans, but she couldn't let her little cousin suffer this way. Lorenna was too good and sweet and childlike to be ignored.

"Listen, 'Renna, don't ever let the things Cousin Beatrice says upset you. Mothers are like that. When their daughters are fifteen they think they'll never be beauties. But give it time. Another year or so and you'll fill out nicely. As for your hair, the boys will notice you especially because you'll stand out from all the others. You don't want to look exactly like everyone else, do you?" She laughed and squeezed Lorenna's hand. "And, if you ask me, I think beagles have beautiful eyes."

Lorenna giggled delightedly. She sat up and threw her arms around Cami's neck. "I'm so glad you're here. I wish you were my really, truly sister." The younger girl leaned back then and looked Camille straight in the eye. "Tell me, now. Please! I'm dying to know."

Cami frowned. "Know what?"

"Who you're going to marry, of course. I heard

Father tell Mama that you had to make your choice this very night. I want to be the first to know." A new degree of excitement crept into Lorenna's voice. "If I were you, I'd marry . . ."

"No! Don't tell me," Camille interrupted, holding her hands up in front of her to stop her cousin's words. "Whoever it is, *you* go after him. I have other plans."

Camille got up and started undressing, stripping off ivory lace and satin, pearls and silks, which she carelessly tossed about the room in her haste.

"What are you talking about?" Lorenna asked, distressed. "What kind of other plans? Oh, Cami, Mama hasn't talked you into entering the convent?"

"Heavens, no! Me? A nun? Can you imagine such a thing?"

Cami flipped her fan open and gave Lorenna a flirtatious, lash-fluttering glance over its lacy edge. Then she hiked up her petticoat to display a stunning length of bare, shapely thigh.

Lorenna giggled wildly and covered her eyes. "You're *terrible*, Cami! No convent, you're right. So what about a husband?"

Camille let her fan and petticoat drop. She shook her head. "It's simply that I can't marry any of those boys your father has been trying to force upon me. Honestly, I feel like a slave wench on the auction block. I want a husband, yes, but I have to find my own. And when I do, he'll be a man, not some simpering, terrified boy."

As she said those words, a picture of the tall, dashing stranger, Victoine Navar, flashed through Camille's mind.

"Oh, Cami, I'd be so afraid of a *man*!" Lorenna

97

wailed. "Are you sure you know what you're getting into?"

"I haven't the slightest notion, actually," Cami answered in all honesty. "But I know what I'm *not* getting into."

"What's that?"

"*Bed* with just any *boy*!"

"Oh, Cami, stop it!" Lorenna gasped, hiding her head under a pillow. "I can't stand it . . . I can't stand it! I don't even want to think about *that*!"

"Nor do I, sweet cousin. At least not until I fall in love."

Rummaging through the armoire, Cami found her favorite riding costume—the one she usually donned when she sneaked off to the swamp alone to go fishing. It was the same outfit she used to wear when she went with her father to search for Lafitte's hidden gold. She pulled on britches, an old linen shirt, and, in her haste, heavy gloves right over the soiled white kid pair she was still wearing. Boots, a slouch hat, and a woolen cape completed her ensemble—a far cry from the pristine laces and satins of moments before. Finally, she stuffed a few clothes and personal items into a carpetbag.

"Ready!" she announced.

"Cami, what in the world are you doing?" Lorenna demanded. "You can't mean to go out riding at this time of night. It's too dangerous. Besides, it's storming."

Camille leaned down and kissed her cousin's cheek. "I can't tell you what I'm doing, 'Renna, or where I'm going. I don't want to get you into trouble. My advice would be for you to tell your parents that you were fast asleep long before I came to the

98

room tonight." She ruffled the younger girl's bright hair and smiled. "Smart as you are, play dumb for once in your life, won't you? It will save us both a lot of trouble."

"But, Cami . . ."

"No buts, my darling 'Renna! Cousin Morris says I must choose a husband. Well, that's exactly what I mean to do. But he won't be one of those goggled-eyed, panting plantation boys. When I find the right man, I'll marry him, quick as you please. But I'll marry for love, nothing less."

"Oh, Camille," Lorenna moaned, "you sound just like a character out of one of Mama's romantic novels. Let me go with you. Please?"

"Not this time, 'Renna." Cami pinned up her long, jet hair and plopped one of her father's old felt hats on her head. "Too dangerous, as you said. But once I find what I'm seeking, I'll send word." She bestowed a reassuring smile on her cousin. "And when your time comes, we'll find just the right man for you, too. Don't let them marry you off in the meantime."

The girls embraced, then Cami opened the window and climbed down the sturdy wisteria vine that grew up the side of the house. Actually, she mused, she would have been perfectly safe leaving by the front door since everyone else was sleeping by now. But somehow the start of a grand adventure seemed to require this dramatic touch.

Moments later, Camille was at the stable, saddling Voodoo, the wild stallion her father had saved from destruction, then taught his daughter to ride. Now that Edouard Mazaret was gone, no one but Camille dared try to mount the horse. The high-strung animal danced with energy, sensing excitement in Cami's every move.

"Quiet, big fellow," she soothed. "We're going for a little ride, that's all."

Lightning flashed and thunder rumbled through the night. But Cami felt fearless as she mounted, then urged Voodoo out of the stable. The storm only added to her sense of adventure.

"Free!" she cried as she whipped the bat-black horse into the night. "Free to live . . . to love!"

The cold rain on Cami's face and the excitement of the moment should have kept her wide awake. But even as she drove Voodoo to top speed, she felt drowsiness setting in.

As Cami dozed off, Carol awoke.

A sharp jolt—the pirogue bumping the dock—made Carol sit up straighter.

"You back now, mam'zelle."

The tall ferryman, Choctaw, leaned over her. He took her hand in his leathery palm to help her mount the ladder from the boat to the dock. As he did so, he pressed the gold coin back into her hand.

"You come again," he invited. "Anytime."

"Choctaw, how could this happen?" Carol asked, frantic. "What about Cami? I left her out in a storm all alone."

"She be waiting, that one, when next you return."

Dawn was just breaking over New Orleans. Was this the same day or some time in the future? Carol wondered.

As she hurried back to the hotel, she picked up a morning edition of the paper. A Friday paper—February 28, 1992. Waves of relief washed over her.

Not until she was safely back in bed at the Hotel Dalpeche did Carol realize that she remembered in sharp detail every moment of her time as Camille Mazaret. With that realization came another—that she fully intended to take Choctaw up on his offer. She vowed to return to Cami's time, to help Cami find her true love.

Chapter Five

The alarm clock had just rousted Frank Longpre out of bed. He ambled across the room to open the curtains and check the weather, but a figure below drew his attention.

Standing at the window of his second-floor apartment, Frank spotted a woman hurrying across the empty courtyard. Had it not been for the upturned collar of her trench coat and her furtive glances this way and that, he probably wouldn't have given her a second look. But she moved like a criminal-type—a drug dealer looking to make an early morning score or a cat burglar on the prowl. He frowned and rubbed a hand over the bristly blue stubble on his chin. Something about her seemed familiar, but she was too far away for him to get a good look.

As the woman drew closer, she glanced up toward his window. There was no mistaking her identity then.

"Carol Marlowe!" Frank frowned.

All sorts of lurid pictures of "women-in-trouble" flashed through his mind and they all wore Carol's face. New Orleans was no place for a lone female to be roaming around before dawn. He picked up his wristwatch from the bedside table.

"It's not even seven o'clock yet," he muttered. "Where the hell's she been?"

Frank continued to watch until she disappeared into her ground-floor door across the way. Then he shrugged and headed for the bathroom. She'd probably just been out for some early sightseeing, he figured. After all, this was her first trip to New Orleans, and she hadn't seen much the night before. Still, she shouldn't have gone alone.

He turned on the shower and stepped in. The jets of water pelted his hard body like a wall of hot needles. Grabbing the soap—his own giant bar, not one of the hotel's dainty cakes—he lathered his neck and torso, working his way down. A quick glance at the erection he'd sprouted brought a grim laugh.

"Hello there! Haven't seen *you* up this early in quite a while. Maybe I should have taken a cold one this morning."

Minutes later, he stepped out of the shower stall and toweled off. Then he turned on the taps at the sink and got out his shaving paraphernalia. The tiny bathroom was steamed up. Frank had to squint at the blob of white lather in the mirror, trying not to cut himself as he made quick, even swipes with his razor. The problem was, his mind wasn't on what he was doing.

He was very confused. The sight of Carol minutes before—her glossy-brown curls wind-tousled and her cheeks rosy with the morning chill—had stirred up a lot of feelings he'd thought he would never experience again. Since Eileen's disappearance, he's guarded his emotions like a pit bull standing watch over a vault door. He'd rather fight than let another woman take his wife's place. But there was something about Carol . . . something that crashed through the wall of defenses he'd erected over the years.

"You're a damn fool!" he told the half-shaved, bleary-eyed guy in the mirror. "Carol Marlowe's a professional—not interested, out of bounds, cool as a cucumber. You just leave her be, ole boy!"

Having given himself a good talking-to, Frank analyzed the situation rationally. He and Carol had hit it off right away, enjoyed a nice, casual evening. That was all—end of story! Now, he had to go and muddy the waters with something that amounted to a schoolboy crush.

"Damn mid-life crises!" he growled, trying to ignore the niggling worm of embarrassment he felt. "Longpre, you're acting like a starry-eyed, pimply-faced teenager."

They had to work together, he reminded himself, and he didn't want anything interfering with the case. Work came first. Always had, always would, did now!

He belted out a laugh suddenly. It came so quickly and unexpectedly that he almost took a chunk out of his left earlobe.

"Sure, buddy, *work!*" he said sarcastically. "As if that's all you've got on your mind."

Well, at least he was being honest with himself. He'd hardly slept at all last night, but his restlessness had little to do with that long-dead Jane Doe lying over in the morgue. It was the flesh-and-blood female who had just drifted into his life from her lofty Mount Olympus in North Carolina that had his gut tied in knots.

Guilty! That's how he felt, he realized suddenly, as if he were sneaking around with another woman behind Eileen's back. He hadn't even had to be careful all these years to keep himself from getting involved. Yet he *wasn't* involved, he reminded himself silently. He sure wanted to be, though.

So, what was he going to do about it?

In a flash, he decided. *Nothing!* "Not one damn thing!" he murmured flatly. "Just hang in there, do my work, and let nature take its course."

He'd go to his meetings this morning, then pick Carol up at noon as planned. They had a lot of ground to cover, more than enough to keep his mind on the case. He figured she'd want to go to the morgue first thing.

"Real romantic, eh, buddy?" He grimaced at the mirror.

Still, as determined as he was to stick strictly to business, Frank couldn't help casting a glance toward Carol's closed door when he passed through the courtyard a little while later. He paused for a second, thinking he might pop in to say good morning. But she was probably sleeping. He paused a minute longer, then forced himself to move on.

* * *

Actually, Carol wasn't sleeping and would have welcomed Frank's company. She needed desperately to tell someone about the confusion of thoughts cluttering her brain.

Shortly after she'd returned to her room, Carol had given way to a serious attack of nerves. Until she took off her coat and gloves, she'd been fine. But when she looked at her hands and found that she was still wearing Camille Mazaret's long, white evening gloves under her own woolly mitts, realization struck with a mighty blow. She had *not* imagined it all! This wasn't one of her visions. It had really happened! And the stain on one of the gloves from Gerome Arneau's greasy hand was proof-positive.

She sat curled up in a chair, staring at those gloves. They lay crumpled on the bed where she had tossed them after quickly stripping them from her trembling hands. They seemed almost alive to her—as alive as Camille Mazaret had been such a short time before.

What on earth was happening? What did it all mean? She'd experienced more than her share of psychic phenomena over the past few years, but this episode boggled her mind. Although Carol could recall everything about her time as that younger woman, she realized now that while she was "the entity Camille," as mediums usually put it, Cami had absolutely no consciousness of Carol Marlowe's existence.

"And why would she?" Carol said aloud. "I wasn't even born back then, so how could she possibly have any inkling that I ever would be?"

106

Carol leaned her head back and closed her eyes. Very deliberately she went over the whole sequence of her morning in her mind—bit by bit, detail by detail. While she had been in the past, her entire identity had been submerged. This had never happened to her before. She had had visions of past occurrences many times, but always as an outside observer, never from the inside looking out. How could such a thing possibly be?

"This is weird stuff," she told herself. *"Too weird!"*

Her lack of rest and fretting over her strange pre-dawn trip finally took their toll. She drifted off to sleep—peaceful, dreamless sleep that she very much needed.

A knock at her door woke her shortly before noon.

"Carol? Are you in there?"

She started awake at the sound of Frank's voice. A glance at the clock told her she'd been asleep for over two hours in the lumpy antique chair.

"Just a minute, Frank."

As she passed the vanity, she ran a brush quickly through her hair and smeared on some lipstick. No need to dress, she figured, for a visit to the morgue. She shuddered, dreading the next couple of hours.

The moment she opened the door, Carol could see that something was different about Frank. He, too, was dressed casually, in jeans and a faded denim shirt. But that wasn't it. There was something in his eyes, perhaps a question he didn't quite know how to ask.

"I woke you?" he asked, glancing pointedly at his wristwatch.

Carol tried to laugh off his half-question, half-accusation. "I've been ready for hours," she insisted, "but traveling always does me in. I must have dozed off while I was waiting for you."

"You're ready, then."

Carol took a deep breath. "As ready as I'll ever be. I have to admit, Frank, I'm not looking forward to this."

Her confession obviously made him ill at ease. "Well, you don't really have to see her, do you? I mean, what good will it do? It's not likely you'd recognize her. I can tell you anything you need to know. Or you could just look at the photos we took and skip the rest."

Carol raised her palms to stop him. "No, no! I really do need to have a look. To touch her, actually."

Frank's mouth formed a grim line. "Why?"

Carol shrugged. "It's hard to explain, Frank. I guess the closest comparison would be a bloodhound getting the scent from a fugitive's clothes. I need to touch the body to pick up her vibes, if you follow me."

Frank shuddered slightly. "Lunch before or after?"

With a forced laugh, Carol replied, "I want to go do this thing right now, Frank, and get it over with. As for lunch, food can wait."

"Okay. But you may want to wait quite a while."

Carol noted a flicker of emotion as their eyes met for a moment and she watched his darken as if a shadow passed over his face. She felt a little curl of warmth inside her. It seemed as if, by his change of expression, Frank was letting her know that she was not alone in this, that whatever she meant to do, he'd be right beside her all the way.

"Carol?" he began as she was locking her door. "There's something I'm curious about."

"Yes, Frank?" She turned and looked at him, ready to answer any question he might put to her. The expression on his face, however, gave her a moment's pause. She had the fleeting feeling that he knew she had left the hotel and that she was keeping something from him. She steeled herself, sure he was about to ask probing questions that she really wasn't yet ready to answer.

But he waved it off. "No. Never mind. It'll keep."

The morgue was every bit as chilling as Carol had expected. She felt as if she had stepped into one of the old black and white *B* movies she loved to watch. It was a sterile setting—all stainless steel and ceramic tile—but it seemed she could almost feel something lurking in the very chill of the air.

"Are you okay?" Frank whispered when he saw a shiver run through Carol.

"I'll be fine," she whispered back.

Whispering seemed the thing to do in such a setting.

"We're ready, Mac." Frank nodded grimly to the white-coated attendant.

The man went to a steel drawer at the far end of the room. Carol noted as she followed that they had interrupted his lunch. A plastic dish of spaghetti and meatballs sat cooling on a nearby table. Her stomach churned at the the sight.

"Here she is," the attendant announced matter-of-factly, pulling the drawer out full-length. "And, by the way, Frank, we're a mite cramped for space around here. How much longer before you plant this one? I hear tell the case is already closed."

"When I'm damn good and ready, and convinced I can't do any more," Frank snapped. "Then I'll see she gets a decent burial, Mac. Not before!"

Carol wasn't listening to the two men. She closed her eyes for a moment, bracing herself for the ordeal. She opened them in time to see the nonchalant morgue attendant whip back the sheet. She gasped softly in spite of her determination to remain calm and in control.

Frank gripped her arm. "Steady," he murmured.

"Let's just get this over with." Carol stepped up to the slab, her hand outstretched to touch the mummy. She looked down and another, louder gasp escaped her.

"What's the matter?" Frank asked, concerned.

Carol stared at the dark, shriveled skin, stretched like old leather over the skull. As she watched, features imposed themselves over the mummified remains. The brown, weathered flesh became soft and pale. Long hair the color of a raven's wing draped the partially-bald skull. Black, feathery lashes formed a spidery pattern on the pale-rose cheeks. An instant later, those very lashes fluttered. A moment after that, Carol found herself staring into lovely, liquid eyes of deep indigo blue.

Soft laughter filled the cool chamber, then the mummy's lips moved and a familiar voice asked, "Whatever are *you* doing *here*? We have business, you know, at Fiona's."

Trembling as if she had palsy, Carol touched the woman's arm. She had expected warm flesh, but

110

felt only cold, taut leather stretched over ancient bone. Carol cried out and jerked her hand back. Tears streamed down her flushed cheeks. Her heart was pounding so rapidly, she felt as if she might faint.

"That's enough," she heard Frank say. "Cover it up!"

Suddenly, Carol found herself in Frank's arms. She was weeping hysterically, crying, "No! No! No!" over and over again.

"Carol, take it easy," Frank pleaded. "Let's get you out of this place. What's wrong? What happened?"

He sounded as frantic as Carol felt. It was as if she had just seen her own corpse. Her whole body ached. Suddenly she was dying of thirst. Her left leg throbbed so painfully that she couldn't stand on it. Frank had to literally carry her from the room.

Moments later, in a comfortable office away from the dreadful morgue, Carol came back to her senses. The pain in her leg stopped throbbing. The weakness went away. She stopped crying and stared up at Frank, who looked as pale as a corpse.

"Carol, thank God you're all right." He was kneeling before her, chafing her cold hands.

She stared down at his long, tanned fingers gripping hers and a little shiver ran through her. There was something in his touch that warmed her, calmed her. But she couldn't think about that now. Frank was talking to her, firing questions.

"What the hell happened to you in there?" he demanded. "I knew this wouldn't be a tea party, but I never expected you'd go all to pieces like that. Did you have another vision?"

"Give me a minute, Frank," she begged, gulping

deep drafts of air. "Could I have a glass of water? I'm *so* thirsty!"

"Sure! Take all the time you need." He walked across the room, filled a tumbler from the pitcher on the desk, and handed it to her. His hand lingered on hers, sending that feeling through her once again. "God, Carol, you scared the hell out of me!"

"I'm sorry," she said between gulps. "It's just that I saw . . ." Even with her thirst quenched, the words simply refused to come.

"What, Carol? Tell me," he begged.

"I know who she is . . . was. I'm sure of it! She spoke to me, Frank."

Frank stood up abruptly. Staring down at Carol, he snapped, "You're putting me on, right? I didn't hear a thing, 'cause dead folks don't talk. And there's no way anybody could actually recognize what's left of that woman in there. Come off it, Miz Marlowe! This isn't some kind of game we're playing."

Carol didn't blink. "I'm very serious, Frank. No games! Her name is Camille Mazaret. Her family owned a sugar plantation somewhere around here called Elysian Fields."

Frank's mouth gaped. She could tell by the look on his face that he still didn't quite believe her. Actually, Carol herself found it all pretty hard to believe and she certainly didn't understand any of it. She just hoped Frank wouldn't ask her to explain.

"Her father's name was Edouard Mazaret," Carol added. "Check it out, Frank. His name must be in some old records somewhere."

The creases were easing from Frank's face. His

black eyes began to glitter with excitement. "All right! We'll do that! We'll check it out right now." He grabbed Carol's hand to pull her up from the chair, ready to be on his way instantly.

"Hey, give me another minute to catch my breath, won't you?"

"Yeah . . . sorry!" His voice was actually shaking, he was so eager to get on with it. "I don't suppose you'd like to tell me how you know all this stuff?"

Carol shrugged and offered a weak smile. "You probably wouldn't believe me if I told you. Let's just say I have an anonymous source."

"Good enough for me." He gave her a lazy smile. "Hey, I'm sorry I snapped at you before. Are you feeling well enough to travel now?"

"Sure! Let's get going."

Frank took her hand and helped her up. His scowl of disbelief was gone. He looked as eager as a kid about to set out on a scavenger hunt.

A short time later, the two of them were poring over old records in a musty courthouse storeroom. The task seemed endless and hopeless to Carol. The more they searched through the crumbling record books, straining their eyes over faded flourishes of ink from the past century, the more discouraged she became.

"I wish I had a date," she said at last.

Frank glanced over and grinned. "Honey, I'll take you on a date wherever you want to go as soon as we find out about these Mazaret folks. I never figured you'd be able to come up with something so fast."

Carol couldn't help but laugh. "That's not what I meant and you know it! I mean *a date!* . . . 1860 . . . 1854 . . . 1898. I have no idea when Camille died."

"Well, you said you knew from this 'anonymous source' of yours that Elysian Fields was a sugar plantation. If that's so, we can narrow it down. I happen to remember from studying my history books that Étienne Bore harvested the first profitable sugarcane crop in 1796. So we don't need to look any earlier than that. And the War Between the States finished off the big plantations. That would mean we're looking for a date pre-1860s."

"That's not narrowing it down much," Carol answered. "Oh, I just remembered something else, Frank."

She had his full attention. "Tell me!"

"Camille's father found some of Jean Lafitte's treasure buried somewhere at Elysian Fields. So it had to be after pirate times."

"Let me think a minute." Frank bowed his head, closed his eyes, and tapped at his forehead with the pencil he was holding. When he looked up again, he was grinning. "Lafitte left here shortly after the Battle of New Orleans. That was in 1815. So we can knock a few more years off our search. Edouard Mazaret really found treasure, no foolin'?"

Carol nodded. "I've seen a piece of it." She hedged, not telling him that she actually had one of the gold doubloons.

"Really?" Frank sounded more than mildly skeptical.

"So have you," Carol reminded him. "Didn't you say the mummy was wearing a gold doubloon around her neck? Cami's father had that made into a necklace for her here in New Orleans. It was part of the treasure he found."

For some time, Frank remained silent, staring out the dusty window of the storeroom. Then he swung around toward Carol, his head tilted and one eye squinting. "You know, if I'm supposed to believe all this, sooner or later you're going to have to tell me how you know so much. I mean, I *am* a policeman. I work with evidence, not speculation. Are you ready to divulge your anonymous source?"

Carol pursed her lips tightly and shook her head. "Right now, Frank, you wouldn't believe me if I told you. I think our best course of action at this point is to turn up a deed or something with Edouard Mazaret's name on it or find Elysian Fields on some old map."

"A map, of course!" The lights were dancing again in Frank's black eyes. "We should have gone there first thing instead of wading through all these crumbling old files."

"Where, Frank?"

"The Historic New Orleans Collection."

"What's that?" Carol looked up at him quizzically as she blew a dust-streaked strand of hair out of her eyes.

"It's a museum and research center on Royal Street. They can probably turn up names, dates, and maps in a flash."

"Great!" Carol cried. "Let's go!"

For several moments, she studied Frank as he worked at replacing files and old ledgers. There was something about that profile . . . the long, slightly crooked line of his nose, the high forehead, the way his mouth drew down just a bit at the corners even when he smiled. She'd seen a face like his on some other man. Recently. But who?

Black Vic! Carol almost said the name out loud, but caught herself in time. Instead, she mentioned casually, "There's another name we need to check out. Victoine Navar. I think he may have figured prominently in Camille's life. If my guess is correct, they came to mean a great deal to each other."

He glanced toward her, unsmiling. "Your *guess?*"

"You'll have to be patient with me, Frank, and give me more time before I can be certain. Guesswork is part of what I do. I get my information in ragged pieces sometimes. It's like fitting a jigsaw puzzle together."

Frank glanced at Carol and smiled, his eyes lingering on the soft curve of her lips. "Hey, I'm not complaining," he assured her. "You haven't been here twenty-four hours yet, and you've told me more already than I've been able to dig up in two months. You're the boss, lady. I promise to be patient from now on."

His words, simple as they were, struck a chord deep in Carol's soul. There was something so kind and vulnerable about Frank. She wondered fleetingly what his wife had been like. Surely, their marriage had been special. With a man like Frank, how could it have been otherwise? He was, as Jesse had said, "a sterling fellow."

"All set?" Frank asked, slamming a drawer and sending up a cloud of centuries-old dust.

"Ready for anything!" Carol answered with a smile.

The walk to Royal Street from the old government building where they'd been searching the records was delightful. The sun was shining and there was an early hint of spring in the air. Jamming the banquettes, the Carnival revellers—most from out-of-town—were doing their best to enjoy every minute of their visit to the old city.

"Is New Orleans always like this?" Carol asked.

"This time of year—yes. Actually, it's pretty lively all the time." Frank grinned down at her. "I love the place—tourists and all. It's hard to explain. The French Quarter is like another country. Have you ever been to Havana?"

Carol shook her head.

"I was there a long time ago. I was just a kid, but I remember the noise and the color and the smell of the place—perfume and rum and bananas. Just like New Orleans. Key West runs a close second, but I guess the French Quarter reminds me most of Cuba."

Frank's mention of Key West brought to mind Carol's broken engagement and shattered the warm spell between them. She was trying so hard to forget about that unpleasantness. Most of the time, being with Frank helped. He was easy to be with. Fun to have around. Still, his mention of Key West cast a pall. Carol fell into silent thought.

As they walked on, she glanced into the shop windows along Royal Street. The glittering displays of antiques quickly improved her mood. Suddenly she froze in total thrall before one of the shops, oblivious to the fact that Frank had hurried on.

"Carol?" Frank called back over his shoulder when he realized she was no longer at his side. "Come look at this."

Frank stood beside her a moment later, his eyes following the direction of her gaze. "Yeah, what?" he asked. "It's just a bunch of old jewelry—not nearly as flashy as what women wear nowadays."

"That necklace and the matching earrings—the tiny tiers of seed pearls in the faded red velvet box. Look at the card beside it. The set belonged to Mary Lincoln."

Frank said something in response; Carol had no idea what. Her thoughts were adrift in time and space. Her body was still on Royal Street, but her mind and soul were elsewhere.

Quite suddenly she found herself in a dark theater. Hearing an excited whisper pass through the audience, she glanced around. The President's pretty, dark-haired wife, her pearls glowing softly in the footlights, settled herself beside her tall husband in the flag-decked Presidential Box to the right of the stage.

A hush fell over the audience once more and the play continued. But Carol's attention was glued to the late arrivals, her eyes fixed on the dainty pearl necklace.

In ladylike fashion, Mrs. Lincoln laughed behind her fan as Harry Hawk, playing the comic backwoodsman in "Our American Cousin," delivered the line that Carol knew was destined to become the world's best-remembered and most horrifying cue: ". . . you sockdologizing old mantrap."

Carol heard a shot ring out and jumped. "What was that?" she cried.

"Just some kids shooting off firecrackers down the street." Frank caught Carol's shoulders and turned her to face him. "Where were you just now? I got this odd feeling, as if you were here, but you weren't."

She tried to laugh it off, but Frank's face remained solemn. He demanded an answer. Finally, she gave up trying to deceive him.

"Bear with me, Frank. Occasionally, I have out-of-body experiences. Mary Lincoln's necklace." She pointed toward the shop window. "Seeing it just sort of transported me back in time."

Frank's frown deepened. He continued gripping Carol's arms as if he meant to keep her in the here and now.

"You mean you actually went . . . ?"

She nodded solemnly, reading his thoughts before he could get the words out. "I've just come from Ford's Theater in Washington where I witnessed President Lincoln's assassination. His wife was wearing those pearls."

"You mean, you *imagined* seeing it," Frank stated.

Looking straight up into his eyes, Carol shook her head. "No, Frank. It was very real. I was there!"

He still couldn't comprehend. "You actually witnessed the whole thing?"

"No, not all of it. I heard the shot, but the firecrackers going off at the same time snapped me out of it. Thank goodness, I didn't have to stay this time!"

"*This time?* Carol, what are you talking about?" Frank sounded frantic—almost angry—as if he was afraid she was losing her mind.

"Take it easy, Frank," she soothed. "I know you

119

don't understand. I don't know how these things happen either. All I can tell you is that they do."

"Not often, I hope."

She answered quietly, "More often than I care to admit. Now how about getting on with normal business."

"Normal!" He laughed nervously, trying to lighten the mood. "I'm not sure anything about you is normal, Miz Marlowe. You better just watch yourself around these parts or people will start accusing you of being a latter-day Marie Laveau."

"The voodoo queen?" Carol chuckled. "No, Captain Longpre. Thank you just the same, but I want no part of the black arts."

The Historic New Orleans Collection was housed in two buildings, the Kemper townhouse built around 1880 and the 1792 Merieult House. The moment Frank and Carol entered, a trim, tailored woman in her late fifties came toward them, her hand outstretched.

"Captain Longpre, I believe." She smiled at the look of surprise on Frank's face. "You've no need to be embarrassed. We haven't met before, but I've seen your picture often. I'm Louise Thibodaux. How may I help you?"

Frank introduced Carol as a friend visiting the city for the first time to do geneaological research. No need, he figured, to bring up either the mummy or Carol's strange powers.

"Well, I'm sure we can be of assistance, Miss Marlowe." She turned a warm smile on Carol. "Come along to my office."

Once the three of them were seated comfortably, Mrs. Thibodaux asked, "Now, how can I help you, my dear? Perhaps if you tell me what you know of your ancestors already, we could start from that point."

"There are two facts that have eluded me so far," Carol began, "the exact location of a sugar plantation called Elysian Fields and what happened to a young woman who was raised there until she was sent away after both her parents died."

"Her name?" Mrs. Thibodaux inquired.

"Camille Mazaret. Her father was Edouard, her mother, I believe, was called Adele."

Excusing herself, the tall woman with graying hair rose and left the room for a moment. When she returned, she was carrying a large portfolio.

"There should be a map here that will show us exactly where *Champs Elysées*, or as you call it, Elysian Fields, was."

"You mean the plantation house no longer exists?" Carol asked, remembering how vividly she had seen it—first in ruins, then in all its glory.

"I'm afraid not. Look here." Louise Thibodaux pointed with one neatly manicured nail to a spot on the map below New Orleans on the river. "Elysian Fields was located at a place in the river called *Detour à l'Anglais*, or English Turn. The spot got its name back in 1699 when Bienville encountered a British ship headed upriver. The Frenchman persuaded the English captain that a great fleet of ships was following his and would attack any British vessel that attempted to approach New Orleans. The English ship turned around and fled, hence the name."

"That's an interesting history lesson, Mrs. Thibodaux, but what about Elysian Fields?" Frank asked, guiding the woman back to the original subject.

"I'm afraid this appears to be one of those cases of an old family simply dying out. Without heirs to take over, the property fell into neglect. For some years the house stood empty. What was left of it was severely damaged in the hurricane of 1915. Shortly after that, the river reclaimed house, land, everything. Whatever is left above water is swampy area now."

"You say the Mazaret family died out, Mrs. Thibodaux. Can you tell me what happened to Camille Mazaret?" Carol asked, sitting on the edge of her seat.

The historian, her dark eyes glittering as if she were a detective on a hot scent, reached into a drawer of her desk and drew out a book bound in worn leather. "This should be of help. It's a history of all the early plantation families, complied by one of their own. Let's see." She thumbed through the volume until she found the *M*'s. "Mazaret, here it is." She glanced up at Carol. "Camille, you say?"

Carol nodded.

" 'Edouard Mazaret, born 1798, died 1838. In 1820, married Adele Tessier, born 1802, died 1832 of accidental drowning.' " Mrs. Thibodaux looked at them over the rims of her reading glasses. "Interesting!" she commented with a knowing smile. "The fact that Adele's death is listed as 'accidental' means that it probably wasn't. Great pains were taken by this author to cover up for these old Creole families since he was related by blood or marriage to most of them."

Carol nodded, but held her silence even though she was dying to blurt out the truth as she knew it—that Adele Mazaret had caused that accident herself rather than carry her husband's child to term.

"Let's see . . . there's more," Louise Thibodaux went on. "Ah, yes, here's what we're looking for. 'One daughter, Camille, born 1822, died circa 1840.'"

Frank was frowning. "*Circa*," he repeated. "That means nobody knows exactly when or how she died?"

Mrs. Thibodaux nodded. "Exactly, Captain Longpre."

"But how can that be?" Carol queried impatiently.

"Let me look up the detailed family history," Mrs. Thibodaux said. "That should tell us more. Ah! Here it is. I won't read it all right now. I'll just give you the salient facts." She scanned the page quickly, then frowned. "Oh, dear! I'm afraid you couldn't possibly be descended from the Mazarets, Miss Marlowe. You see, Camille was the very last of the line. Her father died only a few years after her mother, leaving no other heirs. Shortly after Edouard Mazaret's death, Camille was sent to live with distant cousins, the Pinards . . ."

"I know," Carol interjected. "Morris and Beatrice Pinard of Mulgrove Plantation."

"Why, yes! That's exactly correct." The woman looked impressed.

"But what happened to Camille?" Frank questioned.

The woman read on, then sighed and clucked

123

her tongue. "It seems she became something of a social outcast. This old history does not go into great detail, but I can tell by what the author left out that Camille had acquired a rather shady reputation before she disappeared."

"What do you mean?" Carol asked.

"Well, it states quite plainly that at one time she was engaged to be married. The name of her fiancé is omitted, which tells me he was not thought to be 'socially correct.' Then there's reference to a duel between her 'lover,' "—Mrs. Thibodaux looked up, one brow arched to show her shock—"yes, the author actually uses that term! Between her lover and her cousin and guardian, Morris Pinard. The duel ended in a family scandal. It seems Pinard retired from the field of honor in disgrace after seriously wounding his opponent."

"It doesn't give the man's name?" Carol asked anxiously.

"Oh, no, my dear!" Again the historian made a clucking sound. "That would further besmirch the young lady's name, for generations to come. That sort of thing simply wasn't done back when this book was written."

"I'll bet I know his name," Frank offered. "Victoine Navar!"

Both women turned to stare at him. Carol realized instantly that Frank had to be right.

Mrs. Thibodaux quickly thumbed back to the *N*-section, then shook her head. "There is no Navar family listing, Captain Longpre."

"Figures!" Frank mumbled.

There was little more information that Mrs. Thibodaux could offer. Camille had returned to Elysian Fields, scandalizing the whole population of New Orleans by running the vast plantation alone. There had been rumors of a man and a boy living there and helping with the duties, but again, no names were given. Could this man, too, have been Camille's lover? Carol wondered. Could the man have been Black Vic?

"I'll keep searching," Louise Thibodaux assured them as they rose to leave. "If I turn up any more information, I'll be sure to let you know, Captain Longpre."

They thanked the lady, then left.

"We should have come here first," Frank said once they were out on the street again. It would have saved us those two hours in the dust this morning. That was certainly a waste, knowing as we do now that Camille Mazaret is a dead end anyway."

"Don't sound so down, Frank," Carol said softly. "This could very well prove what I believe, that your mummy is, indeed, Camille. If she disappeared without a trace, that could mean that now, at least, she's been found."

"Sounds good," Frank answered, "but how do we prove it?"

For a blinding instant, pain shot through Carol's left leg again, just as it had when she was in the morgue earlier. She grabbed Frank's arm to keep from falling.

"Hey, what happened?" he asked, concern in his voice and his dark eyes. "Watch the cobbles. They've sprained many a dainty ankle."

"I didn't turn my ankle, Frank." Still leaning heavily on his arm, Carol said, "There's something I forgot to mention. This pain in my leg started when I touched the mummy. It's like hot poison shooting through me. Is there any way you can check to see if Camille was bitten by something? Perhaps a poisonous snake," she added, remembering the loathsome reptile in her vision.

"We can check the corpse more carefully," he replied. "I reckon we could have missed something. After all, we weren't looking for anything like a snakebite. You're right—that would be the most likely. Why don't I take you back to the hotel, then I'll go on over to the morgue again and ask some questions. There's no need for you to put yourself through that again."

Carol was about to agree when she spied a red tignon in the crowd. Her heart raced even as her blood ran cold. "You go on now, Frank," she insisted. "I can find the hotel on my own."

"You're sure?" He was still clutching her arm, supporting her.

"Positive!" she replied. "Now, get going. It's late."

"Okay," he answered. "I'll see you back at the hotel in a couple of hours."

Frank was only a few yards away when Carol felt a dry hand touch hers.

"Choctaw, he be there for you in the morning. Cami needs you."

"Tell me your name," Carol begged.

She received no reply. As abruptly as the old woman had appeared, she vanished into the crowd.

"Damn!" Carol moaned. "I had a dozen questions I wanted to ask her."

It seemed, though, that Carol would have to wait and get all her answers directly from Camille Mazaret.

126

"Tomorrow morning," Carol repeated. "Again? So soon? I'm not sure I'm ready."

But even as Carol voiced her doubts, she realized she would meet Choctaw in the cold, misty hours before dawn. She could no more stop herself from going than she could stop herself from taking her next breath. She could no more ignore the old woman's words than she could ignore the growing warmth and closeness she felt for Frank Longpre.

They *both* needed her—Cami *and* Frank.

As she wandered back toward the hotel, the fleeting thought crossed her mind that she should have stayed tucked atop her mountain in North Carolina—safe from danger, safe from love. But in a flash she realized the truth. She had been drawn by destiny to New Orleans, to Camille Mazaret, *and* to Frank Longpre. The two of them were intertwined through Carol's life—*my lives*, she corrected mentally.

"I wonder when—*if*—Frank will realize what's happening to us?"

Chapter Six

Carol was exhausted and emotionally wrung out by the time she returned to the hotel. Her early-morning jaunt into the past had deprived her of much-needed rest. Then Frank had kept her on the go all day. As for the mental strain, most of that came first from seeing Camille Mazaret's mummified corpse, then later from hearing that the young woman's date, place, and cause of death were all unknown. Carol's visit with Choctaw to Elysian Fields and Mulgrove had made her understand that somehow she and Camille were linked. She knew it was crazy, but it almost seemed as if they shared some profound affinity. She tried to sort out her feelings, but found that thinking about the fragile bond between herself and Cami only brought on more confusion.

Carol entered her room and glanced about. The maid had been in to tidy up. The bed looked especially inviting.

"If I could just catch a quick nap . . ."

No sooner had Carol uttered the words than the phone rang. It was Frank.

"Hey, I'm sorry, but I've got to meet with some out-of-town politicians for dinner this evening, Carol."

In spite of her weariness, she felt a pang of disappointment at the thought of not having dinner with Frank. She'd been eager to talk over the day's findings with him.

She frowned into the receiver. *Admit it!* she thought. *You were eager to see him, be with him, tonight. And it has nothing to do with the case.*

She was careful to hide her growing feelings and her disappointment, however. "Don't worry about it, Frank. I'm really done in. I think I'll just call room service, eat a light supper, then get some rest."

"You're sure you'll be all right alone? I hate to run out on you like this."

He sounded so concerned that Carol almost laughed—not at Frank, but at the sheer delight it gave her to have someone worry so.

"Really, Frank, I'll be fine."

"If I could get out of this dinner meeting, believe me, I would. I'd much rather spend the time with you." He paused and cleared his throat nervously, as if he'd said more than he'd meant to. "I mean, we have so much to talk over."

"Don't worry about it," Carol insisted, pleased to hear that he was as disappointed as she was. "Any word on the snakebite?"

"Nothing yet," he answered. "They're working on it. Maybe I'll know something by morning. I'll meet you in the coffee shop for breakfast at eight sharp tomorrow. Okay?"

Remembering the woman in the red turban, Carol paused before she answered. "That's awfully early, Frank. How about ten?"

"No, no!" he insisted. "We have to get an early start. I've requisitioned a boat to take us down to English Turn. I figured it might help you to see the spot where Elysian Fields once was, even if there's nothing there any longer."

"Yes, that could be helpful," Carol agreed. "But so early, Frank?"

"Once you've had a good night's sleep, you'll be raring to go again. Trust me on this, Carol."

"If you say so." She sighed. There was simply no arguing with the man.

She was about to say goodbye and hang up when Frank spoke again. "Carol, I've been wanting to tell you something all day . . . what I mean is, I had my doubts before you got here, but . . . well, I'm no good at saying exactly what I'd like to. I just want you to know that I'm *real* glad you're here—not only because you're helping so much on the case. I mean, I'm really, *personally*, glad you're here."

Carol held the phone in stunned silence for a moment, trying to think of a reply. Before she could, Frank said a quick " 'Bye now!" and hung up.

His unexpected sentiment left her with a warm, cozy feeling. She smiled, stretched out on the bed, and closed her eyes.

* * *

Carol never remembered anything about that evening after Frank's call. She retained no recollection of ringing room service or of drifting off to sleep after she ate supper. Nor did she recall getting up before dawn to go the the foot of Barracks Street. She could only assume later that Choctaw had met her and taken her back through the years.

It seemed only moments after Frank's phone call that she found herself—or rather, Camille Mazaret—right where she had left her, riding alone through the night, escaping from Mulgrove Plantation.

Once again this was a different time, a different place. And Carol was a different woman.

Thick mist rose in humid clouds from the nearby swamp as its night creatures signaled to each other in an eerie medley of peeps, screams, and grunts. Mulgrove seemed a haunted place on such a night, and the storm only added to its sense of mystery and danger.

Cami bent low over Voodoo's neck, urging the powerful stallion to go faster. But the muddy, rutted road proved treacherous. Realizing the need for caution, she eased off on the reins, letting her mount select his own pace. At a turn in the path, the plantation house slipped behind a tall line of oaks.

"You can relax now," she said aloud to herself. "You're safe. No one but Lorenna saw you leave."

Camille was mistaken. A second pair of eyes had watched her every move since the moment she spurred her father's huge black stallion out of the stable and toward the levee road. A gray curtain of rain and some fifty yards now separated her from her pursuer. The trailing rider, who could have overtaken her at any time, held back purposely, not wanting to spook his prey.

"Steady, Lucifer," he said to his horse in a low whisper. "We'll keep them in sight, but we don't want to get too close just yet."

Victoine Navar had suffered one minor defeat tonight, and he had no intention of losing this second opportunity. He meant to capture this runaway slave he'd spied slipping off from Pinard's place. He could certainly put the reward money to good use.

Black Vic chuckled softly, humorlessly. "When am I not in need of ready cash?" he reminded himself.

The ball at Mulgrove had been only a lark. He had not really expected to gain *entrée de la maison*. Getting stuffy old Pinard in a huff had been entertainment enough, he mused, smiling grimly. Besides, it would have seemed such a waste not to use the handsomely engraved invitation after he'd won it in a game of craps from young René Gireau.

A low laugh rumbled in his chest. "*C'est un gentil garcon!* Such a well-bred young man!"

That, the boy was, Vic reminded himself, but René had needed to be taught a lesson. A man's game required a man's skill and cunning, and a player should never wager more than he can afford to lose. Young Gireau now understood that fine point of gambling. Perhaps because of the lesson he'd been taught—the ball he had missed—René might be spared what Victoine had had to learn the hard way. Ten years ago, Vic had lost far more than a single evening of lavish food, fine wines, and flirting with pretty women. He had learned the hard way about the gaming tables. By wagering unwisely, Vic had lost *everything*—his plantation, his family, his entire birthright.

"Ancient history," Navar muttered, pulling his hat lower over his eyes to keep out the rain.

His attention focused once more on the lone rider up ahead. This venture was surely much more to his taste than trying to get some prissy Creole virgin to toss her glove his way. He'd been a fool to waste precious time on such silly sport. This present pursuit could prove highly profitable. He needed money *now*. And that runaway slave up ahead would likely fetch a fat reward, especially since the foolish fellow had stolen one of his master's prized stallions in order to make his getaway.

Vic tipped his hat to the blurred image in the distance. "I thank you and my creditors thank you," he said with a bemused smirk.

Cami shivered—wet to the skin and aching with weariness—but she refused to stop. A creeping sense of alarm prickled along her spine. She had neither seen nor heard another soul since leaving Mulgrove, but she felt as if someone was watching her, following her. Several times she glanced back over her shoulder. All she saw were distorted shapes in the blackness—tall oaks like ghostly sentinels guarding the road behind. Still, the feeling persisted, like a phantom riding double on her saddle. She could not ignore this sixth sense that never failed to warn her when danger was close at hand.

A mixture of blind panic and stubborn determination drove her now. This was a crazy thing she was about to do. But, she reminded herself, drastic situations required drastic measures. Truly, Camille was fed up. Cousin Morris's unreasonable demands had finished things as far as she was concerned. She had endured the unending lines of boring fortune-seekers that the Pinards forced upon her, but she refused to endure their threats.

The moment Cousin Morris demanded she choose a husband was the very moment that had sent her dashing through this stormy night, headed for New Orleans, headed for the little house on *rue d'Amour*.

"The Street of Love," she whispered. "How appropriate!"

The house at number ten was where her father had known love, where Camille hoped she, too, might find the secret to this greatest mystery of life. Surely, the woman named Fiona would be willing to help the daughter of the man she had loved so deeply for so long.

But as the hours crept by and Camille neared New Orleans, her resolve began to falter. What if Fiona refused to see her? What if Fiona hated her for being the offspring of her lover's wife? And, most seriously, what if Fiona scoffed at Cami's plan and refused to help her? Where would she turn then?

"Don't think about that," she warned herself. "Just ride on and keep hoping."

Black Vic still hung back. He was enjoying this cat-and-mouse game, even if the little rodent up ahead had no idea it was under close scrutiny. He had a plan in mind. He would shadow the runaway, but not overtake him too soon. If he went after the slave now, the hapless fellow might make a dash for the swamp and lose himself in that murky den. A search of that quarter would prove highly taxing and extremely unpleasant, especially on a night like this. And after all, Vic wasn't exactly dressed for a search through the swamp. He was wearing his only remaining suit of evening clothes. He couldn't afford to ruin them. A gentleman must dress properly to sit at a poker table.

"No. I'd best wait," he muttered. The slave was headed for New Orleans. He probably had friends there who would hide him. Vic decided to hold off until he reached the city. Then, if he needed help, he'd find it close at hand. The reward would still be his for tracking and apprehending the fugitive.

In the eerie pre-dawn light, the marshy site of the Battle of New Orleans was coming into view ahead. The old Chalmette Plantation. Vic felt an odd twinge whenever he came near this place. His own father had died here back in January of 1815, defending the city he loved against the British invaders. Vic had been a brash youngster then, but he'd been forced to grow up fast after his father's heroic death.

Shifting in the saddle, he bowed his head and tried to say a prayer. No words came. Somehow he no longer felt worthy of the honor his father's death had placed on the family name.

However, he more than deserved the epithet, "Black Vic," he reminded himself. But how he longed to feel worthy once more of the revered family name, Navar.

* * *

Cami breathed a sigh of relief. Her muscles ached with tension after such a long, unpleasant ride. She allowed herself to relax slightly. The worst, she hoped, was behind her. Ahead, she could see the outskirts of town. Even though the lazy sun still slept behind boiling, purple-black clouds, New Orleans was coming awake. Street lamps still glowed, but the first peddlers were starting their rounds. She heard their melodic calls—sing-song wails echoing through the quiet streets of Faubourg Marigny. Just knowing that other human beings were once more close at hand made her feel safer.

She decided to follow the river to Esplanade. That wide avenue should be safer at this early hour than the narrower back streets favored by the city's drunken sailors, prostitutes, and thieves. Once on Esplanade, she had only to ride to its junction with Rampart to find the Street of Love.

"Giddap!" she cried and her powerful black stallion streaked toward New Orleans.

Cami let her guard slip as she rode into the city. Just up ahead, she could see the first great homes that lined either side of Esplanade.

"Almost there," she said with a sigh of relief.

The comforting aromas of Creole coffee and fresh-baked French bread drifted by, mingling with the moss-humid smells of old bricks and river dampness. A breeze brought a sweet waft of oleander from a courtyard. Another stirring of air made Cami wrinkle her elegant nose in distaste—an overflowing gutter nearby—reminding her that New Orleans was, indeed, a city of vast contrasts. To live

136

in the Crescent City, one must be prepared to take the bad with the good, the ugly with the beautiful, the poor with the rich. As for the love Cami sought, she knew she must guard herself well against the lurking lust of this city of sin.

For a moment, Cami's own thoughts frightened her. What was she doing here, anyway? New Orleans was a dangerous place in the best of seasons. No one came to the city in the summertime, and those who lived here had left for healthier climes until the first frost. The Pinards' townhouse in Toulouse Street was closed and shuttered until the fever-ridden months of heat and stench had passed.

"All the better," she said aloud, trying to bolster her spirits. "They won't dare come into the city to search for me. Cousin Beatrice is far too terrified of contracting yellow fever."

She glanced from side to side. The great homes of fine old Creole families looked like so many ghost houses this late in June. Not until now had she realized she might be in any real danger—a woman traveling alone up this wide, deserted avenue. It seemed almost as if she were lost in some city of the dead. She urged Voodoo onward.

Black Vic picked up his pace as well. He could easily overtake the rider now, he assured himself. The street of unoccupied houses would work to his advantage. No interference from outsiders could be anticipated, and all doors would be locked against the fellow if he ran for help. Yes, now was the time, Vic decided.

Had he brought along his pistol, he might have simply fired a warning shot to halt the runaway. However, the only weapon he had on him was his *colchemarde*. His trusty sword-cane came in handy in a polite, gentlemen's disagreement, but it was of little use in this instance.

"Damn foolishness!" he growled. "No guns allowed at balls!"

He resigned himself to taking the fellow by manual force if it came to a struggle. He would hardly have wanted to shoot the slave in any case. Owners seldom paid the full reward when one damaged their property before returning it.

Camille heard the hoofbeats thudding behind her. Her heart leaped with fear at the sound. Grabbing her hat, she whipped it viciously at Voodoo's quivering flank. The pins in her hair flew out, giving the wind free rein with her dark tresses, but Cami never noticed.

"Faster!" she urged. "Go, boy, go!"

Had Victoine Navar been on foot, he would have stopped dead in his tracks when he saw her long, black hair whipping over her shoulders. As it was, he reared back in the saddle and gasped, "Good God, it's a woman!" Then he chuckled to himself and leaned close down on his horse's neck. "This could turn out to be as entertaining as it is profitable."

Cami heard the rider closing on her. She was so frightened she could hardly breathe. He drew nearer every second. A moment later she could actually feel his horse's hot breath on her back.

"Go, Voodoo!" she cried. "Go!"

"Whoa there, boy," a deep voice rasped.

The other horse drew abreast of Voodoo, who bucked and stamped angrily. A hand shot out and wrenched the reins from Cami. The next moment, a strong arm imprisoned her waist.

"In something of a hurry this morning, aren't you, missy?"

Cami stared at the dark figure towering beside her. The slouch brim of his hat hid his face in shadows. But the set of his features mattered little. Handsome or grotesque, he was a terrifying threat. All that mattered at the moment was that she escape, and she knew she couldn't match his strength.

Cami stopped fighting him and let her body go limp, hoping he would relax his tight hold. She had to get away. She had heard terrible tales of women being kidnapped in the city and never being seen or heard of again. She trembled, remembering one tale she had heard from the servants at Mulgrove about a lady from a fine Creole family who had been abducted and shipped off to a brothel in some distant city.

"I'll bet you're a pretty thing when you're all cleaned up." The tall stranger leaned closer, his hot breath warming her cold cheeks.

Cami tensed as he tested the size of her waist with strong fingers. Still, she didn't fight him. She must feign surrender until her chance came. *Rue d'Amour* was only two blocks away. Providing Voodoo could outrun the man's horse and providing Fiona was at home and would let her in, Cami figured she might have a chance.

He was talking to her, but she wasn't listening. The sudden mention of her cousin's name brought her attention back to what the man was saying. "I'll wager you're one of old Morris Pinard's bed-warmers." He punctuated his words with a clucking sound of pity. "If that's the case, girl, then I can't blame you for running."

"Bed-warmer?" Cami gasped. What on earth was

139

the man talking about? "I don't know any Morris Pinard," she shot back.

He only laughed. "No? Then why did I see you riding off his place? Perhaps you ran away from another plantation and only stopped by Mulgrove to steal this fine horse. In that case, I'll collect two rewards. A nice night's work!"

"The horse is mine!"

"Come, come! Slave wenches don't own anything, not even themselves."

A sick feeling twisted through Cami's stomach. At last she understood. The man was a slave-catcher. He'd seen her leave Mulgrove in these ragged clothes and assumed she was a runaway—not from a threat of marriage, but from a life of bondage. Had she not been so frightened, she might have smiled at the irony. Were the two so different, actually?

In the next instant, however, realization struck with a mighty blow. Camille's whole life flashed before her eyes. Young Juno, one of the Pinards' houseservants, had run away last fall. Cami had helped nurse her back to health after the bounty men finally brought her home. They had taken their time about returning her, using her first for their own pleasure in their swamp hideout. The filthy brutes had kept her for nearly a month before they tired of their sport and brought her back to Mulgrove to collect their reward.

"I am *not* a slave!" Cami protested. Then before she thought, she added, hoping to throw him off the track, "I'm a free woman of color. I have rights."

He stared at her in silence, then drawled, "Not many."

140

"You let me go!" she cried, trying to wrench her arm free from his iron grip.

Once more he laughed at her. "Feisty little spitfire, aren't you? If you are what you claim, let me see your papers."

Cami stared blankly at the man, straining to see the face hidden deep in shadow. "Papers? I don't understand."

"If you were truly free, you would. My guess is you're a liar and a poor one at that. Old Pinard will pay plenty to have you back in his bed. Come along quietly now."

"No, please . . ."

He reached out and touched her cheek. "Soft," he murmured. "So soft. If I weren't strapped for cash at the moment, I'd be tempted to let you go. A pretty octoroon like you shouldn't have to put up with a fat bastard like Pinard. I might even try to talk you into coming home with me. It's been quite a while since I had . . ."

His words trailed off wistfully. He leaned closer, and the next thing Cami knew his mouth was on hers. She struggled to pull away, but he held her in a vise-like grip. His kiss, though, was soft, almost tender.

Pretending to react to his surprising gentleness, Cami turned her head slightly as if she meant to place a kiss in his palm in a plea for mercy. Instead, she sank her teeth into the fleshy part of his hand, so deeply that she tasted his blood and felt it dribble down her chin.

He roared with pain and rage, but he released her as she had prayed he would. In that instant, Cami dug her heels viciously into Voodoo's sides.

The big stallion reared, then shot off like a devil chased by angels.

"Damn you to hell, come back here!" he yelled. "When I catch you—*and I will*—you'll be sorry! You wait and see, you blasted wench!"

Cami felt inclined neither to wait nor to see. All she wanted was the safety of number ten *rue d'Amour*.

The pure shock of her actions worked to her advantage. By the time the man recovered, she was far ahead of him, already turning into the street called Love. Frantically, she searched the doors of the trim, white, shotgun cottages for the right number. Just as she heard his horse approaching the intersection of Rampart and Esplanade, she spotted Fiona's house.

Camille leaped off Voodoo and gave his rump a smart whack. "Go home, boy!" she commanded.

Too spooked to fumble with the gate latch, Cami leaped over the low cypress board fence. She raced up the narrow walk and pounded at the door. By now she was frantic.

"Answer, Fiona!" she begged. "Oh, please, open up!"

The door opened as if on command. Standing before her, however, was not the beautiful octoroon she had expected, but a handsome young man with reddish-brown hair and the bluest eyes she had ever seen.

Startled, Cami lost her voice for a moment. Then hearing the sound of approaching hoofbeats, she cried out, "You must help me! I am Edouard Mazaret's daughter. Please, let me come in."

The young man only stared at her with a vague

expression of surprise, as if he were not quite awake yet. Then from somewhere inside the house, a woman's voice called, "Show mademoiselle in, Prospere."

The man named Prospere stepped aside, making a gesture that allowed entry if it did not exactly exude welcome. Cami threw herself across the threshold, then slammed the door behind her, bolting it securely.

"Fiona?" she gasped.

A diminutive, alabaster-skinned beauty stood before Cami. Only the woman's dark hair hinted at the drop of black blood somewhere far back in her ancestry. Eyes like pale amber, she was as light-skinned as the young man beside her.

"You are Camille Mazaret?" Fiona's passive features and tone betrayed none of her doubts as she gazed at the wild-eyed, rumpled creature's bloody mouth.

"Yes," Cami answered breathlessly, "and there's a terrible man chasing me. He'll be here any moment. I'm in grave trouble and you're the only one who can help me. Please, Fiona, for my father's sake? Hide me!"

Fiona's features remained calm and expressionless. "Take her to the back bedroom and stay with her there, Prospere. If he comes, I will handle the situation."

Prospere nodded, then showed Camille through the four rooms to the back.

Even though Cami was safely hidden away with Prospere to protect her, she whimpered, terrified, when she heard the pounding at the front door.

"Don't let him take me," she sobbed hysterically. "Please, oh, please!"

Prospere closed the bedroom door and motioned for her to sit down.

"You will stay quiet now," he told her in a heavily accented voice. "Trust Fiona."

Cami was more than happy to do that. She sat very still, trying to imagine what was happening between Fiona and the bounty man. Although she could hear muffled voices from the front room, she could make out nothing of what was being said.

"Open up, Fiona, I know you're in there!" Black Vic shouted.

Fiona, accustomed to a quiet, tranquil life, allowed herself a mild curse at all this sound and fury so early in the morning. What on earth was happening? First, that ragamuffin who claimed to be Edouard's daughter. *Ridiculous!* And now, if she was not mistaken, that was Victoine Navar attempting to beat down her door.

Unbolting the latch, which she never locked, Fiona opened it to find the very man she had expected. What she hadn't anticipated was the sight of his hand dripping blood all over her porch.

"Victoine!" she gasped. "What has happened?"

"Damn slave wench bit me!" he exclaimed, holding out his injured hand to her as a puppy might offer a hurt paw.

"Come in," she said. "Let me see to that while you tell me, please, what this is all about."

She showed Navar into her cozy sitting room—a room furnished to her elegant tastes with Edouard

144

Mazaret's generous gifts. The injured man slumped down on the pink brocade sofa.

Fiona brought brandy—for drinking and for healing. Having poured him some and doused his hand liberally, she wound a fresh strip of linen about his wound. He would live.

"Now, M'sieur Navar, an explanation, please. From the beginning, if you do not mind."

Black Vic confessed to his evening's escapades, starting with trying to crash the ball at Mulgrove and ending with the runaway slave wench sinking her sharp fangs into his hand, then slipping out of his clutches. He had no idea she was hiding in Fiona's bedroom, and the lady made no attempt to enlighten him.

"Dammit all! I even let the black stallion get away," he lamented. "He would have brought *some* reward money."

"Victoine Navar, when are you going to get control of yourself and your life again?" Fiona scolded gently, her large eyes soft with sympathy. "You simply cannot live in this careless hand-to-mouth fashion any longer. Tell me this—if you had captured the runaway and the horse, and if M'sieur Pinard had paid you a more than generous reward, what then would you have done with the money? Paid your debts? Put it in the bank to save until you have enough to buy back Golden Oaks?"

He looked directly into her honey-warm eyes, his own wide and alight with a peculiar, dark fire. "There's a poker game scheduled at Gaspard's tomorrow night. Big stakes! I could win enough to set me up for life, Fiona. I might even be able to buy back my home."

Fiona made a soft clucking noise—tongue against

teeth—and shook her head sadly. "Vic, poor Vic. Will you never learn?"

"I *did* learn, Fiona!" He scowled at her most unpleasantly and his black eyes lost their fire, turning hard and cold. "Don't you think I learned my lesson when that bastard cheated me out of Golden Oaks in that game ten years ago . . . when Madelaine went away and took our son, Pierre . . . when everyone turned from me? I learned then that nothing matters, nothing lasts, and that no one can be trusted. What more do I have to learn?"

"You trust *no one*, Victoine? Not even me?"

Hearing her injured tone, Vic answered quickly, "Of course I trust you, Fiona, but no one else." His head drooped and his voice became quiet. "You tell me, Fiona. Is there anyone else in the world I can trust or love ever again? My love of the gaming table is all I have left. I've always been a passionate man. You can't ask me to give up the one passion left to me." He scowled at his injured hand and shook his head. "I won't, Fiona. I can't!"

She touched his dark, tousled hair with her fingertips—not the touch of a lover, but the caress of a mother for a child in pain. "There are still other passions worth pursuing, *mon cher.*"

His head jerked up and he gave her a piercing stare. "If you're talking about love, forget it. If I did find a woman I cared for, what then? I have nothing to offer. I'm not even sure I'm free to marry again. As far as I know, Madelaine is still out there somewhere—hiding, keeping my son from me, refusing to be my wife, yet denying me any other."

Fiona ached for her friend. For so many years he had suffered. Other Creole men had entered

146

loveless matches. Her own Edouard was a prime example. But none she had ever known had been so battered and hurt by the old custom of arranged marriages as Victoine Navar.

As the only son of the great war hero and plantation owner, Philipe Navar, Vic had accepted his rightful place in the world when he was barely twenty. Ordered by his family to do so, he had married a noble Creole daughter, who had soon given him every man's dream—a son to carry on his name. At the age of twenty-three, Victoine had already become a leader in plantation society. He was admired by many, envied by some, tricked by one villain who remained unpunished to this day. The scar on Vic's face and the deeper one on his heart were the only things Domingo Cadella had left him after their duel at the gaming table.

Navar's mind was still on his one passion. "Yes, if I could only get a stake for that game tomorrow night, then I could . . ."

Vic's muttering interrupted Fiona's troubled thoughts, and suddenly she remembered some gossip she'd heard at the market. "Have you been away from the city for long, Victoine?"

"Almost a month," he replied. "I was on a riverboat that put in late yesterday. That's where I won the invitation to Pinard's fancy ball. I left the city immediately to ride out to Mulgrove, figuring I had as much right as anyone to woo his rich little cousin. But then—now that I think of it—I suppose I was wrong. Madelaine's been gone so long that sometimes I forget she ever existed or that I'm *still* a married man."

Fiona reached out and touched his arm. "Victoine, there's something you obviously haven't

147

heard since you got back. A stranger is in town looking for you. He claims to have come to New Orleans seeking revenge."

Vic's eyes went steely. "If I had a centime for every man who comes looking for me to make trouble, I wouldn't have to gamble any longer. I'd be rich, Fiona. Forget this idle gossip."

She shook her head. "I don't think this man can be dismissed so easily. He claims you killed his brother. It seems it happened some time back. A card game, as usual, but this one ended in violence."

Vic frowned. So many years, so many card games. Which one was she talking about? Then he remembered. "The bastard who accused me of cheating," he said. "Yes, I remember that night. Your Edouard sat in on the game with two brothers named Lazano from up Natchez way. One of them marked the deck. Edouard caught on to their cheating and called them on it. The older chap said it was my doing—probably trying to protect his guilty brother. Then he pulled a pistol on me and fired . . . missed, though, by a country mile. I wasn't going to let him get off a second shot."

"You killed this man, Lazano?" Fiona asked softly.

"What'd you expect me to do? Sit there and let him kill me and Edouard like he threatened? For Chrissakes, Fiona, it was self-defense!"

She stared at him gravely, tears gathering at the corners of her golden eyes. "You saved Edouard's life, *mon cher*? I never knew."

"Aw, hell! I was saving my own skin, Fiona." Vic's cheeks went ruddy with embarrassment as he protested his valor.

148

Fiona gripped his hand. "You will be careful, won't you, Victoine? The man could be dangerous."

He laughed and held up his injured hand. "I'm always careful except when I get around women. Looks like I'd learn, doesn't it?" He shook his head and sighed. "Well, I guess that slave wench is long gone by now. Just as well. I figure the poor girl was being forced by old Pinard to perform more than her fair share of duties."

"You are generous to let her go, Victoine. Perhaps she might even escape to the North, to freedom."

"Not likely, but I wish her luck." Vic rose and started for the door, then turned. "Thanks, Fiona."

"For what, my friend?"

He smiled. "For just being here. For just being you, sweet lady.".

"You should smile like that more often, Victoine." Out of habit, Fiona batted her long lashes. "It makes you such a handsome rogue."

Vic bellowed a laugh. "Handsome, you say? Ah, Fiona, you're such a cunning liar and such a woman! Were it not for my respect for your lingering feelings for Edouard, I would take you up in my arms this minute and haul you back to the bedroom for a long, lazy day of infinite pleasure. I would make you my *placée*."

A smile curved her soft lips. "Ah, no, m'sieur. You would not. You cannot afford me, remember?"

He shook his finger at her and winked. "Someday, mark my words! I will have enough money to win the finest lady in this town. She will be the envy of every other man's woman."

"Not if this Lazano has his way. Be gone with you now and take care."

Dawn was creeping down the narrow *rue d'Amour* when Fiona opened the door for Black Vic. She stood on the porch until he waved, mounted his horse, and rode off down the street. His fate lay heavy on Fiona's heart as she watched him go. Having Victoine around always made Edouard's memory seem more alive. The two men, although they had never known each other while Vic was still the respected owner of Golden Oaks, had become close through their common passion for wagering. Now that her lover was gone, she could not bear it if anything happened to his friend.

Suddenly, she remembered her other early visitor. Gathering the silk folds of her dressing gown about her, she retied the sash with a sharp jerk of conviction. She *would* find out the truth about this young woman—slave or free, black or white.

With determination in her every stride, the woman who still loved Eduoard Mazaret with all her heart headed toward the back bedroom to confront the girl who claimed to be his daughter.

Cami cried out when the door flew open, fully expecting to be confronted by her dark pursuer. Instead, the most delicate of beauties stood before her, her ecru silk dressing gown caressing the soft curves of her slender body. Cami now understood how her father could fall in love with such a woman. Fiona seemed the very essence of softness and femininity. Cami had been horrified when she first learned that her father kept a *placée*. It had seemed a scandalous thing, the way her bitter mother had explained it. But now she knew more, now she un-

150

derstood this yearning to love and be loved in return.

Smiling at Fiona, Cami held out her hand. Her father's mistress stared at her coldly, ignoring the offer of friendship.

"Now, young woman, you will tell me the truth. Obviously, you are *not* Eduoard Mazaret's daughter. Camille's beauty is legendary throughout this city and all surrounding parishes. Also, I happen to know for a fact that the young lady in question is at this very moment with her cousins at Mulgrove Plantation some miles from New Orleans. So who, pray tell, are *you*? And what do you mean, invading the sanctity of my home?"

Taken aback by Fiona's brusqueness, Camille could not think of an answer.

Fiona's eyes flashed a darker, more ominous hue. "Tell me at once or I shall send Prospere for the authorities."

Camille swallowed several times, trying to find her voice. A new fear swept through her. Fiona might not be the gentle, understanding woman she had envisioned. It seemed Cami had escaped the slave-catcher, but would Fiona send her back to Mulgrove, to her slave-trader of a cousin, with his panting boys all waiting in a row?

"Go, Prospere!" Fiona ordered. "Summon a *gendarme*."

"Please, no," Camille begged. But they were the only words she could speak as she stared into Fiona's cold, golden eyes, her own flooding with tears.

* * *

Only a moment later, or so it seemed, Carol found herself alone and weeping on the deserted wharf at the foot of Barracks Street. Although she could see nothing through the thick morning fog, she could hear Choctaw's oars as he pulled away into the river.

"Wait!" she called. "I can't leave Cami like that!" But she knew it was useless even before she cried out.

With tears as desperate as Cami's streaming down her cheeks, Carol turned and headed slowly back toward the hotel, her mind whirling with all that she had seen and heard and done during the night. She wandered the French Quarter for a long time, thinking. The sun came up; the streets came alive.

She looked at her watch suddenly. "Eight-thirty!" she gasped. "Frank's going to be pissed!"

Chapter Seven

"Dammit! Where the hell could she be?"

Frank was long past frantic. He checked his wrist-watch for the umpteenth time in the past half-hour, swore under his breath, then paced across the courtyard again. A sharp blade of pure, cold fear stabbed through his gut. He knew he was being unreasonable. Carol was late for a business appointment, that was all. It could happen to anyone, he tried to tell himself. But he was beginning to realize that Carol Marlowe wasn't just anyone. Add to that growing awareness his painful memories of Eileen's disappearance and you had the makings of a man teetering on the edge.

What if she'd wandered out alone again early this morning and run into some kind of trouble? The thought kept nagging him: *It's happening all over again—just like with Eileen. Carol's gone—gone for good!*

He couldn't decide which way to turn, what to do next. At eight-ten, he'd knocked gently on Carol's door. At eight-fifteen he'd pounded. No response in either case. Five minutes after that, he'd ordered the hotel manager to use his pass key to open her suite. What they'd found had been anything but reassuring. Carol hadn't slept in her bed. Her purse was there. Nothing looked out of place or suspicious, yet the entire situation seemed powerfully suspicious to Frank.

He had to find Carol. But where could he look?

Impulse told him to call headquarters and have an immediate All Points Bulletin put out for her. That was crazy and he knew it. He certainly couldn't declare her a missing person when she was only a half-hour late for an appointment.

"Eileen was just a little late, too," he reminded himself grimly. He tried not to think of that, tried even harder not to make any connection. Still, there it was. The painful comparison kept gnawing at him. "Maybe if I'd shown more concern for Eileen sooner . . . yeah, *maybe, maybe, maybe!*"

White-hot rage mixed with his frustration. Frank spent both on a discarded beer can lying in the courtyard. Giving the dead soldier a mighty kick, he sent it tumbling out onto the banquette. He followed its trajectory until he stood outside the hotel entrance. Hopelessly, helplessly, he scanned the street up and down.

"Not a sign of her. Damn!"

He was about to turn around, his mind made up to call the station and spread some kind of alarm, when he spotted Carol ambling toward the hotel at

154

a lazy, haphazard pace, seemingly oblivious to how late she was or how badly she'd scared him.

When she got close enough for him to see her plainly, Frank cursed again—louder this time. "What the hell . . . ?"

Carol had blood on her face.

Carol spotted Frank ahead and quickened her step. Even from half a block away she could see that he looked drawn and pale. Maybe something had happened while she was away. Perhaps he'd heard some news—a real break in the case. He headed toward her almost at a trot.

"You're hurt!" They were Frank's first words.

"No, I'm fine," Carol insisted, wondering what made him think she wasn't.

"You're bleeding! Don't tell me you're fine!"

Carol licked her lips. She did taste blood. "I don't know. Maybe I bit my lip or something. Really, it's nothing, Frank."

Before she realized what he meant to do, Frank enveloped her in a smothering bear-hug—right there on the busy banquette with all the tourists watching. The embrace was so unexpected that Carol almost went faint in his arms. She forgot the gaping onlookers, the early hour, even the predicament in which she'd left Camille Mazaret. Frank's urgency seemed her only reality at the moment.

She could actually feel his body trembling against hers. Only then did she realize what hell she'd put him through. Ashamed and contrite, she tried to apologize, but her words came out a muffled whisper against his shoulder.

A moment later, Frank released her. Glaring at

her with fierce, black eyes, he demanded, "Where the hell have you been?"

"I'm sorry I'm late, Frank." Carol tried her apology again, but he didn't let her finish.

"*Sorry?* Sorry won't cut it, Miz Marlowe!" He seemed to tower over her, bearing down with all the wrath of an outraged lover. "I've been going crazy, wondering where you were, what might have happened to you. And all you have to say for yourself is that you're sorry?"

Carol felt her cheeks flame. She hated scenes. She glanced about at the curious crowd that had gathered.

"Frank, please," she whispered. "Can't we go somewhere else? People are staring."

Frank slowly and deliberately turned his glare on the ogling spectators. "I don't give a damn who hears!" he growled.

The crowd scattered in the face of his anger, but Carol had no intention of continuing the heated discussion on the street.

"Come on, Frank." She grabbed his arm and all but dragged him through the arched entry to the courtyard. "Your room or mine?" she demanded.

Silenced now by her quick actions, Frank stared at her and motioned toward his apartment. Without another word, they went up the stairs to the second floor. Not until Frank unlocked the door and they were both inside did he speak again. His tone was more civil now, but still taut with tension.

"I apologize, Carol."

Trying to lighten the mood between them, she asked, "For what? Giving me hell or hugging me out there in front of God and all the old people?"

He didn't laugh as she'd hoped he would. Instead, he reached for her hand and pulled her close once more. His embrace this time was much gentler than before. Not knowing what else to do, she let her arms glide around his neck. She closed her eyes and languished in his arms, sighing at the wonderful feeling of being this close to a man once more. For a time, she forgot how angry he had been only moments before.

While Frank cradled her to his broad chest, rubbing his cheek against hers, an odd collection of thoughts tripped lightly through Carol's mind. Maybe Frank Longpre was the real reason she had come to New Orleans. She'd always figured that her psychic powers were useless as far as giving her any help romantically. Look at that last fiasco, for instance! But this time could prove the exception. What if all the business about Camille and the mummy was simply fate's excuse for bringing her here to meet Frank? Perhaps the reason none of her past relationships had worked out was that she and Frank were meant for each other all along.

He was still holding her, almost desperately, as if he were afraid she might disappear again the moment he let her go. She could feel his heart pounding rapidly against her breasts. From time to time, he drew in a deep, shuddering breath like a man who'd just run a race or reached an especially satisfying climax.

"Frank," Carol whispered, touching his face with her fingertips, "I never meant to upset you so. I really am sorry."

"So am I." His voice was deeper, huskier than usual. "It's just . . . when you didn't show up . . .

when I couldn't find you, it was like I was reliving Eileen's disappearance."

A lump in Carol's throat choked off words. She tried, but couldn't speak. Tears welled in her eyes. What a dummy she was! She could have hurried back to the hotel and been nearly on time. Why hadn't she realized earlier how upset Frank would be if she turned up missing? Had all her psychic powers fled along with her compassion and understanding?

"Oh, Frank," she finally managed, "I feel terrible about this."

Now it was Carol's turn to hug him with every bit of the tenderness she could muster. When she sensed Frank's passions rising in concert with her own, she quickly stepped away. She felt awkward suddenly, embarrassed for both their sakes. This simply wouldn't do. After all, they were professionals. And here she was acting like a starry-eyed teenager with her first crush just because Frank—frantic with worry—had hugged her.

Suddenly, Frank caught her by the shoulders. Holding her in his solid, steel-like grip, he stared into her eyes. "Carol, do you realize what's happening here?"

Her voice was as calm as she could make it under the circumstances. "Yes, Frank, I think I do. I've upset you again without meaning to. By being late, I made your past come back to life. I wasn't the one you were worried about. I realize that now. It was Eileen all over again."

His olive-dark face turned ruddy at her words. "You have it all wrong. What happened to Eileen certainly triggered my fears, but it was *your* disap-

158

pearance that scared the hell out of me," he said bluntly. "So, what are we going to do about that?"

She shrugged and tried to smile, not sure exactly what he was trying to tell her or what he expected in the way of a response. "I don't think there's much we *can* do about it."

"Me either," he mumbled, shying away from her steady gaze.

"Is it so terrible?" she asked. "That you worry about me, I mean."

The pained expression on his face and the terror—still ebbing from his dark eyes—answered that question for Carol. Frank hadn't simply been worried when she was late, her tardiness had put him through a special brand of hell.

"It isn't fair," Frank murmured.

"Life isn't always fair, Frank," she whispered. "But please . . . I am *so* sorry."

He went on as if he hadn't heard her apology, as if he were talking aloud to himself. "When you didn't show up this morning . . . when I went into your room and saw all your things there . . . I can't begin to describe the way I felt." He looked into her eyes, his own a dense, smoky black. "I went crazy, Carol."

"Surely you knew I'd come back."

"Eileen never did." He paused—a long, still silence. "I was sure I'd never see you again either, that I'd have to spend the rest of my life searching for Eileen *and* for you, Carol."

"Oh, Frank!" Carol longed to hold him again and soothe him, but his mention of Eileen held her at bay. What good could come of getting involved with a man who still had a wife, even if it was in name only? Frank had to let Eileen go before he could ever really resume his life. And certainly love would be out of the question for a man so obsessed. Carol wondered if she might be falling once more for someone incapable of loving her in return. If so, life was, indeed, far from fair.

"Tell me where you went, Carol," Frank demanded. "Today *and* yesterday."

She caught her breath when he mentioned her early-morning jaunt the day before. "How did you know about yesterday?"

"I saw you coming back to the hotel just as I was getting up. What's going on, Carol?"

Carol sank down on Frank's antique brass bed. She bit at her lower lip, trying to decide how to explain everything.

Suddenly, Frank laughed, but there was little humor in his tone. "I sound like a jealous lover, don't I? Well, you'll have to pardon that, ma'am. I know I have no right beyond our professional association to demand explanations, but, to be right truthful, Carol, I'm afraid for you. You may be getting in over your head on this case."

So much for the lame explanation she'd planned to use—that she had gone out early to see the sights or go window shopping. Frank had his own ESP working here.

"It's a long, complicated story," she began.

"I've cancelled the boat to English Turn. We have plenty of time. Want some coffee?" he asked. "Maybe that would help us both settle down."

Carol nodded and smiled. Frank poured out two mugs of black Creole coffee with chicory. One sip of the strong, hot brew brought Carol's jumbled thoughts into instant focus.

She began her explanation with her arrival in New Orleans and her first encounter with the anonymous woman in the red tignon. She told him of the shadowy ferryman named Choctaw. When she tried to explain about Camille and how she actually became the young woman when she went back in time, Frank frowned, obviously finding it difficult to believe the things she was telling him.

"Don't look at me that way, Frank. I know it all sounds bizarre. But it really happened—every last bit of it." She paused for a moment, trying to think of some way she could prove her story. Her eyes lit up when she remembered something. "You said you were in my room. Did you notice the long, white evening gloves on the dresser?"

He nodded. "Yeah, as a matter of fact, I did."

"Those belong to Cami. She was wearing them when I left her yesterday. I had them on when I got back to the hotel. There's even a stain on one of them. One of her dancing partners had dirty hands."

He cocked his head and squinted at her skeptically. "You really believe all this, don't you?"

"Yes, every word of it. You'd better believe it, too. And there's more." She licked her lips, tasting again the faintest trace of blood. "Victoine Navar—I've seen him twice now." She grinned, embarrassed suddenly. "In fact, I . . . that is, Cami had a fight with him a short while ago. She bit him—*hard!* Drew blood, in fact."

"You're trying to tell me that's Navar's blood on your face?" Frank gave her another skeptical frown.

"It must be. The taste of it is still in my mouth." Quickly, she explained to Frank all about Cami's

161

escape from Mulgrove and how Black Vic mistook her for a runaway slave. "If Cami hadn't sunk her teeth into his hand, she'd be back with her scheming cousins by now. Of course, Cami didn't realize the guy giving her trouble was actually Navar, the hunk who tried to crash the party earlier. She just figured he was some bounty man out to pick up a quick reward. In fact, he told her as much."

Frank leaned closer, all attention now that he knew these phantoms of Carol's imagination could actually bleed. "Tell me more."

"I'm sure now that he must be the man who eventually became Cami's lover and fought a duel with her cousin, Morris Pinard. But when Vic left Fiona's house he still believed that Cami was a runaway slave."

Even to Carol, who had been part of it all, the tale sounded just too weird. She fully expected Frank to laugh in her face or at the very least shake his head and tell her she'd gone bonkers. His reaction came as a total shock.

"I don't like this—not a-tall! What if you go back there and get stuck? I'd never even know what happened to you. There'd be no way on God's green Earth that I could do anything to help you. So, next time you go to meet Choctaw, I'm going with you."

"I don't think you can do that, Frank."

"Why not?" he demanded.

She shrugged. "I'm not sure Choctaw will come unless I'm alone. And even if he does, you have no gold doubloon. That seems to be my key to returning to the past. He has to see it before he'll let me get in his boat."

Frank rubbed a hand over his chin, thinking.

Then Carol saw a new light in his eyes. "You forget," he said, "that the mummy was wearing a similar coin around her neck. If my Jane Doe is really your Cami, as you believe, then her doubloon should be good enough to pay my passage. If not, then it seems to me that would prove that that's not Camille Mazaret lying over in the morgue. I'm going, Carol! Damned if I'm not!"

His determination worried Carol. She wasn't sure how she actually managed to cross over that invisible line into the past, but she was fairly certain her psychic powers enabled her to make the trip. If that was the case, there was no way Frank could accompany her. And what if, on seeing Frank with her, Choctaw disappeared and never returned?

"I don't think this is a good idea, Frank," she repeated.

Instead of arguing, he reached down and slipped one hand around the back of her neck, massaging gently. "Good idea or bad, I'm not going to let you run any more risks alone. I'm not sure I believe that all you've told me is anything but a dream, some sort of vision. However, if it is true and you are traveling back in time, I mean to be right beside you from now on."

They spent what was left of the morning in Frank's room, drinking coffee and talking, really getting to know each other. Carol figured that was only right if they were going to be traveling through time together.

Frank told her about his motherless childhood, spent mostly in military schools. He'd been a loner back then just as he was today. His father, embittered after his wife died in childbirth, had never forgiven his son. During Frank's formative years, no closeness grew between farther and son. Carol ached for him as she listened in silence to Frank's boyhood stories. The year he entered The Citadel, his father died. A heart attack—sudden, unexpected, final. There had been no "Granny Bess" in Frank's life. No one at all in the way of family. Not until he married Eileen did Frank even begin to realize all the love he had missed, had ached for, all his life. Then—suddenly, unexpectedly, tragically—she, too, was taken from him.

Frank told his long, sad tale without emotion. He didn't feel sorry for himself, but Carol felt sorry enough for both of them. She was verging on tears by the time he finished. She had the greatest urge to take him into her arms and comfort him and tell him everything would be all right from now on. Yet she sensed that Frank was not a man to accept sympathy gracefully.

"You hungry?" he asked finally.

Carol nodded. Actually she was starved. She'd had only a light supper the night before and no breakfast at all.

"How about some eggs?" he said. "I can scramble some up in a jiffy on the hotplate."

"Sounds good!" Carol agreed.

She busied herself setting the table while Frank went to work in his kitchenette, still rambling on about domestic bliss with Eileen.

A knock at the door and the maid's voice put a sudden end to one of Frank's stories right at its middle. Annoyed by the intrusion, Carol shot a mean glance at the door.

Noticing her reaction, Frank said, "It's just the maid bringing me some fresh towels."

164

His simple statement almost brought the tears Carol had been fighting. Imagine a man at Frank's stage in life who lived so impersonally that he didn't even own his own towels. His life was exactly the way she had envisioned—a Christmas tree with no presents, a mailbox with no letters, a bathroom with no towels. She stifled her pity, knowing it was the last thing Frank would want.

All intimacy between them vanished with the maid's interruption. Frank suddenly grew silent and withdrawn. Carol felt almost uncomfortable with him now, as if she were intruding on his deep need for solitude. She wanted desperately to ask him if something was wrong or if she had offended him in some way. But she sensed that he would not welcome any questions right now.

Sense his mood was all she could do, she realized with a start. She'd been able to read Frank's thoughts with ease since their first contact over the phone. Suddenly, she was being blocked. She had no idea if Frank was doing it consciously or if something in her psychic system had gone on the blink. At any rate, the loss of this power gave her an odd feeling, as if she were now placed at a distinct disadvantage.

Silently, they sat down across the table from each other and passed the salt and pepper, then set upon their food. The tension between them—tension that Carol could not comprehend—grew with every wordless moment.

"Eggs okay?" Frank asked laconically.

"Fine!" she answered too quickly, too loudly. She realized that she was almost pathetically happy that he had finally spoken to her again. "They're delicious, really," she added in a more composed tone.

"Well, eat up, then. I know you must be worn

out. I have to dress and go to my office for a while—some things I need to pick up. You'd better head on back to your room and catch some shut-eye. I'll come back for you around five and we'll go to a little Cajun joint I know." He'd been staring down at his empty plate and rambling on as if he were talking to himself. He paused and looked up at Carol, his face so dead-serious suddenly that her heart raced from fear of what he was about to say. "You like Cajun? Real spicy?"

Carol nodded enthusiastically. "Love it!" Actually, she had no idea whether she liked Cajun or not. But faced with Frank's strange mood shift, she would have told him her favorite dish was snake eyeballs with 'gator-tail gravy, if he'd asked.

"Good. Then we'll do it."

He rose and began clearing dishes from the table, stacking them in the tiny sink in his kitchenette.

Carol got up, too, scraped her plate, and positioned herself in front of the sink, ready to finish the domestic chores.

"Hey, the maid'll do that," Frank said suddenly.

"I don't mind."

He caught her elbow and directed her away from the dishes and toward the door. "But I do," he told her. "I can't afford to get the maid spoiled. I pay her extra to do housework for me."

He gave Carol no opening for argument. At the door, he said simply, "See you about five," then he hustled her gently outside.

Frank leaned his back against the closed door with a long, pent-up sigh, then muttered, "Damnation!"

166

He bent forward and put his face down in his hands, then ran his clutched fingers up through his hair, grinding his teeth as he did. He felt a sudden killing rage that threatened to engulf him. He wanted to kick butt, scream obscenities, smash some guy's face to a bloody pulp.

"Why?" he growled. "Why in hell is this happening to me?

He remembered once when he was a kid of about eight and he'd gotten into a fight with one of the other boys from school, a cop had spotted the two of them slugging it out. The hefty Irishman had caught each of them by the collar and hauled them up off the ground until their fists and feet were thrashing blindly through the air.

Frank recalled how scared he'd been at that moment, sure he was about to be hauled off to jail because of his hair-trigger temper. In spite of his present pain, he gave a wry chuckle and said, "I almost pissed my pants!"

But the big cop hadn't turned them in. Instead, he'd taken the two young rascals to the backyard of his own house in the Irish Channel. There he had armed the boys with a boxload of empty mayonnaise jars, pointed them toward his board fence, and ordered, "Fire away, lads!"

Frank and his sparring partner had spent the next twenty minutes heaving mayonnaise jars at that back fence, giggling their fool heads off and whooping gleefully each time a direct hit sent bright bits of glass flying. By the time they ran out of things to throw, the two of them had worked out their frustrations and were laughing and joking with each other and the cop. Neither of them could even remember what their fight was all about.

"I could use about a million mayonnaise jars right now, and a board fence twenty feet high." Lacking that Frank took his anger out on a nearby chair, kicking it halfway across the room.

It didn't help. He sank down on the bed, his face buried in his hands again.

"Eileen, Eileen!" he moaned.

He could barely remember his wife; it had been that long. Yet whenever he started to feel something for another woman, the guilt came washing over him, turning any affection he felt into something dark and twisted and ugly. Eileen wouldn't have wanted it that way and he knew it, but there was little he could do to change things. His gnawing guilt led to frustration and that frustration to impotent rage.

"Not *this* time!" he said through clenched teeth.

Flopping back on the bed, Frank closed his eyes. He could still smell Carol's perfume—not a scent purchased over a department store counter, but the warm, earthy essence-of-woman that was her own delicious trademark.

Frank inhaled deeply, then let his mind go blank to wander as it would—he hoped it would be away from Carol Marlowe and the need he felt building inside him every time she came near.

He tried to concentrate on Eileen. "Yeah, think it through," he said, "figure it all out. What happened? Why? Whose fault was it?"

Frank squinted hard, trying to bring a picture of Eileen to mind. He could visualize her long, blond hair, her nice figure, her smile. But individual features remained indistinct in his mind. He recalled that last day—how they'd made love before he left for work. He hadn't wanted to, afraid it might harm the baby she was carrying. Eileen, playful and coaxing, had insisted that it would be perfectly safe until she was much further along. He'd been more than willing to take her word for it. Afterward, she'd cooked him breakfast—his favorite, French toast and link sausage—hurriedly ironed him a fresh shirt, and kissed him goodbye for the day.

"No, not for the day," he reminded himself with a moan. "*Forever!*"

He'd come home that evening to find everything neat and tidy. Eileen had been a wonderful housekeeper and she was so proud of their first real home, which they had moved into barely a month before her disappearance.

He'd known the minute he unlocked the front door and stepped inside that something was wrong. Eileen loved to cook. She had told him at breakfast that she'd be trying out a new recipe for dinner. "Creole pot roast," she'd said, "with lots of spices and a thick, red gravy. I just hope all the neighbors don't show up to join us. I figure on smelling up our whole block, cooking it all day like I'll have to."

Neither Eileen, who always watched for his car, nor any spicy, mouth-watering aromas had greeted him that night. The fact that his dinner wasn't cooked should have been his first clue that something was very wrong. But he'd been young then, and so innocent of the cruel tricks life can play. He'd told himself Eileen must have decided to go to a movie or do some shopping at the new mall. He'd waited hours before alerting authorities to her disappearance. Those wasted hours might have been crucial in finding her, and he—her own husband—had allowed the trail to go cold.

Now, all these years later, that trail was even

colder. Frozen over, in fact. No answers. No clues, except his name scratched on a pad of paper beside the phone, then crossed out. Just this same old soul-shattering remorse and guilty rage when he tried to tell himself it was all right for him to feel something for another woman.

"I still have a wife," he murmured. "I do! She's out there somewhere."

Carol crossed the courtyard hurriedly. She felt like every eye was on her and had seen her coming out of a married man's room. That was ridiculous, of course. After so many years, Frank was no more married than she was. Besides, they hadn't done anything really—a couple of hugs and a lot of talk. But it wasn't anything they'd done that made her feel this way. No, it was what she felt growing between them. She had been aware of Frank as a handsome, sexy man from the first moment she laid eyes on him.

Cancel that, she mused silently. His husky, southern-tinted voice over the phone had been the first thing about him that turned her on. She had to admit that Frank Longpre was one of those men who attracted women without even sensing his power over them. More often than not, she found herself avoiding direct eye contact because when she looked at him his gaze set up a little licking flame down inside her. She had a feeling that if she let him feed that flame it might just burn her alive. There were other things, too. The way the dark hair on his chest curled up toward his neck, looking so inviting when he wore his shirt unbuttoned at the collar. She found herself longing to reach up and stroke those glossy strands, to feel her fingers gliding over the coarse texture.

The more she thought, the guiltier she felt. She had the uncomfortable feeling that everyone in New Orleans knew and disapproved of the fact that she had just come from Frank's room and was now thinking such intimate thoughts about him. She knew it was silly. She also knew that Frank's mood when she'd left him contributed to her own guilty feelings now. She still couldn't figure what had come over him, but she had no intention of letting his moodiness stand in the way of what could well be the dawning of a new and wonderful relationship.

It had been a long time since Carol had been so moved by and attracted to a man. She quickly corrected that thought in her mind. *I have never felt this way about anyone before*! It was truly scary.

The quiet security of her own room came as a vast relief. Quickly, she shut the door, locking the troubling world outside. She needed some time alone to think everything through, not only this new turn of events with Frank, but all that had happened during her most recent visit back to Camille's lifetime.

Only after Carol had relaxed in a hot tub, brushed her teeth, and washed and dried her hair did she realize how exhausted she was. Frank had said he'd come for her about five. She glanced at the clock, hoping she could catch a couple of hours' sleep before then.

With a sigh of pleasure, she turned back the covers, climbed into bed, and stretched out, almost purring it felt so good. She was gone the minute her head touched the pillow.

For a time, she drifted in blissful, restful nothingness. But soon the dream began.

Carol herself played no role in the troubled wanderings of her mind this afternoon. The main character was another woman—a beautiful, blond housewife, who looked to be in her mid-twenties. Carol hovered, unseen, as the other woman went about her morning chores in the modern, ranch-style house. She made the bed, did some laundry, put the breakfast dishes into sudsy water in the stainless steel sink. This seemed to be the quite normal routine of a quite normal domestic engineer. Carol couldn't accurately judge the date by the woman's attire—faded, low-slung jeans and a purple stretch-knit turtle-neck. Then she glimpsed a 1980 calendar hanging on the kitchen wall. It was turned to the month of May. She read several notations jotted down on various dates—doctor's and dentist's appointments, a church picnic, laundry to be picked up.

Nothing sinister, nothing threatening. Yet Carol reacted to the ordinary in this case as if she were in the throes of the most terrifying nightmare. She tossed and turned in bed, moaning in her sleep as the young housewife went about her everyday tasks.

When the beige wall phone rang in the tidy kitchen, Carol cried out in her sleep. The woman, on the other hand, answered it calmly, smiling as if she had been happily anticipating this call.

"Hel-lo-o," she answered musically.

Her smile immediately faded, replaced by a business-like expression.

172

"No. I'm sorry. My husband isn't here right now. He won't be home till this evening. You might try him at the station."

She paused, listening to the caller for a moment, then reached for a pencil and pad. Although Carol had no idea what she wrote down, it seemed to be only one word.

"May I ask who this is?" the woman inquired politely. "I'll take your number, if you like, and have my husband return your call as soon as possible."

Whoever the caller was hung up abruptly at that point. The young woman stared at the receiver in her hand with a look of exasperation on her pretty face.

"Probably some insurance salesman," she said, scratching out whatever she had written on the phone pad. "They never leave a name or number. Then they call back just in time to interrupt supper."

The scene dissolved, leaving Carol to sleep peacefully for a time.

When the dream returned, Carol saw the same house, but from the outside. She could see the woman through the window, hurrying to the side door to answer the doorbell at the carport entrance.

"Coming," she called out. "Just a minute!"

After the woman's words, Carol heard only silence, saw only the closed door before her, but the hair rose at the back of her neck. She was in the carport now, but had yet to glimpse the person who had rung the bell. As she lay sleeping, however—waiting for the woman to open the door—she became aware of several things. There was the sound of labored breathing, like someone who smoked

173

heavily, was overweight, or who had recently exerted himself in some way, perhaps running or lifting weights. Yes, he was a smoker. Carol could smell a cheap, rank cigar even now. Another odor—no less pleasant—mingled with the tobacco smell. An unwashed, heavily perspiring body.

Still, the door remained closed; Carol's fear mounted. Her eyes stayed trained on the screen. She heard the tap-tap of the woman's footsteps inside as she hurried to answer the bell. The closer she came, the more terrifying the dream. Carol tossed and moaned.

The caller grew impatient. With her eyes still fixed on that closed door, Carol saw a thick hand, the back furred with black hair, reach for the button to press the bell again. Her eyes gazed on broken fingernails clogged underneath with black grease. The man had a tattoo on his right forearm—a dagger piercing a woman's breast. Underneath the gory flesh-picture were the words: "My Heart Bleeds." As the hand rose higher, she noted the peculiar way he rang the bell, using his middle finger with the two on either side tucked under, turning the mundane task into an obscene gesture.

"Don't . . . don't!" Carol groaned in her sleep. "Don't come! Don't open it!"

Then, as if in slow motion, Carol watched the knob turn. Inch by slow, agonizing inch, the door opened inward. The woman inside was smiling as she had been before. But, again in slow motion, Carol saw the muscles in her smooth cheeks tighten with fear. The corners of her mouth drew down. Her green eyes went wide and wild. One hand clutched at her stomach, the instinctive reaction of a pregnant woman trying to protect her unborn child. At the same moment, Carol watched the woman's mouth form the wide *O* of a scream.

Carol heard the throat-tearing sound. But when she jerked awake and sat up in bed, shaking and sweating, she realized immediately that the scream had come from her own mouth. The woman was gone.

"Gone forever," Carol whimpered miserably, having no idea why she said those words.

A moment later, however, in a sudden flash of mental clarity—a psychic burst—she understood everything. She knew who the woman was and what she had just witnessed in her dream.

"Oh, please, no!" she begged some unseen force. "I don't want to know about this. Don't show me," she murmured, tears streaming down her cheeks. "If I know, then I'll have to tell Frank, and I don't think he can handle this."

There was only silence. But somehow Carol knew that what she had just witnessed was the beginning of the end for Eileen Longpre.

Chapter Eight

Frank seemed preoccupied and subdued when he
came by for Carol at five. As for Carol herself, she
had yet to recover from her terrifying dream. The
images of Eileen and the tattooed man still swam
in her head—sharp and clear and frightening. If
only she could believe that it had been *only* a dream!

They walked the few blocks from the hotel to
Jackson Square in silence. Still, Carol could feel the
heat inside her rising with Frank so close again. She
glanced up at him once when they stopped at a
corner. She'd been wondering if he was even aware
of her beside him or if he was still lost in his own
thoughts. When she looked up, he was staring
down. Their gazes locked for a moment and Carol
actually felt her heart race in that instant. Quickly,
she shied away, knowing she was blushing. The

moment passed. Her pulses calmed. But Carol remained very much aware of the man beside her.

"We're almost there." Frank pointed toward the far side of the park over the heads of a wave of party-goers. "The *Laissez-Les-Bons-Temps-Rouler-Café.*"

As they shouldered their way through the Carnival throngs, headed for the Let-The-Good-Times-Roll-Café, Frank suddenly brightened and made an effort at conversation.

"I'll bet you can't guess who flew into N'Awlins last night."

Carol laughed as tourists pressed in around them. "About a million more people?" she ventured.

"Aw, you probably don't care anyway," Frank said with a shrug. "I'll bet you never even watch the Monday night comedies on TV. Too tame!"

"I do, too," Carol informed him. " 'Evening Shade', 'Major Dad', 'Murphy Brown', 'Designing Women', 'Northern Exposure'—start to finish, every week."

Frank smiled his approval. "I guess you would care, then. Gerald McRaney, 'Major Dad,' is here. His wife, too. He'll reign as Bacchus XXIV tomorrow night."

Carol's eyes glittered with starstruck awe. *"Really,* Frank? But you didn't actually *see* him, did you?"

Frank's dark eyes twinkled as he gave her a gloating grin. "Oh, you think not? Well, you bet I did! Saw him and shook his hand! As for proof, I'll tell you a little secret." He dropped his voice to a whisper. "Delta Burke's gone blond."

Carol gasped, then fell silent, mulling this over,

her earlier grim thoughts upstaged by Mrs. McRaney's drastic new hair color.

They skirted the cathedral, walking down Pirates Alley into Chartres. Jackson Square was a mob scene, a carnival in itself, with a jazz band playing in the middle of the street, tourists jiving to the throb of an African beat, tap-dancers cavorting, artists stroking canvas, souvenir vendors hawking Mardi Gras masks, and a mime dressed all in black and white doing his own thing beside General Jackson's statue.

"The cafe's over there in the Pontalba building," Frank said.

Actually, there was no need for Frank to point out the place. Carol's nose had already picked up the spicy aroma of the Cajun eatery and she could hear the distinctive music of the old fashioned Acadian band, playing the traditional fiddle, accordion, and triangle.

They arrived before the dinner rush, so they got a table immediately. The rotund, mustachioed owner, recognizing Frank even before they entered the open front door, hurried forward to show him to his regular spot. Soon they were seated in a relatively quiet back corner at a small table covered with a red-and-white checked cloth.

Carol glanced about as they settled themselves. The high-ceilinged old building offered a perfect setting with its white marble floor, shadowy rafters, and tall windows that looked out over Jackson Square. Strings of dried red peppers and snowy garlic added bright touches to the dim interior, and Cajun music plunked and rollicked through the spice-laden air.

"M'sieur Frank?" the owner asked with a quirk of his shaggy brow. *"Le menu?"*

Frank smiled up at the man, but shook his head. "No need for a menu, Papa Joe. Just bring us the works."

"Oh, *oui*, M'sieur Frank!" The man shared his pleased grin with Carol, smoothed his hands over his white-aproned girth, then called toward the kitchen, *"Le spécialité de la maison pour M'sieur Frank et la mademoiselle. Immédiatement!"*

In spite of her earlier bleak mood, Carol didn't have to force a smile. "Such service! I'm impressed, Frank."

"You needn't be." He shrugged. "Restaurant people know me. I eat out a lot."

"It's more than that," Carol said. "Papa Joe likes you. In fact, everyone we've met seems to admire you greatly."

"Aw, cut it out, Carol," he said, obviously embarrassed by her observation. "I'm a cop. Everybody either likes us or hates us. If they stay on the right side of the law, we're great guys, keeping the peace and upholding their rights. They want to stay on the good side of us in case they ever need help. The rest—the bad guys—hate our guts. Once we've put them away, most of them would as soon slit our throats as give us the time of day."

Carol shivered slightly. "You sound so cynical, Frank. Surely you can't believe that anyone who's nice to you has an ax to grind, or that every criminal you've ever brought to justice is out to get you afterward."

"Can't I?" He looked her straight in the eye, unsmiling.

"You mean, there are really guys out there who might come after you?" She shuddered at the thought. "People who might try to do you harm?"

Frank simply nodded, his face expressionless, showing his lack of interest in this particular topic of conversation.

"But doesn't that make you nervous, Frank?"

"Not especially. It comes with the territory. I can't jump at every shadow or I'd never know a peaceful minute." He looked thoughtful, then added, "I'm one of the lucky guys on the force. I don't have a family to worry about. It's when the ex-cons come after a fellow's wife or kids that it really gets scary. Still, the good folks outnumber the bad, and they treat us real fine to get what they want."

Frank's cynical attitude, his whole grim demeanor, made Carol more uncomfortable by the minute. She hesitated, but decided she had to ask. "Do you think I want something from you?"

He looked blank for a moment, like he couldn't figure what she was talking about. "No, Carol, not you," he said quietly. "You're an exception to my rule."

He mumbled something at the end of that last sentence that Carol didn't quite catch. She thought he said, "In more ways than one." She frowned, puzzled by the words. Maybe she'd been mistaken.

When she glanced at Frank again, her frown deepened. He looked utterly miserable. She regretted asking the stupid question. She was acting like a pouty teenager, fishing for compliments. Why hadn't she just come right out with it: "If I let you have your way with me, will you still respect me afterward?" How silly could she be?

She smiled at him reassuringly. "Don't mind me, Frank. I'm just a little edgy this evening."

"Me, too," he admitted. "Carol, I've got to tell you something."

"Go ahead," she urged expectantly, hoping they might clear the air and have a more pleasant evening.

He shied away from her eager gaze. "It's about this morning—the way I acted. I shouldn't have thrown you out that way."

"You didn't exactly throw me out, Frank, but I did wonder about your sudden change of mood," she confessed.

Frank had been staring down at the table, tracing a line of red checks with one finger. He glanced up at Carol, then slid his hand across toward hers, until their fingertips touched.

She felt a thread of heat pass from his hand into hers. It raced up her arm before flowing into her chest to flood her pounding heart. She had to force herself to breathe normally.

"I'm sorry, Carol," he said simply. "You're the nicest lady I've met in quite a while. I reckon I've just about forgotten how to treat someone like you. Hell, I never was any good with women. I think Eileen married me out of pity, figuring I'd never find a wife otherwise."

He looked up at Carol with a lopsided grin, and she thought: *Sure, my sexy friend, and all these vibes I'm picking up are coming from some guy across the room!*

"Mostly, what I wanted to tell you, Carol, was that I'm afraid our business relationship is breaking down." Frank paused to take a deep breath. "Hell, I'm messing this up every which-a-way. What I mean to say is that there's something between us that's getting in the way of business." He paused and grinned. "Something real nice!"

Carol felt herself blush with pleasure. What a neat thing to say! What a neat guy!

"Anyway, Carol, I just hope I haven't offended you. I'll try to keep things professional, but . . ."

Professional, ha! Carol thought. Before Frank could finish what he was saying, Carol closed her hand over the warm fingers that had been toying with hers.

"Frank, look at me," Carol said, and he did as she commanded. She was smiling. Her expression chased the worry lines from his face. "I'm not real sure what's happening either, but I know I don't want to fight it. In fact, I tried. I *can't* fight it! Let's just be friends and let nature take its course. Okay?"

His whole tough-handsome face lit up, the smile starting deep in his dark, liquid eyes. "You bet, honey! We just won't worry about it."

For a time, they sat silently—holding hands across the red-checked tablecloth and staring into each other's eyes. Carol felt so choked up she didn't dare try to speak. This couldn't be happening to her, but it was. Frank Longpre, man of her dreams—the good ones, that is—was holding her hand, gazing into her eyes, and sending out enough signals to turn her to warm jelly. Lord, warm jelly felt nice!

It took an outside influence to snap them out of their mellow trance. Papa Joe himself waited on them, bringing a drink in an Old Fashioned glass for Carol and branch water with a twist for Frank. "*Lagniappe*—on the house," he told them.

"What's that?" Carol asked, wondering about Papa Joe's strange word as she eyed the frosty tumbler.

"*Lagniappe* means something extra," Frank explained. "In this case, it's one of Papa Joe's special Sazerac cocktails. I think he likes you, Carol."

A moment later, the smiling Cajun was back with a tempting array of hors d'oeuvres—tiny green tomatoes and okra pickles, shrimp canapes, hot pepper jelly, and pink pickled eggs. Carol found both her cocktail and the plate of delicacies to her liking.

Frank nibbled at a piece of okra as he watched Carol dive in.

"Back to this afternoon," he said at length. "There's something else I have to tell you before I lose my nerve."

Carol set aside a shrimp canape and gave her undivided attention to Frank. "Yes? What is it?"

"After you left—no, really, it started before you went to your room—I got to feeling so bad, honey. I mean, low-down, gut-twistin', swamp-water bad. It hit me so quick . . ."

"What on earth, Frank? Was it something I said or did?"

"Hell, no!" He cleared his throat and stared down at the napkin he was about to twist in two."It was me, Carol, all me. That's why I have to tell you about it. See? If there's any chance of us ever getting together," he paused and glanced at her, cleared his throat, then added, "—in the biblical sense—you've got to understand from the start that I get in these foul moods. Real blue funks."

"Depression, you mean," she ventured. "Have you seen anyone about this problem, Frank? There are drugs now that can work miracle cures on people who suffer drastic mood shifts like yours." She thought for a moment before she offered her next suggestion, not sure how Frank would take it. Finally, she decided to give it a shot, regardless. "Or you might consider a psychiatrist to get to the root of the problem."

"Waste of time and money!" he growled. "Hell, I know the problem, and talking to a shrink about my rotten childhood isn't going to make it go away." He looked up at Carol, his dark eyes so filled with pain that her heart ached. "It's guilt, honey, plain and simple."

"What on earth do you have to feel guilty about?"

Frank shook his head almost imperceptibly. "My wife. You see, it's a *husband's* guilt I'm feeling. Eileen's gone; I know that and, most times, I accept it."

His mention of his wife sent a tremor through Carol. She'd been trying not to think about the nightmare she'd had this afternoon, but hearing Frank speak Eileen's name brought all the details and the terror back into sharp focus. Luckily, Frank seemed not to notice Carol's reaction.

"It was years after her disappearance before I even thought about another woman," Frank continued. "Every day—with the help of a few stiff drinks—I'd convince myself she'd be home before dark. That seemed to keep me going somehow. But then, when Eileen had been gone about five years and I finally got my act together—sort of—I met a real nice lady. I took her out a few times—dinner, movies, that sort of thing. Finally, things came to a head. I had to make my move or lose her to another fellow." His eyes soulful, Frank looked at Carol and gripped her hand again. "I tried; I couldn't. I mean, we were in the damn bed!" He shied away from Carol's steady gaze. "I could not do it! It was like Eileen was somewhere waiting for me and I was cheating on her."

"And afterward?" Carol asked gently.

He shrugged. "Afterward, she married that other guy and I gave up trying to form any kind of normal relationship." He glanced up at her again, his eyes heavy with sorrow. "And now there's you. And now there's guilt—more than I can live with. I want to promise you everything will be different. God, how I want to! But I honestly don't think it will be. So I figured I'd better warn you right up front."

Carol felt herself blushing again, but for Frank's sake this time. At least he was being honest. He had already told her earlier that he felt something was happening between them. How sweet that had been to hear! Now he was, in effect, telling her that he doubted anything would come of it. Good take-off; shitty landing!

"Don't worry about it, Frank." Her words dropped like rocks in the silence.

He shook his head sadly. "I just want you to understand that it's got nothing to do with you, Carol. It's me. Me and my guilt because I could never find my wife, never bring her home where she belonged."

"That was a long time ago, Frank," Carol said, groping for some way to comfort him, to give herself hope.

He sighed. "You don't have to tell me. But I guess to me it will always seem like only yesterday. I don't

185

know how to fight it, Carol. I do know, though, that I want my chance with you."

"I'm glad you told me all this, Frank. I promise you, I'll understand." Carol said every word slowly, evenly, trying not to betray her raging emotions. "Ordinarily, I would have been able to read your mood swing for what it was." She glanced at him; he seemed calm. She dared to confess, "Up until this morning, I could read your thoughts."

"Oh, God!" he groaned.

"Don't worry about it. You keep 'em pretty clean." She tried to smile, to make a little joke, but the subject was far too serious. "But then suddenly you blocked me out. I figured you had some ESP of your own and you were using it to shield yourself from me—not wanting me to know what you were thinking."

"We better put this conversation on hold. Here comes our dinner." Frank nodded toward a huge, brimming tray headed in their direction. "I hope I haven't killed your appetite."

"No way!" Carol answered with forced enthusiasm. In truth, she felt less than hungry at the moment.

As he placed steaming plates and bowls on their table, Papa Joe explained in a mixture of French, English, and Cajun patois that he was offering them his Acadian Sampler. He named each dish, pointing it out proudly: "*Filé* gumbo, garfish boulets, crawfish *étouffée*, oysters Bienville, Turtle On The Bayou, baked 'coon and sweet potatoes, zucchini squash with dill sauce, stuffed cucumbers, and fried green tomatoes." He also tossed a huge salad at the table with his "secret Cajun dressing," then sliced

186

thick hunks of hot French bread for them before bowing away from the table to allow them to "Enjoy!"

"We'll *never* eat all this!" Carol cried in dismay.

"Sure, we will," Frank told her, piling his plate high. "We've got all evening. Why do you think I wanted to get an early start? Other folks eat to live, but here in New Orleans, we live to eat."

"I believe it!"

Carol passed on the "'coon and 'taters," as Frank called the dish, and dipped into the spicy, steaming gumbo instead.

After over two hours of Cajun feasting, walking it off seemed their only salvation.

"I've never eaten that much at one sitting in my entire life," Carol moaned.

With almost schoolboy caution, Frank slipped his hand into Carol's. She stopped on the Moon Walk as if she meant to gaze out over the silvery river. In truth, the mere touch of Frank's flesh against hers left her weak-kneed and breathless. Holding hands with him was, she realized suddenly, as physically arousing as having some other lover kiss her nipples or stroke her thighs. She was trembling all over.

"Let me know when you're ready for the good part," Frank said.

Carol's breath caught and she glanced up at him through lowered lashes, inviting come-what-might. She was ready for the "good part" *now!*

"Dessert is my favorite part of any meal," he added. "I figured we'd stop in at the Café du Monde for coffee and beignets."

Carol moaned and laughed aloud at her own disappointment. "Talk to me about dessert next week this time. Okay?"

A cool breeze off the river sent a shiver through Carol. Frank slipped his arm around her shoulders and pulled her closer. Their eyes met for a moment and Carol held her breath. Was this it? Was he going to kiss her? Or would he shy away at the last instant, afraid of facing his guilt if he let his longing show.

Frank's hesitation lasted long seconds, a minute. Carol held perfectly still. She dared not even blink. Her breathing grew shallow and quick. His dark, liquid eyes were kissing her—a deep, probing, wet kiss that set her senses reeling and left her feeling almost faint. This was one of those extraordinary moments when time simply stood still. Carol held her breath—waiting, longing, aching for his kiss.

Finally, almost in slow motion, Frank leaned down—Carol meeting him halfway—and their lips met. It was no great, passionate production number, no fondling of breasts or thrusting of tongues. Just a simple, brief, tender kiss, but it had all the dramatic impact Carol could have handled at the moment. Her whole body warmed in that instant and she felt an earthquake of pleasure mingle with the desire that burned through her body.

From the startled look on his face, Frank must have experienced the same pleasant jarring of the senses and jolt to the soul. For several minutes, they neither spoke nor moved, but stood close together, staring off into the distance. The electric moment passed gently away.

"I couldn't help myself," Frank whispered.

Carol tried to laugh brightly, but the sound came out a fractured, high-pitched trill. "I don't think you need any help, mister."

"You're not offended? I didn't mean to rush you."

God! Rush her? This man had burst into her life like a sexual sonic boom. Wasn't he even a little bit conscious of his own vibes? Couldn't he tell she ached she wanted him so?

"I'll let you know if I feel like I'm being rushed, Frank." Carol glanced up at him and grinned. "That was the best dessert I've had in ages. Thanks."

"My pleasure," Frank answered in a halting, boyish voice.

They strolled on, hand in hand. Carol tried to think of something more to say, but it seemed to her that the moment needed nothing more than their companionable silence.

Finally, Frank was the one who broke the silence. "What about tomorrow morning?"

Carol couldn't think what he was talking about. Here, at this moment, with this man, tomorrow had ceased to exist for her.

Before she figured out his question, he asked another—one that quickly yanked her out of her euphoric state. "Are you going off again with that guy, Choctaw?"

"Oh, that! I don't know, Frank."

"If you are meeting him, I'm *definitely* going with you."

Carol had been so caught up in so many other things all day that she'd almost forgotten about Camille Mazaret, Choctaw—anything having to do with her real reason for coming to New Orleans in the first place.

"I honestly don't know, Frank," she answered. "I haven't seen the woman in the red tignon today. It seems like she's the key to these mysterious jaunts."

"Well, if you see her, you tell her that from now on I'm in, too. I'm not going to let you go traipsing off to God-knows-where without me. Understand?"

Carol could tell by his tone that he was dead serious. But as much as the thought of her traveling all alone through time frightened him, the idea of Frank trying to go scared her even more. He had no psychic powers that she could detect, other than the average amount of ESP. On top of that, Carol wasn't even sure Frank believed her. If he was not convinced that she really could go back in time, then there was little chance that he could accomplish that transition. His attempt to do so might well put an end to her ability to make these trips.

"Frank, I really don't know about this." He started to argue with her, but Carol held up her hand to silence him. "No, hear me out! I *know* that I have a place back in time. Suppose you did manage to go back with me. What would happen then? I would become Camille the minute I get there, but you would probably remain Frank Longpre, misplaced man from the twentieth century. Do you see the problem we have here?"

He was scowling at her, obviously ready to do battle before he'd let her go alone again. "Okay, tell me this: how'd you get to be Camille? Did you pick her out and jump into her body or something when you decided to go back?"

Carol shook her head, frustrated with trying to

make Frank understand. "First off, I didn't *decide* to go back. I was *sent* back. As for how I become Cami, I have no idea. One minute I'm me, the next minute I'm her. And, as I've told you, when I am Cami, I have no conscious memory of ever having been anyone else—of ever having lived in any other time. It's not until I return to this century that I'm able to see the whole picture."

Frank was silent for a time, mulling all this over. Finally, he said, "Maybe I'm Black Vic." He grinned at her, his excitement growing. "Yeah! I think I could be Black Vic."

"About as easily as you could be Rex the Carnival King and sing 'If Ever I Cease To Love,' standing on your head on top of St. Louis Cathedral!" Carol replied scornfully. "That's not the way it works, I keep telling you. You don't just pick a character from that other time and become that person because you want to. Frank, this isn't a game."

"I know that," he answered. "I just thought . . ."

"No, I don't think you thought at all!" was Carol's sharp retort.

He pulled her almost roughly into his arms then and kissed her with much more force and passion than he had displayed moments before. If he meant to shut her up, it worked. Like a charm! She couldn't have spoken a single syllable when he released her. She was that shocked by the kiss, that overwhelmed.

"Dammit, there's something you have to understand!" Frank said. "I'm not letting the woman I love go running headlong into any more dangerous situations alone. I don't care what happens, if you go with Choctaw again, I'm going, too."

191

His declaration of love stunned Carol more than his rough kiss. In movies maybe it happened this way sometimes, but not in real life. It had been her experience that those words had to be pried out of a man, usually through much effort, cajoling, and pleading. She almost wondered if he could be serious, he sprang it on her so quickly.

She stared at his face, her mouth slightly agape. Serious, he was—dead serious! There was no doubting it when she gazed into his eyes. He looked as vulnerable as a child, as open to love and to hurt as any man she had ever seen. In that instant, she knew that fate had sent her to New Orleans, to Frank.

"You win," Carol said softly, still staring into those wonderfully dark eyes. She reached out and touched his cheek. "And, Frank?"

"What, darlin'?" he whispered.

"I guess I love you, too."

He blew out a long breath and pulled her into his arms. "Well, I'm sure glad that's all settled!"

Carol wondered what he meant. Was it settled that she would let him accompany her and Choctaw or settled that they did, indeed, love each other?

She was still mulling this over when she heard a harp playing off in the distance. She glanced about, hoping to see a musician performing in the square. She did not. What she spied instead sent a chill through her.

"What's wrong?" Frank asked, feeling Carol tense in his arms. "You're ghost-white."

"Nothing." She tried to deny the apparition. "Nothing at all."

"Tell me," Frank insisted. He followed her gaze, then exclaimed, "The woman in the red tignon!"

192

His words shocked Carol out of her stupor. "You see her, too?"

"Right there by the fence, big as day," he answered. "So that must mean you're supposed to meet Choctaw tomorrow morning. And since I can see her, too, my guess is that they want me to come along," he added with no small amount of triumph in his voice.

Carol slipped her cold hand into Frank's and gripped it tightly. She was shaking all over, but the chill came from inside.

"Don't worry, honey," he whispered. "I'm not going to let anything happen to you."

She couldn't answer. How could she tell Frank that she knew she'd be safe, it was his uncertain fate that had her scared out of her wits?

Carol didn't tell him anything. Instead, she turned to him and slipped her arms around his waist, then buried her face against his chest. He reached down and cupped her chin with his fingers, bringing her lips up to his. Holding her close, there on the Moon Walk, he gave her a long, lazy, very thorough kiss. By the time he finished with her, she was limp in his arms.

"Ready to go home, darlin'?" he whispered. "If we don't find some privacy right soon, I'm afraid I might get us arrested."

"But, Frank, what about . . . ?"

Sensing that Carol was going to ask him if he was willing to bear the guilt in order to be with her, Frank cut her off before she could say the words. "Don't you worry about that, honey. That's my problem; I'll handle it."

When they turned and headed back toward the Hotel Dalpeche, Carol experienced a strange feeling of being somewhere else—another time, another place, but with the same man. She glanced up at Frank. Could this possibly be happening to her—to them? And had love, she wondered, been theirs to share once before, long ago?

A short time later, they had all the privacy they needed back at Frank's place. Once the door closed, Carol realized she felt as nervous as if she'd never done this before. She had a genuine case of virgin's jitters.

Frank seemed to sense her problem as clearly as if he were the psychic. Then, too, he was experiencing his own nagging fears. They needed a little time together to think things through before they took the plunge.

"Want some wine?" he asked. "I bought a bottle of your favorite and put it on ice."

Carol stared at him, incredulous. "You mean you planned all this?"

Frank shrugged. "I never plan anything much. I just like to be prepared for any emergency. Comes with being a cop."

He held up the smoky bottle so Carol could examine the label.

"Nice," she said. "Good year." Now her smile was nervous only around the edges.

Frank uncorked the wine and poured a glass for Carol. He brought it to her, put it in her hand, then watched as she tasted it.

"Good?"

Carol closed her eyes, tossed her head back, and hummed her pleasure through a smile. "Wonderful!" she sighed. "Want a taste?"

Frank frowned and was about to decline when

he realized she was offering him a taste from her lips. He leaned down and draped one arm around her shoulders. The next moment a tremor ran through Carol's body when she felt Frank's tongue glide softly over her moist lips. She opened slightly, inviting him in. But he drew away.

"Tasty wine," he whispered. "Tasty lady, too. Smoky and mysterious."

Carol took another sip and raised her face toward his. "Want some more?"

He closed his arms around her and murmured against her hair, "I want it *all!*"

Frank eased Carol back toward the bed, his mouth covering hers, tongue licking at her winey taste. She slipped her arms around his shoulders and held him tightly as they kissed. Once more Carol felt as if she were traveling through time and space. But it wasn't Choctaw's boat that swept her away.

For a long time, they lay on the bed in each other's arms. Carol was conscious of Frank's desire. It fed her own. It had been too long for both of them. Right or wrong, they needed each other. And it seemed that need could be held at bay no longer.

Their lips still joined, their tongues doing velvety battle, Carol felt Frank's hand slip between them. Slowly, he undid the buttons on her shirt. A moment later, she felt the warmth of his palm pressed to the throbbing flesh of her bare breast. A hot flood rushed through her body, cresting and intensifying at her very center of longing.

"Frank?" she murmured. "What's happening to us?"

"I'm not real sure," he whispered back, his voice

husky with passion. "But I sure as hell mean to find out. I have a feeling this has been waiting to happen since the beginning of time."

Afterward, Carol could never remember exactly how or when they undressed. It didn't matter. Moments after their last coherent words to each other, they were lying naked in each other's arms—hot, hungry flesh pressed tightly.

Carol's mind swam with a rainbow of bright colors as Frank kissed and caressed her breasts. His lips passed lightly downward, ever downward. Far off somewhere Carol heard a harp playing and a sad little voice calling Cami. But these sounds proved no distraction to either her need or her pleasure. Right now, Frank filled her whole consciousness. He possessed the very essence of her being. He was, she realized suddenly, the eternal soul-mate she had searched for all her life—perhaps through many lifetimes.

"Oh, my darling!" Carol gasped when his body moved into place over her writhing form. The long-awaited thrust came at that very instant. She had given her virginity long ago to a boy in college she'd thought she loved. But the lack of pain only enhanced the pure, sweet joy of the moment. He whispered soft words of love to her as he transported her to the very pinnacle of passion.

Carol couldn't think where she was the next morning when the alarm clock woke her. Before she opened her eyes, she knew that the bed felt comfortable, but unfamiliar. Then, too, there was the odd warmth next to her. She sniffed the air—

196

shaving cream, the lingering aroma of chicory, and the distinct, wonderfully male scent of Frank. She smiled and reached over to touch him. He roused and snuggled close.

"No time for that this morning, love," she warned him. "We have a boat to catch. Remember?"

"Damn!" he cursed softly, pulling her toward him.

As much as she was tempted to stay and give him what he so obviously wanted—what they both wanted—Carol leaped out of bed and pulled the covers off him.

"Got to get up!" she ordered. "Now!"

"Aw, hell! Why does this guy have to come so early?"

"I don't make the rules," Carol said. "I just play by them. Now, are you coming with me or not?"

Carol noted as they got dressed and quickly downed mugs of coffee that Frank's mood was different this morning. The "blue funk" she had expected after last night's ecstasy had yet to take hold of him. She crossed her fingers and said a silent prayer that she had somehow managed to break this dark spell of his.

A short time later, they were both dressed warmly, ready to leave for the dock. "Oh, wait a minute!" Frank said as he was about to lock the door. "The gold coin. I picked it up at the station yesterday, just in case."

He dashed back inside and came out patting his shirt pocket. All set at last, they headed for the river.

The morning was chilly, dark, and foggy. As they made their way toward the Barracks Street dock,

197

Frank continued protesting the early hour and the fact that he'd been rousted out before he could enjoy a leisurely repeat performance of last night's lovely love-making.

Carol, delighted and relieved that he was in such a good mood, laughed at his complaints. "If you hadn't kept us both up so late last night, you wouldn't have had such a hard time getting out of bed this morning."

"*A hard time!*" Frank growled. "Boy, you hit the nail on the head, darlin'. Things are about as hard as they get right now."

"Fra-ank!" Carol protested, feigning virginal modesty.

They reached the end of the dock. Choctaw was nowhere in sight.

"Well, where the hell is this guy?" Frank fumed. "What does he expect us to do—stand out here in the cold and freeze our buns off?"

Carol pressed his arm. "Take it easy, Frank. You aren't having a change of heart, are you? You do still want to go along?"

"Hell, yes!" he snapped. "I just want to get on with it."

"Sh-h-h!" Carol cautioned. "Listen. I'm sure we'll hear him coming any minute now."

Sure enough, a moment later they both heard the movement of water and the soft splash of oars as a boat approached. Suddenly, Choctaw's tall, skeletal form emerged from the thick river fog.

"I'm here," Carol called.

They both heard and felt the soft thud when the bow of the pirogue nudged the dock. Choctaw reached his long arm up to steady Carol as she descended the ancient ladder. "Mam'zelle, be careful, you," he cautioned.

"It's okay, I won't let her slip." Frank's deep voice came like the crack of a pistol on the still air.

"Wait, you!" Choctaw answered in a threatening voice.

"This is my friend, Frank," Carol explained quickly. "He's coming with us."

"Sez who?" Choctaw countered.

"Sez *me!*" Frank answered. "I saw the woman in the red tignon the same as Carol did. And here . . ." He thrust the doubloon toward the scowling ferryman. "Here's your gold coin."

"I'm pretty sure he's supposed to come along this morning, Choctaw," Carol said in a placating manner. Then her tone and her attitude turned stubborn. "If Frank can't come, then I won't either."

The boatman seemed to consider the matter for several minutes, then he motioned them both to come aboard, but with a sound deep in his throat that let them know he was permitting this only grudgingly.

Carol glanced toward Frank, her heart suddenly in her throat. Now that she knew she loved this man, she was more afraid for him than she had been before. What was she getting him into? What if he could go back, but had to remain there? Wild, terrifying scenarios flooded her mind. She was about to cry out to Choctaw not to go when she realized it was already too late. Carol's heart sank and fear gripped her troubled soul.

Chapter Nine

From the moment Frank settled in the boat next to Carol, he felt odd. It was almost as if the fog formed a wall around him—shutting him off from the world, even from Carol. His gaze focused on the gaunt ferryman, who loomed in the stern of the pirogue like some specter rising from the grave.

Carol remained silent and nervous. Frank could feel her tenseness as her hand gripped his. He wanted to talk to her, to try to comfort her. After all, wasn't that the reason he'd come along? But it seemed that some unseen force kept him from speaking. He could only sit quietly, waiting . . .

Waiting for what? he wondered.

Murky light shone around them. Frank could see that they had left the river, following a narrow, twisting bayou into the swamp. Still held by Choctaw's dark, fixed gaze, Frank watched the man raise one arm and point off to the left. Frank turned his head slowly.

Like a spotlight, a ray of sunlight suddenly brightened one area of the swamp. In that brilliant setting, Frank spied a handsome lad astride a fine bay gelding. The boy of ten or twelve was dressed in an immaculate riding costume down to his shiny black boots. As young as he was, the child handled his mount with expertise. While Frank remained mesmerized, a second rider entered the scene. The coal-black hair and jet eyes of the older man mirrored those of the boy. Father and son, Frank assumed correctly.

As the man reined in beside the lad, Frank noticed for the first time that they were at the edge of a cane field. Suddenly, the man stood in his stirrups and blew one long, sharp note on a conch shell. The tall, waving cane parted here and there. Black faces, gleaming with sweat, peered out at the father and son.

"Come closer, all of you," the man's voice boomed in the humid stillness. The slaves—fifty or more—crept nearer.

Satisfied that he had an attentive audience, the dark-haired gentleman spoke. "You all know my son, my heir, the future master of Golden Oaks. From this day forward you will obey him as if his words came directly from my mouth. You will help him learn the ways of this great plantation."

Frank glanced toward the boy. He sat straight and tall in the saddle, his young face as serious as his father's. Frank sensed neither fear nor embarrassment in the lad. He seemed remarkably bright, composed, and mature for one so young.

Again, Frank tuned in to what the father was saying to his field hands. "The British Dragon is threatening our land, indeed, our very way of life. We may soon be called to defend New Orleans against those accursed lobster-backs. If that time should come, I shall heed the call. Should I fall in battle, my son will be your master in my stead." He turned toward the boy, who showed the first sign of any childish emotion. His father's speech had brought an unmistakable brightness to the lad's eyes, although not a tear escaped to betray him. The handsome father—proud and erect—said softly, "Victoine, invite them to pay their respects."

"*Oui*, Papa." The boy raised his hand, beckoning to the slaves. One by one, they hurried forward to press young Victoine's hand, stroke his boot, or simply bow. Over and over Frank heard their murmured words: "Bless you, Massa Vic . . . We be yours now, young massa . . . We work hard for you, little squire, make good cane."

The line of slaves was still coming toward the boy and his father as the scene faded. Frank gripped Carol's hand more tightly. He tried to turn to her to tell her what he'd seen, what he now knew. But before he could say a word, another bright spot gleamed among the tall cypresses.

An eerie sound caught Frank's attention before he could distinguish anything within the bright light. The wailing made his skin crawl, his hair stand on end. Then, suddenly, he recognized the high-pitched scream—bagpipes! Smoke swirled through the bright patch in the swamp. Frank saw that he was viewing a battlefield, and out of the thick haze marched the entire British army, their white cartridge belts forming perfect targets across their red-coated chests. They marched in regulation, gentlemanlike fashion across the marshy reaches, straight for the American lines.

Frank had read all about this in history books. Every child raised in or around New Orleans knew the story well. This, he realized immediately, was the final day, the final conflict of the Battle of New Orleans. He even recalled the date: January 8, 1815.

Two men just behind the American lines came into sharp focus before Frank's eyes.

"Damned if Lord Pakenham hasn't provided us with his whole army to use as target practice."

From museum portraits Frank had seen, he recognized the tall, craggy-faced officer who spoke as General Andrew Jackson. The man next to him seemed familiar, too—black hair, dark eyes, large frame, but his features were lost in the shadow of his broad-brimmed hat. However, the moment the officer spoke, Frank knew him. Not his name, but the fact that he was the master of Golden Oaks.

"This should be a fine day's work, General, and an end to it. Why, this time tomorrow, I fully expect to be home at Golden Oaks with my wife and son, telling them all about our triumph over the British."

Somehow, Frank knew that the man's hopes were destined not to come to pass.

Just then, another startling sound filled the air. It was a growling swoosh that sent a chill down the spine. Following the awful noise, the battlefield erupted with bursting red glares. The Americans might have panicked had not General Jackson spread the word down the lines: "Easy, boys. It's the Brits' new Congreve rocket. Scares the hell out of you, I know, but it can't hurt you unless the eight-foot shaft catches you on the way down. Keep your eyes peeled."

The master of Golden Oaks moved among the terrified men, trying to calm the ranks, spreading Jackson's consoling words. As Frank watched and listened, he heard the wail of one of the monster-rockets as if it were coming straight for him. He ducked. He looked up again in time to see the blood-red flare of an explosion, then the fatal impact at the moment the deadly rocket shaft struck young Victoine's father full in the chest. Frank could tell the man was dead before he hit the ground. The bloodied shaft writhed off through the underbrush like a demented snake, then burst with an ear-splitting bang and a great puff of black smoke. Frank looked back to the man. He lay in the mud, his eyes wide, staring at nothing. His chest was laid open to the backbone. Frank wanted to weep. It was as if he had watched his own father die.

Carol's trip this time had been less eventful than the last one. She watched the swamp glide by. She saw nothing out of the ordinary, only the duck-weed, the cypresses, the water oaks.

She noted that Frank remained silent and tense all the way, no doubt wishing he'd stayed home in bed. From time to time, she was tempted to say something to him, but he seemed to be so deep in thought that she quelled the urge. They drifted on in total silence except for the water rippling against the sides of the pirogue and the occasional scream of a swamp creature.

The sudden bump of the boat against a wooden dock made them both jump.

"We be here," Choctaw informed them.

"Where?" Carol asked.

Before she received an answer, she noticed that the fog was rolling in again. She'd never seen it this thick. Why, she could hardly make out Choctaw's tall form at the other end of the boat.

"Come on, Frank," she urged. "This is where we get off."

Carol scrambled out of the boat, then turned back to urge Frank to hurry. To her horror, all she could see was his hand, reaching out to her through a narrow hole in the fog. She could hear him calling her name, but the sound seemed to come from far away.

"Frank, for God's sake, grab my hand!" she cried, leaning out over the water. "Hurry, Frank!"

Sudden terror gripped Carol. Something had gone wrong. Frank wasn't going to come with her after all. She could only watch, helpless, as he desperately tried to grab hold of her hand. She lay down on the dock, straining to reach him. The hole in the fog had narrowed until only the very tips of his fingers showed through.

"Frank!" she screamed. "Take my hand!"

For an instant, their fingertips touched. But it was no use. The next moment, the fog closed in completely.

"Frank?" she wailed. "Frank, where are you?"

She cried his name over and over again until her throat ached from calling. Nothing! He was gone—she was forced to admit—vanished, sucked into some black void in time.

Carol's voice and her will ebbed away. She stood on the lonely dock, stunned. She was still staring at the spot where she had last seen the boat, Choctaw, and Frank. Nothing remained any longer except a swirly gray curtain of mist. Frank was really, truly *gone!*

A tremor ran through her. Waves of cold closed in around her heart. Then the hysteria began. Great, awful, wracking sobs threatened to strangle her. Hot tears blinded her eyes. Her heart pounded until pain burned in her chest. Through it all, she fought the heavy haze that had taken Frank and was even now trying to whisk her away. She struggled on, hoping to fight her way out of the blackness, but it was no use. At last, she crumpled to a heap on the dock and lay there, weeping miserably. She closed her eyes. If she couldn't see Frank's face, she had no desire to see anything at all.

"Do as I say, immediately!" A woman's heavily accented voice issued the stern command.

Carol caught her breath and her eyes shot open. Gone was the fog of the damp morning, gone the bayou and the swamp. She was conscious only of the hard glitter of the woman's golden eyes, like twin doubloons shining coldly.

"Fetch a *gendarme* this moment, Prospere!"

In the blink of a startled eye, Carol forgot all about Choctaw, the strange swamp, and the frightening fog that had engulfed her. Even Frank slipped from her memory. In that fraction of a heartbeat, she forgot completely that Carol Marlowe existed or that she ever would. Once again, she was Camille Mazaret. And Cami was every bit as frightened and miserable as her counterpart had been moments before ... every bit as frightened and miserable as she had been when Carol last left her to face Fiona alone.

"Please, wait!" Cami cried, stretching pleading hands toward her reluctant hostess. "Won't you at least hear me out, Fiona?"

Prospere was at the door, ready to carry out the woman's order to bring the authorities. Fiona hesitated, then made a slight sign for him to stay.

Cami exhaled a pent-up breath. "Thank you," she murmured.

"You have nothing to thank me for yet," Fiona countered, her beautiful amber eyes still narrowed in suspicion.

"But I truly am Edouard Mazaret's daughter," Cami insisted, spreading her hands before her now in a gesture for mercy.

Fiona remained unmoved. "I do not believe your tale for an instant, girl. The man who came here looking for you said that you are a runaway slave. Only because I believe *him* have I not sent Prospere for the law. If you need help to escape from your master, to run to the North and freedom, then I may be of some assistance to you. But, I warn you, do not sully the name of Edouard Mazaret with your wicked lies."

"I am *not* a slave! I told him that. He merely believed what he wanted to think."

The girl's evaluation of Victoine Navar almost brought a smile to Fiona's lips. This young woman—whoever she was—had Black Vic figured out already. He was never a man to deal well with reality or logic. But this discussion did not concern that man and his many peculiarities. Fiona remained firm and resolved to find out the truth from this ragged girl once and for all.

"Well? I am waiting," she said impatiently.

Cami had feared few things in her life, but she found herself quaking with fright before this tiny woman with the eyes of an angry swamp cat. Cami hugged her arms across her chest, trying to stop her trembling. She had to get control of herself, to think of a way to make Fiona believe her.

Cami glanced toward the handsome young man named Prospere, as if help might come from that quarter, although she sensed that was hopeless. He and Fiona were obviously very close and he would side with her. His presence here puzzled Camille. Everyone knew that her father's *placée* had sworn to remain faithful to the grave. Yet here was this handsome gentleman and here was Fiona, and both were in their nightclothes. Prospere had obviously spent the night with Fiona. How long, Cami wondered, had her father's mistress waited after his death before striking a bargain with this young replacement? His very presence made Cami nervous and resentful.

"Have you lost your tongue, girl?" Fiona demanded. "Speak up! This instant!"

"Please, could we talk alone, Fiona?" Cami asked, still fighting to regain her composure.

Fiona gave a nod and Prospere left without a word.

nicely, but you'd never know it at the moment. I must look a mess, Fiona."

Never one to be less than honest even for the sake of tact, Fiona smiled and nodded her agreement. "That you do, my child. But we will make things better. Shuck those filthy rags this instant!" She went to the door and called, "Prospere! Please tell Ellie to heat water and bring the tub. Quickly, now, my love!"

Camille frowned. It still bothered her that Fiona had taken another protector after her father's death. But who was she to deny another woman the very thing that she herself had come to New Orleans in search of—someone to love?

"Now, Camille, we shall see what lies under all that dirt." Fiona wrinkled her dainty nose and added, "It is no wonder you were taken for a runaway slave in those old rags."

Cami laughed. "Well, I couldn't very well ride Voodoo all the way to New Orleans in my satin and lace ball gown, could I?"

"You rode your father's wild horse all the way from Mulgrove? But why, *ma chère?* Why have you come to New Orleans?"

"Cousin Morris was going to force me to choose a husband, Fiona. I refuse to marry a man I can never love. I hoped you would help me."

A worried frown clouded Fiona's smooth face. "Your guardian will likely come searching for you. What then?"

Cami thought for a moment. Fiona was right. After all, Cousin Morris had a stake in seeing that she married a man of his choice so he could keep some control over Elysian Fields.

"Perhaps I could send a letter," Cami suggested, "telling him that I am all right, but not telling him where I am. I could say simply that I'm staying with a friend until I make my decision regarding a husband. He meant to force me into making a choice this very morning, you see. But I can't, Fiona. I refuse to marry until I fall in love."

Fiona clucked her tongue over Cami's dilemma and quickly agreed to have the letter sent once it was written. Privately, Fiona assured herself that Camille would not be long in her care. Edouard's daughter didn't belong here, but Fiona couldn't simply send her on her way. It must be Camille's choice to return to her proper place, if she was to accept her lot in life gracefully.

Moving about the room, Fiona took soap and oils and powder from one of the bureau drawers, lilac-scented towels from another, and a dressing gown of peach-blush silk from the cedar-line armoire. She handed the filmy robe to Camille.

"This will be small for you, since it is mine," Fiona said, "but never mind. Only Prospere and I will see you wearing it and we'll not tell a soul."

"I brought a few things with me," Cami said. "In the bag over there."

Fiona picked up the muddy satchel with two fingers, holding it away from her as if it were diseased. She opened it and dumped the contents on the bed. Then her tinkling laughter filled the room.

"Ball gowns, *ma chère*?" She turned a glowing, but slightly patronizing, smile on Camille. "And where did you plan to wear all these fine silks and laces?"

Standing in her muddy underthings, tangled hair straggling about her dirty face, Camille felt slightly

212

ridiculous. She might have brought more sensible clothes had she had more time to think before her escape.

Cami shrugged. "I packed in such haste." It was the truth, after all. "I just grabbed any old thing and threw it into the bag."

"Well, dear child, we'll have to buy you some school clothes if you plan to stay long in New Orleans."

"Fiona!" Camille purposely spoke the name in her most adult voice. When the woman turned to her, Cami had slipped her chemise over her head and stood before her new friend, naked to the waist. "My school days are long since behind me. I am *not* a child!"

Fiona stared at the amazing sight before her. Camille Mazaret was indeed a child no longer! Her breasts were full and proud, the nipples large and darkly shaded. Her waist curved gently in above a woman's softly rounded hips, ripe for childbearing. Fiona herself had often longed for such a lush and lovely figure.

"My mistake, surely," Fiona said, her cheeks tinting faintly as she smiled at Edouard's beautiful daughter. "How old are you, Camille?"

Blushing from the woman's appraising stare, Cami held up her camisole to hide her naked breasts. "Old enough to be married and nursing my second or third child. I am eighteen now, but I'll turn the calendar again in September."

Camille heard a sharp intake of breath from Fiona. "And *never* married?"

"Never *anything*!" Camille answered firmly.

"Still a virgin at almost nineteen?" Fiona mut-

213

tered, as if the fact made her seriously nervous. "*Mon Dieu!* But, forgive me, my dear. Tell me your problem. Surely, we can figure out something, you and I. Or perhaps a doctor I know could help."

Cami laughed. "I don't think so, Fiona. Not unless your doctor friend sells love potions. Marriage would be no problem. Cousin Morris would be more than happy to arrange that. Love, however, takes a bit more time and effort, it seems."

"Ah-h-h!" Fiona's golden eyes glittered with understanding. "Now, I see. You are, indeed, Edouard Mazaret's daughter."

The whole tale tumbled out then as Camille told Fiona about the endless balls, the endless boys, and her cousin's demand that she forsake all thoughts of love and choose a husband immediately so that Elysian Fields would have a new master.

"So, I ran away," Cami finished. "I don't want to be like my mother, my Cousin Beatrice, or any of those Creole ladies who settle for less than their fondest desires."

Fiona sighed in sympathy, realizing at the same time that it might be more difficult than she had imagined to convince Camille to return to Mulgrove.

"And have you a man in mind, *ma chére*? Someone who stirs your passions?"

Camille's whole face lit with pleasure and a winsome longing when she answered. "Yes, Fiona, I have found such a man—one who completely captured my heart when first our eyes met. I mean to marry Victoine Navar."

For a moment, Fiona looked totally confused. Surely, Edouard's daughter could not have fallen in love with the man who chased her through the night, the man she bit so viciously.

"I saw him at the ball last night," Cami continued wistfully. "Oh, Fiona, he is such a man! I've never seen another like him, and I know he's the only one for me."

"*Oh . . . my . . . God!*" Fiona gasped. "Anyone, anyone but Black Vic!" she cried. Then her eyes narrowed to slits and she leaned close to Camille's face. "You say you love Victoine Navar and yet you claim to be still a virgin? I do not believe it!"

Cami shied away from Fiona's piercing gaze. "It's true! Actually, I don't know him very well yet. That is, I didn't exactly meet him at the ball. Cousin Morris refused him entry. But when I saw him from a distance at Mulgrove—when he looked at me—that one glance was enough."

Fiona moaned her relief that Edouard's daughter had given nothing but her heart to the married man. She knew from firsthand experience what pain such a love could bring. "God has been kind to you, Camille. See that you keep your distance from that one at all times. He is not right for you."

"I don't care if he has no plantation, no fortune, no standing in society," Cami declared vehemently. "Those things mean nothing to me. I have all that. I only want the right man to share my life. And Black Vic is definitely the husband for me!" She turned a pleading gaze on Fiona. "If you understood the way he made me feel, only gazing at me from a distance. Oh, Fiona, please don't try to discourage me. Believe me, it was love at first sight."

Cami felt a shiver run through her as she recalled

those few moments with Black Vic. A warmth spread through her thighs and she went weak with emotion. She sank down to the bed.

Fiona cursed softly in French and turned away.

"Fiona, you don't understand," Cami whispered. "I admit that I am inexperienced with men. Still, I felt something the moment I saw Victione Navar. Something powerful. Something that will remain with me forevermore. It would be so wonderful to go through life feeling that deep glow every day and every night. I tremble just thinking about his black eyes, the way his mouth twitched as he stared at me as if he longed to kiss me. The things he seemed to be saying to me without ever speaking a word. He looked dashing and hungry and *evil*."

Fiona cast her gaze toward heaven and muttered, "Mother of God, keep this child safe." It was one thing to be Black Vic's friend, but quite another to trust him with Edouard Mazaret's innocent daughter. The very thought sent a shiver of dread through Fiona's slender body. She looked back at Camille, her eyes as sharp as talons, ready to snatch the full facts out of the girl. "Evil, you say? Well, there are many who would agree with you, most of them fathers of foolish, beautiful, once-innocent daughters. You are certain he never touched you, Camille?"

Cami shook her head. "Never touched me, never even spoke to me, but, oh, Fiona, how I burn for him! I would be eternally grateful if only you could arrange to have us introduced."

"Impossible!" Fiona gasped. "Never! I do not want to hear his name mentioned again as long as you are under my roof. Do you understand, Camille?"

216

"Yes, Fiona," Cami answered disconsolately, yet in her soul she remained determined.

A knock at the bedroom door interrupted their conversation. Fiona's fat little maid, Ellie, scurried in, carrying a tin tub and a bucket of steaming water.

Relieved to be done with all talk of Black Vic, Fiona helped Camille into the shallow hot-tub. "This will have to do for now. But later I will have Ellie boil enough water for you to have a real bath."

The hot water felt wonderfully relaxing to Cami's tired muscles. Lilac-scented bubbles tickled her skin, and the French-milled soap felt as soft as satin. She might have fallen asleep if Fiona had left her alone, but the woman was bursting with questions, mostly about Edouard Mazaret. Did Cami remember the way he loved to sing? Had she ever seen a man with eyes so blue? Was he as sweet and kind to his daughter as he had been to Fiona herself? Did he really teach Cami to ride that devil-horse, Voodoo?

Finally, washed, dried, powdered, and perfumed, Cami slipped into Fiona's peach silk dressing gown. It proved a scandalous fit, but it felt wonderfully cool and smooth against her bare skin.

"Now, for some food," Fiona said. "You must be starving, dear. Come. We will eat in the front parlor."

Cami hesitated, shy at the thought of having that man, Prospere, see her in the scanty dressing gown.

Realizing the cause of her guest's distress, Fiona laughed and said, "Don't mind Prospere, darling. He has been away in France, and, believe me, there is little he has not seen these past months. I assure you, the cut of your gown will go totally unnoticed."

Too famished to resist any longer, Cami followed Fiona to the front room of the house. There they found silver, crystal, and china gracing the table. Warm, sticky pastries, crusty French bread—hot from the oven—and *café au lait* awaited their pleasure.

Camille sipped her coffee and munched on a deliciously flaky apricot pastry while Fiona and Prospere entered into a spirited conversation, mostly in French. Although Cami had spoken the language since childhood, she much preferred the English her father had taught her. Still, she had no trouble following Prospere's exciting tales of his recent adventures in Paris.

"When I go back," he said to Fiona, "I plan to take you with me. There are no lines of color there. You would be free to live as you choose."

Camille felt another twinge of jealousy for her father's sake as she watched Fiona reach over and cover Prospere's hand with her own. "Ah, *mon coeur*," the woman whispered, "I live as I choose already."

"That must be nice," Cami interjected with more sarcasm than she'd intended.

Both Fiona and Prospere looked at her, shocked by her tone. Cami felt her cheeks flush with embarrassment at her outburst.

"I only meant," she attempted to explain, "that some of us are not so fortunate. We are forced to follow the rules others set for us."

"Ah, Prospere, our Camille has a serious problem," Fiona confided. "She longs for love, but has yet to find it. If she does not, her guardian will soon force her to marry, regardless."

For the first time, Cami became conscious of Prospere actually looking directly at her, appraising her. She clutched the robe to cover the swell of her bosom.

"But Camille is a beauty, no?" Prospere observed objectively. "Even the lovely women who attend the *Bals du Cordon Bleu* at the Orleans Ballroom would pale beside her.

"The *Bals du Cordon Bleu*?" Camille queried.

"It is the best . . . the *only* place here in New Orleans where a respectable young woman can go to seek and find the love her heart desires," Prospere explained. Cami noticed the merry twinkle in his sky-blue eyes, but thought nothing of it as he continued. "Young men of good family and mature gentlemen alike attend the well-chaperoned balls three times weekly. They all go there in search of love. Everyone says it is the gayest affair in all the city."

Cami's eyes lit up with excitement. She had never heard of the Orleans Ballroom, but what a wonder it must be! Why had her Cousin Morris never told her about this or encouraged her to attend the *soirées* there?

"I brought ball gowns," Cami reminded Fiona breathlessly. "And perhaps I would meet someone who is perfect for me there."

"No, no, no!" Fiona protested. She shot a warning glance toward Prospere. How dare the devilish scamp bring this up in front of Edouard's daughter? "You should not have mentioned this," she told him sharply.

"But why not?" Camille insisted. "It sounds perfect."

Fiona rose from the table. "Will you excuse us now, Prospere? I think Camille and I should have a little chat alone."

He smiled and nodded, obviously pleased with his mischief as he poured another cup of coffee.

"Come along, Camille," Fiona ordered. "It is time you and I got a few matters straight between us."

Even as they walked through the house and out into the tiny garden in back, Fiona's mind was working. She was angry with Prospere for teasing Cami that way, but perhaps he had given Fiona just the idea she needed. Once she explained to Camille about the Orleans Ballroom and the *Bals du Cordon Bleu*, better know as the Quadroon Balls, she was certain the girl would be horrified by the very thought. No doubt, Edouard's lovely daughter would go running back to Mulgrove Plantation where she belonged for fear of being forced into such a daring masquerade.

Fiona glanced back at Camille—so ripe and slender and beautiful. *And innocent*, the woman reminded herself with a sigh. It was a shame Edouard had put these ideas of love into her head. She would have made a wonderful wife and mother before, but this rebellious spirit fostered by her own father's words and actions could only cause her grief. There seemed only one way Fiona could help her. She must frighten Camille into putting aside her dangerous thoughts and accepting her proper role as a Creole wife and mother.

Sensing that Fiona was deep in thought, Cami followed her in silence. When they reached the garden—a small but lovely fenced plot ablaze with a rainbow of cosmos and zinnias—Fiona finally turned to her and smiled.

220

"Prospere is a dear young man, but I'm afraid he talks too much." She smiled apologetically at Cami.

"I found his stories fascinating. I only wish he had told me more about the Orleans Ballroom."

Fiona gripped Cami's hand and squeezed. "Actually, although I scolded him for mentioning the balls in your presence, I'm glad now that he brought up the subject. I'd been thinking myself of that very thing, but I was not sure how you would react. I know you'll find my idea shocking at first, but at least consider it, Camille. It may be your only chance for finding true love."

Cami laughed, hugged herself, and twirled in a circle, her heart suddenly light and gay. "Fiona, do you know what it means to me to be told that I even have a chance? Tell me your plan. At once!"

Fiona led Camille to a marble bench and they both sat down. The older woman took Cami's hands in hers. "I'm so glad you are at least willing to listen, my dear. The Quadroon Balls are quite respectable. As Prospere pointed out, only gentlemen of the best social standing are allowed to attend. And they must pay two dollars to gain entry to the Orleans Ballroom—twice the amount they would pay to enter the *white* balls in town."

Camille's smile faded for a moment. "The Quadroon Balls? The white balls? I don't understand, Fiona."

Pretending nonchalance, Fiona picked a large purple zinnia and twirled it between her slender fingers. She stared at it, not wanting to meet Camille's eyes. "Surely you must have heard of these affairs, my dear. I met your own father at such a *soirée*. Only the most beautiful free women of color in the city are invited to attend. Gentlemen from all over come to the Quadroon Balls to choose their *placées*." She turned then, and looked squarely at Camille.

"Free women of color?" Cami echoed, slightly dazed by Fiona's explanation.

"Such as myself, dear." Fiona smiled gently. "The members of my family have been free from the earliest days of New Orleans. It is said that one of the founders of this city, Jean Baptiste le Moyne, Sieur de Bienville, chose an ancestor of mine to be his mistress. Ever after that, the women of my family have been free and have used the Le Moyne name. From the crudest beginnings of this town on the river, we have followed in each other's ways, taking only the most worthy gentlemen as our protectors. Men such as your own father, Camille. Our daughters follow our lead, while our sons are sent to Paris, where they receive the finest educations. Some stay there for life. Others, like my own son, Prospere, return to set up business in New Orleans."

Camille's eyes went wide. "Prospere is your *son*, Fiona?"

The woman nodded and smiled. "A son to be proud of."

"But I thought . . ." Cami stumbled over the words, catching herself just before she admitted exactly what she had thought about Prospere and his relationship with Fiona. Quickly, she changed directions and asked, "How old is Prospere?"

"Almost twenty. Can you believe it?"

Cami felt a wave of relief, yet, she had to admit, some regret at Fiona's answer. Edouard Mazaret had always wanted a son. Prospere's blue eyes, his ready smile—it might have been. But not if he was approaching twenty. As far as Cami knew, her father had not met Fiona Le Moyne until at least a year later—after her own birth.

"So? What do you think?" Fiona asked.

"I think Prospere is extremely handsome and quite charming."

Fiona laughed and reached up to tuck the purple zinnia into Camille's shining hair. "His mother thanks you, dear. Actually, though, I meant—what do you think about attending the Quadroon Ball? Your dark hair would work to your favor. But then, octoroons and quadroons come in all colors, with eyes as light-gold as mine or as blue as Prospere's. I could tell everyone that you are my niece, sent here by my sister in Mobile to find a proper protector."

Fiona held her breath, awaiting an outburst of righteous indignation from Camille. At the very least, she anticipated an outraged visitation from the angry spirit of her dear, departed Edouard.

Instead, the bees buzzed on in the garden, the butterflies continued kissing flowers, and Camille turned a glowing countenance on Fiona, her eyes fairly sparkling.

"It's perfect!" Cami cried, throwing herself into the woman's arms. "How can I ever thank you for thinking of this? I'll go to the ball. I'll find the man I love. Then I'll tell Cousin Morris that I've decided upon a husband. Won't my intended be surprised when he discovers this grand masquerade and that he has found himself a wife instead of simply a *placée*! Oh, Fiona, you're brilliant!"

Fiona felt like moaning aloud. What had she

done? Camille was either calling her bluff or she was actually delighted by the bizarre scheme. Silently, Fiona begged Edouard Mazaret's forgiveness from beyond.

"Are you certain you wish to do this, Camille?" There was true pleading in Fiona's gentle voice. "I would never want to force you into anything."

Cami was on her feet, practically dancing with excitement. "Force me? Just try to keep me away. When is the next ball? What shall I wear?" Suddenly, she turned toward Fiona, her indigo eyes sparkling with blue and violet lights as she whispered, "Why, Fiona, at the Orleans Ballroom I might even get to meet Victoine Navar!"

The anguished moan Fiona had been holding in finally escaped her. "Mother of God, what have I done?"

Still, just seeing Camille's happiness and excitement was like being a part of something magical. Fiona smiled in spite of herself.

"When may I go?" Cami begged.

"On Thursday evening next, if that suits you, Mademoiselle Mazaret."

Camille whirled around, making the peach silk gown fly in the breeze. "Oh, yes! It suits me well, Madame Le Moyne!"

Chapter Ten

"Carol!" Frank yelled. Then he yelled and yelled some more. No use! She had simply vanished in an angry whorl of fog. He stared off into the veil of black nothingness, his face a mask of anguish.

"God, she's gone off into this swamp alone and I never even remembered to tell her about the snake." Frank had found out last time he stopped into the office that forensics had, after closer examination, discovered two tiny puncture wounds in the mummy's left ankle, made by the fangs of a poisonous swamp-rattler. Now, Carol had gone off into that other time—to God knows where—without so much as a warning. If Carol had become Camille Mazaret again, and if the mummy had once been that same Creole lady, then sooner or later that deadly snake was bound to cross Carol's path.

"Damn! How could I have forgotten something that important?" Frank cursed. He lifted his voice once more in a long, pleading wail for Carol. Still no answer.

Frank had figured he couldn't sink any lower than he'd been when the alarm clock woke him earlier this morning. Now, however, he knew he'd been dead wrong. In the last five minutes, he'd sunk lower than a swamp-rattler's belly.

What had happened? What had gone wrong? He thought back over the morning's events trying to figure it out.

Before the clock woke Carol, he'd been lying in the dark next to her, trying to rationalize how he could wake up feeling so rotten after he'd gone to sleep believing—thanks to Carol—that he owned the whole damn world. The two of them seemed so perfect together. So why did this miserable, gut-gnawing guilt have to mess things up?

Frank had figured that Carol didn't need to know what a lousy mood he was in. So he'd put on a grand show for her, pretending that his personal black cloud had vanished for good. Once they settled in the pirogue and got going, his mind had eased somewhat or at least been diverted. He had focused his attention on the strange scenes Choctaw had shown him. He'd all but forgotten where he really was. He had actually felt like he was a part of the past. Damned if he wasn't beginning to believe that he *was* Black Vic!

Then, only moments ago, Carol's voice, telling him they'd arrived, had jolted him back to his senses. It couldn't be more than five minutes ago that he was watching the Battle of New Orleans.

Now, here he sat, still groping for Carol's hand through the dense fog, knowing all the time that it was useless.

Carol was gone and he was in the pits!

Frank turned and glared at Choctaw. The big Indian—or whatever he was—stood in the stern of the boat, poling as lazily as before, as if nothing had happened.

"What the hell did you do with Carol?" Frank demanded. "You bring her back here or, so help me, I'll wring your scrawny neck!"

Choctaw said not a word. He just kept poling. Enraged, Frank made a sudden move toward the stoic figure. The pirogue tipped, Frank lurched. The next minute he hit the cold, black water and plunged under, going deeper and deeper. He tried desperately to swim back to the surface, but his arms and legs seemed totally useless, paralyzed. Frank's lungs felt like they would burst. His eyes shot open. He saw a thin, wavering light glowing down through the murky depths. Holding his breath—still trying to swim—he concentrated on that one bright spot. If he could just make himself stop fighting and relax, maybe he would float effortlessly up to the top of the water—to air and life.

Maybe, hell! Maybe he'd drown!

That thought seemed to take the fight out of him. He closed his eyes and actually smiled. At least he wouldn't have to deal with the damn guilt any longer. And besides, if Carol was gone, what did he care about living?

The instant Frank gave up, the light engulfed him. Brilliance wrapped him and warmed him and brought him up for air. He gasped several times, filling his aching lungs until he felt dizzy and disoriented. But how sweet it was to breathe again!

Frank's euphoria vanished the minute he opened his eyes. He wasn't merely at the surface of the water. He was in another world entirely. He knew this place, yet he didn't. Frank found himself walking down Decatur Street in New Orleans, headed toward the French Market. The day was hot and muggy under a brassy summer sky. He was sweating inside his heavy clothes and suddenly longed for the cool, black water he'd left moments before.

"Just wait a damn minute!" he said, stopping so abruptly that a big, black woman with a basket balanced on her head ran slap into him. He failed even to notice as he stared about in amazement. "This isn't any New Orleans I've ever seen—except in old paintings."

"*Bonjour, M'sieur Navar.*" A passing stranger tipped his high silk hat to Frank.

"Yeah, you have a good one," Frank answered absently, still numb with shock.

He glanced about, desperately searching for something—someone. "Carol!" he exclaimed under his breath. "That's why I'm here. I've got to find her. She must be nearby."

But all thoughts of Carol vanished in the blink of an eye. With his next breath, Frank heard himself speaking excellent French, asking the fellow— Monsieur Reynard—if he knew of any upcoming card games to be held at Gaspard's.

Reynard replied, again in French, that he did indeed know of a game. "Scheduled for this very evening, it is, with high stakes and an opening for one more player should you be interested, Navar."

The two men chatted amiably for several minutes, then Frank tipped his own top hat and said, "*Au revoir*." Only he wasn't Frank Longpre any longer. He'd never even heard that name. This was Victoine Navar who strode with purpose in his step toward the French Market. Perhaps he might glean some tidbits of gossip concerning Lazano, the man Fiona had told him was threatening his life.

Before reaching the market, Vic turned into a dim barroom. The rough sign over the door identified the place as "*Le Bleuet*," "The Blue Bottle." Owner and proprietor, Ignacio Bleu.

Early as it was in the day, Black Vic needed a drink. He'd been up all night, first riding out to Mulgrove, then chasing after that "runaway," who'd turned out to be a sharp-fanged hellion in disguise. He glanced in disgust at his bandaged hand. It still throbbed like hell. The pain in itself was enough to justify an early shot of brandy.

"Ah, M'sieur Vic!" It was Ignacio Bleu himself who welcomed his faithful customer. "Good to see you. You've been away some time. On the river?"

"*Oui*, Ignacio, for the past month." Vic dropped a coin on the rough counter, which consisted of an old door placed atop two wine barrels. He was a regular; Ignacio knew what he wanted without having to ask.

The short, round man poured Vic two fingers of brandy from a dusty bottle, asking, "Any luck in those floating gaming parlors?"

Vic lifted his glass to the light and savored its rich amber tint. *A shade darker than Fiona's eyes*, he mused silently. Then in answer to Ignacio's question, he gave the man a Gallic shrug. "The luck comes; the luck goes. You know how it is."

The barkeep shook his bald head and sighed

deeply. "Luck, she is no lady to treat us so badly, eh, M'sieur Vic? Often I wonder why we bother to tempt her, when we know all the while she will do us wrong."

Vic drained his glass, then set it on the counter, smiled, and nodded for a refill. Leaning closer, he said, "Ah, but, *mon ami*, we must always give the lady one more chance. Who knows when her flirting and teasing may turn into something more pleasing, more productive? Tonight could be the night."

The barman belted out a deep rumble of laughter and poured Vic another. "So, you know already of tonight's game at Gaspard's. I should have guessed." Then the man cocked one brow and glanced about even though they were alone before he continued in a quieter voice. "But have you heard who is playing, M'sieur Vic?"

Black Vic raised his brimming glass in a silent toast to luck. "That matters little. You see, the lady will be at my side this evening. I feel it in my bones." He winked at his friend. "Besides, I have had such a losing streak—*mon Dieu!*—it is my turn to win."

Ignacio pursed his thick lips and nodded sagely. "As you say, M'sieur. But you should know that one of the players tonight will be that scoundrel Hector Lazano."

A frown distorted Black Vic's handsome features. He did not fear Lazano's threats, but he had been counting on a civilized game this evening. This man, whose brother Vic had been forced to kill so long ago, was a known cheat. The evening and the poker would surely go badly with him at the table.

"Do you happen to know where I might find

Hector Lazano?" Vic asked of the barkeep. "The old score we have to settle should not ruin the game for everyone else."

Ignacio nodded quickly, his rheumy eyes gleaming at the thought of a possible duel. "*Oui, M'sieur!* He is staying with a woman named Ivory at her house in Dumaine Street. Will you be needing a second to go with you to the oaks, sir?"

"Thank you, my friend, but no," Vic answered. "I face only *gentlemen* on the field of honor. I will deal with Hector Lazano in some more suitable fashion."

"Should I come along . . . as a witness?" Ignacio suggested, all eagerness, pulling off his apron. "I was about to close for a noon nap, you see."

"A wise thought," Black Vic answered. "Let's be off, then. I want to settle this affair quickly so that tonight's game will not be spoiled. I mean to play while I still feel lucky."

The two men charged out into the bright noon sun—Ignacio eager to witness this possibly violent showdown and Victoine fired by the brandy in his blood and his keen appetite for revenge. *Yes, revenge!* he told himself. After all, Lazano had besmirched what little was left of his reputation by spreading his vile lies.

The old city seemed unusually quiet to Black Vic. The narrow streets were nearly bare of horse-drawn traffic and only an occasional pedestrian passed them on the banquette. Houses were shuttered and deserted until cooler, healthier weather returned. Only those on urgent business came to the city in the summer. Only those too poor to leave remained through the sweltering, fever-ridden

231

months. Victoine Navar qualified in both categories, but he hoped all that would soon change.

By far the shorter of the two, Ignacio had to hurry to keep up with Black Vic's long strides. Even the barkeep's best pace proved inadequate, however.

"Please, M'sieur, I am not a racehorse," Ignacio called. "This heat . . . my bad heart . . ."

Vic realized he was sweating heavily himself inside his evening clothes and cape. He slowed to let the other man catch up. They were almost to Ivory's house anyway—a house and a woman Vic knew well by reputation, though not firsthand. When Victoine Navar required such services from a lady he seldom found it necessary to pay for them.

Ignacio stumbled up, huffing and puffing, red in the face. He leaned heavily on Vic's arm until he caught his breath.

"Too hot," the little fat man gasped. "Too goddam hot, she is!"

"We don't have much farther to go. The house is just down there," Vic said, pointing to an old West Indian-style structure that leaned tiredly over the banquette.

"*Oui!* I know the place well," Ignacio answered, grinning up at his tall friend and giving Vic a poke with his elbow and a sly wink. "It is like a second home to me."

"You old cocksman!" Vic laughed. "I thought you well beyond the age for such sport. And what about your bad heart?"

"Are you telling me, M'sieur Vic, that you plan to retire yours when it reaches a certain age?" Ignacio's eyes went wide in disbelief and he made a clucking sound of disapproval. "Me? Never! When my heart stops, let it cease beating at the exact moment I have shot my seed into the hot depths of some lovely, panting female."

Vic roared with laughter. "You have a good point, my friend. I do apologize for underestimating your swordsmanship. Now, shall we get on with this?"

The shutters of Ivory's cottage were closed and no sign of life indicated that they would find anyone at home.

"Mam'zelle Ivory will likely be sleeping now," Ignacio informed Vic, as if he knew her routine intimately.

"Then we'll wake her," Black Vic replied, pounding at the painted cypress door.

Moments later, a sharp-edged female voice yelled out, "Who the hell is it? Go away! You're disturbing me."

"See? I told you," Ignacio said, turning to leave the narrow gallery.

But Vic only pounded harder. "It's Victoine Navar," he called. "Open up, Ivory! I have business to discuss with your friend."

Vic heard the bolt sliding, then the door opened a mere crack. A moment later, Ivory stepped out to greet him.

"M'sieur Navar," she said. "So, at last you have come to visit Ivory, eh?"

Vic couldn't help smiling as he gazed at her. She was, indeed, a beautiful woman in spite of the hard life she'd lived. It was rumored that she had been a clergyman's daughter, but when her lover got her with child, she was cast out by her family. No money, no friends, nowhere to go. From that time, she had followed the only occupation left to her. What her real name was no one knew. She was called Ivory because of her pale skin and long, silver-blond hair. Now, however, the angelic beauty of her face was marred by an angry purple bruise across one cheek. Her hair, Vic noted, was still as fine and silky as a girl's. Only her eyes—the color of cold sapphires—betrayed the hurt in her body and soul. They were lifeless, lightless, and totally devoid of emotion as if too much pain lay there to allow any of it to show.

God, she is a beauty! Vic thought as he viewed her exquisitely voluptuous figure outlined inside the sheer white silk of her negligee. *Yes, Ivory, you are quite a woman!*

"M'sieur?" she said in a throaty voice of invitation when Vic kept staring at her dumbly. "Please, won't you come in?"

Remembering Ignacio, Vic glanced over his shoulder at his friend. Ivory's gaze followed Vic's and she scowled at the little barkeep. "Go away, you!" she hissed.

Ignacio scurried down the steps as if he were a filthy cockroach she'd just whisked away with her broom.

"I won't be long, Ignacio," Vic called. "Wait for me, won't you?"

"But, of course, M'sieur Vic," Ignacio replied with all the decorum he could muster after Ivory's harsh rebuff.

Ivory took Vic's arm and guided him inside to her front parlor. "Please, have a seat. I'll tell Tessa to bring us something cool to drink. It is *so* hot!"

To illustrate her words, Ivory fanned herself with one hand while she used the other to adjust her silk wrapper, pulling it lower to expose a vaster expanse of luscious, sweating bosom—and more bruises. Black Vic frowned, wondering who the brute might be who'd left his ugly mark on such tender flesh.

He took the seat she indicated, a narrow couch of purple and gold brocade. Ivory yelled orders to her maid, then sank down next to Vic, letting her gown fall away from her long, silk-clad legs.

Vic's gaze strayed down the length of her shapely limbs. He sensed her object. On some lighter occasion he would have been tempted to play along with the game, but at present he had only one thing on his mind. He cleared his throat and eased slightly away from her.

"Ivory, I've come here on very specific business."

With the tip of one finger she traced the scar down Vic's right cheek. "But, of course, M'sieur. For you, I am always open for business. I had hoped you might come long before now."

Black Vic was getting more uncomfortable by the minute. That sword slash on his face was the most sensitive part of his body. It still pained him at times, so he was surprised to realize that Ivory's light stroke on that tender flesh proved quite an erotic sensation.

"Ivory," Vic began, "you don't understand." Trying to think how to get out of this gracefully, he finally blurted out, "I haven't a picayune to my name at present. So, you see, it's other business that brings me to you."

She only smiled and clucked her tongue in sympathy. "You needn't worry about paying me, darling. A girl must have some pleasure now and then."

"No, Ivory!" he said determinedly. "I haven't come here for *that*. I've come looking for Hector Lazano. Is he here?"

A flicker passed over Ivory's face, and for the first time Vic noticed how nervous she seemed. He was about to ask what was wrong. Before he could get the words out, however, he was rudely interrupted.

"Damn right, I'm here!" snarled a whiskey-rough voice from the hallway.

Vic looked up to see the vaguely familiar face and shock of greasy gray hair. The man lounging against the door frame wore filthy trousers that he had obviously pulled on in haste. His hairy chest glistened with sweat. He held the stump of a half-smoked cheroot clenched between uneven, yellow teeth.

"You lookin' for me, Navar?" he growled.

Vic turned to face the man directly. "That I am, Lazano." Navar's voice was calm but forceful. "I hear you've been spreading lies about me throughout the city. I demand that you stop this slander immediately."

"Who's gonna make me? Besides, they ain't lies. You kilt my little brother, Navar."

"Your brother was cheating at cards. Furthermore, he threatened my friend's life. Now, you can either leave town peacefully of your own accord, or I will assist you. Either way, you shall depart New Orleans immediately."

"I ain't going nowhere till after the big game tonight."

They stood staring at each other, a few feet apart.

Vic's face was grim, his dark eyes steely. Lazano's eyes narrowed and a muscle twitched angrily in his unshaven jaw. He made a slight move toward Black Vic.

Ivory quickly jumped between the two men. "Not in my parlor, you don't!" she cried. "If you mean to spill blood, you'll do it outside."

This interruption proved just the distraction Lazano needed. Quick as a flash, he pulled a bowie knife and went for Vic. The two men tussled about the parlor, overturning tables, smashing fragile bric-a-brac, creating general chaos in their wake. Ivory, frantic for fear they would destroy everything, tried once again to get between them. She screamed when the tip of Lazano's knife slashed her shoulder. It was little more than a prick, but blood seemed to be everywhere.

Lazano fell on Vic then. The two men grappled, fighting for possession of the knife. In the scuffle, Vic gave his opponent a jarring blow to the chin, then shoved him away before the man could find a mark for his deadly blade. Lazano stumbled and tripped over Ivory, who lay crouched in the middle of the floor sobbing and bleeding. In the next instant, the burly man fell on his face with a heavy thud.

Lazano gasped, made a choking sound, then fell silent after a final twitch of his thick body. When Vic turned him over, Hector Lazano lay on the floor in a pool of his own blood, the bowie knife through his heart. Sure that he was dead, Vic turned from the corpse to help Ivory to her feet.

"Oh, God!" she moaned, shielding her face with crossed arms. "Don't kill me!"

"It's all right now," Vic murmured, trying to

soothe her. "Lazano fell on his knife. That one's palmed his last ace. Now, let's see to you."

Vic picked up the sobbing woman and started down the hallway. Wide-eyed Tessa, the maid, pointed out Ivory's bedroom.

"Bring some water and toweling," Vic ordered, "and some whiskey to clean her wound."

By now Ivory was hysterical. She kept shielding her face with her bloody arms, crying, "No! Don't hit me! Not again . . . please!"

Vic shook her gently. "Ivory, snap out of it. I'm not going to hurt you. I only want to help."

He eased her back on the pillows and held her close until she stopped fighting him. Finally, she opened her eyes. For a time, she only stared blankly at him. Then the lines of terror eased gradually from her face.

"You're not the one!" Ivory cried, tears of relief suddenly streaming down her bruised face. "You're Victoine Navar!"

"Of course I am. Now, lie still so I can see to this cut."

Ivory glanced at her bloody shoulder, then laughed—a short, sharp sound. "He's done a damn sight worse to me than that little pinprick." Then she heaved a great sigh and relaxed. "But it's over now. He's dead, isn't he? He won't hit me ever again."

Vic touched her cheek gently. "You mean, Lazano did this to you?"

"That and a lot more," she answered with a shudder, remembering.

"Then why on earth did you let him stay?"

"*Let him?* Like hell I let him!" She leaned up on

her elbow, staring hard into Vic's face. "He blew into town out of nowhere last week, came here like any regular customer. Shit, I didn't know him from Adam's housecat. I did him and he paid me. When the last John left at dawn the next morning—same as always—I came back to my bedroom to get my beauty sleep and here he was, stretched out big as you please. And with his filthy boots on my satin spread! I told him to get the hell out or I'd yell for help. The next thing I knew, he was off the bed, giving me a beating like I haven't had since my old man kicked me out. He said he was staying. He even made Tessa turn the cat in the window."

"The cat?" Vic stared at her, puzzled, thinking that her recent beatings must have addled her brain.

"*Oui*. It's a special china cat that a sailor gave me a while back. He said they're all the rage at sporting houses in England. The thing has two faces, two sets of eyes. If the green eyes are showing, I'm open for business. But if the red eyes are toward the street, then my regulars know not to knock. Classy, huh?"

"So, Lazano has been virtually holding you and Tessa prisoner?"

"That's it in a nutshell. I was sure happy to see you come to the door."

"But you told me to go away," Vic reminded her.

"Lazano had that knife. He told me he'd cut me if I let anyone in. Then, when you said your name, he told me to open up, but that I wasn't to let Ignacio in, only you, M'sieur Vic." She looked away, her tears flowing again. "I'm sorry. I could have gotten you killed."

"Don't fret over that, Ivory. I'm just glad it's all over for both of us now."

Tessa came in with a bowl and pitcher, several towels, and a bottle of rye whiskey on a big tray.

"Put everything there on the table," Vic instructed. "I'll see to your mistress."

Still looking fearful, young Tessa did as she was told, then curtsied and left the room.

Vic eased the sticky silk down from Ivory's shoulder. The wound was not long, but it was deep. Wetting the end of a towel he cleaned her shoulder and arm. "Looks like you'll live," he quipped.

"Wonderful!" Ivory replied sarcastically.

When Ivory saw Vic soak the tip of a towel with whiskey, she shied away.

"This won't hurt," he told her.

"It already hurts like bloody hell! Give me a swig of that before you do anything else."

Vic obliged. Ivory took a long gulp from the bottle, then handed it back to him. "You look like you could use some of this, too," she said.

Never one to pass up an offered bottle, Vic helped himself. On top of the brandy he'd had earlier and all the activity, he felt an immediate buzz behind his ears. He took another sip, then smiled at Ivory.

"Are you ready now?" he asked gently.

She snuggled down into the pillows. Her eyes half-closed, she smiled back at him. "More than ready, M'sieur Vic. You can do whatever you want with me now."

The invitation in her voice was as thinly veiled as her voluptuous body. He tried to ignore the appeal, but there was no way he could deny his growing fascination with this woman.

240

"All right, then," he said evenly. "I'm just going to press this to your shoulder. It will sting, but it won't last long."

"Can I squeeze your hand?" She sounded like a frightened little girl.

"By all means," Vic answered, twining his fingers through hers. "Squeeze the hell out of it, if that helps."

She did! She moaned and writhed and made whimpering sounds. And, oh, how she squeezed! However, the moment Vic took the whiskey-soaked cloth away, her pain turned instantly to something far different, though every bit as fierce. She caught Vic in a headlock and pulled him down to her. Placing her mouth on his neck, she sucked long and hard, sending fire surging through his taut body. Then her lips were on his, her satiny tongue teasing him to open to her. Ivory guided the hand she'd been squeezing to her bare breast. Before Vic ever realized he meant to do it, he was naked, in the bed with Ivory, partaking of her many charms and loving every minute of it.

He'd been several months without a woman—his lack of finances being mostly at fault. Granted, he almost never paid outright for love, but in order to get it the other way, a certain amount of wooing was required and that, too, took cash. In short, Ivory was a godsend.

Conscious of what she had been through with Lazano and the wound in her shoulder, Vic was especially gentle and tender with her. He took great pains to pleasure her well.

When at last they were done, Ivory lay next to him purring with satisfaction. "You are even better than I had heard," she told him frankly.

Vic stared at her, feeling the color rise in his face. "My God, you mean ladies actually discuss this among themselves?"

Ivory laughed softly. "Well, perhaps *ladies* don't, but my friends and I do pass along interesting tid-bits to amuse ourselves." She paused and stroked his cheek. "You needn't worry, though, M'sieur Vic. I'll tell no one about this afternoon. I mean to keep it all to myself, you see."

"I don't blame you," Vic answered in a surly voice—annoyed only at himself. "You wouldn't want the word to get around that you take in charity cases." He looked over at her, his darkly handsome face gone serious. "Ivory, I really didn't mean to take advantage of . . ."

She placed one finger over his lips. "Sh-h-h! Not another word. It is I who should pay you—a reward for saving me from that awful man."

Ivory rose from the bed, gliding across the room in all her magnificent nakedness. Opening a filthy carpetbag, she fumbled inside, then drew out a fat leather wallet. "Ah, here it is! Lazano showed me his stake for the poker game tonight. He bragged to me about how he'd cheated some poor fellow out of his life savings and even the ring he had bought for the woman he meant to marry. The bastard stole all this from him. I want you to have it now, M'sieur Vic."

With a bow and a smile, Ivory placed the bulging wallet and a delicately wrought gold wedding band on the bed beside Vic.

"Oh, no," he replied, shoving the things back toward her. "I can't take any of this. You keep the money."

She shook her head. "The police are certain to

242

search the house once we summon them to remove the body. They would only take everything to the station 'for safekeeping.' Then neither you nor I would see any of it ever again." She handed the wallet to Vic; the ring, with its single ruby glittering in the light, dangled from the tip of her little finger. "I want you to have all this. There are many things I need in life, but money is not one of them."

Vic could hardly believe his good fortune. He felt understandably odd, being paid by a prostitute afterward rather than giving her money for her services. But he did need a stake for the poker game.

"Whatever I win tonight, I'll split with you," Vic offered. "And, here." He slipped the ruby ring on her finger. "You must keep this to remember our time together."

"*Oui*. If you wish," she whispered, "I will keep the ring, *mon cher*. But use whatever funds you win tonight to put your own house in order. As for sharing, should you ever care to share *yourself* with me, you'll know where I am." Then she gave him a sad-sweet smile. "I think, though, that our paths will not cross again. I have served my purpose in your life. Fate surely willed it so. You need a woman, Victoine Navar, but you must find one who can be all yours, to keep and to love all your life."

"I had a wife," he answered sharply. "She left me, took our son. Now I have no one. I don't need anyone."

"We all need someone, *mon ami*. Open your eyes and look about. You will find the right woman, M'sieur Vic. You have only to claim her. Already, she loves you."

"You're a witch!"

243

Ivory shook her head and smiled. "No, but I do have dreams. Last night you were there while I slept—you and a lovely, dark-haired woman whose eyes shone with love when she gazed at you."

Vic wanted to believe. He ached to believe.

Ivory gave Victoine Navar far more than money that day. He knew he would remember her for all time.

A short while later, Vic found himself out on the street again. Once he had dressed, Ivory insisted that he leave immediately. "You have no need to be mixed up in this," she'd told him. "The authorities will think nothing of finding a drifter's body in this house. I will show them my bruises, tell them what he did to me. I'll say that we fought over the knife when he tried to kill me. That will be the end of it. Now, go!" She had refused any and all arguments on the subject.

Ignacio, weary of waiting in the hot sun, had gone back to the Blue Bottle, Vic was sure. He turned and headed toward the bar to tell his friend all—or *almost* all—that had happened.

When Vic finished his story, Ignacio slapped the counter and grinned. "Lady Luck, she is with you, just as you said, my friend. Otherwise, you might be lying dead in Mam'zelle Ivory's parlor at this very moment, spilling your guts on her nice carpet. But, you see, here you stand—not a scratch on you and plenty in your pocket to wager on the game tonight. And what will you do when you win this great fortune, eh?"

Vic thought hard for a minute. He was sure he

would win, but Ignacio was right; he needed a plan of investment. "You know I've always wanted to buy back Golden Oaks."

"*Oui!*" Ignacio nodded. "But that would take a great fortune, indeed. Why, you would have to *save* money to do that, M'sieur Vic, and you are a gambler."

"You're right," Vic said, his dream deflated. Then his dark eyes lit up and he smiled broadly at the ruddy-faced barkeep. "Perhaps it is time I had a woman in my life again, Ignacio."

The shorter man frowned. "But you have a wife, M'sieur Vic. You cannot marry twice."

"I never said anything about taking another wife," Vic replied. "No law says I can't have a mistress, though."

"Not Ivory!" Ignacio looked horrified at the thought, afraid of losing the woman to his friend.

Vic shook his head. "No, no! That would never work. I mean a young woman, an innocent woman. One with hair as dark as night and eyes that shine only for me," he said, remembering Ivory's words. "One whom I can shape and mould. I'm talking about taking a *placée*, Ignacio. I'll win enough to buy myself a fine new suit of evening clothes, then on Thursday night I'll go to the Orleans Ballroom. Surely there must be some young, lovely child who could make even this cynical gambler happy."

"Oh, *oui*, M'sieur Vic! What a grand scheme! And you will set her up in your house in Condé Street? Ah, I can see it all now—you coming home late after a hard night at the gaming tables and this beautiful, delicate flower waiting with open arms to pleasure you. A pretty picture, no? Shall we drink to it?"

Black Vic smiled and winked at his friend. "Indeed! A toast to my lovely love."

Frank shook his head, trying to clear the cobwebs. His temples throbbed. His mouth and throat burned like he'd just drunk fire. He hadn't had any booze in a long time, but you never forgot that sensation, that taste. He coughed and sputtered, feeling his head spin like a merry-go-round gone berserk.

"What the hell?" he muttered.

He blinked repeatedly, fighting off murky visions. For a time, he thought he was still under water; he was that wet and cold. Yes, he could hear the sound of it rushing all around him. Then something touched his hand—something damp and dead-feeling.

He jerked around, ready to fight his way to the surface. At that moment, he realized the water was below him. He was standing high and dry on the dock at the foot of Barracks Street. And through the fog, he could see a face to close to his. It looked ghostly pale in the dim, predawn light.

"Frank?" Carol's quivery voice reached his ears. "Oh, Frank, is it really you?"

The next minute she was in his arms, sobbing with relief, hugging him, kissing him, begging him to say something.

"Oh, God, Carol!" he moaned. "What the hell happened? I lost you! I thought you were gone for good. And I was gone . . . gone somewhere else. I was in New Orleans, but I wasn't. Damn, I'm not making any sense, am I?"

He hugged her tightly, never wanting to let her go again.

"Come on, Frank," she whispered, still clinging to him. "Let's go home now. Why, you're soaked to the skin and shivering!"

Numb from all he'd been through and a little drunk as well, he took Carol's hand and stumbled along with her back to the hotel, to his room.

Once they got there, Frank sank down on the bed, staring at Carol, trying to think how to begin. He had to tell her everything—all the sights, the sounds, the feelings, the passions . . .

"Don't just sit there," Carol ordered. "Go change out of those wet clothes. You'll catch your death. I'll put on some coffee."

She was right. He was water-logged and so cold his bones ached. It felt great to peel off his wet clothes and pull on a warm, dry robe. Moments later, Frank was back on the bed, watching Carol as she moved about the room. He still couldn't quite believe she was real.

Carol handed him a steaming mug. "Drink this," she ordered. "You look like you need it. Then, when you *sober up*, I want you to tell me *everything!*"

Chapter Eleven

"What do you mean, 'sober up'? I don't drink anymore," Frank reminded Carol. "You know that."

She looked at him askance. "Maybe Frank Longpre no longer indulges, but I have the feeling you haven't been yourself of late, my friend."

"You can damn-sure say that again!" Frank shook his head, bewildered by the odd fragments of memory tossing around in his brain.

Carol sat down next to him. "Then you did go back?"

"Yeah, I guess. How about you?"

Carol nodded.

"Well, where the hell were you?" Frank queried. "I thought we took the boat together so I could be with you. I was supposed to protect you when we got back there. And I forgot to tell you about the snake."

"What snake?"

"You were right about the mummy, Carol. She probably died of a poisonous snakebite. The marks are there." He paused and searched her face, his eyes tense with worry. "You're okay, aren't you?"

"I knew it!" she cried. "I was sure that awful pain in my leg meant something. But don't worry, Frank. There were no snakes this trip. In fact, there was no danger of any kind. I was with Fiona Le Moyne and her son, Prospere, the whole time."

"Fiona?" The name made Frank think of golden eyes, as dark as brandy, but his recollection went no farther.

"She was Edouard Mazaret's *placée*. Remember? I told you about her."

Frank rubbed his hands over his face. He still felt strangely disoriented, as if he were only half here while the other half remained somewhere back in time. Something Carol had said struck a familiar chord. He strained, trying to recall what it might be. No use, he decided. He couldn't make the connection. Maybe it would come to him later.

"What happened between you—I mean, Cami—and her father's lover? Seems to me that would be a pretty uncomfortable situation all around."

"It was, at first. But Fiona soon took Cami under her wing and they became wonderful friends. And I think that through Fiona Cami is finally going to get to meet Victoine Navar."

Frank moaned and rubbed his aching temples. "All this stuff is making me crazy!"

"Not so crazy," Carol answered with an accusing

glance. "You've managed to keep me talking about what I did while telling me absolutely nothing about your experiences. I want to know everything, Frank. Right now!" She gave him another sharp look to match the tone of her voice. "You might start by telling me who the woman was."

Frank's head shot up, his dark eyes wide. "How'd you know about her?"

Carol reached out and pressed one fingertip to his neck. "Right there!" she said. "That's a monkey-bite, if I ever saw one."

"A *what*?"

"A love-bite, a hickey. Don't try to play the innocent with me. You know very well what I'm talking about. We both know how a person gets a mark like that, and I damn-well mean to find out who gave it to you!"

Frank smiled innocently, adorably. "First off, Miz Marlowe, as you keep pointing out to me, when you go back in time what happens to you is really happening to another person. So, even though I may have brought this hickey back with me, by rights it belongs to someone else. Am I correct?"

"Who?" Carol demanded, about to burst with curiosity.

Frank grinned, savoring his secret a moment longer. "Well, if you must know, Cami's ole buddy, Black Vic."

"No!" Carol gasped. "Why, I didn't even see him this time. How could Cami have done that without my knowing about it?" Again, she poked at the discolored mouth-print on his neck.

"Did I say Cami did it?"

Carol caught her breath, shocked. "You mean *my* Vic was with another woman?"

"Carol, Carol, Carol," Frank moaned in exaggerated frustration. "Black Vic is not *yours!* In fact, at the point in time when I was there, Cami wasn't even around. Good ole Vic saved a lady named Ivory by fighting a scumball who'd been holding her prisoner and knocking her around. It was only natural that she should want to show her gratitude after Vic shoved the bastard and he fell on his knife. Don't you agree?"

Carol groaned at Frank's grin. She threw up her hands in dismay, then rose and paced across the room. "Oh, Lord, I don't believe this! Here I thought you and I really had something together, Frank. Then I let you out of my sight for an hour and you fall into bed with some floozy named Ivory." She turned and faced him, her hands on her hips. "This really hurts, Frank. I mean, all that stuff you told me about your guilt. What am I supposed to think now? *Ivory!* Who was she anyway—some prostitute you and Black Vic picked up on Bourbon Street?"

"Carol!" Frank placed one hand over his heart and drew back as if the accusation both offended and bewildered him. "Why, darlin', you cut me to the quick!" Then he laughed.

"Frank, you obviously aren't taking any of this seriously."

"Sure, I am."

He tried to put his arms around Carol, but she moved away. Dream, vision, whatever he'd experienced—it was making for jolly fun, teasing Carol. He decided to have a bit more sport with her.

"Ivory was better than your common run-of-the-mill prostitute," Frank confided. "She had her own house in Dumaine Street—a real neat place. And she had this china cat in the window—the most amazing invention . . ."

"Oh, be quiet!" Carol stormed. "I don't give a damn about her house or her cat!" Carol knew she was being unreasonable, but she couldn't help herself. She really felt so much for Frank, and she'd been so terrified when he disappeared. Now, come to find out, all that time he was off gallivanting as Black Vic, lolling around in bed with a damn hooker! The very thought of him with some other woman drove her wild. The fact that he had been Victoine Navar at the time made little difference. "You'd just better tell me what happened, Frank Longpre. Every detail! I mean it!"

"Oh, I couldn't," Frank said with a quick shake of his head and another boyish grin. "A gentleman doesn't kiss and tell. It's just not kosher."

Carol turned back to him, the green of her eyes demanding the truth. "Are you saying that's all that happened? You *only* kissed her?"

"Well, actually, there was more, but . . ."

Carol freaked. With a most unladylike curse she threw a pillow at his head, then lurched toward him. "You no-good two-timer . . . you . . ."

Figuring he'd teased her enough, Frank met her halfway. After a brief tussle, he managed to get hold of her. Gripping her upper arms, he pulled her almost roughly to him. His kiss was hard and sweet and quite convincing.

"Do you think I could ever want any other woman now that I've met you? If so, then, darlin', you must have lost your psychic powers somewhere along the way. I love *you*, Carol, *only* you."

Carol tried to laugh, but it came out as a soft,

little sob. "I'm being foolish?" It was both a question and a declaration. "You're right, of course. None of this really happened to you. It was Black Vic—the scoundrel, the rogue, the skirt-chaser!" She ended her tirade in a contrite whisper. "I'm sorry for doubting you, Frank."

Frank's joking and teasing ended abruptly. "How much do you know about this Navar character, Carol?"

She thought it over for a second. "Not much, really. Cousin Morris told Cami that he came of good family, but managed to lose everything. Fiona was horrified when Cami said she wanted to marry Vic."

Frank raised an eyebrow. "That's not surprising."

"What do you mean?"

"He's already married."

"No, he can't be!" Carol felt the words twist her heart as if that part of her still belonged to Camille Mazaret. She was stunned. How cruel fate could be! She had sensed that Fiona was keeping something about Vic from her. Now she knew what it was.

"You really didn't know?" Frank asked. "But how can that be? I thought you knew everything that was going on back then, even if Cami didn't get the whole picture."

Carol sighed. "I guess I didn't want to know," she admitted. "It's a pretty painful fact to face, caring about what happens to Cami the way I do. If I knew, I must have just blocked it out."

"Well, I'm sorry to be the one to tell you, honey, but he's married all right. His wife left him several years back; I think it must have been around 1830. Their long separation doesn't change the legality of the marriage, though. Unlike nowadays, marriage back then was *forever*."

Frank had a sudden clear flash. How similar Black Vic's dilemma was to his own!

"The hardest part for Vic must be that his wife took their son," Frank continued. "Vic's searched for both of them for a long time. I gather, though, that he's about ready to give it up. So now I guess he's in a real bind. Divorce wouldn't have been a consideration in those days, so he's stuck with a wife who really isn't one. You can't blame the poor guy for bedding down with a willing beauty when he gets his chance."

"Ivory was beautiful?" Carol asked, feeling another jealous twinge.

"A damn goddess!" Frank cried enthusiastically. "Long blond hair, real pale blue eyes, and she was built like the Great Wall of China!"

"And you—I mean, Vic—actually took her to bed?"

"It was more like she took him." Frank grinned, remembering. "And I'm here to tell you, that lady knows a few interesting tricks."

"Oh, Frank," Carol groaned. "I hate this! I can't stand hearing about you with that woman. Don't tell me another word." She covered her ears so she couldn't hear if he did say something more. Then the next minute she demanded to know, "How was she? Really?"

Frank moved close to Carol again and nuzzled her neck. "Not as good as you, darlin'." Then his smile changed to a thoughtful expression. "Oddest damn thing, though. I mean, I know I was Vic at the time, but after it was all over—that was the great part. I didn't have to deal with any guilt. I told you what hell I go through. Well, with Ivory there was none of that. Afterward, there was just a nice, satisfied, happy glow." Frank paused and shook his head. "I liked that, you know?"

"Oh, Frank!" Carol put her arms around him and held him close. She knew exactly why he had experienced no guilt, no depression. When he'd been with Ivory, Eileen had yet to be born, much less disappear. But she decided not to bring up that painful subject. Instead, she gripped his hand and whispered, "I wish I could give you that. I do want to make you happy."

"Ouch!" he exclaimed, pulling his hand from hers. "That hurts!"

"I'm sorry. What did I do?" She reached gently for his hand. "Let me see."

When she turned his hand palm-up, Carol gasped at the discolored, puckered flesh around the distinct imprint of several puncture wounds. "What on earth did this, Frank? Why, those look like teeth marks!"

"The real question is: *Who* did it?" Frank answered. "I think this injury actually belongs to Black Vic. Nobody bit him while I was there. At least, not in the hand." He paused and chuckled, remembering Ivory's little love nibbles. He pulled a straight face when Carol glared at him. "Hey, didn't you tell me you bit him?"

"Oh, dear God!" Carol gasped, remembering the vicious bite she'd inflicted, not realizing at the time that her victim was Black Vic. "Yes, the blood on my face . . . it was the night Cami ran away from Mulgrove and arrived at Fiona's. But that was before you went back. You weren't Vic then."

Frank sighed and winced as he moved his sore

fingers. "Well, it sure carried over. I guess if I'm going to bed his women, I'm going to have to suffer his pain as well."

"I really do apologize for taking a chunk out of you, I mean Vic," Carol began. "But he deserved it. If he hadn't grabbed me and kissed me, I wouldn't have . . ."

"That bastard kissed you when I wasn't there?" Frank exploded. "That settles it; you're not going again. He can't be trusted. Carol, there's a lot you don't know about this guy. The fact that he's married is only a small part of his sordid tale. He's also a drunk, a womanizer, a gambler, a murderer . . ."

"*But,*" Carol interrupted sharply, "in spite of all that, Cami is going to fall in love with Vic, Frank. With us or without us, it's fated to happen. Maybe by being there we can make things better. Maybe we can save her from ending up in that swamp."

Frank gazed at Carol, a bewildered look on his face. After a time, he admitted grudgingly, "I reckon you're right. But how did you and I get involved in all this in the first place, Carol? That's what's buggin' the hell out of me."

She looked up at him, her hazel eyes misty and glowing. "Haven't you figured it out yet, Frank? I knew the minute I touched her there in the morgue. I *was* Camille Mazaret, and through some magic—maybe my psychic powers—I've been given a miraculous second chance to go back in order to change Cami's fate—my own fate in that lifetime. If I'm right about this, I firmly believe that improving Cami's former life can only mean that Carol Marlowe's present life will be better, too."

"And Frank Longpre's as well?"

Carol nodded solemnly. "I'm convinced of it. This is at least our second time around, Frank."

"Then I guess we don't have much choice about returning to the past, do we?"

"I don't think so, Frank. I believe it's something we *must* do."

"Okay, darlin', I'm with you. But you just watch that guy when I'm not around."

Tense silence fell over the room as they both considered the incredible task before them. Carol was determined, but Frank still had his doubts.

Trying to change the subject, to get them on safer ground, Frank plucked the wilted flower from Carol's hair. "Hey, what's this?"

Carol uttered a cry of surprise, then smiled. "It's a purple zinnia. Fiona put it in Cami's hair when they were in the garden, when Cami said that she wanted to go to the Orleans Ballroom." Carol giggled. "Actually, I can hardly wait to go back, Frank. Fiona and Cami have cooked up this wild masquerade. Fiona plans to take Cami to the Quadroon Ball and pass her off as a niece from Mobile. That way, Cami will get to look over the eligible men in New Orleans and take her pick. If she does fall in love, then she'll tell the gentleman of her choice the truth—that she's not a woman of color who can only be his *placée*, but the daughter of a fine old Creole family, with a fortune in her own right, ready and willing to marry him. Have you ever heard of anything so wonderfully romantic?"

All of a sudden, Frank's whole body jerked as if he'd been shot. "Oh, my God!" he groaned, his memory finally triggered by the word *placée*. "That's it! I know what's going to happen, Carol.

The same thing all over again. I don't want you to be there."

"Frank, what on earth's gotten into you? What are you talking about?"

He held her as if he could keep her in the present by sheer force. "Black Vic's going to that same ball. It's on a Thursday night, right?"

Carol nodded, dumbfounded.

"They're going to meet and he's going to set Cami up as his *placée* in a house on Condé Street. Don't you see? It all fits—what Mrs. Thibodaux told us about Cami's reputation being ruined. It's about to happen, and Black Vic's the sonofabitch who's going to ruin her."

"Impossible!" Carol stated flatly. "Fiona would never allow it. She's told Cami already to forget about Victoine Navar, and, believe me, Fiona Le Moyne is a very strong-willed woman."

"Big deal!" Frank scoffed. "When have you ever known a teenaged girl who listened to what she was told, especially if the warning involves a man? If you don't go back, Carol, then the ball will never take place and Vic won't get to meet Cami right now. So, that settles it! You're staying right here with me where you belong until Black Vic is a free man."

"It doesn't work that way, Frank," Carol reminded him. "Whatever happened at that ball took place over a century ago. If I stay here, then that's that. It's over and done with and that unidentified mummy will meet her appointed, ghastly fate. But if I go back, I may be able to change something. Cami's a sweet girl; she deserves better. I'd like a shot at fixing things so her life will be happier."

"Well, I'm not going!" Frank announced flatly.

"If I'm not in the picture, Cami can't meet Black Vic. So there!"

"Wrong again, Frank," Carol said. "If you don't go back, Vic will still be at that ball. You simply won't have any chance to change the course of his life. But, you're right. Having one of us there should be enough. Besides, I have to admit that I'll feel much easier with you and Ivory in two different centuries."

"Now, you just hold on . . ." Frank paused to give the matter serious consideration. He'd figured if he refused to go back, Carol would stay put, too. He should have known better.

Suddenly, Carol interrupted his brooding. "Frank?" she whispered, her face glowing when he looked at her. "I've just had the most intriguing thought. If we both go back, and if Cami and Vic do meet and fall in love at the ball, then you and I will become lovers in another time. Aren't you even a little bit curious about what that would be like?" Warming to the idea, she added, "I mean, it couldn't be better than what we have now, but it surely would be different. And—just like with Ivory—there'd be no guilt afterward. I know all this must sound silly to you, but I'd love to . . ."

Convinced and aroused by her words, Frank took Carol in his arms and kissed away the rest of her sentence. When he drew back from her lips, he smiled and whispered, "I hope I haven't forgotten how to deal with a virgin, darlin'."

Carol laughed shyly. "I hope I haven't forgotten how to act like one."

* * *

A short time later, Carol returned to her room to change before rejoining Frank for breakfast. The oddest thing happened when she reached the door to her suite. Suddenly, it wasn't the painted cypress with its worn brass knob she knew so well. Instead it was an aluminum screen door with a button doorbell beside it. She caught her breath and took a step back. In that instant, the whole vision she'd had of Eileen Longpre and the faceless, tattooed man flashed through her mind like a TV rerun. A moment later her door looked perfectly normal again.

The minute she got inside, she went straight to the bedside phone and dialed Atlanta. Luck was with her. Jesse Calhoun answered his home phone immediately.

"Well, hey, Carol! How you doing with ole Frank? Any leads on that mummy yet?"

"We've made some progress—nothing to shout from the rooftops, though."

"You like Frank, do you?" Carol could hear Jesse's grin through the phone.

She smiled and admitted it. "Very much! Maybe you should give up police work and go into matchmaking, Jesse."

"Hot damn!" he bellowed into the phone. "When's the wedding?"

"Hey, don't rush me, pal! If anything like that develops, you'll be the first to know—okay? But right now I don't have much time to talk, Jesse. I'm meeting Frank in a few minutes, and I'd really rather he didn't know that I'd called you."

Jesse got serious, too. "So, what's up, Carol?"

"It's something Frank said to me about ex-cons

coming after the cops who put them in jail, sometimes threatening their families as well."

"Yeah, it happens."

"Was anyone out to get Frank when his wife disappeared?"

There was a long pause while Jesse thought back through the years. "Jesus, Carol, that's been a long time! I'd have to go back through the files—check some names and dates. My memory's not what it used to be."

"Maybe I can help," Carol suggested. "Do you remember a man with a tattoo on his right forearm?"

"They *all* got tattoos, Carol."

"Not like this one—a woman's breast with a knife stabbed through it and underneath it the words, 'My Heart Bleeds'."

There was a silent pause. Then Jesse said, "Damned if I don't remember that particular tattoo! And it *has* been a while. Hang on a minute, honey. Let me check something."

Carol held the phone for what seemed an eternity. She could hear the click of computer keys in the background as Jesse searched for the right file. She tapped her foot impatiently. Any minute now, Frank would knock on her door. What would she do then—refuse to answer or hang up on Jesse? She was still wrestling with her imagined dilemma when Jesse came back on the line.

"I got what you're looking for right here, Carol. The guy goes by about a dozen aliases, but his real name's Orville Percy Jones. Back in 1977, he slaughtered a whole family—mother, father, grandmother, and three little kids, one just an infant—at their farmhouse in Jefferson Parish. He took one of the kids, a fourteen-year-old girl, with him. Kept her for a few weeks before he cut her up, too."

Carol felt ill. "Never mind the gory details, Jesse. Where is this guy now?"

"Let's see. Frank was the arresting officer in 1978. Jones was convicted of the murders and sentenced to death by lethal injection. But there were appeals and stays and the usual bureaucratic red tape and crap so the sentence wasn't carried out right away. He escaped in March of 1979, but they picked him up after a few weeks. Uh-oh! Here's something . . ."

"What?" Carol asked impatiently.

"In January of 1980, he overpowered the two guards moving him from one prison to another and escaped again. Got clean away that time."

Carol's heart sank. "Then he's somewhere out there, on the loose."

"No, hold on a minute. He was recaptured a few months later, again with Frank's help. Yeah, I remember that now. Jones swore he'd get Frank or die trying."

"Oh, God!" Carol groaned.

"Hey, there's nothing to worry about. Jones has been safe and sound behind the bars of the Louisiana State Pen ever since. No way he's going to get at Frank, so you just stop worrying your pretty little head over such things."

Ignoring Jesse's slightly patronizing tone, Carol went on with her questions. "I'm not clear on the chronology. Where was Jones when Eileen Longpre disappeared? That's what I really need to know."

"I don't quite see what you're getting at, Carol,

but he was on the run when Eileen disappeared, right enough. That would have been shortly after his second escape."

"Thanks, Jesse. I've got to go now."

"Hey, wait a minute! How'd you know about that tattoo? You haven't seen this guy, have you?"

"Not in the flesh, Jesse. I'll call when I have more time to explain everything. I just needed to know. Thanks!"

Jesse was still firing questions when Carol hung up, but she couldn't afford to stay on the phone a second longer. Frank would be here any minute and she certainly didn't want him to know she'd been talking to Jesse about Eileen.

In spite of her need to hurry, she sat back staring at the phone for a time, mulling over all that Jesse had said. Finally, she forced herself to get going.

"Poor Eileen," she murmured as she got dressed. Then, "Poor Frank!"

An hour later, Carol and Frank were in one of the light and airy dining rooms at Brennan's enjoying a sumptuous Creole brunch. Beyond the window they had a perfect view of the bubbling fountain in the courtyard. So far, Carol had managed to keep up an acceptably cheerful appearance. There was no way she was going to let Frank know what a bad feeling she had after talking to Jesse Calhoun—or even that she had called him.

When they'd arrived a short while earlier, the popular restaurant was already filled to capacity with Carnival tourists with a line waiting along Royal Street to get in. But once again, Frank had been recognized and immediately shown to a table. They lingered over their fancy poached eggs, broiled fish, and a sumptuous Carnival confection called king cake—sweet dough baked in the form of a wreath, topped with icing and purple, green, and gold sugar sprinkles.

Carol took a generous forkful of cake and popped it into her mouth, smiling at its warm, moist sweetness. Suddenly, she stopped chewing and grabbed for her napkin, a stricken look in her eyes.

"What's wrong, Carol? Are you choking?"

Frank half-rose and lifted his hand to slap her on the back, but Carol waved him off. A moment later, covering her mouth with her napkin, she extracted a tiny pink plastic doll.

"Ho, ho! You found the baby!" Frank exclaimed.

"I certainly did," Carol agreed, holding up the sticky little toy to inspect it more closely. "So, what's it doing in my piece of cake?"

"There's a baby in every king cake." His tone made it clear that Carol must be the only human being in all creation who didn't know that.

"Why?" she questioned.

Frank looked at her blankly. "Damned if I know!" Then he laughed. "This is New Orleans and it's Carnival time. You aren't supposed to ask why, you just go with the flow, darlin'. But since you found the baby, that means you throw the next party and buy the next king cake."

Carol opened her mouth to ask why again, but Frank cut her off. "Tradition!" he stated flatly.

"I think I'll name it Jane," Carol said, still examining the naked pink doll.

"You don't name king cake babies."

"I do," she answered. "Poor little Jane—yes, that's her name."

"I hate to ask this," Frank admitted. "But *why?*"

Carol grew serious suddenly. She gazed fixedly at Frank as if pleading for him to believe what she was about to say. "I told you that among the other strange manifestations of my psychic powers, I sometimes hear voices."

Frank nodded, encouraging her with his silence to go on.

"There's one in particular that has plagued me since I first had the nightmare about that Louisiana swamp. There's this pitiful little voice—a little child, a girl, I'm sure—and she's always calling for Cami, begging her to come back. I call the voice 'poor little Janie.' "

"That purely gives me the shivers, Carol."

"It shouldn't," she answered. "I'm convinced that a child named Jane has something to do with Cami and with that body the fisherman found."

"Then I'd say, from past experience, that you're probably right."

"I know I am," Carol answered softly, still fingering the tiny baby doll. "I only wish I understood the connection."

They both lapsed into meditative silence. After a time, Carol looked up at Frank, smiled brightly, and asked, "So, what do you have planned for today? More digging through old files? A boatride down to the old plantation site? Or perhaps a visit to the dock to see if you can get Choctaw's fingerprints?"

Frank laughed softly. "I doubt your ferryman has any fingerprints, so that would be a waste of time. As for digging . . . I'm not in the mood. What say we take the day off? Relax. It's Sunday. There'll be parades and all kinds of fun going on in the Quarter today. We might as well join in. How 'bout it?"

Carol sipped the last of her giant Bloody Mary and grinned at Frank. "That's a great idea! I've hardly seen anything of the city. But don't we need costumes if we're going to join in the festivities?"

"Yep, we sure do, but we can buy those tomorrow. We'll look around for some today. And I'll bet you need to buy something to wear to the ball, too."

Carol's eyes sparkled, remembering her lovely vintage gown. "That's all taken care of."

"Hey, you mean I'm not going to have to stand around in a ladies' shop for hours while you pick out something, then get it fitted? You're a wonderment, Carol Marlowe!"

"Just wait till you see this gown. It's—well, different."

"Not giving away any hints, eh?"

"Not a one. I want to surprise you." She gave him a sly smile.

"So, anything in particular you'd like to see, honey?"

Carol thought for only a moment before she asked, "Is the Orleans Ballroom still open?"

Frank nodded. "Open and thriving, but not for Quadroon Balls. After the War Between the States, it was purchased by the Sisters of the Holy Family as a convent and school. They moved out in 1964, and now it's a hotel—the Bourbon Orleans. The ballroom's been totally refurbished. It's supposed to be just like it was back in Cami and Vic's time."

266

"What luck! I'd love to see it, Frank."

"I guess we might as well check the place out since it seems we're both going there next Thursday."

After a short, pleasant stroll, they stood outside the impressive wall of French doors that opened from the hotel onto Orleans Street. Carol paused to read the historical marker on the building at number 717. It told briefly the same facts that Frank had given her back at Brennan's. Glancing up, she spied the white wooden balcony on the second floor just off the ballroom.

As Carol continued staring upward, the bright sun seemed to go behind a cloud. The boisterous Carnival sounds in the street faded with the sunlight. She heard music—harp music—and gay laughter tinkling on the still air. She blinked, then looked again. A tall man in evening costume and a beautiful, dark-haired young woman in a shining ball gown stood together on the balcony, sharing an intimate moment.

At first, Carol couldn't hear what they were saying. Then she saw the man slip his arms around the young woman's waist. She came hesitantly into his arms, as if she were a bit awed or possibly a little afraid. When his lips touched hers, Carol experienced the sensation of a phantom kiss. It lasted only an instant, then the man drew away.

"You needn't be shy with me," Carol heard him say. "I will take good care of you, *ma chère*. You will be loved—no, *adored*."

The words affected Carol as if the man had just stroked her intimately. A warm shiver coursed through her.

"You must speak with my aunt," the young woman answered shyly.

"But of course. She and I shall settle all the arrangements, if it is your wish."

"What of *your* wishes?" the Creole beauty said, obviously torn by her feelings.

Once more, he took her into his arms, bending over her, ready to kiss her again. "This very night, my little love, you will be mine, if I have my way."

Again, Carol felt his kiss as he sealed his pledge. She closed her eyes, savoring the sweetness of his lips on hers.

"Carol! Carol!"

Her eyes shot open. Frank was shouting her name, his face drawn and pale.

"It's all right, Frank. I was only . . ."

"You don't have to tell me what was happening. It was just like when you saw Mary Lincoln's necklace. You slipped away. God, you scare the hell out of me when do that! I hate your out-of-body experiences. Where were you this time?"

She pointed overhead. "Up there."

He gave her a hard look. "I don't get it. You mean in the ballroom?"

"No. I was on that balcony. I'm pretty sure I was Cami for a moment and that it was Black Vic who kissed me."

"Damn! Him again! Looks like he'd stay under wraps when I'm not back there. I don't like him fooling around with you when I'm not him."

Carol giggled. "Do you know how crazy that sounds?"

Frank's face was a thundercloud. "You still want to go inside?" he grumbled.

"Of course! More than ever."

"Well, all right. But he'd better be gone!"

Stepping through the doors into the hotel was like entering a grand French drawing room. Velvet drapes hushed the noise from outside. A grand piano played softly in the background, mingling its chords with the soft strains from Carol's phantom harp. She almost expected to see ladies in period costumes come gliding down the broad sweep of the stairway.

"The ballroom's up that way," Frank directed.

Carol drifted up the stairs, still not quite herself. In spite of Cami's earlier insistence that she meant to marry Black Vic, Carol could tell the young woman secretly feared what loving him might bring. She ached for Camille, aware now of her doubts and her total naivete about what it would mean to be kept by a man.

Carol's gaze took in the vivid colors of the portraits on the walls above the staircase, but no distinct features impressed themselves on her consciousness. Not until they entered the old ballroom did she feel totally aware of her surroundings once more.

"Oh, Frank!" she cried. "How elegant!"

She stood in the center of the room—a chamber much smaller than she had expected—staring up at the allegorical murals covering the ceiling. There was Neptune, surrounded by his bounty, the Old and New Worlds, the Muses, a soldier, and the banner of religion. Then she focused her gaze on the antique portraits around the walls. Fashionable ladies in their period gowns stared haughtily back.

Suddenly, Carol gasped and gripped Frank's

arm. "It's Cami!" she cried, hurrying toward one of the portraits. "Cami!"

"Are you sure?" Frank asked, skeptically eyeing the lovely, sad-eyed young woman inside the ornate gold frame.

"I know that face as well as I know my own."

Camille Mazaret was pictured seated at a golden harp, her dark tresses caught up in a cascade of curls in back. Her indigo eyes seemed alive in her perfect but unsmiling face. She wore a shimmering gown of violet brocade. And around her neck hung the gold doubloon.

As Carol stood staring at the portrait, transfixed, it almost seemed she could see Cami's delicately shaped fingers move on the strings. The harp music swelled until Carol could feel its vibrations in her heart. Unbidden tears spilled over her lashes.

"What's wrong, darlin'?" Frank asked gently.

"It's Cami. She's so sad. So terribly, irreparably heartbroken. Oh, Frank, I can feel her pain, her hopelessness." Carol was gasping suddenly. "Frank, I can't breathe!"

"Let's get out of here."

Without giving Carol a chance to argue, Frank took her hand and hurried back to the stairs. By the time they reached the lobby, she was sobbing. People turned to stare.

Out in the sunshine again, Frank put his arms around Carol, trying to comfort her.

"I'll be all right in a minute," she murmured tearfully. "For a moment in there I was Cami. I must have been. Otherwise, how could I have felt her pain so sharply?" She gazed up at Frank through thick, wet lashes. "Oh, Frank, if we don't go back

270

and help her, Cami is going to lead such a miserable life. She wants Black Vic. She *needs* him so desperately. Yet I have the feeling that she's terrified of him, too."

"With good cause, I'd say. My guess is it's Black Vic who put that sad expression on her face."

"I don't think Vic would ever cause Cami pain on purpose," Carol countered.

"I don't like this, Carol. I don't like what it's doing to you. If I'd known the mess I was getting you into, I'd never have called for your help."

Carol reached up and pulled Frank's cheek down to her own damp face. "Don't say that. Can't you see that I was meant to come here? And you were meant to bring me to New Orleans. If you hadn't called, Frank, then we might never have met . . . in this life."

He stared into her eyes, his own dark and somber. "You really believe that, don't you? That we're doing all this again."

"And *better*, I hope, than before."

Frank glanced about, nervous suddenly. "I wish we knew more about Victoine Navar. Carol, there's somewhere I need to go, if you're willing to come with me. I'm not brave enough to go back there alone."

In control of her emotions once more, Carol looked at Frank with concern. Certainly he was as brave a man as ever lived. She couldn't imagine anything that would shake his courage.

"Lead the way, Frank," Carol whispered. "I'm with you."

"Aren't you even curious about where I'm going to take you?"

"Of course, I am. Tell me . . ."

271

Chapter Twelve

Frank rubbed a hand over his mouth, embarrassed by his own idea. He shied away from Carol's curious gaze.

"I know it sounds crazy, but I can't seem to get Ivory's place out of my mind. I swear, Carol, it looked familiar. I remember that Black Vic said he knew the place. But it's not *his* memory that's bugging me. I think that house is still standing on Dumaine Street."

He glanced at Carol to see how she had reacted to his mention of Ivory. They'd had such a pleasant breakfast, he didn't want to get her riled again. He realized now that he shouldn't have teased her so much. To Frank's relief, the only emotion Carol's face belied was one of glowing curiosity.

"Let's go see if we can find it! Imagine, if it's still

there . . ." She rubbed her arms suddenly. "It gives me goosebumps thinking about it."

"Well, I'm not sure I'm as eager as you to find this place. But if I don't go, I'll keep wondering about it."

"You shouldn't be nervous about seeing it again, Frank. I don't understand."

"I'm not sure I do, either," he admitted. "It's hard to explain. I guess I haven't quite convinced myself that all this is real. If we walk over to Dumaine and find Ivory's house still standing, then I'll have to admit that I really did travel back in time and that I'll probably be forced to go back again."

"Was it such a terrible experience?"

He laughed and winked. "Only the part when you gave me hell for letting Ivory give me a hickey."

"Oh, you! Come on. Let's find it. I've never been in a house if ill repute." She cast Frank a playful glance. "Not in this life, anyway."

He scowled.

The going was slow since they had to fight their way through the crowds on Orleans and Royal Streets. But once they reached Dumaine, the battle was won in the blink of an eye. Ivory's house was easy to pick out from the others crowding the banquette. It was a different style of architecture— what was called a "raised colonial cottage." Frank immediately recognized the place by its West Indies flavor—the shuttered French doors, living quarters above the elevated basement level, and wide overhanging roof topped by twin dormers.

"Well, there it is, almost exactly as I remember it." Frank sighed, obviously regretting that he'd ever suggested this search.

"What a quaint place!" Carol exclaimed. She pointed to a small sign in the window. "And look, it's a museum now. Let's go in."

Carol headed straight for the stairs, but Frank hung back.

"What's wrong? Come on," she urged.

"I don't know if I want to go back in there, Carol. It gives me the willies just looking at it from out here. What if I step inside and nothing's changed and I'm suddenly Black Vic again?"

"Oh, Frank, don't be silly! It doesn't happen that way," Carol assured him. "I want to see where this fabulous Ivory lived. And you need to see if it's the way you remember."

Finally, resigned if not happy, Frank followed Carol up the stairs. Everything he'd seen and done here before flashed through his memory. He half-expected Ivory herself to answer their knock.

Instead, a frail woman in period costume met them when they entered. Her white hair hung down about her shoulders, reminding Frank of Ivory's pale tresses. Her ice-blue eyes seemed familiar as well. Frank did a double take, then realized there was no way she could be Ivory as an old lady. He was merely allowing his imagination to run wild.

"Welcome," the elderly curator said. "I am so pleased to have guests this morning."

At the same time that she called them "guests," her eyes shifted to a basket on the marble-topped hall table with its small calligraphy sign indicating that "donations" were six dollars per person. Frank quickly fished out his wallet and deposited the required number of bills.

"My name is Madame Yvette. Welcome to my home," the woman said politely. "Would you like

274

me to tell you the history of my little cottage or would you prefer to look about for yourselves?"

"Oh, please, tell us the history," Carol begged.

Yvette smiled at her. Frank was nervous and fidgety. The present mistress of Ivory's house seemed set on ignoring his seeming disinterest.

"The original house was begun around 1730, but not finished for nearly fifty years," the woman began. "It is believed that a Spanish pirate from Barataria by the name of Zeringue contracted with a famous architect to build a beautiful cottage for his bride. Unfortunately, as the legend has been handed down, she died of a fever on the very eve of their marriage. Her fiancé went mad with grief. First, he tried to burn the house down, but heavy rains put out the blaze so that it was only partially destroyed. Tormented, the man, who had sworn to give up his wild life once he married went on a rampage after his lover's death, murdering twenty innocent people before he was finally captured and hanged."

Carol shuddered. "How terrible! I hope the next occupant had a happier life."

The elderly lady patted Carol's hand sympathetically. "If you want happy tales, my dear, I'm afraid *Maison d'Ivoire* is not the place you should have come."

"The House of Ivory," Frank translated. For the first time, their tour guide seemed to have captured his undivided attention.

"Yes." Madame Yvette flashed a grateful smile. "The name of Ivory has been linked with this house for many years. She was a great lady, so they say. But, I get ahead of the story."

"What happened to Ivory?" Frank queried.

"Please, sir," the woman said reproachfully. "The story must be told chronologically. I will tell you of Ivory, all in good time."

"Do go on," Carol insisted, with a warning glance at Frank.

"Let's see. Where was I? Oh, yes. After the fire, the house was thought to be haunted. Some believed that the ghost of the pirate's bride roamed the unfinished corridors on stormy nights. Others said the pirate himself returned, searching for the woman he loved. People heard things here—moaning, crying—and saw lights at the windows on dark nights. Whoever the ghosts were, everyone agreed that this house was cursed with restless, unhappy spirits." She leaned closer to them, glanced about, then whispered. "As well it may be, my dears. There was at least one murder within these very walls."

Frank felt the hair rise on the back of his neck. They were still standing in the entryway, but just down the hall on the left was the room where Hector Lazano had died.

"Are you sure it was murder?" Frank asked in a rather surly tone. "Maybe the guy fell on his own knife."

The old woman sniffed indignantly at being interrupted and at having her facts disputed. "On what authority do you base this assumption, sir?"

Frank was about to say that he'd been there and witnessed the whole thing and the bastard deserved to die anyway, when Carol nudged him in the ribs. Although he was anxious to carry the argument further, he kept quiet.

"But again, I'm getting ahead of the tale," said Yvette. "The ruined cottage was at last purchased

276

by a French sea captain, Jean Claude Blanchet, in 1779. He had the place completely rebuilt, adding many of his own distinctive touches—the marble fireplaces, the crystal chandelier in the front parlor, the twin mirrors you see on either side of the hall, all brought from Europe aboard his own ship."

"And this captain, he lived happily with his wife and family here for many years?" Carol asked hopefully.

The woman's smile rapidly faded. She shook her head. "Alas, no, my dear. The captain drowned at sea in a storm. His wife and six children all died in a yellow fever epidemic."

Carol sighed, but Frank leaned closer, all attention now. Surely the woman was about to arrive at Ivory and her story.

"The house stood vacant until 1835. No one wanted to live here, afraid the very walls still carried the taint of Bronze John—what they called the fever in the old days, you know."

"Then Ivory . . . she bought it. Right?" Frank stammered excitedly.

"Yes." Yvette uttered a sigh and inclined her head toward Frank. "You are partially correct, sir. But Ivory herself did not purchase the property. She arrived in New Orleans penniless, alone, and *with child*." Madame whispered the last two words, and when she spoke of that long-ago shame, bright spots of color appeared on her wrinkled cheeks. "With nowhere to go, no one to turn to, Ivory was at the mercy of fate."

"Aren't we all?" Carol murmured to herself.

"How'd she get the house, then?" Frank asked impatiently.

"Please, sir!" their guide replied. "Any tale worth the telling deserves to be told properly."

"By all means, continue, ma'am," Frank replied with forced courtesy.

"Poor Ivory!" Madame Yvette sighed dramatically. "Cast out by her own family, deserted by the man she thought to wed, alone in a strange and wicked city. Can we blame her for what she did?"

"What did she do, dammit?"

"Frank!" Carol hissed, gripping his arm. "Just listen, won't you?"

Their thoroughly annoyed guide shot Frank a hostile glance, then said to Carol, "Thank you, my dear. Now, if I may continue?" She stared at Frank pointedly.

"I'm sorry, ma'am," he mumbled.

"Ivory met a man!" The woman emphasized each word. "Of course, he knew that she was to give birth to another's child imminently. Still, he placed her under his questionable protection. He purchased this cottage, sent one of his own servants to care for her . . ."

"Yes, Tessa." Once again, Frank interrupted and was forced to endure glares from both Carol and the storyteller, but this time Madame Yvette's stern look was mingled with curiosity.

"Have you been here before?" she asked.

Frank cleared his throat. "Yes, but it was quite a while ago."

"Well, I hope I'm not boring you, sir."

"Not at all," he said eagerly. "Please, continue."

"Ivory's daughter was born a short time after she moved in. I'm sure she was relieved and happy to have her baby and a roof over its little head. Truly, life must have seemed nearly perfect for Ivory on the day she gave birth. But happiness was ever a fleeting emotion for poor Ivory. You see, the moment the infant was born, she was taken from her mother's arms by the man who had promised to take care of them both. He placed the child with nuns to be raised. Ivory was allowed to visit her daughter, but they could never be together for more than a few hours at a time. It was a sad arrangement for both of them. Still, the child was well cared for and grew up to be a beautiful girl."

"Pardon me, ma'am," Frank said hesitantly. "But you were telling us about Ivory. We must hear the tale chronologically. Remember?"

She smiled sweetly. "Of course. Ivory. Poor, dear Ivory! The man who had seemed so kind when they first met, used her cruelly after the child was born. He allowed her to stay on in the cottage, but only as long as she would entertain for him."

Carol frowned. Madame Yvette was obviously trying to treat a disturbing topic with delicacy. But she was being delicate to the point of becoming obtuse. "Entertain? I'm not sure I understand."

"Come on, Carol," Frank groaned. "The guy was a pimp!"

"One might say that," Yvette answered, raising a delicately arched brow. "This man visited Ivory regularly to collect any monies she had received for her . . . ah, entertaining."

"And this man's name was Hector Lazano, right?" Frank blurted.

Yvette stared at him blankly. "Why, no! I've never heard of anyone named Lazano in Ivory's story. Legends tell us that her *pimp*, as you so blatantly put it, sir, was a scoundrel called Black Vic, who had a heart as dark as his name."

"That's a lie!" Frank all but yelled the words at poor Madame.

Carol dug her fingers into Frank's arm to shut him up. In a minute, he'd be revealing everything about Vic and Cami and Ivory and Choctaw. Madame Yvette would no doubt call the authorities and Frank would end up in a rubber room somewhere.

"Frank, *please!*" Carol urged in a whisper.

"Well, it's not true and I can prove it."

"Would you like to tell me *how?*" Carol demanded, still whispering. "You had better watch what you say."

Madame Yvette, obviously hard of hearing anyway, tilted her head to try and catch some of the whispered discussion between her two customers. But the look of consternation on the old woman's face told Carol that Yvette hadn't heard enough to make any sense of their conversation.

"If you will please follow me now," their guide urged.

Madame Yvette went as far as the doorway to the parlor and stopped abruptly. She pointed one arthritic finger down at the floor. "*There!*" she said in a deep, dramatic voice. "That dark stain on the floorboards is the very spot where the murder victim fell. His blood seeped into the wood to mark the place forevermore."

"You're right about the spot," Frank blurted out, "but dead wrong about it being murder."

Yvette turned and glared at him, sniffing indignantly as she raised her chin higher. "And would you like to tell me, sir, exactly how you know that?"

"Ouch! Because I'm a police detective," he said in reply as Carol pinched his arm.

Refusing to argue with Frank, Madame turned her back on him and walked into the parlor toward the fireplace. She reached up to the mantel and stroked a fancifully painted figurine.

"This is an interesting piece," she went on. "It's called a Chelsea cat. Sailors often brought them home to their sweethearts. We believe this one was a gift from Captain Blanchet to his wife."

"Wrong again!" Frank stated bluntly.

Carol fully expected Madame Yvette to eject them from her premises at that point—six dollar donations or no.

"Well, perhaps you would like to tell me about this cat," Madame said to Frank, her sugary tone overlaid with sarcasm.

"That was a gift from a sailor, all right, but it never belonged to the Blanchets. It was Ivory's." Frank went over to the mantel and picked up the fragile antique cat, bringing a gasp from Madame. There were calligraphy cards everywhere, reading: "Please do not touch!"

"See?" Frank said, ignoring Madame's fierce gaze. "Two sets of eyes—green on one side, red on the other. This cat sat in the window, right over there." He pointed to the place. "If Ivory was open for business, the green eyes were turned to the street. Red eyes forward meant stop—don't knock."

"Well, I never!" Madame Yvette cried. "I have been showing my home for nearly thirty years, but no one has ever been as rude as you, young man. I believe this is the end of the tour. You may retrieve your donation from the basket on your way out."

"Oh, please, Madame Yvette," Carol begged. "You must forgive him."

"For what?" Frank demanded. "For correcting the fallacies in her tale? Seems to me she'd be grateful. This is the way history gets written all wrong, by people not telling it right. Ivory was a nice lady! And if her story's going to be told, it ought to be told accurately."

Tears were brimming in Madame Yvette's eyes. She reached out a trembling hand to touch Frank's sleeve. "Why, sir, you come gallantly to my great-grandmother's defense as if you knew her personally."

"Your great-grandmother?" Frank stared at Yvette, his mouth agape.

She patted his arm. "Yes. You are a kind man. Forgive me for being sharp with you. I'm afraid we lose patience as we grow older."

Frank stared down at the withered hand on his arm. His eyes went wide when he noticed the ring for the first time. "Where did you get that, Madame Yvette?"

She held up the slender gold band for both Carol and Frank to inspect. Its single ruby caught the light and flashed blood-red. Carol murmured over the delicate piece of antique jewelry.

"It was hers—Ivory's," Yvette explained. "She told my grandmother, who told my mother, who told me that it was given to her by the only man she ever truly loved, my great-grandfather."

Frank was about to argue again, knowing that Black Vic had given Ivory the ring or at least insisted that she keep it after Lazano's death. Then another thought struck him. Instead, he said, "So,

Ivory finally married the man who fathered her daughter? What did he do, come to New Orleans to find her?"

Yvette shook her head. "Oh, no! That first child died as a young woman. So far as I know, Ivory never saw the girl's father after her parents drove her from their home. Ivory never married, but in her diary she recorded the name of my great-grandfather—his last name, at least. She lamented that though she had loved him from afar for many years, she had spent but one afternoon with him. Then he departed from her life forever."

"Oh, no! How sad!" Carol cried. "You mean, he died, too?"

Again, Madame shook her head. "He remained in and around New Orleans for many more years. But Ivory recorded in her journal that once they had been together, she sent him away to find someone he could love as she loved him. She wrote that she had seen a vision of him with a lovely, dark-haired woman. He never knew that he gave Ivory a daughter. Where he went to find that ebony-haired love or if he ever found her, we can only guess."

As Yvette's words sank in, Frank felt a chill. The old woman standing before him was his own—or rather Black Vic's—flesh and blood.

Frank pressed Yvette's hand for a moment. "Thank you," he said solemnly. Then he caught Carol's arm and said, "Let's go."

"Oh, must you leave so soon?" Madame asked. "Don't you want to see Ivory's lovely bedchamber?"

"I've seen it already," Frank told her, turning quickly toward the door.

"Will you come back sometime so I might finish the tour? There'll be no charge."

"Perhaps," he answered in a whisper, "perhaps, Yvette Navar."

Outside on the banquette, Carol turned on Frank. "Why did we have to rush out of there? I wanted to see the rest."

"Carol, don't you understand?" He was trembling all over as he gripped her hand. "Black Vic was Yvette's great-grandfather. Ivory herself told me— him—that he should go find someone to love. We both know where Vic went."

"The Orleans Ballroom," they said in unison.

"Then why does Madame Yvette believe that Black Vic was the man who treated Ivory so badly?" Carol queried.

"Because the story's been handed down and changed for generations. Madame said that Ivory recorded only the last name in her diary. No one nowadays knows that Black Vic and this lover named Navar are even the same guy. Poor ole Vic! History's sure given him a bum rap."

"Why, Frank! That's the first kind word I've heard you say about Victoine Navar."

"Well, maybe he wasn't such a hard case after all. Who knows?" He looked down at her, his face solemn. "But he'd better keep his nose clean when he's around Cami. I mean it! I'm not going to put up with any funny business."

Carol laughed. "If you could hear yourself . . ."

Frank took Carol's hand and led her back toward Bourbon Street, where most of the Carnival action was taking place.

"So, when do we do it?" Frank asked suddenly.

"Do what?"

"Go to this ball." Then he stopped and frowned down at Carol. "Or has it already taken place without us? You said you saw Vic and Cami on the balcony of the ballroom. Maybe they couldn't wait for us to get back there."

"No, no," Carol assured him. "I think that was sort of like a preview at the movies or a teaser in the front of a novel. I got a glimpse, but there's a lot more to come."

"When?"

"I'm not sure. We could try going to the dock in the morning, but I haven't seen the woman in the red tignon. I have a feeling she won't show herself again until Carnival is over."

Eager to be on with it, Frank turned to Carol with an impatient sigh. "Now just how do you know that?"

Carol laughed. "I'm psychic! Remember?"

"How could I forget?" Frank groaned.

For the next two hours, Carol and Frank rambled around the Quarter. The whole area was one huge party. Every bar on Bourbon Street was overflowing with merrymakers. Dancing in the streets seemed the thing to do. At Jackson Square a band was blaring Beatles tunes. "Help!" wailed through the air, echoing off the façade of St. Louis Cathedral, then bouncing back and forth between the Pontalba buildings. The whole area in front of the Cabildo was crowded with gyrating bodies in all manner of dress and undress.

One of the musicians recognized Frank. "Hey,

Cap'n!" he called, waving frantically. "Get down, man!"

Frank threw back his head and laughed, then caught Carol's hand and swung her into a Sixties-style bop.

Carol beamed as she watched the subdued sway of Frank's torso. This man, who exuded sensuality from every pore as it was, set off a sexual sonic boom when he moved to music. Warming to a fever pitch, Carol followed him bump for grind.

"Hey, I didn't know cops danced," she said over the blare of the music.

"Cops do a lot of things, darlin'." He gave her an inviting half-smile and a wink. "Stick around. You'll see."

Just then, the band slowed its pace to a brassy rendition of "Yesterday." Frank whirled Carol into a close embrace. She sighed and slipped both her arms up around his neck. They snuggled into a cozy body-hug, oblivious to the rowdy crowd all around them. Carol could feel the heat rising between them. She sighed again.

"A doubloon for your thoughts," Frank whispered.

"I was just thinking how nice this is and wishing that we could go on like this forever. No mysterious mummy . . . no ghosts from the past . . . no lonely cabin on a mountaintop that I have to go back to."

"I thought you loved your solitude."

"I do when life has nothing better to offer."

Frank smiled. "Thanks," he said. "It's good to hear that I'm better than nothing."

"Oh, you!" Carol reached up and nipped at his lips. "You're a lot better than anything I've ever had in my life. I could go on dancing like this until . . ."

"Until what?"

Carol shrugged in his arms. "I don't know. I just could." She looked up at him, her eyes growing misty. "Frank, I don't want it to end. What's happening to me? I've never felt this way before."

"It's Carnival," he answered softly. "It does strange things to people. The glow will fade once Mardi Gras is over."

Carol shook her head. "No," she said solemnly. "This glow will never fade, and it has nothing to do with Mardi Gras."

They danced on in silence, a slow, graceful caress of tingling flesh, of twining arms, of joined bodies.

For a long time the rest of the world was simply a colorful blur around them. Then something crashed through that euphoric barrier. Carol's eyes were still half-closed when she saw it. She froze in Frank's arms. Her head jerked off his shoulder. Eyes wide, she tried to spot it again, but the ever-shifting dancers pressing in all around them blocked her view. It was gone as quickly as she had seen it.

"What's wrong?" Frank asked.

"Ah-h-h," she stammered, trying to think up a suitable fib. She certainly couldn't tell him what she'd seen or that she was suddenly terrified because she knew his life was in danger. "This is embarrassing, Frank, but I *have* to find a john. *Fast!*"

Convinced by the feigned urgency in her tone, he glanced about. "We could try one of the restaurants over there. You may have a wait, though, with this crowd."

"Let's just head back for the hotel. That would be quicker."

They turned toward the Dalpeche, setting off at a near-trot.

Carol had thought up the perfect white lie. If she had insisted on returning to her room for any other reason, Frank would undoubtedly have come in with her. Short of slamming the door in his face, there would have been no way to keep him out. But he simply left her at the door and asked her to give him a call when she was ready to go out again.

"Sure, Frank," she answered, taking a few hurried steps toward her bathroom.

The minute he closed the door, she headed straight for the phone. She dialed Jesse Calhoun.

"Thank God I caught you," Carol said as soon as he answered.

"What's up, honey? You sound—I don't know—strange."

She felt strange all right—confused, nervous, just plain scared. "Jesse, I think you'd better check your reports on the latest whereabouts of Oliver Percy Jones."

"Slow down, Carol. What do you mean?"

"I mean, I think I just bumped into him at Jackson Square. Frank and I were there in the Carnival mob just a few minutes ago. I looked up and suddenly I saw it—that tattoo, big as life, only a few feet away from us."

"Maybe it wasn't Jones. There could be lots of those tattoos. What did the guy look like, Carol?"

"I didn't see him, Jesse. All I saw was that hairy arm and that awful picture."

"Come on, kid! How could you see the arm, but not the man?"

MORE PASSION AND ADVENTURE AWAIT... YOUR TRIP TO A BIG ADVENTUROUS WORLD BEGINS WHEN YOU ACCEPT YOUR FIRST 4 NOVELS ABSOLUTELY *FREE* (AN $18.00 VALUE)

Accept your Free gift and start to experience more of the passion and adventure you like in a historical romance novel. Each Zebra novel is filled with proud men, spirited women and tempestuous love that you'll remember long after you turn the last page.

Zebra Historical Romances are the finest novels of their kind. They are written by authors who really know how to weave tales of romance and adventure in the historical settings you love. You'll feel like you've actually gone back in time with the thrilling stories that each Zebra novel offers.

GET YOUR FREE GIFT WITH THE START OF YOUR HOME SUBSCRIPTION

Our readers tell us that these books sell out very fast in book stores and often they miss the newest titles. So Zebra has made arrangements for you to receive the four newest novels published each month.

You'll be guaranteed that you'll never miss a title, and home delivery is so convenient. And to show you just how easy it is to get Zebra Historical Romances, we'll send you your first 4 books absolutely FREE! Our gift to you just for trying our home subscription service.

BIG SAVINGS AND FREE HOME DELIVERY

Each month, you'll receive the four newest titles as soon as they are published. You'll probably receive them even before the bookstores do. What's more, you may preview these exciting novels free for 10 days. If you like them as much as we think you will, just pay the low preferred subscriber's price of just $3.75 each. *You'll save $3.00 each month off the publisher's price.* AND, your savings are even greater because there are never any shipping, handling or other hidden charges—FREE Home Delivery. Of course you can return any shipment within 10 days for full credit, no questions asked. There is no minimum number of books you must buy.

4 FREE BOOKS

TO GET YOUR 4 FREE BOOKS WORTH $18.00 — MAIL IN THE FREE BOOK CERTIFICATE T O D A Y

Fill in the Free Book Certificate below, and we'll send your FREE BOOKS to you as soon as we receive it.

If the certificate is missing below, write to: Zebra Home Subscription Service, Inc., P.O. Box 5214, 120 Brighton Road, Clifton, New Jersey 07015-5214.

FREE BOOK CERTIFICATE

4 FREE BOOKS

ZEBRA HOME SUBSCRIPTION SERVICE, INC.

YES! Please start my subscription to Zebra Historical Romances and send me my first 4 books absolutely FREE. I understand that each month I may preview four new Zebra Historical Romances free for 10 days. If I'm not satisfied with them, I may return the four books within 10 days and owe nothing. Otherwise, I will pay the low preferred subscriber's price of just $3.75 each; a total of $15.00, *a savings off the publisher's price of $3.00.* I may return any shipment and I may cancel this subscription at any time. There is no obligation to buy any shipment and there are no shipping, handling or other hidden charges. Regardless of what I decide, the four free books are mine to keep.

NAME

ADDRESS _____ APT

CITY _____ STATE _____ ZIP

TELEPHONE ( )

SIGNATURE _____ (if under 18, parent or guardian must sign)

Terms, offer and prices subject to change without notice. Subscription subject to acceptance by Zebra Books. Zebra Books reserves the right to reject any order or cancel any subscription.

"Easy! It's Carnival time, Jesse. Have you ever been down here for Mardi Gras?"

"Okay, okay! I get the picture. I'll check again and call you right back. You're at your hotel?"

"Yes. And, Jesse, Frank doesn't know anything about this. He's not here right now, but he's liable to pop in at any moment. So, if I call you Aunt Belle or something when I pick up, I'm not crazy, just covering. Okay?"

"Gotcha, Carol!"

Carol hung up and sat for a moment staring at the phone. Five minutes ticked by. Her nerves went from ragged to raw. She stood up and paced the length of the bedroom and back, never taking her eyes off the phone.

"This can't be happening," she told herself, "but it is. I *know* what I saw."

The phone rang. She nearly took a nosedive in her haste to answer it.

"Carol?" It was Frank's voice. "Are you all right now?"

Frantic to free the line, she snapped, "Give me a few more minutes, won't you? I'll call you."

She slammed the receiver down, not even allowing Frank to say goodbye.

More pacing, more hand-wringing, more ticking of the clock. *Finally*, the phone rang again.

"Jesse?" Carol cried instead of saying hello.

"Yeah, Carol. It's me." He cleared his throat, seeming nervous. Then he gave a low whistle through his teeth before telling her what he'd discovered. "I'm afraid you may be onto something. Jones escaped from the Louisiana State Pen three days ago. It makes sense that he'd run to New Orleans to hide out in the Mardi Gras mobs. There's an All Points Bulletin out on him, but you're the first to spot him. Of course, I'll pass that information on to the authorities down there."

"Oh, Jesse! Do you have to?"

"Of course I do. This guy's dangerous, Carol, a mass murderer."

"I know, I know. I'm just so scared he's after Frank."

"All the more reason to get him back behind bars as quickly as possible."

"You're right, Jesse. I'm not thinking too straight at the moment. But when you report this, do you have to use my name? Can't you just tell them that someone reported this anonymously?"

There was a long pause on Jesse's end of the line while he thought it over. "Yeah, I guess I could do that. I'm not sure I understand why you want to stay out of it. You know Frank's going to find out the guy's on the loose, if he doesn't know already."

"I just don't want *my* name connected with this right now."

"But what difference could that make?"

"Don't you get it, Jesse? Frank and I have a good thing going. In fact, it's so damn good that I don't want it messed up. I saw something the other day— something scary."

"What?"

"It was sort of a vision, and it had to do with Eileen Longpre. The day she disappeared, I'm pretty sure."

"Good God!"

"And I think this Jones is the fellow who murdered her."

"*Murdered?* Carol, nobody's ever found her body.

For all we know, she could have decided to run off to South America or been picked up by a UFO. Do you realize how many people just vanish into thin air every year?"

"I don't think that's the case here. I'm convinced Eileen died a horrible death at the hands of that man with the tattoo. If I'm right, and if Frank ever finds out, he'll never be the same. He would blame himself forevermore. We might as well let Jones kill Frank. It couldn't be any more painful than his finding out the truth about Eileen."

"Jesus! What a mess! But you're right. Frank's been on the edge for years. If your vision was accurate, the news could send him right off the deep end."

"Then you'll keep my name out of it?"

"Only if you promise to call me the minute you see anything else, Carol."

"You have my word on that. I'd better go now. Frank's waiting for me."

"Hey, Carol, you two be mighty damn careful."

"Right."

Frank knocked at Carol's door just as she hung up.

"Coming," she called after taking a moment to regain her composure.

When she opened the door, Frank stepped inside and took her in his arms. "Let's see, where did we leave off?" he murmured, nuzzling her neck as he danced her slowly into the bedroom.

"Please, Frank. We can't dance here."

"Why?" he demanded. "Not enough people watching? If that's the case, then I'll take you right back to Jackson Square, darlin'."

His mention of returning to the spot where she'd seen Jones froze her blood. She wanted to lock her door and keep Frank inside until that creep was back on death row where he belonged. But she knew that was impossible.

Still, for tonight she could keep him here. That thought gave her a moment of calm, but only a moment. Tomorrow Frank would expect to mix and mingle with the Carnival crowds all day. And somewhere in that milling throng of thousands, a crazed killer was waiting to end Frank's life.

Keep him here! Keep him safe! The two thoughts kept running through Carol's mind. She slipped her arms around Frank's neck, went up on tiptoe, and pressed her lips to his.

"If we stay here instead of going back to Jackson Square, I know what we could do," she whispered, coaxing him toward the bed.

"I thought you wanted to go see Gerald McRaney in the Bacchus parade. If you smiled pretty and yelled real loud, he'd probably throw you a go-cup, doubloons, cards—all kinds of goodies."

"All the goodies I need are right here," Carol purred.

Frank needed little encouragement. In moments, they were undressed, lying on the bed in a hot tangle, their need as sweet and urgent as ever.

The afternoon sun sank low, turning the room from gold and scarlet to bronze, then velvety-purple. Not until darkness closed in did the two of them drift off in a wonderful, satisfied haze—Carol to her place back in time, and Frank to his.

They traveled together this time.

Chapter Thirteen

The oppressive heat was the first change Carol noticed—that and the sticky humidity as if someone had suddenly thrown open all the windows to the night air. Then there was the cloying mixture of odors. The sweet scent of French perfumes fought to overcome the less pleasant aromas of cigar smoke and perspiring bodies. Her own among them, she quickly realized as a bead of moisture trickled down between her breasts.

Only a moment before, Carol had been lying in Frank's arms, her eyes closed, her senses tingling. She'd been more than half-asleep. When she opened her eyes, she found a totally different scene. In that split second, everything had changed. Her own identity had vanished. She felt strange, drugged, not sure where she was.

Then, in a flash, she knew—*The Orleans Ballroom!*

She glanced about. A dozen or so young women—all lovely, all gowned in virginal white—sat about the room on dainty gilt chairs. Beside each of the debutantes hovered an older woman, all darting eagle-eyes assessing the possibilities and the competition. These mature ladies seemed to fade into the wallpaper, however, as Cami concentrated on the graceful, snowy-gowned beauties—her rivals.

A more winsome gathering she had never encountered. They put the Louisiana planters' daughters to shame. But then, she mused, most of these young ladies had been fathered by those very Creole gentlemen. The taint of their mothers' blood, however, added a touch of the exotic that was lacking in the blue-blooded belles she knew.

Cami wasn't sure what she had expected of these free women of color, but to the last one they were beauties, their flawless complexions ranging from pale ivory to golden-cream. Some flashed dark glances, but others had eyes as blue as her own or the subtle amber shade of Fiona's. Some had hair as dark as hers; others were redheads or even blondes. They held themselves like queens, and wore their silks, satins, plumes, and jewels as if they had been born to European royalty.

The ballroom provided a perfect setting for these exquisite young women. The long, lofty-ceilinged chamber was a wonder with its fantastical murals, crystal chadeliers, costly paintings, and polished dance floor of oak over three thicknesses of cypress. The prospective *placées*, Cami mused, looked like an expensive collection of china dolls arranged perfectly in a lavishly ornate display case.

Even as Cami gazed about her, awestruck, the first group of men arrived from the card rooms below. Her pleasant thoughts turned to sudden anxiety as she felt the men's eyes playing over her.

"Smile, *ma chère*," Cami heard Fiona command under her breath. "One of the gentlemen will come this way any moment. He will no doubt ask my permission to dance with you. Remember, though, you are to pretend you hear nothing that he says. You must appear to see right through him. Should you look at him directly, such forwardness could be construed as flirting. An unpardonable sin!"

Flirting was the last thing on Cami's mind. She only prayed she didn't look as awkward and uncomfortable as she felt. She had so looked forward to this evening. Now suddenly it took on the aspect of the purest form of torture. The full weight of her actions had finally sunk in. By merely being in this place, at this ball, she was announcing to one and all that she was fully willing and capable of handling men and sex and any situation that might arise accordingly—be it marriage or, more likely, an unsanctioned liaison. She had also—simply by coming here—ruined any chance of entering into a more orthodox relationship.

Fiona noted Cami's sudden attack of nerves. She thought this a good sign. After all, a young woman should never be too sure of her charms. The very fact that Camille was having second thoughts meant that she would behave in a properly cautious manner.

She eyed her lovely young charge, who was gowned in a gorgeous confection of silver and white tissue silk with a beau-catcher of fragrant, waxy lime blossoms nestled at her bosom and gardenias in her sweeping cascade of night-black hair. Camille looked like a fairy princess, and, suddenly, Fiona felt like a wicked witch for bringing her lover's innocent daughter into this sordid world of the Orleans Ballroom. Edouard would never have approved.

Fiona sighed, but said nothing. It was too late now.

A tall figure started toward them. "Put on your prettiest face, Camille," Fiona whispered.

Cami's pretty face ached from smiling when she felt more like sobbing. Inside, her heart fluttered like a frightened dove, but she did her best to follow Fiona's instructions.

"Good, Cami, good!" Fiona murmured. "You look properly demure."

Her eyes cast down, Cami glanced up through her lashes to steal a peek at the imposing stranger coming toward them. Her breath caught. Her heart picked up speed. He was tall and bold, dressed all in black except for his ruffled white shirt and the gold embroidery gleaming on his vest. Most of all, however, she was struck by the dark gleam of his eyes and the livid scar across his right cheek.

Victoine Navar! Cami thanked her stars that she was expected to remain silent. She could not have found her voice with Black Vic so close at last.

"M'sieur Navar, this is an unexpected pleasure." Fiona's cool tone belied her words. Cami felt the woman stiffen.

He swept a low bow, his gaze remaining on Cami although he spoke directly to Fiona. "Madame, the pleasure is mine entirely. Might I beg an introduction to this lovely young lady?"

Fiona turned to stare at Cami, as if trying to make up her mind what she should do. To give herself more time, Fiona fluttered her fan and her eyelashes in unison while she glanced wildly about the room.

"I suppose a simple introduction will do no harm," she said at length.

Cami mumbled her way through the formalities with Victoine Navar. All through their small talk, she could feel Black Vic's smoldering eyes on her—eying her charms, scheming, planning her seduction, she surmised. The thoughts brought a hot flush to her face and shoulders and even more heat beneath her shimmering gown.

"Might I be permitted a dance with Mademoiselle Cami?" Vic asked at length.

Fiona gave him no answer. Instead, she beckoned Vic to accompany her to the balcony for a breath of fresh air. He followed, as silent as she.

Frank smelled the hot, humid air before he felt it. He opened his eyes, fully expecting what he found—Carol gone, himself in another time and place. His last conscious thought as Frank Longpre was: *Where the hell has Carol gone now?*

Vic stood on the tiny balcony staring down at Fiona. Her smile had vanished. He guessed what she had on her mind and he was absolutely correct.

"It is most kind of you to ask Cami to dance, but you are a married man as I recall. My niece is here to secure a protector. She is little more than a frightened child and I could see that the very sight of you terrified her, as well it should. Why not leave the poor girl in peace, Victoine? There are many other beautiful women here tonight."

"I wish to dance with Cami, Fiona. You know I'll treat her gently." He smiled down at the lovely woman in her bright silks and red tignon. "She seems as sweet as she is beautiful."

"Beauty is as beauty does," Fiona snapped, changing her tactics, frantic now to protect Camille. "You'll find her quite awkward, I fear. She may look the part of a woman, but she's extremely immature for her age."

"All the better for molding into a proper lady," Vic said with a stubborn smile.

Fiona hesitated. "I shouldn't allow this."

"One dance is all I ask." He waited, but received no answer. "Please, Fiona, for the sake of our friendship. I'd never harm the girl."

"Oh, very well," Fiona conceded. "Dance with her, and do be kind even if she bores you."

Black Vic had no fear of being bored. Impatient to claim his charming partner, he bolted through the door, back into the ballroom. He was thunderstruck by the girl, but dared not let Fiona know that.

"Mademoiselle, your aunt has given her permission." Vic offered Cami a low bow, then a winning smile. "May I have this dance?"

Panic-stricken when faced with this man she had admired for so long, Cami could find no words as her heart raced in her breast. She glanced toward the door. Fiona entered, unsmiling, but nodded her approval.

"*Oui, m'sieur,*" Cami murmured, trembling inside with a mixture of terror and excitement.

She all but swooned when Black Vic took her

hand. At close range, he was even more handsome, so manly. Just looking at him made her want to turn and flee for fear of what she might say or do. His slightest touch electrified her. His low, husky voice caressed her. His power and grace as he led her confidently through each step of the dance made her feel totally dependent, a virtual captive of his masculine spell. But the more entranced she became, the harder she fought the attraction. She was determined not to let Vic know how he had mesmerized her. *No man* should be allowed to do this to her!

Although permission for one dance was all that Fiona had given, Vic refused to give up his claim on Cami, monopolizing her for the entire evening. More than simply a beautiful young woman, she became his ultimate challenge. He could feel her holding herself aloof. She seemed all ice, yet the cooler her attitude, the more fascinated Vic became.

Cami, meanwhile, found it more difficult by the minute to keep her icy distance. Black Vic, no matter what her Cousin Morris had said, was a true gentleman—polite, charismatic, even gentle. And there was no doubting his maleness, through and through. The harder he tried to make her relax and enjoy his company, the more she worried over all the things he was making her feel, all the things he was making her long for. Fiona had told her of men and love and the shocking things that went on behind closed bedroom doors. And when she thought of Black Vic doing those very things to her, she shuddered inside with horror, but with a delicious sense of anticipation, too.

As the evening wore on, Cami became increasingly aware of Black Vic's amorous intentions. His loving attack began slowly, slyly. A bit more pressure on her gloved fingers, a casual touch to her cheek, a whispered endearment now and again. Then, during one intermission, he launched a direct assault. He enticed her out onto the balcony with a promise of a cool breeze off the river. It was there, on the second story balcony overhanging Orleans Street, that Victoine Navar made his bold move.

At first, Cami had no idea what he meant to do. He sidled closer—so close she could feel his warm breath on her face. When his hand slipped around her waist, she caught her breath, frozen with fearful uncertainty. Granted, they had touched while they danced, but this was far different. This time they were alone and there was no music to use as an excuse for his casual intimacy. She held rigidly still as she felt his arm surround her. Very gently, he forced her to turn toward him. He said nothing. He only stared down at her—his face solemn, almost tense, and his dark eyes gleaming with an unsettling emotion.

Cami moved hesitantly. What did he expect of her? Fiona had given her no warning that this might happen. When he brought her closer still, his hot breath kissed her cheek. She felt quite weak. For a moment his nearness made her joyously dizzy.

And then it happened! Afterward, Cami told herself that she could have stopped him, but deep down she knew that was not true. She had no warning, no inkling whatsoever of his intentions until it was too late. One minute she was standing before him and the next his lips were on hers. The kiss lasted only a moment, but it left its imprint scorched into Cami's soul.

"You needn't be shy with me," he whispered. "I will take good care of you, *ma chère*." His words were solemn—a heartfelt promise. "You will be loved—no, *adored*."

The true meaning of his words struck Cami with a staggering impact. This was it—the moment she had planned and schemed for. If she could love any man, that man was Black Vic. She wanted to tell him so many things—how he made her feel, the thoughts that his nearness put into her head and her heart. But the words simply refused to come. And what did it matter? As much as she wanted this, she knew that Fiona would never allow it. Hadn't she ranted and raved each time Cami dared mention the name Victoine Navar?

"Is something wrong, Cami?" His voice was low and caressing.

"Fiona." Cami's voice quivered as she said the name. "She'll never grant permission."

"Do you need her permission to take a lover? Someone who will take care of you and adore you from this night forward?"

Cami caught her breath. Never had she expected him to state his case so directly.

Before she could answer, he added, "Tell me what *you* want, Cami."

"You *must* speak with my aunt."

He smiled down at her, taking her words as assent. The light in his dark eyes fairly danced. "Certainly. She and I shall settle all the arrangements, if it is your wish."

She wanted to cry for joy and throw her arms

301

around him. Instead, she kept a level head and an even tone. "What of *your* wishes, m'sieur?"

In answer, Black Vic swept Cami into his strong arms. She could feel his heart pounding against her quivering breasts. She could also feel enough of the rest of his body to know, from the things Fiona had explained to her, that he was dangerously aroused. When he kissed her again, she knew she should struggle against him, but instead she gave in to her own desires.

Another kiss, and then another. He held her tightly, teasing her lips before slipping his tongue into her mouth. The shock was too great for Cami to fight him. She should have guessed. She should have been on guard all the while against this. Fiona had told her about this tongue-kissing that Frenchmen liked so well. Cami had been horrified at the time, thinking it must be a disgusting practice. But it wasn't so bad, she found, stroking tentatively at his tongue with her own. The gentle, moist contact sent a hot shiver through her body.

Feeling her tremble in his arms, Vic broke away. She barely had time to experience a fleeting sense of disappointment before his lips touched her bare shoulder. She tensed, hardly daring to breathe as she felt his tongue draw small, damp circles on her burning flesh.

At last Vic drew away, leaving Cami weak and totally breathless. For what seemed like an eternity, he simply stared silently into her eyes. When he spoke at last, his voice was deep and hot and rough. "This very night, my little love, you will be mine, if I have my way."

The words sent a tremor straight through Cami's body to her heart. Even though she feared the

302

things Vic might do to her, a part of her burned with a passionate fury to be his.

As if reading her confusion, he said gently, "You needn't worry, *ma chère*. I could never demand that you come to me before you are ready. I promise to be patient with you." As a whispered aside, he added, "At least, I will try."

She wanted to tell him that no man would ever force her . . . that only love could make her give herself, and that she felt that love for him and would come willingly. But she was far too shy to admit her thoughts. She could only stare at him, while fear and desire fought within her.

"Come, we must speak with Fiona at once," Vic said.

The moment they returned to the ballroom, a slightly drunken young man approached them. He stared hungrily at Cami with glassy green eyes, then reached out to take her hand. "Madame Le Moyne gave her permission for me to dance with her niece," the tipsy fellow announced.

His face stormy, Vic drew Cami away from the man and put himself between them. "I think not, sir!"

"Damn you, Navar!" the tall, wiry man bellowed. "It's not your place to say. This is *my* dance!"

"Mademoiselle Cami's dance card is filled," Black Vic insisted, his deadly tone warning the other man as clearly as his words. But the fellow refused to be put off.

"Why don't you come with me to St. Anthony's Square behind the cathedral, Navar? Bring along your second. After we've finished our business, then I'll have my dance with mademoiselle."

Hearing a duel in the making, Fiona quickly intervened. "M'sieur Navar, I must take my niece home now. Will you see us downstairs to our carriage?"

Cami's would-be suitor stared hard at Fiona. "Madame, you are interrupting. Navar and I have our own business to tend to. It is time Black Vic made arrangements for his funeral."

Cami felt fear race through her veins like fire. Surely she had not found the man she wanted only to lose him before they ever had a chance to be together. But Fiona leapt to the rescue.

"M'sieur Labot," she said in a shocked tone, "you can't mean that you would desert this lovely ball, all these beautiful young ladies, simply to have M'sieur Navar pierce you through with his *colchemarde*?" She pulled a sad face. "What a waste that would be! You are such a fine young fellow. Why, any lady here would love to dance with you."

"I mean to dance with Mademoiselle Cami!"

"Perhaps some other time," Fiona replied archly. "You see, we were just leaving. Now, you had better be on your way while you still have a chance. M'sieur Navar, as everyone knows, is the finest swordsman in New Orleans, but his temper leaves something to be desired."

Young M'sieur Labot opted for discretion rather than valor. He moved off quickly, leaving Fiona, Vic, and Cami staring after him.

"That was close," Vic said. "Why are these young fools so eager to die?"

Cami stared up at Black Vic, a new kind of horror rising in her. "You actually would have killed him rather than allow him to dance with me?"

"I would have had little choice if he forced the

issue," Vic answered. "A duel at St. Anthony's seldom leaves both participants in good health. In other words, it would have been him or me. As for me, I have some rather urgent plans this evening."

"I would have danced with him," Cami insisted.

Vic's eyes flared with anger. "You would *not* have because I would not have permitted it, Cami."

"What are you saying, Victoine?" Fiona gasped.

"That you and I, Fiona, have important arrangements to discuss."

"*Mon Dieu!*" Fiona's words were only a faint whisper.

"I want Cami for my *placée*. She has agreed to my proposal."

Fiona said nothing. She still felt that Cami would back out at the last moment. Saying she wanted this and actually committing to it were two entirely different things. She guessed that any moment now, Cami would lose her last shred of courage, beg Fiona to take her home, then never speak of Victoine Navar or the Quadroon Ball again. If Fiona's calculations were correct, Camille would soon be back at Mulgrove where she belonged.

Cami's next words shocked Fiona. "Yes, I suppose I did agree," she said with only slight hesitation, all the while gazing up at Vic, her eyes dewy with longing.

"We have only to settle matters," he replied, slipping his arm once more about Cami's slender waist.

"You can't be serious about this, Victoine," Fiona hissed under her breath. "She's a child. She doesn't know what you're proposing or what she wants."

"I am not a child!" Cami protested. "And I told

you what I wanted when I arrived in New Orleans, Fiona. I want love!"

"And you shall have it!" Vic's dark eyes blazed as he stared down at Cami.

Stunned, Fiona motioned them to follow her downstairs to one of the empty card rooms. How had she lost control of this situation? What would become of Cami now? Perhaps she should put an end to this masquerade by telling Vic Cami's true identity, by confessing to Cami that Vic was a married man. No, things had gone too far for that. Besides, she had the feeling that neither Vic nor Cami would back out, even if the truth were known. She could only hope that Camille would come to her senses before she allowed Victoine Navar to further soil her reputation and ruin her life. There was still time—the courting period.

Once they were seated at the table downstairs, Vic launched his campaign. "You know I have the house ready, Fiona. I would like to take Cami home this very night."

"*What?*" Fiona cried. "No courting? No time for Cami to come to know you first?"

Vic smiled down at Cami. "We know each other well enough. You're willing to come to my house tonight, aren't you, my darling?"

Fiona tried to cover her shock gracefully. "A house is one thing, Victoine, but what of the rest of the settlement? Can you afford to keep my niece in style? What of clothes, jewels, a carriage, servants?"

Cami's head was spinning as the two dickered back and forth. They talked as if she were not in the room, ignoring her presence as they bartered her flesh for gold. Somehow she had been sure earlier in the evening that it would never come to this. She'd been certain that Fiona would never allow it. But it seemed to Cami that her father's former mistress had launched herself into this haggling with fierce enthusiasm.

After nearly an hour, Black Vic rose, smiling. "Then it's all arranged. Now, may I take my darling home?"

"Home? Now?" Suddenly, Cami felt afraid once more.

Fiona thought she saw a slight ray of hope. Cami might still back out. "M'sieur Navar has settled handsomely for you, Cami, but it is not too late. Have you changed your mind?" Her golden eyes glittered as she pleaded silently with the girl. "We would both understand, child."

"Speak for yourself, Fiona!"

At Vic's angry tone, Cami turned to look at him. His face was a mask of manly determination. She had gone too far for him to allow her to turn back now.

"What about my clothes, my other things?" Cami asked, knowing her attempt to stall would most likely fail.

"I'll send someone over to Love Street for your belongings the first thing tomorrow morning," Vic answered.

"Fiona?" Cami turned her gaze on the woman, but it was obvious there was nothing more she could do. Cami had gotten herself into this. It was too late for second thoughts.

Vic slipped his arm about Cami's trembling shoulders and hugged her close to his side. "Come to think of it, Fiona, don't look for my servant to arrive *first thing* tomorrow. I expect Cami and I will be occupied through the morning."

Everything was moving so fast. Cami's head was spinning. She had imagined this moment for so long, but now that it was actually here, she wasn't at all sure she was ready. What would she do when they arrived at Black Vic's house and she found herself alone with a man for the first time in her life?

With a sorrowful shake of her head, Fiona said good night, kissed Cami's cheeks, then left. Alone with Black Vic, Cami felt as awkward and tongue-tied as she had been that night she first saw him at Mulgrove. And if she'd thought he looked at her that night as if he'd enjoy doing indecent things to her, right now he gazed down as if he meant to devour her whole, on the spot. Instead, he led her outside to his waiting coach.

They rode all the way in silence, Cami lost in her unsettling thoughts. Suddenly, Vic's hand touched hers and she all but jumped out of her skin.

"We're home," he said softly.

Cami looked up. "Home?" she repeated tonelessly.

"Yes, mine and yours, *ma chère*." He pressed her hand. "Come. Let's go in."

"Wait!" Cami whispered, knowing that there was no way she could stall, but nervous at the thought of actually entering his house—his bedroom.

"Come, little love," Vic said quietly. "It's time for us to vacate this stuffy coach and get safely inside. I don't trust the night air. I myself am immune to the city's fevers, but I wouldn't want you to breathe the miasmas for too long." He slipped his hand into hers and squeezed. "You are far too precious to me, Cami dearest."

Cami felt a little thrill run through her, yet she drew her hand away. "Very well, m'sieur. Whatever you say."

Cami had to bite her lip to stay her tears once they were inside. Now she felt truly alone and at Black Vic's mercy. She wasn't ready, but how could she explain that to him?

"Well? Do you like it?" Vic asked. He seemed unaware of Cami's trembling.

"Yes, m'sieur. It's very nice."

They were in the green and gold *petite salon*. Vic turned to Cami, he dark eyes pleading. "Won't you please call me Vic? You sound so very formal— more like a servant than a . . ."

"Than a what, m'sieur?" she challenged.

"A lover." When he said the word his voice was deep and warm and caressing. The sound sent a new kind of shiver through Cami.

She shied away from his direct gaze after a moment. So, there it was! She must face that fact. He wanted her not as a wife, but as a woman to do his bidding. Only one question remained: When would he strip the gown from her and demand that she bend to his will? She almost wished that he would force the moment so they could be done with it forever. It would serve her right, she reminded herself. After all, she was the one who had run away from her safe, dull life to find adventure and romance.

Suddenly, Cami remembered her conversation

with her Cousin Lorenna the night she left Mulgrove. She had told 'Renna of her wish to find a man to love her. Well, now she had that wish and the very man she had set out to capture. Only the tables had turned. She was the prey now and he the pursuer. Very well, now that she knew her role, it was time they discussed the rules.

"Fiona told me exactly what will be expected of me," Cami said with more courage than she thought she possessed. "I am to be at your beck and call, day and night. I am always to smile—even when I'm unhappy—to act in a pleasant manner, and to do your bidding, m'sieur. So what do you wish of me?"

Black Vic smiled at her pretty speech, but ignored her forthright question. Instead of answering, he handed her a small glass of wine. "Would you like something to eat before we retire? I've no servants here at present, but I'm sure I could manage a plate of fruit or some pastries from the pantry."

Cami sipped her wine, staring at Vic over the delicate crystal rim. So, she mused, he had this all planned. No servants. How convenient! He had her all to himself, to ravish at his leisure, with no one to hear should she cry for help.

"No, thank you," she answered, then allowed herself a ladylike yawn behind her hand.

"I'm rather tired tonight, too," he confessed. "Why don't I show you to the bedchamber? You can change and then . . ."

Cami's blood froze in her veins when he let the sentence trail off unfinished.

And then *what?* As if she didn't know!

Sure enough, a moment later he came toward her. She recognized that dark flame in his eyes. She had seen that same look on the balcony just before he assaulted her with his tongue. She moved slightly away from him.

Setting his wine glass aside, Vic reached for Cami's as well. Then he placed his hands on her waist. As he held her at arm's length, his gaze traveled over her. She trembled when he looked at her breasts, straining at the filmy white fabric of her gown. This was the same lazy, bold perusal he had given her that night at Mulgrove. The sensation left her breathless and confused.

Finally, his eyes locked on hers and Vic said, "Cami, you're so lovely. If I had my way, I would sweep you up in my arms this minute and carry you to my bed."

Fear made Cami catch a ragged breath, but she determined not to let him know how much his words frightened her. She decided her best defense was to cast off her demure façade and match him shock for shock. If he meant to take her here and now, he would know that she was a woman of spirit, not some shy child who quaked at his touch even as she welcomed it.

Tossing her head so that her hair whipped back over one shoulder, she glared at him, smiling. "I hope you don't intend to tear off my lovely new gown, ripping it from my breasts as your eyes seem to be stripping it away at this very moment."

"Rip your gown?" He drew back, an expression of amusement and horror on his handsome face. "Of course I'd never do such a thing!"

"Ah!" She nodded as if she could read his every

thought. "Then I suppose you will now show me to your chamber where you will lounge on the bed—hot and ready—while you command me to undress before your hungry eyes. Well, if that is your plan, m'sieur, do not expect me to tremble before you and plead for mercy. Although I appreciate my privacy, I am not ashamed of my body."

Stunned at first by her outburst, Vic was now almost ready to burst out laughing. This girl was no shy violet as Fiona had claimed. She was a fiery-tempered minx who would no doubt make him pay far more than gold for her love.

"You have a body no woman would be ashamed of," he fired back, still smiling. "And you've a fine flare for the bizarre as well. I certainly will not expect you to disrobe before my leering eyes." He cocked a brow and looked thoughtful. "At least, I hadn't planned it, but if you're willing . . ."

Cami's face went scarlet. At that moment, Vic realized she was merely putting on this feisty front. It dawned on him that she was truly terrified of what he might do to her.

Careful to keep his distance, Vic said, "Cami, what are you afraid of?"

The soft tone of his words crumbled her bold façade. She put her face in her hands with a long-suppressed sob.

"Please don't," Vic said almost coldly. "I've done nothing to make you weep, nor do I intend to. I thought you found me pleasing or I would never have brought you here. I had hoped, Cami, that in you I had finally found a woman who could love me. If I'm mistaken, then you have nothing to fear. I'll never touch you again."

Now a new kind of terror surged through her. She tried to stop the flow of tears, tried to find her voice to explain, but it was hopeless.

"Come," Vic ordered. "I'll show you to your room. I believe you'll find anything you might need there—toilet items, night clothes. You needn't worry about my invading your privacy tonight. You may even lock the door, if you wish. Tomorrow I'll see that you return safe and sound and untouched to your Aunt Fiona."

All of the things Fiona had told Cami about the proper conduct of a *placée* came back to her in a rush. "You must be at all times trusting, willing, giving, and loving if you expect happiness in return. A Creole man may be unfaithful to his wife, but never to his mistress. Theirs is a relationship more sacred even than marriage. With the right man I found perfect bliss. Perhaps in time you will, too, Camille."

Time! Yes, time was the key, Cami realized.

"Please, Victoine!" Cami forced herself to use his name, her words only a bare whisper. "Don't send me away. Only give me a little more time, won't you?"

She reached out one trembling hand in a pleading gesture. When his fingertips touched hers, it seemed to Cami that something like a flow of life force passed between them. At that moment, in her mind's eye she could see the two of them as if she were floating somewhere high above, the image caught forever of a man and a woman reaching out to each other. There was a vast sense of yearning, needing—a sense of longing to share pain and joy and love.

"Time?" he murmured quietly. "I would wait days, years, centuries to know your love, Cami. A chance is all I ask."

Slowly, cautiously, Cami moved toward him. His words had touched her deeply. Somehow she must let him know that.

Sensing a change in her, Vic stood frozen to the spot, not daring to move. He couldn't chance frightening her again. She would have her time—all she needed and more. God, how he ached to take her in his arms and make mad, passionate love to her this very minute! But he would guard himself well until she was ready and willing to come to him.

A moment later, Cami stood so close to Vic that she could feel his heat and hear the soft hiss of his breath. She stared up into his face. A nerve twitched in his square jaw, otherwise his features remained passive. Slowly, she went up on tiptoe, but she still could not reach his lips.

"A kiss to seal our bargain?" she begged, her velvety voice trembling with emotion.

Black Vic leaned down to her, his hands still at his sides. When their lips touched at last, Cami felt such a dizzy longing that she almost stumbled away. Instinctively, her hands went to his waist. At first, she meant only to steady herself, but a moment later her arms slid around him and she pressed her body close to his. Their kiss went on and on—a sweet, gentle pressure that first warmed Cami's toes, then weakened her legs. Soon her whole body suffered the tender impact. She let her hands glide up and down the muscular contours of Vic's back, pressing him more firmly to her breasts. She could tell Vic was holding back. His arms remained at his

314

sides. All intimate contact between them was her doing. She gave him the kiss. She held him close. Only one part of him responded, seemingly with a will of its own.

By the time Cami released Vic, she felt as if a fever had gripped her. She knew she wanted more from him. Her mouth longed for the caress of his tongue. Her breasts ached for his touch. And something deep inside her burned for more of him than she cared to put a name to. After all she had been through in the past hours, would he now make her beg? No! She couldn't!

Her indigo eyes pleaded as she gazed up at the placid mask of his face. Then something moved— the twitch of a muscle beside his mouth. Surely, he was about to say the very words Cami longed to hear.

Instead, Vic said, "It's been a very long day. Come, Cami, I'll show you to your room. And tomorrow . . ."

"Tomorrow?" she asked in an uncertain whisper, but Black Vic never finished the thought aloud.

Chapter Fourteen

Cami's long day stretched on into a long night. Lying in the big empty bed in the room next to Vic's, she went over everything that had happened in her mind a thousand times. She reviewed her fears, caused, she was certain, by the intimate things Fiona had told her that men did to women. Somehow, though, those things seemed far less frightening now, when she thought of sharing such experiences with Black Vic Navar.

She glanced across the room. He was sleeping in a chamber that connected to her own. A few steps, the turn of a doorknob, and she would be there with him. How great the temptation!

Just before dawn, Cami rose from the tester bed and tiptoed, barefoot, to the door that linked their chambers. Vic would be sleeping, of course. She wouldn't wake him. She'd simply peek in to make sure he was still there.

The first faint pearly rays of dawn inched across the floor as Cami leaned against the door to listen. All was quiet on the other side. Summoning her courage, she slowly turned the knob. To her relief, the door opened silently. His room was filled with shadows, but she could clearly see his dark form on the big bed. He was sleeping on his back, his arms thrown over his head. A sheet covered him to the waist, but his chest was naked, darkly furred with man-hair.

Fascinated by the sight of him, Cami eased a few steps into the room. She gazed intently at him. He looked much younger with his facial muscles re-laxed. His scarred cheek was turned away from her. His thick, black hair was rumpled, glistening with night-sweat. She had so many questions about Black Vic. What had his life been like when he was younger? What were his hopes and plans for the future? Then another thought crossed her mind— what would he think if he suddenly woke and found her staring at him? That question almost sent her running back to the safety of her own bed, but her curiosity was too keen to allow her to leave just yet.

Before Cami knew what was happening, she stood over Vic's sleeping form, staring down into his handsome face, so peaceful in sleep. She let her gaze explore this awesome male, from the dark tousled hair pressed damply to his forehead, to the strong arms and broad chest. Vic shifted slightly and the sheet slipped down, an inch past his waist. Cami stared, fascinated by his lean, hard form. She could only imagine what lay hidden from her eyes.

Once more, she let her gaze travel to his face. In that instant, she could have died of shame.

His eyes wide, staring at her staring at him, Vic warned in a husky voice, "You're treading dangerous territory, Cami love."

She tried to think of some reply, but found there was simply no explanation for her being there. When she meant to turn and flee, she met with the same lack of success. She could only stand dumbly next to the bed, still staring down at Black Vic.

She watched a smile spread over his face. At the same time, something rose beneath the sheet to form a tent over his lower body. Realizing what it was, Cami gasped.

Vic reached out and placed his hand on her thinly-clad hip, caressing her until an ache burned through her lower body. She wanted so to run back to her room and hide there forevermore, but his touch held her mesmerized.

"Come lie with me, won't you?" he begged. When she hesitated, he promised, "I only want to feel you close. You needn't fear me, Cami."

Far from certain she was doing the wise thing, Cami eased onto the bed beside him. She sat erect with her back to him, not daring to lie down. A moment later, she wished she had. Both Vic's hands gripped her waist—kneading, massaging, sending wonderful thrills all through her.

"Won't you lie with me, Cami darling?" he begged again.

Without further prompting, she lay back on the pillows, her whole body stiff and motionless.

"Ah, that's better," Vic sighed. "This bed was made for two. It doesn't fit right otherwise. But the pair of us fill it nicely, don't you agree?"

As Vic talked, his fingers trailed up and down Cami's bare arm. He was driving her crazy.

"I'd better go," she said suddenly.

"As you wish," Vic replied.

He was under the sheet—part of him at least—and she was on top of it. He did nothing to force her to stay. Yet Cami found herself unable to move. His warmth felt so nice, his hand on her arm so pleasant. She began to relax beside him. Before she knew it, her eyes closed. For some unnatural reason, it suddenly semed perfectly natural that she should fall asleep in Black Vic's bed, next to his hot, naked body.

The shock would come when she awoke a few hours later to face her situation in the full light of day.

Vic never went back to sleep. How could he with such a soft and tempting female stretched out beside him? This was a hell of a note! After all he'd been through with Cami during the evening—and finally having to swear that he'd not touch her until she was willing.

"Dear, trusting Cami," he said softly, staring down into her face, as pretty and innocent as a child's. He was quite sure he was about to be forced to kiss those sweetly pouting lips. But the moment before his mouth would have covered hers, he drew away, frowning.

"Damn!" he swore quietly. "Why does she have to believe that promise I made?" The fact remained, however, that she did believe him and she did trust him. "And she isn't ready," he added aloud.

If any other woman had come sneaking into his

319

bedroom at dawn, they would both be sleeping now—exhausted by a long, frenzied period of love-making. That, of course, had been Vic's first thought when he woke to find Cami standing over him. In that lovely, waking instant, he had believed she was only a vision—a beautiful, leftover fragment from his erotic dreams. But one touch had told him she was all too real. When his hand had grazed her hip, he had felt her warm flesh quiver beneath his fingers like the shank of a nervous filly.

"I wanted you then," Vic told her sleeping form. "You'll never know how much. I wanted to hold you and calm you and make you purr beneath me."

Her eyelids fluttered slightly. Still, Cami slept on.

Seeing that his quiet talk did nothing to disturb her, Vic went on. "You've come into my life to drive me mad, haven't you? For one awful moment last night, I thought you might be one of those cold women. But, thankfully, I was wrong. You're only innocent of love and frightened by the unknown. And, God knows, you should be! I'm hardly the sort of man to protect you, especially from myself."

He reached out, meaning to touch her breast. As with the kiss, he drew back. Instead, he gazed at her, at the even rise and fall of her breathing. The gown she wore had a high neck, but the dark outline of her nipples shone clearly through the thin white batiste. Vic leaned down over her breasts and blew a strong breath across their peaks. He watched, fascinated, as the flesh rose and tightened beneath the nearly-transparent fabric. Very slowly, he bent farther, until his mouth gently pressed the tip of one soft mound. He breathed in and out deeply, warming the flesh between his lips.

Cami moaned in her sleep and he quickly drew away, his own moan echoing hers.

"You stupid bastard!" he said to himself. "What if you'd roused her? She'd never have trusted you again, never have stayed with you."

He lay back beside her, propped on one elbow. He would simply have to force himself to be content with filling his eyes with her. Yet while he filled his eyes, he filled his senses as well. She looked all ivory and ebony, her hair and brows and lashes dark shadows against the pale porcelain of her exquisite skin. The scent of her was pure female—lingering fragrances of lime and gardenia blossoms mingling with that sharp-sweet musk peculiar to a woman who has yet to be loved.

Still fast asleep, Cami turned toward him in bed. As she moved, her gown caught under her. When she settled again, her feet and legs were bare to mid-thigh. Vic had to enforce control when his gaze first took in the sight of her long, shapely limbs, her dainty bare feet, the toes curled prettily.

"Turn once more, Cami," he whispered, hoping against hope that she would hear his command and obey—that her gown would ride just a bit higher.

The bed was bathed in sunlight now. The room grew hot and humid. Vic felt sweat trickle down his back and sides. Summer heat always aroused him, as if he needed that this morning. Cami, too, was perspiring. Her gown grew damp from the skin out. Before long, she might have been as naked as Vic himself. He smiled. She was, indeed, lovely, so lovely he could barely endure the ache that simply looking at her caused.

"When you are ready, my little love, what wonderful passion we shall know."

As if she heard and understood his words, Cami smiled in her sleep. One hand stretched out across the sheet until it came to rest on Vic's chest, a well-shaped fingernail stabbing at his nipple. A sharp thrust of the sweetest kind of pain raced through him.

"No more of this!" he groaned, sliding away from Cami and off the bed. He should dress before she awoke.

A slight tremor shook the mattress. Cami's eyes flew open. For the first moment, she had no idea where she was. Then all of the previous night's terror and embarrassment flooded her senses. She was in Victoine Navar's house. A movement across the room caught her eye. She almost cried out. Holy Mother, she was not only in his house, but in his bed!

And there he stood, facing away from her, as naked as you please. She shut her eyes quickly, wanting to see no more of the straight, tanned back, white buttocks, and long, muscled legs that had been her waking vision. Even with her eyes closed, she found she could not block out that sight. Actually, she realized, she didn't really want to. Seeing him that way had sent shivers all through her. Pleasant little pricks of hot, delicious pain.

Perhaps just another tiny peek . . .

Cami opened her eyes and all but fainted dead away. Vic had turned to face her. Not only did she have a full-face view of him, but it was a full-erection view as well. And he had caught her spying on him. He was staring straight into her wide, amazed eyes.

"Good morning," he said nonchalantly. "Did you sleep well?"

Cami swallowed several times, trying to find her lost voice. "I don't know."

Seeing the focal point of her startled gaze, Vic whipped a length of toweling off his shaving stand and wrapped it around his hips.

"If you don't know how you slept, then obviously nothing disturbed you."

He went to his shaving stand and began preparing for his morning ablutions as if it were a perfectly normal occurrence for a woman to awake in his bed and find him standing naked—and ready—before her.

"How should I know what happened while I was sleeping?" Cami argued, trying to cover her embarrassment. "Why, almost anything might have transpired."

Vic turned to her, his cheeks swathed in shaving lather, but a smile showing through. "Almost nothing did. Take my word for it."

"But how can I be sure?" Quickly, she checked the sheet for blood. Fiona had told her there would be blood.

"You'll find no stains on the bed," Vic told her.

"I wasn't looking . . ."

"Oh, yes, you were! You were looking for some sign that I might have taken advantage of you. Admit it!"

Cami blushed—caught! "I'm sorry," she murmured.

"No, I'm the one who should apologize," he said. "I did take advantage while you slept. I kissed your breast."

"Oh!" The word came as a soft gasp. Cami

glanced down at her thin gown, then quickly crossed her arms across her chest. She was trembling suddenly and she felt she might cry, not because Vic had admitted to his indescretion, but because it had happened while she was sleeping. She had missed it.

"I do apologize, as I said. It was beastly of me." He went on shaving. "But, dammit all, I lost control!"

"You didn't have to admit to what you did," Cami ventured. "I'd never have known."

"I thought I'd better tell you," he said matter-of-factly. "You see, I'm not a very trustworthy sort. Even though I promised, you should beware of giving me such opportunities. I am just a man, after all."

Just a man barely covered it! Cami had seen exactly how much man he was. More man than she could safely handle, she feared.

"I'll be more careful from now on," she assured him.

He turned toward her again, the towel dipping dangerously low on his hips. "Why did you come to my room, Cami?"

"Certainly not to tempt you," she answered quickly. "I don't really know." Suddenly, she realized that she did know, if only she could make him understand. "Have you ever been to the circus, Vic?"

He frowned at her. "What does that have to do with anything?"

"My father took me once. There was a lion in a cage—a fearsome beast who roared and gnashed his teeth. I was so afraid! My mother was angry

324

with my father for taking me. She said afterward that surely I would have nightmares about that vicious lion."

"And did you?" Vic asked, not following her reasoning in the least, but more than willing to hear her out.

"No. I dreamed about him, but they were gentle dreams. I would see myself approaching the lion's cage in the dead of night. He would be sleeping. There were no frightening roars or scary teeth. I would reach through the bars into his cage and rub his great mane."

"Weren't you afraid he would bite your arm off?"

"No, never! While he was fast asleep he was as tame as a housecat. Besides, in my dreams he never woke."

Vic chuckled. "So you came to my room last night to rub my shaggy mane while I was asleep and couldn't gobble you up. Right?"

"Something like that." She pouted at him suddenly. "But you aren't as tame as my terrible lion. You woke up," she said accusingly.

"Please forgive me, Cami dearest." Vic made an exaggerated bow and his towel slipped to the floor. He watched the blood rush to Cami's face.

"I didn't do that on purpose," he assured her. "I'm sorry, Cami."

"Would your *placée* see you that way?" she asked softly.

"Undoubtedly."

She shrugged. "Then you have no reason to apologize to me."

"You've never seen a man before, have you?"

"No," she said.

"Does the sight of me frighten you?"

"A bit. Yes, *quite* a bit," she admitted. She wanted to tell him that because of his amazing size she believed they would be an uncomfortable fit, but she couldn't bring herself to say the words.

He reached for a robe to replace the skimpy towel. "Then I promise to keep myself covered from now on."

Cami felt an odd pang of disappointment once Vic's astounding maleness was hidden away inside his gray silk robe.

"Why don't you go and dress now?" Vic suggested. "Your lion is definitely awake and aroused. I don't think you're quite safe, playing about his cage in your nightie."

His warning sent Cami scurrying back to her own room.

The next few days proved both a wonder and a torment for Cami. True to his word, Vic made no demands upon her. He remained kind, gentle, charming, and at all times attentive. But the very moment she was certain he meant to touch her hand, put his arms around her, or give her a kiss, he shied away, restraining himself with great effort.

Cami began to feel there must be something wrong with her. Perhaps Vic had changed his mind and didn't want her for his mistress after all. The more he held back, the more she became determined to make him love her. She had decided already that she loved him. She even thought that to win him over she might tell him the truth about being Edouard Mazaret's daughter, not a woman of color as she had represented herself. But she dared not confess her true identity until she could be sure that he had accepted her into his heart.

The spiritual side of love was easy enough for Cami to acknowledge. She knew by the way her heart swelled at the sight of Vic that he was meant to be hers. He brought sunshine into the darkest, stormiest afternoon by simply saying her name. He could make her soul sing with a certain smile. Yes, this was love, pure and simple and perfect.

The other side of love, she had yet to experience. But as each day passed, she began to yearn for it more and more. No matter the fit, she had the feeling they were meant for each other. So, what was he waiting for? When would it happen? Surely, they had plenty of opportunity.

Cami and Vic stayed close to the house except the nights that Vic had poker games at Gaspard's or some other gaming establishment. Cami feared that someone might see her with Vic and recognize her, then tell her whereabouts to Cousin Morris. She had no trouble convincing Vic that she should stay inside. The summer fever season was raging with new cases in all parts of the city. Cannons boomed over the waterfront, smudge pots against the disease further polluted the air, and dead-wagons rumbled through the streets at all hours. The whole house smelled like vetiver and camphor, believed to be protection against the disease. Vic was determined to guard Cami well against the dreaded Bronze John.

On one particularly stormy afternoon, Cami joined Vic in a few rounds of Boston, one of his favorite card games. Although he remained intent on his hand, Cami grew restless after only a short while.

"Must we play this?" she asked. "I'm no good at cards."

"That's why I enjoy it so," Vic teased. "I always win when I play with you, darling."

"Why do you call me that?" Cami sounded absolutely peevish.

"What?"

"*Darling!* You say it with such passion—as if you really meant it."

He reached across the table and caught her hand. "But I do mean it, Cami darling. It's a name for lovers. You know I adore you."

"We *aren't* lovers, Vic!" she pointed out hotly. Then her voice fell to almost a whisper. "I'm not sure we ever will be."

"When you're ready, my sweet love, then we will be."

She seethed and burned inside. What must she do? Come right out and beg him to take her to his bed? Well, she wouldn't do that. She couldn't!

"We don't have to play cards, if you don't feel like it," Vic said. "What would you like to do?"

If ever there was an opening, Vic gave it to her. But Cami let it pass. Instead of telling him the truth, she sighed and said, "Oh, I don't know. I just feel so restless and cooped up. Maybe we could go out for a ride."

Just then a flash of lightning lit the afternoon darkness of the room. The thunder that rolled out behind it shook the whole house.

"Not today," Vic replied. "We'd get stuck in the mud for sure. Any other suggestions?"

"Could I have a glass of wine?"

He rose and went to the spirits chest. "Certainly. In fact, I'll join you."

Cami roamed about the room, prowling like a caged beast. After a time, she flounced down on the settee, staring dismally out at the pounding gray rain. "When I was a little girl, I had a special place to play on rainy days. I used to look forward to long, stormy afternoons like this."

"So did I," Vic said under his breath, thinking that days like this were absolutely the best of all for enjoying long, leisurely sessions of love-making. Aloud, to Cami he asked, "Where was your special place?"

"My bed in my upstairs nursery. Mother would let me draw the curtains to make my own little world. I'd bring my favorite toys in with me and we'd hide away from the storm. Sometimes I pretended I was in a harem tent or camping out in a jungle where my fierce lion roamed free. But I was safe behind my barrier."

Vic sat down next to Cami and took her hand. His unexpected touch sent a thrill through her. "And did your lion come and sleep next to you and let you rub him?"

Cami sipped at her wine, her mind vividly alive with childhood fantasies. "Ah, yes! You've guessed my best times."

"And who came when your bed was a harem tent?"

She giggled softly and squeezed Vic's warm hand. "My great, dark master. His black eyes would flash with fire as his gaze swept over me and my dollies. I was always safe. He would choose my beautiful blond-haired china doll. You see, dark sheiks are very fond of fair-haired maidens."

"And was your pretty, blond doll pleased to be the chosen one?" Vic's black eyes glittered at the very thought of an innocent child entertaining herself with such bizarre fantasies.

"Secretly, perhaps," Cami confided. "But my dolly always wailed and cried, begging our master to choose another. It never worked; he would not be refused."

Vic chuckled. "You had quite a vivid imagination as a child. Did this evil master ever choose you?"

"Oh, yes!" Cami's indigo eyes fairly sparkled. "But he wasn't evil. He was very tall and very strong and very grand. I was so happy when he finally picked me . . ." Cami's words drifted off, leaving Vic hanging.

"Then what happened?" Vic was on the edge of his seat. "Tell me!"

Cami shrugged and laughed. "The storm ended and Mother called me down to supper."

Vic refilled Cami's glass, then settled beside her once more. A flash of lightning lit up the room, followed by an especially loud clap of thunder. Startled, Cami cried out and reached for Vic. The next moment his lips were on hers. It was a long, deep kiss—the kind Frenchmen find so pleasing, the kind that Cami had been praying for for many days and nights.

When Vic drew away, he didn't go far. He kept one arm around Cami's shoulder while his other hand toyed with the lace at the bodice of her green silk gown. Cami leaned toward him, enjoying the feel of the fabric tightening over her breasts as Vic tugged at it.

"I'm sorry things didn't work out with your sheik," he whispered.

She shrugged again. "It's probably just as well."

"Why?"

She giggled and twitched her nose. "He had this enormous, black mustache. I'm sure it would have scraped me raw. Besides, I hadn't that much imagination. I could never have done justice to what went on in his tent."

"And could you now?"

Cami sighed wistfully. "Probably not."

Vic rose suddenly, his dark eyes gleaming. "Stay here. I'll be back shortly."

When he left, Cami refilled her wine glass once more. Suddenly the storm didn't seem so terrible any longer. She still had a restless feeling, but now it was a different sort. She paced the room, wondering where Vic had gone and how long before he would return. She wanted *something*, she wasn't sure what. Most of all, she wanted Vic back beside her, playing with the lace of her bodice, kissing her with his velvety tongue. And, yes, she was forced to admit to herself at last, she wanted him to force her to surrender to her own needs—to make her his lover. More than anything, she longed to lie quivering in Black Vic's arms, learning the long-kept secret of this mystery called love.

Even as she admitted her desires to herself, Cami saw the door to the salon swing wide. Before her stood a sheik of sorts, garbed in an old *bal masqué* costume. Vic wore a bejeweled satin turban and a cloth-of-gold cape draped over his broad shoulders.

"What on earth?" Cami cried through a wine-flavored giggle.

"Silence, maiden!" Vic snarled, pointing a commanding finger her way. "Sheik Navar will choose no hysterical, sharp-tongued female for his pleasure. His lover must be as silent as she is passionate. Let me see now . . ." He roamed about the room as if trying to make his selection, gazing first at a lovely figurine of Venus, then at a portrait of a dark-haired woman over the fireplace, and finally at a naked nymph woven into a tapestry that hung between the windows. Suddenly, he turned to Cami, a leer on his handsome face. "I choose *you!*" he cried, with a great swirl of his cape.

Before Cami could react, Vic swept her up in his arms and headed for the stairs. Moments later, he carried her through the doorway into the old nursery. The windows were shuttered, filling the room with shadows. Still, Cami could see that Vic had already been there to prepare the scene. The curtains were drawn around the bed to form a private chamber.

Vic set Cami on her feet, then kissed her again, deeply.

"I can't guarantee the storm's duration, but I promise no one will call you down to supper this time, my darling."

Cami stood staring from Vic to the bed, then back to Vic. Her whole body burned for him as she realized that her moment had finally come.

Releasing her, Vic gazed down into her eyes and smiled. He removed the silly turban and tossed it across the room. His cape soon followed. "Well, my darling?" he whispered expectantly. "Your sheik awaits. Will you surrender your innocence here and now or must he steal it from you?"

Cami couldn't answer. All she could do was cling

to Vic and tremble. This was what she'd been waiting for since the first night she set eyes on him. Now that the moment had come, she felt consumed by her own painfully sweet longing.

She reached up and touched Vic's cheek, tears brimming in her wide, indigo eyes.

"Oh, *mon coeur*," she whispered. "The place, the time, and the man—they are all perfect. At last, I have been chosen!"

Chapter Fifteen

Cami and Vic stood facing each other, frozen as if in a Mardi Gras tableau. The sweetness of the moment held them both. Lightning flashed, illuminating the passion in Vic's face, the soft, glowing innocence of Cami's. Their eyes caressed each other—the black of midnight commanding the gentle blue-violet of dawn.

Slowly, Vic's hand came up to rest on Cami's shoulder. Her flesh quivered beneath his warm touch. One finger traced up her throat to fondle the delicate curve of her cheek. Cami stood still, holding her breath, her eyes closed. Unable to see where her bold lover might touch her next, she found the path of his seeking hand all the more arousing. When his fingers left her for a moment, then returned to fondle the lace at the edge of her bodice, Cami caught her breath. An instant later, his lips touched her shoulder.

"Oh, Vic . . ." she moaned softly. She ached to embrace him, but forced herself to stand perfectly still for fear she might seem too eager.

Her eyes shot open again when she felt the tug of her sleeve as Vic eased it off her shoulder. His eyes glowed like black fire—more flesh to touch, to kiss. And he did.

"Oh, love, you drive me wild," he murmured between light, hot flicks of his tongue. Then "Damn! How do I get you out of this gown? I may be forced to tear it off as you once suggested."

Cami pressed her hands to Vic's chest, gently pushing him away. Then, deftly, she undid the tiny, hidden hooks of her bodice. Vic stood before her, his hungry eyes taking in her every move. When her work was done, she slipped her arms from the sleeves. Only her thin camisole covered her breasts.

"My God, you're beautiful!" Vic gasped.

Once again, his hands reached out for her. He drew her close, kissing her deeply while his fingers kneaded the thin batiste over her straining nipples. Cami truly thought each breath would be her last. His fondling sent tossing storms of pleasure and desire raging through her until she felt weak with longing.

"I'll buy you a new one," Vic groaned, ripping the thin camisole away in his strong grip. "Ah, Cami . . . Cami, my love . . ." He buried his face between her bare breasts, moaning her name over and over.

Cami felt sure she would swoon when Vic caught her breasts between his palms, pressing them forward. When the tip of his tongue touched her nipple for the first time, fire shot from the point of contact to all parts of her body. Her legs almost gave way beneath her. She clung to Vic to stay on her feet as he held her, teasing one breast and then the other.

At last, she could take no more. "Oh, please, Vic," she moaned. "Please . . ."

"Please, what, my little darling?" he whispered against her warm flesh.

His question barely pierced her desire-fogged consciousness. She found it impossible to form words to express her longing. Instead, she slipped her arms around his waist and drew him tight against her, marveling at his heat and the hardness of his body. He pressed closer still, showing her that he shared her readiness.

"Will you come into my tent, then?" Vic asked in his sheik's commanding voice.

"Oh, I will, I will," Cami moaned back.

After some hurried fumbling to shed her petticoats, Cami found herself standing there in only her ruined camisole and pantelettes. Once more Vic raked her with his hungry black gaze.

"My God!" he breathed. "Oh, Cami . . ."

Vic began hurriedly undressing. Averting her eyes, Cami slipped between the filmy bed curtains and stretched out, awaiting for her lover. The wait was brief. A moment later, Vic eased in beside her. He was as naked as she had seen him on that very first morning. And as large, she noted with a momentary tremor.

But all fear was soon forgotten. The bed was small, forcing them close. With skill born of experience, Vic divested Cami of the tattered remnants of her underthings. When flesh met flesh for the first time, Cami experienced an electricity more powerful and wonderful than any lightning from the stormy heavens. Vic held her so close she could feel every hard plane of his torso. The coarse hair covering his chest abraded her breasts, but brought no pain, only burning pleasure.

Vic placed one long leg over both of hers, guiding her into a love-locked embrace. Then, holding her—head to toe—he kissed her, a kiss that went on and on. The deeper he probed, the more savage she became. Gone were all thoughts of Fiona and her warnings, all lurid descriptions of the act. This was not an act after all, but a total, perfect, loving melding of one man and one woman into two halves of the same unique soul. And how Cami's soul ached and burned to mate with Vic's!

The first fierceness of their loving passed after a time. In an instant, Vic turned from wild to tender. His kisses on her breasts and face were light now, his touch, as his fingers trailed over her body, almost teasing. If Cami had thought she might die from wanting him moments before, she was sure of it now. When his hand slipped down between her thighs—touching, stroking, fondling—a new sensation began to build. Later, Cami would think about it and decide that it felt like wading into a warm pool. Right now, she could think of nothing; she could only feel and ache to feel more. As the pleasure built, Cami feared she might lose consciousness. The storm raging outside seemed to have taken possession of her body, whipping her inside with its winds, striking between her quivering thighs with great jagged bolts of lightning, making her heart beat like shuddering thunder. But all the while, she was aware only of Vic—Vic kissing her breasts, Vic clutching her to him, Vic touching some secret spring that opened her very soul.

And then he was there, poised above her. For one passion-filled moment, their eyes met and held. He was not smiling, yet the darkness of his eyes was different—softer, kinder, gentler than Cami had ever seen. He almost seemed to be asking silent permission to complete this wondrous act. Cami was sure that the longing in her own half-closed eyes must have granted him the world and more.

When she felt the first tentative touch of his hot, love-swollen flesh, Cami closed her eyes and caught a ragged breath. Vic paused, giving her a moment to ready herself for his thrust. When she felt him ease in a bit farther, she sighed. Every nerve came alive in her body. The pleasure that had begun as he fondled her built to a new and staggering height.

"Oh, Cami love . . ." Vic groaned. As he said the words, he thrust forward.

Lightning struck, destroying Camille Mazaret's virginity for all time. Tears eased out of the corners of her eyes, but they were tears of pure ecstasy. Whatever pain there might have been was lost in the tumultuous wave of pleasure that consumed them both moments later. Cami clung to Vic, murmuring his name over and over again, wondering that she had survived such a total and overpowering burst of all-consuming bliss.

After a time, they lay still in each other's arms— silent and awed. Vic kissed Cami tenderly, letting his lips trail over her cheeks, kissing away her happy tears.

"It will be better next time, my darling," he whispered.

"Oh, Vic!" Cami turned her face into his shoulder and wept. "I'll die if it's any better."

Carol woke first. She could still feel Cami, tingling all over. Her cheeks were damp with Cami's tears. She gazed at the man asleep beside her. It was Frank, of course, but in her moment of waking he had looked like Black Vic. She shook her head slightly, trying to clear her vision. Then she noticed that Frank's eyes were open. They looked glazed.

"Are you all right?" she whispered.

"Cami," he murmured hoarsely. "Don't cry, Cami, please."

"Frank!" Carol said louder, touching his cheek. "Cami's gone now. It's Carol."

He frowned at her, then rose up on one elbow and glanced about. "Carol? Where . . . ? What . . . ?" He relaxed visibly. "I went away, didn't I?"

"Yes," Carol answered softly. "I went with you. Cami's lost her virginity and Black Vic is a wonderful lover. Thank you, darling."

"It will be better next time." Frank's voice still sounded strange, as if it came from far away.

"I know. Vic said that already. Frank, are you sure you're all right?"

"I don't know. I just feel sort of weird, honey. But good." He smiled at her and stroked her hand.

"Yes, it was good," Carol said wistfully. Then she sighed. "*So good!*"

"I didn't—I mean, Vic didn't hurt you?"

Carol smiled at him. "No. Cami didn't even notice the pain. She loved every minute of it."

"I'm glad. I was really afraid—that is, Vic was concerned about her. He knew he was her first lover."

"And how was it for Vic? As good as with Ivory?"

Detecting no jealousy in Carol's voice, Frank answered honestly. "It was great with Cami, but in a different way. Making love to a woman her first time is a tremendous responsibility. You just can't imagine, Carol. And Vic's really crazy about Cami. He didn't want to do anything to turn her off."

Carol laughed softly. "You don't need to worry about that. He didn't! He sure knows how to turn her on, though. Wow!"

"I didn't think he was all *that* great!" Frank snapped, irrational jealousy flaring suddenly.

"Touchy, touchy!" Carol teased. "Remember, that was you and me back there. And I can tell you, Cami sure had it better her first time than I did—the back of a van, scared to death that campus security might come along and catch us. Enjoying it was the last thing on my mind. God, it was a horror!" Carol shuddered in Frank's arms. Then she leaned over and kissed him deeply. "Thank you, darling. You and Vic have just made up for what I missed."

Frank grinned. "Hey, if you liked it that much, then maybe we ought to go back to their time and stay there." He was only joking, but Carol failed to realize that.

"Oh, we couldn't!" she cried. "You mean just vanish into thin air? What would people think?"

"Who cares? We wouldn't be around to worry about that." Frank was suddenly warming to his own suggestion. "Think about it, honey. No income tax, no polluted air, no war, no Saddam Hussein.

340

Why, I'll bet they didn't even have many murders back then."

Carol was becoming uncomfortable. Frank *was* serious! "They murdered each other in duels. As for war, they've got a big one coming up. Remember?"

"Oh, yeah!" Frank frowned, wondering how it would feel to fight under Robert E. Lee. "I don't reckon it would be too much fun enlisting in the Confederate Army. But, hell, honey, that's twenty years off. Vic would be too old to fight."

"Nevertheless, I think we'd better stay right here where we belong, Frank."

"You mean we can't go back at all? Shoot! Now that we got the big devirgination out of the way, I was hoping we could really relax and enjoy ourselves next time."

Carol laughed out loud. "*You!* You're incorrigible, Frank Longpre."

He leaned over to nuzzle her cheek. "Naw, honey, I'm just lovable. We will get to go back again, won't we?"

"I'm afraid we have no say in the matter. All we can do is wait and see." She hugged him. "And hope," she whispered.

"For now, I'm happy right here."

Frank pulled Carol back into his arms. Snuggled close, they drifted off to sleep again, both exhausted by their long night's journey.

Two hours later, Frank shot up as if an alarm had gone off. He rolled over, ready to get out of bed.

Picking up his watch, he checked the time. "Hey, guess what time it is and what day, Carol. It's Lundi Gras, the day before Mardi Gras and it's already nine-thirty. We're missing everything."

Carol didn't want to get up. All through the night she had kept Frank safe in her room—at least in body, if not in spirit. But this morning would be quite a different matter, unless she could convince him to remain in bed. Oliver Percy Jones was still out there somewhere, and she knew he was waiting for his chance at Frank. She moaned and turned over as if she meant to go back to sleep.

Eager to get her going, Frank gave her bare fanny several pats and said, "Up and at 'em, girl! Time's a-wastin'!"

Carol groaned. "Must you be so cheery first thing in the morning?"

Her question stopped Frank cold. Carol was right—he did feel cheerful. For the first time, his guilt was missing. Suddenly, he went from cheery to euphoric.

"This is great!" he shouted.

"Morning is *never* great," Carol mumbled, pulling a pillow over her head. "I don't do morning!"

"Well, you're going to today, by golly! We've got costumes to buy, parties to crash, and parades to watch. Move it, lady!"

Frank whipped the sheet away from Carol and grabbed her up from the bed. She struggled and snarled, but he only laughed at her protests.

"What you need, hon, is a wake-up shower. Then you'll be ready to hit the streets and party."

A moment later, Frank had the shower taps on and had Carol beside him in the roomy tile stall.

She crouched back in a corner, her hands covering her face to keep the hot spray out of her eyes as she called down curses on Frank's head.

"Turn around!" Frank ordered, then he mumbled, "Damn little soaps!"

The next moment, Carol stopped cursing. Her breasts pressed against the smooth tiles, she purred as Frank soaped her shoulders and back. "Oh, that feels wonderful!" she moaned.

He laughed. "I thought this might wake you up."

Working lower and lower, he soaped her whole back, then turned her to face him. "Here's a bar for you," he said, handing her one of the dainty little cakes.

While Frank lathered her breasts and belly, Carol worked on his arms and chest. Soon bubbles were everywhere—hands and lips were everywhere, too.

"You know, you're mighty sexy when you're slippery," Frank growled, trying to get a grip on Carol to bring her closer.

She giggled and slithered her hands down over his soapy torso. A moment later, all laughter ceased. Frank, at last, got a grip on Carol and, with a mighty, soapy thrust, pinned her to the wall.

"My God!" she gasped, sliding her arms around his neck while he lifted her. She locked her legs around his hips. Silence fell except for the sound of spraying water and the slap-slap of flesh on wet flesh.

Afterward, they stood together under the hot spray for a time, then toweled each other off. Within the hour, they were jeaned and tee-shirted, ready for action.

"I figure we'll head down to Decatur Street first,"

Frank began. "We can grab some beignets and *café au lait* at the French Market, then check out a costume shop or two. Okay by you, darlin'?"

"Sounds great!" Carol answered, putting more enthusiasm into the words than she felt.

But, in fact, the whole morning was great. The weather was a pure delight—bright sun, clear skies, warm air. The Carnival crowds seemed more high-spirited than ever. The coffee and square sugared donuts were delicious.

As they were polishing off their open-air breakfast at the *Café du Monde*, Frank said, "What would you like to be tomorrow? Devils are always fun, but the suits are hot. It's supposed to get up to eighty degrees tomorrow, so I suggest something cooler."

"Like what?" Carol asked.

Frank squinted up at the sky, thinking. "I don't know. Let's go see what we can find."

A short while later, they were knee-deep in colorful costumes at a shop called "Demons-R-Us."

"Hey, this is *you*, Carol!" Frank called, holding up a wisp of gold net and satin, studded with purple and green sequins.

Carol came over and fingered the flimsy costume uncertainly.

"Well, it would be cool all right, but what is it?"

"A harem outfit. See? Here's the mask and veil." He thrust the costume into Carol's hands. "Go try it on. I want to see how you look in it."

Moments later, Carol reappeared. Frank gave a low whistle of approval. "That's you, all right!"

Carol laughed. "Just about *all* of me," she answered. "Won't I get arrested in this?"

The shop owner, a heavy-set, dark fellow, came

over and looked Carol up and down approvingly. "You got all the vital parts hid," he assured her, even though her breasts were barely contained by the tiny gold lamé bikini top. "Besides, on Mardi Gras nobody gets arrested. They take all their damn clothes off and nobody notices."

Carol looked down at herself—breasts bulging, a purple jewel winking in her belly button above gold satin briefs with a voluminous, see-through net skirt.

"Honest, Carol, you look fantastic," Frank told her, grinning broadly. "And I've found just the outfit to match yours." He plopped a shiny turban on his head and swirled a golden cape around his shoulders.

"This goes with it," the shop owner said, handing Frank a huge fake mustache, which he immediately stuck to his upper lip.

Carol howled. "Perfect! I'll wear this, if you wear that."

Their costumes set for the next day's frolic, Carol and Frank ambled back toward the hotel to drop off their packages. It was such a gorgeous day that Carol almost forgot the danger lurking in the city— almost, but not quite. She kept a wary eye peeled for the man with the tattoo. He could be anywhere. He could threaten Frank at any moment.

"I figure after we stop by the hotel, we can head on to Bourbon Street for a bowl of red beans and rice," Frank said. "Does that sound right?"

"Sounds super! I'm starving," Carol admitted.

"We can hang around the Quarter and see what's happening, then walk over to Canal Street about four. The floats for the Proteus parade are probably rolling out of their den already. It starts at six, but we need to get there a couple of hours early to find a good spot. There'll be thousands out to watch, especially since Comus and Momus cancelled their parades."

Frank's mention of the thousands of spectators sent a wave of apprehension through Carol, but perhaps there would be safety in numbers. She wished they could go in costume, but Frank had said it wasn't done. "Why, it's downright illegal to dress Mardi Gras before the day!"

The afternoon passed in a dizzying flash of sound and color. Bourbon Street was even more crowded than it had been the night Carol arrived. After lunch, then a couple of Hurricanes at Pat O'Brien's, they made their way slowly toward Canal Street. Shortly before four, they were settled in a prime viewing spot on the neutral ground—the grassy strip down the center of Canal Street. Waiting with them were noisy revellers of all ages, from an old man in a wheelchair wearing a button that read "I'm 100 today—throw me something, mister!" to toddlers tied atop step ladders.

When distant music sent word through the ranks that the parade was coming, the crowd went wild. Carol covered her ears against the din.

The glittering captain of the Krewe of Proteus, mounted on horseback, led the twenty-float parade. On either side of the street, black men marched along carrying naphtha-fueled torches. Frank explained that in the old days of Mardi Gras these *flambeaux* provided the only illumination for nighttime parades.

The volume of noise increased as the king's golden shell rumbled into view. The parade-watchers gasped in collective awe at the shimmering magnificence of the king and his court.

Silver sovereigns, frisbees, and red and silver go-cups rained down on the eager crowd from the masked riders on the tractor-borne floats.

Carol was in the spirit of things. Jumping up and down and waving, she yelled, "Throw me something, mister!" Immediately, she was showered with bright-colored throws.

"Damn, you're a good catcher!" Frank congratulated when she came up with a cup, a frisbee, and several aluminum doubloons.

Floats, horses, dancers, bands—the spectacle stretched on and on. Carol didn't know exactly what she'd expected, but her first Carnival parade was beyond any of her fondest expectations. She felt like a child at her first circus, a teenager with her first boyfriend, a virgin bride on her wedding night. She laughed until her face hurt and yelled until her throat ached.

"Oh, Frank, I've never had such fun!"

He ducked down and stole a kiss. "You think this is fun, just wait till tomorrow, darlin'."

Hours later, they trudged back to the hotel, tired but happy. Fireworks lit the sky; the party was still going strong.

As they walked, Frank kept Carol mesmerized with his vast knowledge of Mardi Gras trivia. "This was a special night for the Crescent Club and the Krewe of Proteus—their one hundred and tenth anniversary. Imagine keeping a party going that long!"

"I wanted to see the king," Carol lamented.

"Nobody sees Proteus," Frank told her. "His identity is always kept secret, his face always covered, even at the ball after the parade's over. You'll get to see the real King of Carnival tomorrow, though. In fact, you can see him right now."

They were passing a newsstand. Frank paused to buy the *Times-Picayune* and held up the front page for Carol to see.

"There he is—local businessman B. Temple Brown, Jr. His queen's a debutante—Elizabeth Fitz-Hugh Kelleher. She's right pretty, too. This says her mother was a queen back in 1964."

They were standing on a corner in the Quarter, Frank reading under a street lamp. The people passing in the dark made Carol jittery. She tried to be watchful, to scan every face, every arm for a tattoo. What if *he* was there in the crowd? She had to get Frank moving—back to the hotel, back to safety.

"Frank, why don't we look at the paper back at the hotel? I can read all about it there."

"Sure," he answered, folding the paper and tucking it under his arm. "We need to get back anyway. We have to be up early tomorrow to put on our costumes, then catch the Zulu parade at eight-thirty before Rex at ten."

"Just how early are you talking about?" Carol asked suspiciously.

Frank laughed. "Oh, about the same time as if we were going to meet Choctaw."

Carol groaned.

A few minutes later, they walked into the hotel courtyard. Frank took Carol to her door, but they parted there after a lingering kiss.

"I'd sure like to come in," he said. "But I reckon I'd better let you get some sleep, darlin'."

Carol watched Frank until he reached his apartment, then waved good night and closed her door. Once she was inside and alone, she realized that her nerves had been wound tight all day. As much as she had enjoyed the parade and all the merrymaking, she felt a great sense of relief knowing that Frank was safely back in his room.

She sighed deeply. "Now, if we can just get through tomorrow."

As weary as she was from their busy day, Carol was sure she would fall asleep the minute she went to bed. Instead, she lay there, jumping at every sound. As much as she wanted to forget all thoughts of Eileen and the man with the tattoo, they kept creeping back to plague her. She tried to soothe them away by going over Cami's wonderful experience with Vic and her own lovely lovemaking with Frank. Things had been so perfect all day.

"*Too* perfect!" she said uneasily.

Now she felt like she was waiting for the other shoe to drop.

Although she longed to believe otherwise, there was no doubt in Carol's mind that her happiness with Frank, their newfound love for each other, was no more than some sort of Carnival-induced magic. Their feelings for each other could disappear as quickly and as surely as the bright fireworks had vanished this evening, leaving the night sky bare and black. More than anything, she realized, she wanted this relationship to work—to last.

"Vic and Cami are so happy now," she murmured, burrowing deeper into her covers. "I want

Frank and me to be like them. No reason we can't be."

Even as she said the words, she knew there were many reasons that loving Frank Longpre might turn out to be a disaster. Carol herself could cause their undoing. She knew secrets about Frank's wife that she would always have to keep from him or run the risk of driving him insane. She also knew that somewhere out there, lurking in the dark streets of the French Quarter, waiting for his chance, was a murderer who had marked the man Carol loved as his next victim.

She tossed in bed, further tangling the sheets, trying to fight her own thoughts as if they were demons she could drive away with sheer willpower.

If only she could talk to Frank—tell him all she knew or suspected. He was the one person in her life with whom she longed to share *everything*. But everything in this case was far too much.

"I wish we really were Vic and Cami," she moaned. "Then our lives would be so simple."

Carol gasped aloud when she realized what she'd said. Her thoughts went back to earlier in the day, when Frank had proposed that very solution. She wondered . . .

"No! It's too incredible! I'm not even going to think about it."

She pounded her pillows, trying to make a more comfortable place for her aching head. Settling in, she willed herself to go to sleep. But she'd sown the seed that would keep growing in her mind for most of the night.

What if they went back? What if they could leave Eileen and her murderer to this century? Could she and Frank correct the mistakes Cami and Vic had made long ago? Could they live happily ever after in another time?

No, she told herself sadly. Such things simply did not, *could not* happen. Tears squeezed out at the corners of her closed eyes as a sense of hopelessness overcame her.

Even as she fell asleep, harp music filled the night. And far off somewhere, a little child kept crying pitifully for Cami.

Chapter Sixteen

It seemed Carol had been asleep only minutes when the phone woke her the next morning.

"Hello?" she answered groggily.

"Up and at 'em, darlin'!" Frank's voice exploded through the phone line with more exuberance than any decent human being should exhibit so early in the day. Carol was just recovering from the first shock when he shouted, "Happy Mardi Gras!" Then the final insult to her auditory system—he tooted a party horn into the phone.

"Yeah, right," Carol moaned. "I get the message."

She hung up on him before he could blast her with his horn again. Inch by weary inch, she dragged herself out of bed. A short while later, she was decked out in her harem costume, her early-morning scowl covered by a sequined veil.

The knock at her door could only be her sheik.

It was, indeed! Frank Longpre transformed—baggy satin pants, bare chest, flowing cape of gold, bejeweled turban, and black mustache.

"Carol, sweetie, you look fetchin' enough to curl hair." He rolled his eyes and twitched the mustache, Groucho-style.

Carol gave him a bump and grind to show off her belly jewel. He roared with laughter. "Do that for King Zulu LXIII and I'll bet you'll get one of their special throws—a Zulu coconut."

"What would I do with a coconut?"

"Treasure it forever!" Frank winked and waggled his mustache at her again. "Now let's get going. I brought breakfast in a brown bag so we can eat on the run."

As they hurried through the breaking dawn toward Canal Street, they munched donuts and drank coffee from plastic cups. It seemed to Carol that the entire population of New Orleans had hit the streets already.

"Don't you people ever sleep?" she asked.

"Not on Mardi Gras. Even the post office closes. Everybody comes to the party."

As they made their way through the crowded streets of the Quarter, Carol tried to keep her eyes peeled for trouble. But the sights she saw—the fantastic, outlandish Mardi Gras costumes—soon distracted her thoughts from the tattooed murderer. When one male reveler jogged by—completely naked, his whole body painted metallic gold—Carol stopped dead in her tracks.

"My God!" she gasped. "Is that legal?"

Frank eyed the golden fellow with far less interest

than Carol. "Hell, *anything* goes on Mardi Gras, honey!"

Soon they were in their favorite spot on the neutral ground, the very air about them charged with a special Carnival electricity. All heads turned as the wild African music and hot jazz of Zulu heralded the coming of the parade. The Olympia Brass Band led the show, along with the Southern University Marching Band and Dancing Dolls. The crowd went crazy, gyrating to the beat.

"This king's a retired postal clerk who's been a member of the Zulu Social Aid and Pleasure Club since he was fifteen years old—James L. Russell," Frank informed Carol, shouting to be heard over all the noise. "His queen's a young lawyer, Ernestine Anderson. Louis Armstrong was king back in 1949. I'll bet that was some parade! Watch for the honor guard, too, the 'Soulful Warriors.' Then there are other famous Zulu maskers—Big Shot, Witch Doctor, Ambassador, Mayor, Province Prince, Governor, and Mr. Big Stuff."

"Should I twitch a hip at them?" Carol asked, demonstrating her earlier maneuver with a wink and a giggle.

"You can do anything your little heart desires, honey. For instance . . ." Frank caught her in his arms and gave her a long, deep kiss, smoothing his hands over her bare hips.

"Frank!" she protested, trying to shove him away. "People are staring!"

The spectators around them applauded, urging Frank on. Carol blushed right down to her belly jewel.

Zulu was crazy and wild and funny and magnificent. The stately king wore flowing robes of purple trimmed in gold while his queen was gowned in white and gold. They made a handsome, glittering pair. The other members of the club were not nearly so elegant in their blackface, fright wigs, and outrageous grass skirts. Carol did indeed capture one of the prized Zulu coconuts for her exceptional hip-swiveling.

Hardly had the thirty-two floats and numerous other units of Zulu faded into the distance before Rex, the King of Carnival, drew into sight.

"For a while, it looked like there wouldn't be a Rex parade this year," Frank said—loudly—to Carol. "When the other old guard krewes pulled out in protest to the new ordinance against discrimination, everybody figured Rex would follow suit. But their motto is 'Pro Bono Publico' and I guess they figured there's nothing better than a parade for the good of the public. It wouldn't be Mardi Gras without the Monarch of Merriment. Shoot! The Krewe of Rex is our symbol. They're responsible for the whole concept of daytime parades, the Carnival colors, and the anthem. For doubloons, too. They threw the first ones." Frank paused and craned his neck. "Here they come, honey!"

Carol stood on tiptoe, trying to see over the ocean of bobbing heads.

Rex's white-plumed captain, astride a snowy stallion, rode proudly at the head of thirty-three mounted lieutenants all garbed in the traditional Carnival colors. The bright sun on their gleaming costumes was almost blinding. Nor was the king's traditional float a less-glittering strain on the eyes.

Carol gasped aloud. "Oh, Frank! It's gorgeous!"

Rex, King of Carnival, wore the costume handed down for over a century—blond wig, bejeweled gold jacket, white tights, gold boots, and a gilt robe edged in ermine. His queen was almost as elegant in her jeweled white gown, collar, crown, and train.

A shower of medallion necklaces, go-cups, and doubloons pelted down on Carol and Frank. Laughing and kissing her, Frank wound a rainbow of plastic beads around Carol's neck.

He fingered one of the necklaces and shook his head. "Back in the old days, they used to toss these real pretty strings of glass beads. You still see them around in antique shops nowadays. But that was before World War II. The necklaces came from Czechoslovakia and when the war broke out the supply was cut off. Since then the throws have all been Hong Kong plastic—not as pretty. But, shoot, it isn't the looks of the stuff but catching it that counts." He grinned at Carol and slipped another necklace over her head. "Right?"

"Right!" she agreed. Then going up on tiptoe, she screamed, "Hey, throw me something, mister!" A grinning masker obliged.

The king's float passed, the Jester float, the Rex Bandwagon, the Royal Barge, and the *"Boeuf Gras,"* the fatted bull, symbolic of the last meat to be eaten before the Lenten season.

Carol felt let down when the parade rumbled off down Canal and the music faded. Frank didn't give her spirits long to sag.

"Now the *real* fun begins," he told her. "Come on. We have to get to Bourbon and Dumaine for the big costume judging—the annual Bourbon Street Awards. Wait till you see this show!"

"Do you think we have a chance to win?"

356

He laughed. "You look devastating, darlin', but, no, I don't think you have a chance. Somebody from one of the gay Carnival clubs always wins."

Carol stopped and stared at him. "They have their own krewes?"

"You bet! There's Polyphemus, Amon-Ra, Celestial Knights, Petronius, Armenius, and Lords of Leather. And this costume contest is better than a Las Vegas show."

A short time later, after they'd elbowed their way to the appointed street corner, Carol had to agree this must be the best show in town. Never before had she seen such glitter, such glamour, such downright outrageousness. Many of the gorgeous drag queens wore headdresses ten to fifteen feet high. Sequins, spangles, beads, and feathers. Carol felt her own costume pale miserably in comparison.

The afternoon wore on through a haze of beer and dancing and good Carnival fun. By three-thirty, Carol was done in—her belly jewel beginning to lose its sparkle.

"Hey, Frank, I think it's time to head home, don't you?"

He looked at her as if she'd lost her mind. "Leave all this?"

"Well, we are still going to a ball tonight, aren't we?"

Just then, a gorilla on the balcony directly overhead called down, "Hey, mister, show us some flesh!"

Grinning up at the guy in the ape suit, Frank threw back his cape, flexing his pectorals.

"You, too, lady! Let's see some skin."

"What does he want me to do?" Carol whispered to Frank. "I've got about all the flesh showing that I care to exhibit."

"He's probably hoping you'll toss him your gold bra for a souvenir."

Carol clutched herself protectively. "Never!" she gasped.

"Well, just do that hip-thing for him then."

Carol complied, but the gorilla still wasn't satisfied. Motioning to a pretty young tourist beside Carol, he called down, "You, redhead! I'll trade you my beads for your tee-shirt."

The slightly drunken reveler never hesitated. Off came the shirt, which she tossed to the gorilla. Then he showered her with almost, but not quite, enough strings of beads to cover her bare breasts.

Carol's mouth flew open; her eyes went wide. "Yes, Frank, I think it's definitely time to go back to the hotel."

"Whatever you say," Frank agreed. But Carol could tell that he would have liked to hang around to see if the ape-man made any more trades.

At six, Carol was gowned in green and gold, waiting for Frank to call for her again. He had explained that the ball they were going to was not one of the tableau balls sponsored by a major krewe, but a private affair at a French Quarter hotel.

"That makes it even better," he'd told her. "We'll really get to dance instead of sitting on the sidelines waiting for a call out."

When Frank knocked at Carol's door, she opened it eagerly, then caught her breath at the sight of him. Gone were his turban, cape and mustache from earlier in the day. He looked so good in his midnight-blue tux that tears actually pooled in her eyes. She laughed and brushed them away.

"My, you do clean up nicely, Captain Longpre!"

He stood staring at her, his gaze traveling over her appreciatively for several moments. Then he reached out to her. "Come here, you," he ordered in a lusty voice. "You look good enough to eat with a spoon. You certainly do that gown justice, Miz Marlowe."

Carol clung to her handsome escort, glorying in the long, tender kiss he bestowed upon her.

"My, my, yes, that is a nice dress," he said after a time, but the shadow of a frown marred his face as he spoke.

"I'm glad you like it, Frank."

Frown gone, smile wide, he said, "I like what's in it even better."

"If you keep this up, we'll never get to that ball," she warned.

"You're right. It's just real hard for me to keep my hands off you, lady." He shrugged, winked, then offered his arm. "If it's okay with you, I thought we'd walk. It's not far to the hotel and it's such a perfect night."

The night *was* perfect, or so it seemed. They wandered, arm-in-arm, through the Quarter, basking in the admiring glances they received from passing maskers. Their looks gave Carol the heady feeling of being someone special on a very special night.

But once again, the coming of dark made Carol more than a little nervous. She caught herself trying to probe behind the masks to see the eyes of passing strangers and taking special note of men's arms as they passed. She was relieved when they reached the hotel and could get off the street into more confined quarters.

Frank had arranged for them to have a table alone in a shadowy corner of the ballroom. "I don't want to share you this evening, darlin'," he whispered.

Romance perfumed the air. They sat together in the glow of the single candle on their table, Carol sipping champagne while Frank kissed her fingertips and talked to her quietly about his dreams, his hopes, and his growing love for her.

When they took the floor for a stately waltz, Carol felt as if she were drifting through a lovely dream. The warm night air, the excitement of Mardi Gras, the soft music, the magic of her feelings for Frank—all these things worked together to transport her to a seemingly mystical, faraway place. She felt like a member of a long-ago royal court.

As she waltzed in Frank's arms, Carol noticed little points of light flitting around them like nervous fireflies. A mirrored ball suspended above the dance floor shot tiny, shining prisms around the room. She half-closed her eyes, imagining that stars had come down to earth to mingle with them.

"I could dance with you forever," Frank whispered, his warm lips brushing her cheek.

"Oh, Frank, I don't want the music to stop—not ever!" Carol felt almost frantic suddenly. "Don't let it stop!"

But it did stop—abruptly.

Still holding Carol in his arms, Frank stared down

into her eyes. His frown was back. She looked familiar, yet she looked like someone else. Her eyes had gone green—not the hazel-green of Carol Marlowe's in anger—but a clear, dreamy green. The green of emeralds, the green of Eileen's eyes. As he continued to stare, the bright color of her irises faded. He blinked. He must be imagining things. A moment later, Carol's eyes had changed color again. Now they were indigo—a wonderful, clear blue, shot through with violet lights.

"Carol?" Frank whispered, wiping his sweating brow. "Carol, something's happening to me."

Before she could answer, the music began again. Frank moved slowly with its rhythm, but he was no longer conscious of anything around him. The ballroom, the mirrored lights, even Carol herself took on a hazy, dreamlike quality.

"Frank? Frank . . ."

He heard Carol calling his name, but her voice seemed to come from faraway in time and space. He tried to answer, but the music grew louder and louder until his voice was lost in the sound.

Suddenly, he felt strange and hot. He fought for breath, trying to call out to her. But there was only the melancholy music of a harp thundering inside his head and the dizziness.

"Carol! Carol, hold onto me!" It seemed to Frank that he was screaming to her, but no sound came. He only mouthed the words in a futile attempt to stop what seemed inevitable. He was leaving her, slipping away into the past.

He thought he heard her call to him, but Frank was too far away to hear anything going on in the twentieth century. He was now in a little shotgun house of the *rue d'Amour*, pacing inside Victoine Navar's body, his face stormy, his mood worse.

"You have to help me, Fiona," he demanded. "I must find her!"

"Mon Dieu! Do you mean to tell me Cami has run away? What did you do to her, Victoine? You knew she was innocent, that you had to be gentle with her."

He stopped pacing long enough to turn and face Fiona. "I'm not talking about Cami. It's my wife, Madelaine. I *must* find her! There's nothing left between us. I want out, permanently."

Fiona gasped. "Surely, you can't mean divorce."

"Annulment, whatever. I mean to marry Cami."

"Marry her?" Fiona paused, her head spinning. Only three weeks ago Victoine had taken the girl as his mistress and now his thoughts were already on marriage. Had Camille told him her true identity?

Vic's voice interrupted Fiona's thoughts and answered her question. "I know, I know. You needn't remind me that she is a woman of color. I'll take her to Paris and marry her there where no laws forbid such a match."

"Have you discussed this with Cami?"

"Not yet," he admitted. "First, I must find my wife and my son. You have connections, Fiona. You know people who could help me. Please, say that you will."

"I can only tell you I'll try, Victoine. But I feel you should talk to Cami first. There are things she should explain to you."

"What things?" Black Vic rounded on the woman, narrowing his eyes suspiciously.

"You must ask Cami for her secrets. They are not mine to expose."

Vic set down his brandy snifter and turned for the door. "Very well. I will. The moment I return to the house."

"Frank? Frank! What's wrong with you?"

Carol was shaking him, there on the dance floor. Frank felt himself literally jerked back from wherever he'd been. Fiona's house . . . yes, he remembered. And some secret that might keep him from marrying Cami. He didn't understand any of it. But he shared Black Vic's feelings. He would move heaven and earth to marry Carol, but, as with Vic, he had enormous obstacles standing in his way to happiness.

"I'm okay now," he said, his voice a harsh, dry whisper. "I had some sort of flashback, but it faded fast."

"You're sure you're all right?"

Frank nodded, trying to smile.

"What triggered it?" Carol asked. "Do you know?"

"I'm not sure. It was real strange, but I think your eyes sent me back. They turned color until it was almost as if I was looking into Cami's eyes and she was pleading with me. For something . . . I don't know what exactly."

They danced on in silence for a few minutes, both thinking about Cami and Vic and how much those two lovers from the past adored each other.

Frank tried to lighten the mood. He didn't want to spoil the evening for Carol. "Hey, did I tell you that sure is a good-looking dress, honey?" He'd only told her that about six times during the evening, but at least the subject was safe, or seemed so. "Where'd you get it, anyway?"

"Oh, this old thing!" Carol laughed, delighted that her vintage costume pleased Frank so and that he seemed to be himself again. "I'd like to say it came straight from Paris, but the truth is it was in a load of stuff I bought from a Memphis dealer a couple of months ago. I don't usually sell old clothes in my shop, but this was part of the deal. If I wanted the garnet jewelry he had for sale, I had to empty his whole truck. When you mentioned the Mardi Gras ball, I figured this dress might be just the trick. I'm glad you like it."

Frank's smile faded instantly. He stopped dancing and stared at the gown. "Memphis, you say?"

"That's right. Is something wrong?" For no reason she could imagine, Carol felt a cold hand close over her heart.

"Eileen was from Memphis. Her mother still lived there."

"Lived?"

"Yeah. She died of a heart attack about six months ago. Eileen's uncle cleaned out the old homeplace, sold most of their stuff. He called to see if there was anything I wanted. Mrs. Doncaster still had all Eileen's things. She said she couldn't bear to part with anything that had belonged to her only daughter. I guess I'm just the opposite, though. I don't like things around to remind me of what happened—to remind me that I'll probably never know what happened. And that dress . . ."

Frank paused—his face pale and frozen—as if the words simply refused to come.

"Yes, Frank? What about my dress?"

"It was Eileen's." His voice broke as he finally managed to say the words. "That's the very dress she wore to the Mardi Gras ball right after we were married."

Carol wanted to die on the spot. "Surely not, Frank! Oh, I'm so sorry!"

"I thought it looked familiar when I first saw you tonight. But, hell, all women's clothes look pretty much alike to me and I couldn't really place it." Although Frank was obviously trying to make light of it, his voice was filled with pain. "You're probably right, Carol. It couldn't be Eileen's even if it did come from Memphis."

Carol followed his lead. "I'll bet there are hundreds of gowns like this. It probably came off some department store rack."

"Not if it's Eileen's," Frank countered. "She had that gown made by a cousin of hers who was a dressmaker. It was one of a kind. There was even a special label in it—'Cassandra Classics.' "

Carol caught her breath. What could she say? What could she do to apologize for this stupid blunder? It wasn't her fault, but all the same she felt responsible for causing him needless pain.

The music ended. Somewhere far off a church bell set up its mournful knell.

"Almost midnight," Frank said. "Mardi Gras will be over in another few seconds. Nothing left but a lot of clutter on the streets and the final toast. Then it's gone . . . all gone."

The sad tone of Frank's voice and the dazed look in his eyes shocked Carol thoroughly. He sounded as if he were talking about some loved one on the brink of death. He looked like he had a short while ago when he'd slipped away. Maybe the gown was the catalyst that caused him to go back, bringing such pain with Eileen's memory that he'd been forced to escape to another time and place. Whatever the cause, Carol had to get him out of here and she had to get out of Eileen's dress. Curses on the gorgeous gown!

"Let's go, Frank," Carol begged. "Maybe we can still beat the crowd."

"Might as well," he muttered, "it's all over now anyway. She's gone, soon Mardi Gras will be gone, too. Nothing left. It's over . . . all over."

Carol gripped him suddenly in a fierce embrace. "No, Frank! It's not over," she cried. "Nothing's over! I'm still here. And I love you, Frank! Can you hear me?"

Frank didn't answer. He seemed caught up in some sort of fog, like a drunk who's gone one drink past his limit plunging instantly from giddy euphoria to deadly depression. That depression, in its deepest form, now had Frank in its deadly grip.

Carol kissed him almost desperately, then caught his hand and headed for the nearest exit. Maybe if she got him out of here the dismal spell would pass.

Clinging limply to her hand, Frank followed. A short time later, they were outside the hotel in the cool, damp air of midnight.

"Breathe deeply, Frank," Carol ordered, realizing that she was treating him foolishly, as if he were indeed drunk.

"I just want to go to sleep," he mumbled. "Just take me home to bed."

A number of taxis were parked nearby, waiting for the Mardi Gras ball to end. Carol hurried to the one at the head of the line. "Take us to the Hotel Dalpeche," she instructed, stuffing Frank in the back door.

"Yes, ma'am," the driver said. "Need any help with him? Looks like he enjoyed Mardi Gras right much. Me? I gotta drive, so no booze."

"He's not drunk!" Carol snapped. "Just get us to the hotel as quickly as you can."

Frank said not one word all the way. He sat next to Carol in the back seat, his face stony, his eyes glazed over. She began to wonder if he had gone back to Vic and Cami's time without her again, and that truly frightened her.

"Frank?" she whispered urgently. "Frank, can you hear me?"

He said nothing, but when they passed under a street lamp, Carol saw that tears were streaming down his marble-white face.

"Oh, God," she moaned softly, then louder to the driver, "Can't you go any faster?"

"Listen, lady, we got laws."

"I think he's going to be sick."

Hearing Carol's words, the cabbie floored it. Within five minutes, they arrived at the hotel. Frank leaned heavily on Carol all the way, but she managed to get him to his room and into bed. He remained stone-faced and silent.

"Frank, answer me! Are you all right now?" Nearly frantic, she leaned over him, trying to get some response. Not a muscle in his face moved. His eyes stared through her instead of at her.

Carol was torn. She was afraid to leave him, but she had to get out of Eileen's gown. Somehow the dress had triggered all this.

"Frank, I'm going to my room for a couple of minutes. You just lie there and rest. I'll be right back."

Nothing! Not a word, not a move.

Carol ran to the door, raced out and across the courtyard. She was breathing heavily as she entered her door, already clawing at the zipper down the back of the gown. Bra, hoopskirt, half-slip, and panty hose went flying about the room like so many odd-shaped UFOs. She pulled on jeans and a tee-shirt and headed back out, still at a trot. Three minutes later, she was back with Frank. He hadn't moved.

Leaning over him, Carol felt his his forehead. He was cold and clammy. She grabbed a blanket and covered him, then lay down beside him, hoping her body heat might help.

"Please, Frank, it's me—Carol," she almost shouted. "Can you hear me, Frank? Answer me, dammit!"

Frank stirred uneasily, giving Carol cause for hope. But when she called his name and gripped his hand there was no response.

"Where are you, Frank? What's happening? Talk to me, darling!"

He settled again, staring straight ahead, but seeing nothing—not the ceiling overhead, not the fan turning slowly, not Carol's tear-streaked face.

Vic found Cami waiting when he returned to the house in Condé Street. But she seemed different somehow. Usually, when he arrived, she rushed to meet him, kissed him senseless, then bombarded him with endless questions about what he'd done while he was away. Today, however, she was quiet and withdrawn. When Vic tried to kiss her, she shied away.

"What's wrong, Cami love? Why, you act as if you're afraid of me."

The girl took a seat as far across the room from Vic as she could get. When he moved closer, she seemed to cringe with fear.

"Cami, what is it? Have I done something to displease you?"

"That is not my place to say, m'sieur," she answered subserviently. "Fiona said it is I who must please you. I fear I do not."

Vic was dumbfounded. "Whatever put such a thought in your head? Of course, you please me. You've given me new life and hope. Why, I couldn't live without you now. Come here to me."

Meaning to demonstrate his words with immediate and passionate action, Vic swept her into his arms and kissed her deeply. No small velvety tongue crept out to stroke his, no gentle hands caressed his neck, no firm breasts pressed his chest. Instead, she held herself coldly away from him.

"What is this—some new game?"

In answer, she merely bit her lip and shook her head. He felt her go rigid in his arms.

"Ah, acting the nervous virgin, are we?" He laughed, thinking the Cami he knew so well was truly playing a game that she hoped would amuse and arouse him. "I know exactly how to deal with you, then."

Swinging an arm down, he caught her behind the knees and hoisted her against his chest. "We'll see who knows the best games, little love."

Vic took her straight to his bedroom where he

369

quickly stripped off her gown. She quivered before him, trying to hide her nakedness with her hands.

Seeing her futile actions, he threw back his head and laughed. "My God, Cami! You're a delight!"

Never for a moment did it dawn on him that she might be seriously afraid—not even when she backed away from him, her face pale, her small hands still attempting to cover far more than they were capable of hiding from his fierce, black eyes.

"Come here to me!" he ordered, her "act" arousing him so that he could wait no longer.

Slowly, she walked toward him, her eyes downcast.

"Get on the bed," he commanded gently.

Trembling, she obeyed.

Still fully clothed, Vic lay down beside her. He chuckled softly as he slipped his hand between her thighs. "You want games, my love? Well, let the games begin."

Ever so gently, his fingers played between her clamped thighs. Always before she had parted them for him at his slightest touch. But today she lay rigid, closed to his pleasure. When he bent to suckle her breast, no moans of pleasure issued from her pretty mouth, only a whimper.

Vic began to wonder what she was about. He understood none of this. Their loving had been so perfect from the very start. Now, suddenly, Cami was as cold as New England ice. But the more she refused him with the stiff rejection of her body, the more he became aroused.

He tried kissing her to softness, but met with no more success than he had encountered earlier. For an instant, he thought seriously of leaving—storming out of the room to let her know his displeasure. But why should he? It was his room and she was his lover!

When he probed her gently with his fingers, she moaned softly. The sound fired his blood.

"Since it seems you aren't in the mood this afternoon, we'll make it quick."

Vic sat up to free himself from his britches. At the sight of him, she gave a frightened cry.

"Oh, please! It isn't night yet. You never come until after dark. Must I fear the day as well?"

Vic stared at Cami, stunned. Could this woman be the same loving, passionate, almost wanton mistress he had come to know over the past weeks? Why was she cringing there before him?

"Daytime, nighttime, it's all the same to me," he said in a husky voice. "When love needs making, the time is always right."

He had to pry her thighs apart to gain entry. She made herself tight, tighter even than she had been their first time. She made no move to touch him, to kiss him, or overtly to deny him. She simply lay there as motionless and as passionless as stone.

Disgusted that he would stoop to force her and confused by this new Cami, Vic spent himself quickly, then rolled away. When he left her, she was crying softly into her pillow.

At the moment he closed the door, the sound of her crying still ringing in his ears, Vic decided what he must do. He'd been wrong about Cami. She'd put up a good front for him until this afternoon. But now he knew her darkest secret—the secret Fiona had hinted at. Obviously, Cami had put on a convincing act for as long as she could manage, but deep down she was cold. Cami could never be able to love any man.

"So," Vic murmured aloud with a sigh, "I'll send her back to Fiona this very evening."

Frank's hand moved. His fingers traced the frightened tears on Carol's cheeks. She uttered a cry of relief.

"Don't cry, Cami. I'm sorry, my little darling. I do love you, you see, and I don't want to send you away." Frank's voice was deeper than usual, not quite his own. And he was begging, pleading, his heart breaking. These were the first words he had spoken since they left the ball. Any words would have made Carol rejoice, but these confused her as well.

"Frank, oh, Frank! Can you hear me? What happened?"

The glassy look remained in his eyes. He turned toward Carol, but seemed not to see her. A haunted look crossed his face.

He laughed aloud, seeming relieved at something. "So, it was a mere dream—more *nightmare*, actually," he said in that same strange voice, yet a voice that sounded vaguely familiar to Carol. "Come here to me, little love."

Carol did as Frank said, sliding closer to him across the bed. His hands gripped her tee-shirt. He stared at the silver "Dollywood" logo across her breasts and chuckled. "What manner of camisole is this?" The next moment, he tugged it off over her head.

Frank's mouth on Carol's breasts felt cool and wonderful. She closed her eyes and sighed.

His hands went next to her jeans. "Britches?" he growled. "My Cami in britches?"

Carol's eyes shot open. She stared at Frank, only she wasn't seeing Frank, she realized. His entire demeanor had taken on the likeness of Black Vic. Even the scar was there—left on Frank's face by a ridge in the bedspread. Or was it?

Carol trembled as Victoine Navar's strong hands gripped her waist.

"You women make this so difficult," he complained good-naturedly. "Take these things off, won't you, Cami? And don't wear them anymore."

Carol obligingly slipped out of her jeans. Meanwhile, Frank—or was it truly Vic?—shed his clothes as well.

Her heart thundered as he pressed his body close, drawing her tight against his erection.

"Ah, that's better, love," he moaned, slipping his hand between her legs exactly as he had done the last time—that strange one-way coupling when Cami had been so cold.

"You won't turn from me again, will you?"

"Never!" Carol answered in a voice choked with excitement and emotion. He was truly doing marvelous things to her.

When at last Vic took Carol, it was a wondrous experience. It seemed she was being loved by two men—as if both Frank and Vic had done everything in their mingled powers to arouse her and then satisfy her. When the perfect moment came, Carol cried out in total, exquisite pleasure. Then her eyes closed.

For a long time, they lay still in each other's arms. Slowly, Victoine Navar ebbed away until only Frank was left in the bed with Carol.

"What the hell . . . ?" Frank's voice jolted Carol, who had nodded off.

"Is that you, Frank?" Carol asked dreamily.

"Well, I should hope to God it's me! I mean, we're both lying here without a stitch on in *my* bed and I'm inside you. Who the hell did you think it might be?"

This wasn't going to be easy to explain and Carol knew it, but she vowed to give it her best shot. Quickly, she filled in the details of their departure from the ball and Frank's strange state. She was careful to skirt any mention of Eileen's gown. "You woke up talking to Cami," she told him. "You must have gone back without me, Frank. Just you and the real Cami and I got left back here."

"Yes," he answered simply. "That's exactly what happened. I remember it all now. It was awful, Carol!"

"Can you tell me about it?"

Before he answered, Frank drew Carol into his arms and kissed her deeply. She copied his tongue strokes hungrily. When he released her, he let out a long sigh.

"Thank God! You're still the same, Carol. Only Cami has changed."

"What do you mean, Frank?"

"I went back . . . yes!" he exclaimed. "First, Vic was at Fiona's. He wants her to help him find his wife so he can get an annulment and take Cami to Paris to marry her there."

"Oh, how romantic!"

Frank shook his head. "I'm afraid not. You see, when Vic got back to the house, Cami was different. She acted like she was scared to death of him. You know all those old tales about how Victorian women put up with their men only to get pregnant and how they really hated sex?"

Carol nodded. "Yes, but I never believed a word of it."

"Well, apparently it's true 'cause Cami sure didn't want anything to do with Vic. She was as cold as frozen marble—made him feel like a real bastard for taking her to bed."

"But how could she act that way? She loves Vic; she adores him."

Frank's dark eyes narrowed as he gazed at Carol. "When *you're* there, she does. But I have a feeling that Cami—all by herself—is a far different woman. Carol, why did you ask if it was me a minute ago?"

She shied away from his direct gaze. "You're not going to like this, Frank."

"Somehow, I had a feeling I wouldn't. But shoot. I can take it."

"You left first while we were dancing, but you were gone only a minute or two. Then after we got back here, you went away again. When you returned, you brought Vic with you. It was uncanny. You looked like him, you talked like him."

Frank leaned up on one elbow and stared hard at Carol. "You're right. I don't like this one damn bit! You mean he was here, in this very room?"

Carol nodded. "Right here, in this bed."

Frank looked down. He'd spent himself and

slipped out of Carol, but he'd still been erect and inside her when he woke.

"Did he do what I think he did to you? Tell me honestly, Carol."

Biting her lower lip, she nodded.

"I'll kill the bastard!" Frank threw off the blanket and got up like he meant to go for his gun right then and there.

Carol caught his arm and pulled him back to the bed. "Listen, it was *you*, Frank! I mean, you and I were the only ones in bed. He was here only in spirit. Somehow he hitched a ride back with you, but he's gone now."

Frank put his face in his hands and rubbed hard. "Shit! This is crazy!"

"I think I understand what happened, Frank," Carol ventured. "If what you say about Cami is true, then Vic came with you looking for the Cami he knows, the Cami who is there only when I'm with her."

Frank thought for a minute, then nodded agreement. "Yeah! That must be right. And if it is, that means that Vic and Cami will never be happy unless you and I go back there and hold their hands. So I say, shove it! I'm sick of a bunch of dead people playing fast and loose with our lives."

Carol experienced a sudden sinking feeling. Frank was right and she knew it. They had no obligation to Cami and Vic. They had their own lives to lead.

"Well, how about it, Carol? Don't you agree?"

"I guess so," she answered half-heartedly.

"Then that's that! Case closed! Come here, you!"

Carol shoved away from him. "No more tonight,

376

Frank. It's been a long day and, actually . . ." she paused, not sure if she should tell Frank the truth, then hurried on, "I'm kind of sore."

"Damn that friggin' bastard!" Frank exclaimed, but he let Carol go back to her room for what little was left of the night.

Chapter Seventeen

Carol couldn't sleep when she returned to her room. After tossing fitfully for a time in the dark, she sat up and switched on the bedside lamp. The first thing she saw was the green and gold shimmer of Eileen Longpre's gown, thrown carelessly across the arm of a chair.

Carol went over and picked it up, turned it around, and ran her gaze along the inside zipper seam. There it was, just as Frank had said, a small label, stitched in gold—"Cassandra Classics." She dropped the dress as if it had suddenly burned her hands. Without turning around, she inched her way back to the bed and sat down.

"What's going on?" she asked aloud as if speaking directly to Eileen's gown, or perhaps to Eileen's ghost. "Don't try to tell me this is a coincidence. I don't believe in coincidences. Everything that happens in life occurs for a reason."

Her only answer came in the form of oppressive silence. Then far off in the distance—or was it far off in some distant part of her memory?—she heard the faint stirrings of harp strings.

Carol sighed and closed her eyes, trying to block out everything. Why was life so complicated? Now that she had finally fallen in love, why was she being forced to do battle with man, nature, and the great unknown in order to hold that love?

"Seems like it would be a simple enough matter," she reasoned aloud. "Frank could have Eileen declared legally dead, which I'm certain she is. We could get married, go on a honeymoon, then come back to New Orleans and settle down to wedded bliss, maybe even have a couple of babies. My shop's no problem—just close up and sell out."

But what of my *problem, mademoiselle?*

The voice sounded as if it came from a man right in the room with her, but Carol's senses and the gooseflesh rising on her arms told her differently. She glanced about just to make sure. She was alone. Besides, she knew that voice, and if that particular guy was here, it was most certainly in spirit only.

"I don't think I can help you, Black Vic." Her answer was as calm as if she were carrying on a normal conversation with a normal person.

You are *my problem!* the voice argued.

"I'm not; Cami is," Carol pointed out.

But you are Cami!

"No!" Carol cried. "I am not! Now, go away and leave me alone."

You will be alone soon, the voice warned. *All alone!*

"What do you mean?"

Only silence answered her. Carol shivered, seized with sudden panic.

"Dammit, you answer me! What are you talking about? I'll never be alone again as long as I have Frank."

My heart bleeds . . . The phantom voice trailed off into deep space, leaving Carol trembling with fear.

She hugged herself and rocked back and forth on the bed like a frightened child. "I am *not* going crazy!" she murmured. "Somehow, all of this is connected. I won't try to find explanations, only answers to why it's happening to me—and to Frank. Poor Frank! I got him into this whirlpool of insanity. If I'd stayed in North Carolina where I belonged, he would have been okay."

But even as she said the words, she knew she was wrong. The mummy from the swamp had drawn Frank into this weird puzzle before he ever knew Carol's name. And everything that had happened since that discovery was connected.

"Everything!" Carol whispered. "Like a drawstring or a noose being pulled tighter and tighter by the minute. Cutting off air and light and breath."

Lost in her morbid thoughts, Carol realized suddenly that she was gasping, trying to gulp for air. Her vision blurred and everything in the room seemed to swim around until the lamps, the chairs, and Eileen's shimmering gown lost form and substance and became no more than a stream of swirling color like a sidewalk chalk picture caught in the rain.

Then, just as suddenly, the chaotic rainbow fused, forming a ghastly scene before her eyes. She saw a woman's ghostly face—nothing else—only the face in light, swimming in a deep pool of darkness. Her green eyes were wide with terror and tears made clean tracks down her dirty cheeks. Her hair was tangled and matted with sweat. Although Carol heard no sounds, she could tell the woman was screaming. At irregular intervals, her mouth opened wide and her features contorted in an awful grimace of pain and fear.

In a momentary flash, Carol saw the rest of the woman's body. Her clothes had been partially torn from her—shirt ripped, jeans zipper torn open, lacy pink panties showing through. She was bound tightly with rope, her arms behind her back. She lay twisted on the swampy ground.

A sudden dark shadow dulled the brightness of the vision. Carol watched, unblinking, as a man's bulk stepped between her and the silently screaming woman. He lashed out—once and then again. And each time he did, Carol got a fleeting glimpse of the tattoo on his right arm. Her stomach twisted. Her heart beat faster and faster.

Sound, at last. Ugly, painful, horrible sound— the man's fist smashing into the woman's tender flesh. Then a surly, drunken voice: "Yell your head off, bitch! Nobody'll hear you out here. Not even your shit-ass husband. After I do you, he'll get his. But for now, it's just you and me for as long as you last . . ."

"Frank, help me!" The woman's scream bounced off the walls of Carol's room and echoed inside her aching skull.

Closing her eyes as tight as she could, Carol covered her ears with her hands and ground her clenched teeth. "No more," she moaned. "Please, no more!"

After what seemed a very long time, Carol dared to open her eyes again. To her vast relief, the horrible scene had dissolved, but still the colors swirled, warning of more to come. Tentatively, she uncovered her ears. Blessed silence!

Moments later, a new scene materialized—the woman again. But this time she was still, silent, as pale as death except for the garish bruises on her face, the blood trickling down her chin. Her green eyes still stared, but now with a glazed, unseeing look. The visionary "camera" drew back, giving Carol a wider shot. She gagged and snapped her eyes shut. The woman was gone. Only her head remained, dead eyes staring at the bloody patch of ground where her body should had been.

Carol must have fainted. When she came around, the first streaks of dawn cast a bloody glow through the window reminiscent of her gory vision. She still felt ill and groggy. She stumbled toward the bathroom to get a drink. The water helped, but not much. She was shaking all over.

Carol was still fighting for control when the phone rang, sending a sharp jolt through her body.

She grabbed the receiver and shouted breathlessly, "Hello!"

"Jesus, Carol, you trying to bust my eardrum?"

"Jesse?" His was the last voice she'd expected to hear. Tears of relief sprang to her eyes. "Oh, Jesse, I'm so glad it's you!"

"Hey, are you okay, honey?"

"Sure, Jesse." Her voice was a quivering whisper. She desperately wanted to tell Jesse what she'd seen, but the words wouldn't come. "Just worn out, I guess."

"Hey, I shouldn't have called so early. I forgot about Mardi Gras yesterday. I guess you and ole Frank were out pretty late, huh?"

"It's okay, Jesse. I was awake. There's something I have to tell you."

"In a minute, Carol. First, let me tell you about this Jones character."

"They caught him? Oh, thank God, Jesse!" At last, something good had happened, Carol told herself.

Jesse soon dashed her hopes. "Afraid not. But we do know for sure now that he's in the New Orleans area. A couple of sightings. He gave the sheriff's guys the slip both times they spotted him. They'll catch him, though. Just a matter of time. Have you told Frank yet?"

"No, Jesse! God, no! And I sure hope we don't have to tell him—ever. Right now, he's so caught up in guilt over Eileen that I'm really worried he might go off the deep end. And it's all my fault."

"What do you mean, Carol, about it being *your* fault?"

"Oh, it's too involved to explain over the phone." She glanced again at Eileen's gown. How she hated the thing! "You just can't tell Frank about Jones, that's all."

"Then you two better lay low for a few days 'cause otherwise Frank's sure to get wind of the dragnet that's out for this guy. Is there somewhere y'all could go till Jones is picked up?"

"Go?" Carol's mind was whirling with the visions she had just seen. She had to make herself tell Jesse. "Oh, yeah, Jesse! There's always somewhere Frank and I can go to get away."

"Well, I'd strongly suggest a little vacation, then. Hey, Carol?"

"Yes, Jesse?"

"You haven't seen anything else have you—weird stuff, I mean?"

There it was, the perfect cue. Now she was forced to tell him. She steeled herself. "Yes, Jesse, I have. Jones is definitely the one who murdered Eileen and I heard him tell her that Frank will be next. What I saw before happened the day Jones took her away."

"Away *where*?"

Carol shook her head and tried to stop trembling so she could continue. "I don't know. Someplace in the swamp. He kept her there, Jesse. He beat her and . . . then he killed her and then . . ." Carol's voice broke. She couldn't go on.

"And *what*, honey? Take it slowly, but you have to tell me the rest. Do you know where we can find the body?"

"The body," she repeated dully. "No. It's gone. I mean, you'll have to search a lot of different places. I can't tell you exactly." Carol spoke every word separately, slowly as if each syllable were frozen in ice.

"Jesus Christ!" Jesse swore softly. "Dismembered? If Frank ever finds out—"

"Dammit, Jesse, he *can't* find out!" Carol broke down on the phone, first screaming at Jesse, then sobbing uncontrollably.

"Take it easy, honey. Are you sure you're okay?"

"I'll manage," Carol whispered, gulping back more painful sobs.

"Good girl! Now you get ole Frank outta there till this all blows over. Call me if you need to talk to somebody."

"Jesse?"

"Yeah, Carol?"

"Frank and I are going away, probably today," she said evenly. "If you don't hear from us for a long time, don't worry. We'll be together and we'll be all right."

"What do you mean by a long time, honey? A couple of weeks? A month?"

"Longer," Carol whispered through her tears. "Much longer. 'Bye, Jesse."

She hung up before he could ask any more questions.

Carol glanced at the clock. Eight-thirteen. Frank was probably still sleeping. At any rate, she didn't want to tell him her plan until she'd made another call. She had a friend in real estate back in North Carolina. Carol started to dial her number, then changed her mind. Better to deal with a stranger, someone who wouldn't ask questions. She checked the business cards in her wallet. Sure enough she had the card of another realtor back home. She dialed him instead.

"Good morning. Wilson Land Development," a secretary answered perkily.

"Mr. Wilson, please."

Within twenty minutes, Carol had arranged everything with the real estate dealer. She told him she was getting married and would not be returning to North Carolina in the foreseeable future. He was to rent her house and her shop for an indefinite period of time. She even provided him with the name of a local lady who had expressed an interest in her antiques business.

"I'm not sure when I'll be back," Carol told Mr. Wilson. "It may be a year or more. If you could simply take your commission, then deposit my rent checks in one of your accounts to be held for me until I return . . ."

He agreed to take care of everything and wished her a happy honeymoon. End of problem! Frank's business matters wouldn't be that simple. But then, Carol reminded herself, she had no guarantee that the two of them could actually stay in the past once they went back. They'd seemed to have little control over their comings and goings during previous visits.

"Black Vic wants me back there," Carol reminded herself aloud. "And if I can convince Frank to go, we're going for good this time. It's the only way. It has to work."

She sighed and got up from the bed. It was time to think of normal, everyday things—bathe, dress, eat.

As she headed toward the bedroom, her eyes lit on Eileen's gold and green gown. With a vicious swipe, she whipped it off the chair and took it into the bathroom. Grabbing the metal trash can from under the sink, she stuffed the dress into it.

"Not good enough!" she said bitterly. "You'll just turn up again if I toss you out with the garbage."

She snatched a book of hotel matches off the back of the toilet, lit the whole pack and tossed them onto the gown. The filmy fabric caught instantly. But this wouldn't do either. Any minute her smoke alarm would start screaming.

Carefully holding the can with its smoldering contents, Carol went out the door and around to the back of the parking lot where the dumpsters were. If anyone asked, she would say that she tossed a burning cigarette into the full can and accidentally started a fire.

No one asked. She stood beside the dumpster until the gold and green fabric was only filmy black ash. Then she tossed can and all into the trash.

Brushing her hands off, she said, "That's the end of that!"

Frank stood at his window, staring out over the courtyard and the parking lot behind it. What the hell was Carol doing now? Burning old love letters? Or maybe it was some kind of voodoo rite. He continued to watch her, frowning as he sipped strong coffee to try to stop the shakes. Oddest damn thing! He'd felt hung over when he woke up a while ago. He knew he hadn't had anything to drink last night. Not that he recalled, anyway. There seemed to be big gaps in his memory this morning. If he was going to have blackouts—shoot!—he might as well go back on the bottle. Just black *everything* out!

Carol turned and started back toward her room. She had an odd expression on her face, and he could tell she'd been crying. What the hell was going on?

"Hey, Carol!" he called, opening his door to wave her up.

She turned and started slowly toward the stairs. He could tell as she came closer that she was fighting for control. Something had happened last night, something that he couldn't remember. Whatever it was, it was serious.

"Hey, darlin'. Happy morning after," he said, forcing a light tone into his voice. He brushed Carol's cheek. When he did, she grabbed him about the waist, clinging tightly, and buried her face against his bare chest.

"What's the matter, Carol? Come on in and tell ole Frank." He was trying to keep things light, but he had a feeling something really heavy had come down while he was out of it.

"Now, what's this all about?" Frank asked as soon as he had led Carol to a chair. "Why the tears?"

Carol hadn't prepared herself to face Frank this soon. She'd meant to go back to her room, wash her face, brush her hair, and look fresh and glowing by the time he woke up. Her plans never seemed to work out, though. She wanted to yell and sob and tear her hair, tell him that the madman who'd tortured, raped, and murdered Eileen was out there somewhere this very minute lying in wait for him. She wanted to beg him to go back with her— back to Vic and Cami's safe, unthreatening lives, where they could love each other without all this danger, this heartache, this guilt. Of course, she couldn't do that. So now she'd just have to make the most of a bad situation.

"Come on, Carol," Frank coaxed. "Out with it!"

Knowing she had to lie, Carol avoided Frank's direct gaze, staring instead at her hands in her lap. "I'm upset over last night, Frank. Actually, I guess it was this morning. We left the ball just before midnight."

"Did we?" Frank mused aloud. "I don't even remember that part of the evening."

Good! Carol thought.

"Do you remember what happened when we got back here to your room?" she asked cautiously.

"Bits and pieces. A lot of stuff jumbled up together." He gave her a lopsided smile. "To tell the honest-to-God truth, Carol, it doesn't make a lot of sense."

Carol prayed that he had forgotten the incident over Eileen's gown, but there was no way to be sure without asking him directly and that would never do. She could only hope that now that the offending garment was gone, it had disappeared completely from Frank's memory as well.

"You don't remember anything about leaving the ball, Frank?"

His eyes went wide and Carol's heart sank. But when he spoke, his words came as a pleasant shock to her. "That's it! I remember now. I went back, didn't I? That's why the evening seems so fuzzy. I was back being Vic . . . playing around with Cami. Of course." He grinned broadly. "That little Cami's something else!"

"Sometimes, she is," Carol answered cautiously. "Can't you remember exactly what happened, Frank? The last time Vic took Cami to bed?"

His grin died a quick death. "Yeah! Why'd you remind me? She'd changed. She was scared and cold. Vic hated it and he hated himself for making her do it. Then I came back too fast and brought him with me. He was here—right in the damn bed

389

with us. Yeah, I remember now, Carol. He better stay where he belongs from now on, the bastard."

"You asked what's wrong with me, Frank. Well, that's it."

Frank whirled around as if he might catch sight of Black Vic. "You mean, he hurt you? By damn, I'll cut his gizzard out!"

"No, no!" Carol rose and placed a restraining hand on Frank's arm. "He didn't hurt me; I hurt him, by not being there when he needed me. Things go all wrong for Vic and Cami when you and I aren't with them, Frank. They aren't themselves—that is, they *are* themselves and that's not good enough. You and I are the rest of the equation. They need a part of us to become a whole, real, loving couple. Without us, their relationship is doomed. And if Vic and Cami never find happiness, you and I won't either."

"I'm happy!" Frank snapped.

Carol answered with a humorless chuckle. "Sure you are! You're deliriously happy and so am I, Frank. Tell me, what are your plans for us?"

"Plans?" He looked at her blankly.

"I can't stay here forever. I have a business to run, a life of my own to lead. Unless you mean to make me a better offer."

"Hey, Carol, don't push me." Frank backed away from her as he spoke. "You know I love you, but . . ."

"But what, Frank? But you can't marry me? Well then, I have a suggestion. Vic is already trying to find his wife and set things in order so he can marry Cami. Of course, none of that will work out unless we go back and help. Our option is to stay here

390

where nothing will work out for us because you aren't yet free. I don't think you ever will be."

Frank heard the tears threatening in Carol's shaky voice and came to her. He put his arms around her, resting his forehead on hers. "I'm sorry, honey. I can't help it. I wish I could."

"I know you can't help it, Frank. That's why I say we should go back and stay as long as it takes."

The full impact of her words took several moments to sink in. When they did, Frank raised his head, staring her straight in the eye. "You mean live back there . . . be those other people?"

"Vic and Cami aren't 'those other people,' Frank. They're us—you and me—in a former life. We'll be the same as we are now, only better, more complete. Don't you understand?"

Frank gave a low whistle and turned away. He went to the window and looked out, but he wasn't really seeing anything. When he swung back around to her, his face was a mask of dismay. "Carol, do you realize what you're suggesting? We can't just vanish like that. Hell, what would people think?"

Carol shrugged. "Darling, who cares what they think? Neither of us has any permanent ties—no parents to grieve for us, no children depending on us, not even a pet between us to go hungry if we disappear forever."

"*Forever!*" Frank gave another low whistle and wiped a hand over his sweating brow. "Do you realize how long forever is?"

"It's as long as I'll love you, Frank, as long as I want to be with you."

He came to her then and crushed her in his arms.

His mouth came down on hers—hot and hungry and bruising. Carol clung to him, as driven by desperation as by longing.

"It's the only way for us," she whispered when he finally released her.

Frank stood silently staring at her for so long that Carol began to tremble. She could almost hear him going over everything in his mind, trying to decide what to do. Finally, he bent down and kissed her briefly, tenderly.

"So, what do we have to do to get ready for this mind-blowing final leap? Should I pack a suitcase? Should I put in for extended leave at the station? And what about the post office—a change of address card? I don't think they deliver to Condé Street any longer. It's been changed to Chartres for a long time now."

"You don't do any of those things, Frank. You sit down on the bed here with me and we talk."

He grinned. "Just talk?" he asked, pulling her down on top of him.

She rolled away. "Talk!" she repeated. "Our biggest problem, as I see it, won't be getting back to Cami and Vic's time, but staying there. We keep getting jerked back to the present. I think before we go, we need to make a pact between us that neither of us will return without the other and that we will stay until Vic and Cami are happily married and settled. At least that long. Maybe we'll never come back, if all goes well."

Frank acted as if he were only half-listening. He was busy at her "Dollywood" shirt again, easing it up to get at her breasts.

"Frank? Did you hear what I said?"

"Every word, darlin'." He rolled the tee-shirt up

under her arms, then bent over her to lick her nipples.

"Frank, this is serious!"

"Sure is, honey!" He was fumbling at her jeans now, trying to get the zipper down while Carol tried, unsuccessfully, to ignore him.

"I think our best bet for getting back in a hurry is to go to the dock tomorrow morning early. Maybe Choctaw will be there."

"Yeah, and until then we can just stay right here," Frank murmured against her breast, sliding her jeans down over her hips.

"Maybe we can and maybe we can't," Carol answered. "An odd thing happened back in my room a while ago. I heard Black Vic's voice. I'm not sure he's gone back. He may still be hanging around."

Finally, Carol's words had Frank's full attention. He sat up and growled, "What the hell for?"

Carol forced her expression to remain dead-serious. "I don't know. Maybe he enjoyed last time so much he's sticking around, hoping you'll get me in bed again."

"Goddammit! That does it!" Frank leaped off the bed, fists up, ready to fight. "Show yourself, you sorry sonofabitch! Right now. We're going to have this out once and for all. What I do with *my* woman in *my* bed is none of your damn business and you just better stay out of it. You hear me, Black Vic?"

"I think they probably heard you all the way to Canal Street, Frank. Hush, now!" she urged. "It's not going to do you a bit of good, taking potshots at a ghost. If you want to straighten Black Vic out, the best way to do it is to go back and be the right kind of person once you're inside his skin."

Frank flung himself back down on the bed beside

Carol and glanced at her "Dollywood" shirt. It was down, covering her again. He decided to do something about that right away and set about stripping it from her.

"Frank, you're ignoring me."

"Oh, no, I'm not, honey." He bent forward and kissed her erect nipples.

"Then you'll go back and you'll make Vic behave himself?"

He looked into her eyes, his own bright with desire. "Do you promise to make Cami act properly passionate when Vic's with her?"

"I do," Carol assured him. "Cami won't be afraid and no one will have to feel guilty," she ended pointedly.

"Well . . ." he stalled.

"Are you willing or not, Frank?"

He was fiddling with her shirt again. "I'm always willing, Miz Marlowe." Frank cleared his throat, then added in a deeper voice, "Or should I say, Mademoiselle Mazaret?"

Carol did a double take, he sounded so much like Black Vic. Had the scoundrel once more slipped into Frank's soul?

Seeing the shock on her face, Frank laughed. "No need to worry, honey. It's just me—ole ever-lovin', ever-horny Frank. Come here!" He grabbed her by the jeans and began tugging at them once more. Carol wriggled her bottom, trying to help him get them off. Then, suddenly, she froze.

"Listen, Frank!" she whispered, straining to hear the music.

"Aw, that's nothing," he answered, giving her jeans a final yank. "Probably just some entertainer playing the harp at brunch."

"You hear it, too?" She turned to stare at him.

"Sure, it's been playing for quite a while now. Ever since you came in. I heard it when I first opened the door."

"That's it!" Carol cried. "That's the music I've been hearing for weeks. Do you know what this means, Frank?"

"It's real hard getting this shirt off you when you don't cooperate," he said distractedly.

She raised her arms over her head to help. "It means we're going back, Frank. Maybe right away. Why, we might not even have to wait for Choctaw!"

He finally had her undressed and was snuggling close, kicking off his own jeans. "Aw hell, honey, I don't want to go back right now. Just give me a little while longer. I'd look right silly showing up back there with a hard-on."

"Frank, stop a minute and listen to me." She tried to bat his hands away from her breasts, but without success. "Frank, are you paying attention?"

"Uh-huh," he whispered.

"As soon as I get back, I'm going to make Cami tell Vic who she really is. You have to make sure that he accepts what she tells him. Otherwise, Vic might do any kind of crazy thing when he finds out she's lied to him. Do you understand, Frank?"

"Jesus! . . . Yes! . . . I understand! Now, will you do something nice to me with that mouth of yours so it'll stop making so much racket?"

Carol did as instructed, and it was ever so much nicer than talking.

Chapter Eighteen

Cami . . . Cami! Come back, Cami!

The child's eerie wail suddenly pierced through the silence. Carol heard it, and she could tell that Frank did, too. Their love-making, at a fever pitch the moment before the sound, slowed to a tense pause when the voice cried for Cami.

"Oh, God, it's happening, Carol!" Frank strained against her, trying to resume their measured rhythm, but it was no use. "Carol, did you feel that?"

"Yes, darling! Oh, yes!" Clutching him tightly, she neared the brink.

"No, that's not what I mean. I can feel *him*—Black Vic. He's here, Carol. He's tugging at me, trying to take me back." Frank gripped her tighter. "Don't let me go," he begged, "not without you."

"I won't, Frank," she gasped, caught up in the throes of orgasm.

Suddenly, Carol's eyes shot open. She had reached the heights, then the wondrous wave of pleasure had receded only to begin building to the crest all over again.

"Frank, what's happening?"

He only moaned in answer. But as Carol stared at him, she saw his features change. His brows grew thicker and straighter—a bold slash above his night-black eyes. His hair seemed longer, wavier. His face looked more tanned. When he raised his head from the pillow, she gasped. There was a scar down his right cheek.

He smiled at her—a slow, lazy, seductive smile. "So, you have come back to me, *ma chére*."

Wildly confused, Carol glanced about. The room was the same, Frank's room. The bed was the same, Frank's bed. But the man himself was no longer Frank.

"Vic?" she asked cautiously.

"*Oui*, my little love. Your very own."

In that instant, Carol realized that she was being given the opportunity she had prayed for. She was with Victoine Navar—very much with him at the moment—and he thought she was Cami, yet she was still herself.

"Vic, there's something I must confess."

He moved inside her—slowly, deeply. "Must we talk *now*, Cami dearest?"

She found herself fighting another orgasm. Clenching her teeth, she tried not to move. She had to hold onto her senses until she could tell him what he needed to know.

"Please, Vic, hear me out. I am not Fiona's niece. This has all been a masquerade. My real name is Camille Mazaret. I am heiress to Elysian Fields—daughter of Edouard Mazaret."

He pulled out immediately. "You are *what*?"

Carol closed her eyes, dreading to face the anger she heard in his voice. "It's true," she whispered.

"Impossible!"

Carol felt him leap from the bed. She opened her eyes to see where he was going, then she gasped. Gone were Frank's clothes, which had been tossed haphazardly about the hotel room. Gone were the familiar electric coffee pot and Frank's hotplate. Gone was the Hotel Dalpeche itself. She was lying in Vic's bed, in his house on Condé Street. She glanced toward the bureau mirror. Gone, too, was Carol Marlowe. Wide, indigo eyes stared back at her from Camille Mazaret's perfect, heart-shaped face.

She turned back to Vic. "It seems nothing is impossible," she replied. "Remember the night of the ball at Mulgrove?"

He nodded, looking stunned.

"You saw me just before you left my cousins' house. I had been hiding and listening while you argued with Cousin Morris. The moment you looked at me, Vic, I knew you were the only man I could ever love, even though I did not yet know your name. That same night, I ran away so that Cousin Morris couldn't force me into marriage. In truth, I set out to find you, Vic. Little did I suspect that you were so near. You followed me, taking me for a runaway slave." She reached out for his hand, brought it to her lips, and kissed it. "I'm sorry I bit you, my love."

398

"You?" he cried. "You were the wench on that devil-horse, riding through the night all alone?"

She smiled sweetly. "But I wasn't alone. You told me you followed me all the way from my cousins' plantation, right to Fiona's house on Love Street."

Carol had to hurry and finish everything she meant to say. She could feel her own will slipping as Cami's grew stronger by the second. And Cami was afraid.

"Vic, I'm sorry I've been so distant of late. I never meant to turn from you. I do love you. I should have told you the truth from the start. You see, I want to be your wife. And now that you know everything about me, little stands in our way."

He groaned as if he were in pain, then turned away from her. "The whole world stands in our way, Cami, more now than before. You see, I have a wife already. And I certainly can't keep an heiress—my own friend's daughter—as my *placée.*"

"I know you're married, Vic."

She wondered suddenly *how* she knew. Had Fiona told her? She couldn't remember. In truth, Carol Marlowe had managed to speak one last line before Cami eclipsed her totally.

Willing herself to remain clam, Cami continued, "But your wife left you long ago, Vic. Surely, you can find her and set things right so that we can be together forever. If we can't marry, I would gladly remain here with you as I am now. What difference does marriage make when we share love?"

"Even if I were free to marry you, I could offer you nothing."

"You could offer me your love, Vic. That's all I need. I have Elysian Fields. It's for both of us. We would be so happy there."

He glared at her. "Do you think I would stoop to being kept?"

She avoided his angry gaze. "I would. I have. None of that matters, my darling. Our love is the only thing."

Without answering, Vic hurriedly pulled on his clothes. He seemed to ignore every word Cami had said. When he turned back to her, fully dressed now, his face was dark with pain. "You may stay here, if you wish, Cami. I will leave immediately." He rolled his dark eyes heavenward. "I wish to God Edouard would come down to strike me dead on the spot! To think that I took his own innocent daughter. I have ruined you, mademoiselle. No other man will have you now."

Cami reached out for him. "Vic, my dearest, I want no other man. You are my one, my only love."

"Stop!" he commanded in a voice filled with pain. "Don't *ever* say that again! Edouard Mazaret's daughter could never love the man who destroyed her reputation. If your father were here now, he would run me through. And I would gladly give up my life on the field of honor to restore your virtue."

"Vic, what are you saying? You love me; I know you do. We were meant to be together."

Slowly, he shook his head. "That doesn't matter now," he whispered. Tears glistened in his eyes, making them look larger and darker than ever. The lines of anguish etched in his face made Cami ache for him—and for herself.

"I bid you farewell, Mademoiselle Mazaret. Never again will I darken your door. I wish you could forgive what I have done. But how can I expect that? I know that I will never be able to forgive myself."

"Vic, wait!" Cami cried.

Again he shook his head. "*Adieu,* my little love!" He turned quickly and was gone.

Cami sat in the middle of the bed, her breasts heaving, tears streaming down her cheeks. An emptiness like death had settled over her heart. What would become of her now? How could she live without him?

Black Vic left New Orleans that very day. In spite of what he had said to Cami about never seeing her again, he knew that he would move heaven and earth to have her for his own. In order to clear the way for their marriage, he had to find Madelaine. If she would agree to an annulment, he could then take Cami to Paris—beyond the reach of scandal— and they could be married.

He headed out of town and up the River Road. He would stop at every plantation, ask every traveller he met. Sooner or later, someone had to have heard the whereabouts of his estranged wife and his little son, Pierre.

"My 'little' son," Vic reminded himself as he rode through the late-afternoon heat, "will be ten years old by now. Nearly a man!" He sighed, then urged his mount faster.

A week later, Vic was still in the saddle. So far, his search had proved fruitless, but now he had a definite destination in mind. Madelaine had distant kin who owned a small plantation called Espérance. Several times in the past, he had contacted these relations, Herbert and Josepha Roche. They had been coldly polite in their letters, telling him nothing of his wife's whereabouts. When Vic had asked after his son, Herbert had said, "My wife is barren. Do you think, sir, that I would be cruel enough to harbor another woman's child under my roof and have poor Josepha suffer the guilt of her own failings every time she looked at Madelaine's son?"

Vic knew he wasn't likely to find Madelaine and Pierre at Espérance. Still, it was at least a starting point.

He arrived at sunset. The fading light almost, but not quite, hid the poor condition of the place. Tall weeds along the lane wanted cutting. Potholes in the dirt road made the going slow and rough. Up ahead, he could see the main house through the avenue of tall oaks. One shutter hung askew and a new coat of whitewash was past due. The Roches were an elderly couple, no longer able to oversee their slaves properly; hence, the poor condition of their home.

Vic shook his head sadly, thinking that if only he had the money to buy back Golden Oaks, he would make his own home shine. He'd purchase sheep to crop his lawn, slaves to work his fields and serve at table. He would tend the place almost as lovingly as he would care for Cami, if only she were his. But there was no need dwelling on such futile thoughts at present. First, he must find Madelaine and Pierre.

A gaggle of geese announced Vic's arrival long before he rode into the yard. Hearing the racket, a small black boy in tattered shirt and britches scurried around the side of the house and peered at Vic with great, fearful eyes.

"You there, boy!" Vic called. "Is your master to home?"

"Me, suh?" the child asked nervously, pointing a finger at his own bony chest. "I wasn't doin' nothin'. I ain't up to no mischief, suh. 'Twasn't me stuffed the turkey gobbler down the well, massa. 'Twas *him!*"

"No one's accusing you of mischief," Vic answered. "I merely want to see M'sieur Roche. Is he here?"

"And who wants to know?" a surprisingly high-pitched male voice called from the gallery.

Vic squinted against the glare of the setting sun. "Herbert? Is that you? It's Victoine Navar, passing through on the way up the river from New Orleans."

"I suppose you'll be wanting to stay the night." Roche's statement hardly sounded like a gracious invitation.

"If it won't be a bother."

The master of Espérance muttered something about all uninvited guests being a bother, but he motioned Vic toward the house with a half-hearted flap of his fleshy hand.

Herbert Roche had changed a good deal since Vic last saw the man several years before. He was completely bald now and stouter than ever. His sturdy cane and rag-bound foot seemed to indicate that he'd contracted gout. However, his dour expression certainly showed that his disposition had changed not a whit.

"I don't suppose you've eaten, either," Roche said in a tone that let Vic know that both his appetite and his presence were a great burden to the folk at Espérance.

Vic pretended he misunderstood. "Ah, how nice

of you to invite me to supper, Herbert. Josepha, as I remember, never fails to set a bountiful table."

With a deep sigh of resignation, Madelaine's obese Cousin Herbert showed Vic into the front hall. "You've arrived too late, you know. I sent my man downriver weeks ago to find you and give you the news. If you wanted to be here for the funeral, Navar, you should have pried yourself away from your gaming table long ago. In this heat, she simply wouldn't keep."

Vic frowned at his reluctant host. "My God, man! You don't mean Josepha's gone? I'm so sorry."

"Indeed not, sir!" a woman's thin voice trilled down from the head of the stairway. "Why, I'm right here, Cousin Black Vic, and fit as the proverbial fiddle, thank you kindly."

"Josepha?" Vic shielded his eyes, trying to make them adjust more quickly to the inside gloom as his gaze followed the wraith-like figure of Madame Roche down the stairs.

The sparrowish woman flitted toward him to plant a wet, toothless kiss on Vic's scarred cheek. She murmured a welcome, then scurried off into another room before Vic could even thank her.

"I'm happy to see Josepha's well," he said to Herbert.

"As well as a woman can be who is unable to give her husband sons," Herbert growled. People had long said that poor Josepha's feathery wits had been made so by her husband's constant harping on her failure as a Creole wife.

"Back to what you said a moment ago, Herbert. I thought you meant someone had died."

"Indeed!" M'sieur Roche replied, brushing at the

tip of his bulbous nose with a delicate, lace-edged hankie. "Didn't you read the letter I sent by my man?"

Vic shrugged and opened his palms toward his host. "Your servant never found me. I've seen no letter. What message did you send?"

"The bleeding black scoundrel!" Roche blustered. "He probably took himself off upriver and is over the border by now." He leaned forward and squinted a small, brownish eye at Vic. "You can't trust them, you know, not a one of them. They'll run off the first chance they get. We pay good money just so we can give them a decent home and an honest day's work, then they bite the very aristocratic hand that feeds them! Bastards, the lot!"

Vic tried to bear with his ill-tempered host, but he wanted desperately to get an answer to his question. "The letter, Herbert! What was in it?"

Brought abruptly out of his tirade, Herbert Roche looked blank for a moment. "The letter? Oh, that letter, of course. Well, 'she's dead' was the message I sent you."

"Who is dead?" Vic could feel his face growing as red as Cousin Herbert's.

"Why, Madelaine, of course—your wife." The man stated the words matter-of-factly, as if any fool should know such news.

Vic was struck dumb. He stood there, mouthing the words silently, his emotions churning. He and Madelaine had barely known each other when they married. Although true love had never flourished between them, theirs had been a good marriage by Creole standards. They had both rejoiced when she

405

gave him a strong, healthy son on her very first try. But everything had changed that night Vic carelessly gambled away his birthright. He had never blamed his wife for leaving him, although he had come to despise her for taking Pierre when she left and for keeping father and son apart all these years. Still, to hear that Madelaine was dead . . .

"When? How?" Vic finally managed.

"Nearly two months ago, it's been." Herbert motioned Vic into the library. "Come, my boy. A dram of brandy might do us both a world of good."

A manservant hovering nearby poured each of them a pony of brandy. Vic and Cousin Herbert settled themselves in the dark room that smelled of camphor, mildew, and mice.

Once Herbert had caught his breath after the exertion of settling his bulk and propping his old, gouty foot, he launched into his tale. "It's best for all she's gone." He clucked his thick tongue. "What a scandal we would have had on our hands otherwise!"

"What the hell are you talking about, Roche? No one has ever spoken Madelaine's name and scandal in the same breath before. She was a fine and proper Creole lady."

"Ah, how noble your defense, sir!" Roche leaned forward and squinted at Vic, his shaggy white brows almost covering his eyes. "She changed, you know. Ah, yes!"

"Changed how?"

"In many ways—in *every* way." The elderly man paused and licked at a drop of brandy that had dribbled out of the corner of his mouth. "She took a liking to one of the stable hands—black as your ace of spades, the boy was."

406

Vic shot out of his chair and paced to the windows. "I don't believe a word of this. You've gone as soft in the head as you are in the belly."

"You think so? Then ask me again how dear Cousin Madelaine died." Vic turned, about to ask, but the man stopped him. Waving his lace hankie and almost grinning in his excitement at being the bearer of such shocking news, he squeaked, "No, no, no! Don't bother to ask. I'll tell you. Your Madelaine died in *childbirth!*" He leaned over his belly and chuckled. "And her bastard was as black as his pa."

Vic felt pain twist his heart. "Poor Madelaine," he said with a deep sigh. "What did I do to you?"

"It's your fault, all right, Navar. If you'd been a proper husband, she'd never have come to such an end."

"And the child?" Vic asked quietly.

"Down in the quarters. I gave him to young Sakie to wet-nurse. She lost her girl-child about the same time."

Vic rounded on the man in a fury. "You mean to make a slave of Madelaine's son?"

"What else would you have me do with a motherless black bastard? He's strong. He'll be a prime field hand by and by."

"My God, man!" Vic cried in disgust. "The boy's your own flesh and blood!"

Roche chuckled and raised his glass for a refill. "So are a lot of the others down in the shacks. Besides, I see the boy as payment. Cousin Madelaine owed me something for all the trouble she caused—she and that young hellion you spawned."

"Pierre!" Vic exclaimed. "My son is here? I want to see him at once."

407

"Oh, you'll see him, all right, Navar. I mean to send the both of you packing at first light tomorrow. I've had my fill of your family. If you weren't such a loser yourself, I'd swear the boy had the devil's own seed in him. But, knowing you as I do, I suppose Pierre comes by his wickedness honestly."

Just then a high-pitched shriek split the twilight stillness. Herbert almost sprawled on the floor trying to lift his vast bottom from the chair.

"It's Josepha!" he shrilled. "Mother of God, what's happened now?"

Vic dashed out of the room and down the hall toward the back of the house. The screams grew ever louder with each step he took. He found frail Josepha standing on the back gallery, sobbing and wailing.

"My Tom! My Tom! Oh, look! He's ruined!"

A fat servant with a dirty tignon on her head stood at the foot of the stairs, holding up a dripping turkey carcass by the feet. The creature was obviously dead, probably drowned by the looks of him.

"What's going on here?" Vic asked, putting his arm around Josepha's thin, quaking shoulders.

"My Tom!" she wailed again. "He's ruined!"

Vic turned his gaze back to the servant. "What happened?"

"This here's Miz Josepha's pet tom turkey. He all the time strut around the yard behind of her, picking up the corn she throw down. Come time to make new feather dusters, ole Tom he allow Miz Josepha to pick him's tail clean 'cause he know if he do that she won't wring his neck for dinner. Now, he done gone and got hisself drowneded."

"How could such a thing happen?" Vic demanded. "I know turkeys are stupid creatures, but that one looks as if he tried to go swimming."

The turkey-bearer rolled her eyes. "Young Marse Pierre throwed old Tom down the well."

"Dammit, Poke, you told!" Vic heard the youngster's voice from around the corner of the house. Then the sound of fists pounding flesh and shrill cries of pain reached his ears.

Taking the steps two at a time, Vic dashed into the yard and toward the sounds of the ruckus. He found two filthy little boys scuffling in the dirt. He grabbed each by the back of the shirt and tugged them apart.

"What's going on here?" he growled, first into one black face and then into the other.

"I didn't tell, suh. I didn't tell nobody nothing! Young Massa Pierre, he got no cause to give Poke a lickin'."

Vic dropped Poke—the boy he'd seen when he first arrived—but kept a firm grip on the other struggling rascal. "Pierre?" he asked, trying to see through all the dirt and spit all over the boy's face. "Are you Pierre Navar?"

"Yeah! What's it to you, mister?" Still swinging his fists, Pierre landed a solid blow on Vic's chin. Vic gave the boy a good shake.

"Stop that and listen to me. I'm your father, Pierre." Vic set the boy on the ground, expecting a hug. He got only a blank, surly stare.

"I got no father—no mother, neither."

"I'm sorry about your mother, Pierre." Vic said the words gently, compassionately, trying to get through to his son.

Tears welled up in Pierre's eyes, but he scrubbed

them away with his fists, leaving smeary white circles on his dirt-blackened face. "She didn't care about me. She just wanted that other baby—that *black* baby. She said it'd be my little brother or sister." He paused and spat on the ground. "Damned if that's so!"

Groping for some way to change the subject, Vic finally asked, "What happened to Cousin Josepha's pet turkey, Pierre?"

For an instant, Vic thought he glimpsed a pleading, frightened look in his son's dark eyes. But it was gone in a blink. "Turkeys, they can't swim," Pierre said matter-of-factly. "Poke said they could. But I proved they can't." He turned and pointed innocently, almost proudly, toward the limp bird. "You can see for yourself, mister. That ole turkey gobbler's dead. He couldn't swim a lick."

"You shouldn't have thrown Tom down the well, Pierre. You must apologize to Cousin Josepha."

Vic—forcing a straight face—was trying desperately to be a proper father, something he knew absolutely nothing about. Pierre was too quick for him, though. The boy caught the suppressed humor in Vic's tone and noted the merry twinkle in his black eyes.

Pierre laughed, thinking correctly that Vic was amused by his high-spirited antics. Then the boy called toward the gallery, "Hey, Cousin Jo, it's too bad about your sorry ole turkey—that he couldn't swim. I know you was real fond of him. But you'll like him, too, stuffed with oyster dressing and greens, and now you won't even have to wring his scrawny ole neck, since I drowned him in the well for you."

At Pierre's mention of eating her pet, Josepha fainted dead away and tumbled down the gallery steps.

"Why, you little . . ." Before Vic ever thought what he was doing, he acted instantaneously on his rage. Dropping the boy across his knee, Vic jerked down Pierre's britches and beat his small, white bottom until it was beet-red. Pierre kicked and twisted, but not a sound escaped his lips, not a tear dribbled from his eyes.

When Vic set Pierre on his feet again, the boy glared at his father with hate in his eyes. Then he turned, and with all the quiet dignity a dirty, beaten, motherless boy can muster, he marched up the stairs and into the house. Vic uttered a weary sigh, knowing that by losing his temper he had lost the first round with his son.

Pierre refused to come down to supper that night. He remained in his room, nursing his wounds.

After supper, Vic took a plate up to the boy. He knocked softly. No answer.

"Pierre? It's your father. I know you're in there."

"Go away!"

"I brought your supper."

"I ain't hungry."

"You need to eat, son, to build up your strength for the trip. I'm taking you with me when I leave tomorrow."

A long silence followed, then slowly the doorknob turned. Pierre, his eyes red-rimmed, peered out. "Where you going to, mister?"

"New Orleans. You'll like it there."

Pierre made no comment. His deep-brown eyes

411

strayed to the plate in Vic's hand, heaped high with ham, corn-on-the-cob, sweet potatoes, turnip greens, and cornbread. Seeing the boy's hungry gaze, Vic offered him the plate. Pierre grabbed it out of Vic's hand and immediately stuffed a whole wedge of buttered cornbread into his mouth.

"May I come in, son?"

"Suit yourself," Pierre said, spewing buttery crumbs with his words.

Vic eased inside and sat down on the foot of his son's bed. Silently, he watched the boy eat. Pierre, Vic noted, had his mother's fine-boned face, her brandy-colored eyes. There was something about his mouth that reminded Vic of Madelaine when she was sad. That look tugged at his heart. Didn't Pierre ever smile?

"How is it?" Vic said at length.

Pierre shrugged and went on eating.

"I'm sorry about this afternoon." Vic really was sorry for whipping his son, but he had to force the words to get them out.

"It ain't the first lickin' I ever had. Won't be the last, I reckon." Then he looked up, accusing his father with an angry, hurt stare. "Still, you had no right. I don't even know who you are, mister."

Vic felt a lump rising in his throat. Pierre was correct. He did not know his father and that was Vic's fault.

"I told you who I am, Pierre. Your mother was my wife. We were your parents. I'm afraid I haven't been much of a father to you, but I hope to change that. We used to be happy—a long time ago. When you were born we lived at a great plantation called Golden Oaks. We had horses and boats and car-

412

riages and peacocks that strutted about the wide lawn. You'd like it there."

"Do you still live there? Is that where we're going tomorrow?"

The hopeful tone in Pierre's voice made Vic shy away. He looked down at his hands. "No, I'm afraid not. You see, I lost Golden Oaks. But someday . . ."

Pierre laughed, but the sound was filled with sarcasm. "Yeah, right!" he answered. "Mother told me all about you and your 'somedays.' She said you were a dreamer, a man who'd make all kinds of promises, but never make any of them come true. She called you *shiftless*."

Vic nodded sadly. "She had a right to say that about me, I suppose. I disappointed her. But I mean to do better by you, Pierre. If only you'll give me a chance. Come with me tomorrow, son."

The boy shrugged. "Reckon I ain't got much choice in the matter. Cousin Herbert says I'm no damn good. He sure don't want me around. Nobody does."

Vic felt himself choking up again. "I do," he murmured. He opened his arms to the boy, but Pierre turned away.

Slowly, Vic rose from the bed. "Good night, son. I'll see you in the morning, bright and early."

Pierre refused to look at his father.

Black Vic's sleep was troubled by dreams that night. Bits and pieces of his whole life returned to haunt him. He relived the day of his father's death, his marriage to Madelaine and their wedding night. Then his wife's form, trembling with a virgin's fear, turned into Cami's pale, sweet body. And then Cami became someone else—a woman with eyes that shifted color, short-cropped hair, and a passion that fired his own. Who was she, this stranger? It seemed he knew her, yet he didn't.

Cami and Vic . . . Carol and Frank . . . His own name and his lover's mingled and mixed with the names of two strangers. Yet that other pair of names struck some vague chord in his memory. Who were they? Why couldn't he think? Why couldn't he understand?

His emotions ranged as widely as his nightmares during the long, turbulent hours of that hot night. When, in his dreams, he was with Cami, he felt whole and calm and loved, while visions of Madelaine brought only pain and guilt.

Vic woke himself at dawn, calling Cami's name. He sat up in bed, wiping a hand over his sweat-stung eyes. His heart was pounding. He'd had an awful nightmare. He'd dreamed he returned to New Orleans only to find Cami gone.

"Wait for me, my little love," he whispered. "I'm coming back to you. Please wait!"

But even as he and Pierre—sullen and anxious—packed up to ride out, the feeling that he had lost Cami continued to nag at Vic. He simply couldn't shake the dreams.

With a deep sigh, he mounted up. Turning to Pierre, he asked, "Ready, son?"

The boy shrugged. "I reckon, mister."

Mister. His son's title for him cut Vic to the quick. But, perhaps in time . . .

Vic waved goodbye to Madelaine's cousins, then they were off. But fear rode with him—fear of what he would find when he returned to New Orleans.

Chapter Nineteen

Victoine Navar had simply vanished from New Orleans after he left Cami that day. Now almost a month had gone by and still there was no word from him, no sign of him. Cami had practically worn a rut in the floor of his house, pacing from the bedroom to the door whenever she thought she heard a sound outside. Each time she convinced herself he had returned, her heart would race, her grim expression would brighten to a smile, and she would feel alive once more. Then when she realized Vic was not there, all the agony would return, doubled and redoubled. She would go back to the music room, to the golden harp, her only solace. For hours on end, her sweet-sad music drifted through the empty house.

On the day Vic went away, Cami had waited for

him, sure that he would have a change of heart and return. She'd given him a second day for good measure. When still there was no sign of him, Cami had hurried to Fiona, hoping she would have some idea where Vic might be.

"So, he has left you," Fiona said that day in a voice that hinted she feared all along this might happen. "It is only a shame he did not go sooner, if he meant from the start to desert you. I should never have trusted fate to keep you safe, *ma chère,* since I certainly did not trust Victoine Navar. I had hoped that fear on your part or conscience on his might save you."

"None of this was Vic's fault, Fiona, it was mine," Cami confessed. "I set out to make him love me and I succeeded. Because of that success, I felt I could wait no longer. I told him my true identity."

"You *what?*" Fiona, who had been standing by the front windows of her cottage, sank to the settee at hearing this news.

Cami would never forget Fiona's shocked tone or how her golden eyes went wide, staring in disbelief.

"Why on earth would you do such a thing, Camille?"

"Oh, Fiona, we are in love," Cami had answered as if that explained everything. "I thought it would make him so happy to know that we were free to wed."

"*You* may be free, but *he* isn't. Camille, Victoine is a married man."

"I know," she answered quietly. "But he could end his marriage. Surely, that's what his wife wants. Then life for us would be so wonderful, Fiona."

"And how did he respond to finding out who you truly are, Camille?"

"Confusingly!" Cami admitted, pacing the room. "Although he saw nothing amiss with taking Cami Le Moyne as his *placée*, the very thought that he had made love to Edouard Mazaret's daughter seemed deeply disturbing. I don't understand, Fiona. Am I not the same person, no matter the name I use?"

"Not in a Creole gentleman's eyes. He saw you for what you told him you were—a young woman of color looking for a protector. As such, I'm sure he did everything he could to make life pleasant for you."

"Oh, he did!" Cami murmured dreamily, tears threatening as she recalled his tenderness and concern.

"*But!*" Fiona's sharp voice snapped Cami back to the painful present. "What he did to you as an innocent Creole maiden is totally unacceptable and unforgiveable in his society. Poor Edouard must be turning in his crypt and Victoine knows that." The woman paused and shook her head sadly. "I share no small amount of the blame in all this. I should never have taken you to the Orleans Ballroom and I should have put my foot down regarding Victoine Navar. In fact, we would all be far better off today if I had sent you right back to Mulgrove and your Cousin Morris the very minute you showed up here."

"No!" Cami cried. "I'll *never* go back there. I couldn't marry another, loving Vic as I do."

A grim expression passed over Fiona's face. "You need have no fear of that, child. Victoine has taken that matter completely out of your hands. Even the promise of Elysian Fields and all Lafitte's golden treasure could not buy you a respectable husband now."

417

Fiona's words sent a shudder through Cami. "You mean, as Vic said, I'm *ruined?* Oh, Fiona, what will I do?"

"It's a bit late for that question, child."

Cami gripped Fiona's hand desperately. "You must help me find Vic. I know he loves me, and, more than that, he needs me. He's known so much pain and sorrow in his life. If we were together at Elysian Fields, I'm sure we would both be gloriously happy. I told him as much before he left. I said it didn't matter to me that he had no fortune. I assured him that I have enough for both of us."

Fiona rolled her eyes and moaned softly. "I'm sure *that* pleased him!" she said sarcastically. "Camille, my dear, you are still such an innocent. No self-respecting man would allow himself to be kept by a woman."

Tears trickled from Cami's indigo eyes. "That's what Vic said," she whispered mournfully.

Fiona rose and caressed the weeping woman's dark hair. "I am sorry for you, Camille. But I'm afraid I don't have any answers. As for Victoine's whereabouts, I haven't the slightest idea where he has gone or when he will come back—if ever. He told me he was going to find his wife and try to get an annulment. That isn't likely to happen, I'm afraid. All you can do is wait and hope."

Patience, Cami learned, was not one of her virtues. After two weeks of waiting and hoping, she made up her mind what she must do.

"I'm going back to Elysian Fields," she told herself with finality. "If I must wait, I will do it in my own home."

Determined to have her way, Cami dressed in a fine new traveling suit of bronze bombazine, had Vic's servant hitch the horses to the carriage with the Navar crest on the doors, then ordered the man to drive her out to Mulgrove.

It was a fine day for the trip—late summer, with the first hint of fall in the air. Soon the plantation families would be returning to New Orleans for the social season. She would have to face Cousin Morris then anyway. No need to put the confrontation off any longer, she told herself.

Cami felt like a new woman as she rehearsed her speech for Cousin Morris. She would tell him that she had decided not to marry, but to take up her role as mistress of her own plantation immediately. She would keep Vic's name entirely out of the conversation. Once she was in possession of Elysian Fields, she could make her own, quiet plans with Vic. She would agree to giving Cousin Morris a portion of her profits, if she was forced to, in order to have her way. She knew the Pinards to be greedy people, not above bribes. Nor was she above paying them, if it meant her happiness.

By the time the carriage rolled up to Mulgrove, Cami felt confident that she would soon have her life in order. This part of it, at least.

Morris Pinard spotted the carriage coming toward the house. Leaving the papers he'd been working on scattered over his desk, he walked out onto the gallery to get a better view. They weren't expecting anyone. He wondered who could be calling this late in the day.

The minute the carriage pulled to a stop, Pinard spied the Navar crest on the door. He bristled.

"What's that bastard up to now?" he grumbled.

419

His shock was total when the coachman handed down a woman to the marble carriage steps. Her fashionable bonnet hid her features, but he could tell by the cut of her gown that she was someone of wealth.

"My dear lady," he said, descending the stairs, "may I be of assistance?"

Cami gave him a wary smile from beneath the feathered brim of her smart chapeau. "Why, thank you, yes, Cousin Morris."

She watched the man pale under his summer tan. His eyes went wide, scanned her head to toe, then narrowed angrily.

"What are you doing in that carriage, Camille?"

She trilled a laugh. "Well, you could hardly expect a lady to ride horseback all this way. I thought you would be pleased to see me, Cousin."

"I *thought* you had gone for good." His emphasis on that word hinted to Cami that actually he *wished* she had gone for good. As well he might. If she had simply disappeared without a trace, he would have inherited Elysian Fields by default.

"I sent you a letter, Cousin Morris, telling you that I was staying with a friend for the time being. I never said I wouldn't return. But you can rest assured I do not mean to remain at Mulgrove. Could we go in out of the sun and talk?"

Anger still written all over his face, Pinard glanced one last time at the Navar crest, then motioned Cami to come into the house. The place was as silent as a grave. No one else was about.

"Where are Cousin Beatrice and Lorenna?" Cami asked.

"Gone visiting for the week."

Morris showed Cami into the parlor and rang a bell for a servant to bring coffee. They settled uncomfortably, facing each other across a low table.

"I expect Lorenna will marry soon," said Pinard.

"Marry?" Cami cried. "But 'Renna's only a child."

"She's exactly the age her mother was when we wed. It is best for a woman to marry young so that her husband can train her properly."

Cami bristled at Pinard's words, but the only outward sign of her resentment was a gently arched brow.

"Who have you chosen as Lorenna's husband?" Cami asked pointedly, expecting to hear the name of one of her own former suitors. The man Morris Pinard mentioned instead shocked her thoroughly.

"Your cousin will soon be Madame Arnaud Savant."

"But how can that be? M'sieur Savant is old enough to be Lorenna's *grand-père*,"

"Age matters little in affairs of the heart, Camille."

"The heart, indeed! Don't you mean the money purse, Cousin Morris? M'sieur Savant may be long in the tooth, but he is also the wealthiest planter in this parish. Poor Lorenna!"

"You have no cause to feel pity for your cousin. Save your sympathy for yourself, Camille. If you had complied with my wishes, you, too, could be anticipating your marriage very soon. I'm sure you would enjoy living in luxury at Elysian Fields once more."

"That's exactly what I've come to tell you, Cousin Morris. I intend to move back to my own home immediately."

Pinard slapped his knees with great satisfaction. "Well, at last you've come to your senses, my girl. Now that you're willing to choose a husband, I won't even question your whereabouts for the past weeks. We'll get right to the business at hand. Tell me the man's name so that I can set the matrimonial wheels in motion."

Cami sighed. Here was the old question once again. "I did not say I plan to marry, Cousin Morris, only that I'm going to move back to Elysian Fields."

"Impossible! No woman can run a plantation all alone."

Cami, though quaking inside, stood her ground bravely. "I believe there is an overseer on the place, as well as a full complement of field workers and house servants. I'm sure I'll manage."

"This is insane—completely out of the question, Camille. I refuse even to discuss it with you."

"There's nothing to discuss. I merely came here to tell you my plans. Now, if you'll excuse me, I want to drive over there and have a look around. I'll inform the overseer—Mister Boggs, isn't it?—of my intent so that he can have everything ready."

Her mention of driving brought the Navar crest on the carriage back to the forefront of Pinard's mind. "That victoria you're in, who owns it?"

"A friend," Cami hedged.

"Perhaps the *friend* you've been staying with in New Orleans, Cousin Camille?"

The incriminating crest never crossed Cami's mind as she answered boldly, "Why, yes, as a matter of fact. I'm allowed use of it whenever I wish. Actually, all my friend's belongings are at my disposal. I have only to ask."

"And, no doubt, you are at your friend's beck and call as well." Cami watched, horrified, as Morris Pinard worked himself into a towering rage. "You may tell your *gentleman friend* that my second will call on him directly. By God, no young woman under my guardianship will be tampered with by the likes of Black Vic Navar!"

Cami set her china cup down with such force that it cracked the saucer. She fled the house and scrambled into Vic's carriage.

"Away!" she called to the startled driver. "Quickly!"

How foolish she had been not to think of the incriminating crest on the carriage. Now her hasty actions had put Vic's very life on the line.

When they reached the road, the driver turned toward Elysian Fields. "No!" Cami called to him. "I've changed my plans. Take me back to New Orleans. And hurry!"

As they sped back toward the city, Cami's mind worked at a furious pace. She knew what she must do. She would go to Fiona and tell her to warn Vic the moment he returned that Morris Pinard knew of their relationship and meant to challenge her lover to a duel. Cami longed to stay at Vic's house and wait for him, but she knew she must take possession of Elysian Fields immediately, now that her cousin knew her plans.

Feeling such a great need for haste, it seemed to Cami that the drive back to New Orleans was endless. She was sure that the road had doubled in length since the morning. At long last, they reached the house in Condé Street.

"I will be needing the carriage at first light tomorrow," she informed the driver. She hesitated, thinking it might be best to go to Fiona's house immediately. Then she changed her mind. She couldn't face the woman with this new and startling news. She would take the coward's way out. "Don't unhitch the team yet," she told Vic's servant. "I want you to deliver a letter to number ten *rue d'Amour*."

She hurried inside and wrote her brief, desperate note to Fiona. Once it was on its way, Cami set about packing her things. By tomorrow this time, she would, at last, be mistress of Elysian Fields.

Vic felt such a vast relief when he reached the outskirts of the city that he might have wept had his son not been with him. All he could think about was getting to Cami, telling her the news, then making her his own.

He glanced toward Pierre. The boy had remained sullen during the entire trip. Vic wished he could read minds. His son told him nothing of his thoughts, but Vic guessed that they were grim. Too grim for one so young. Maybe he'd made a mistake by telling Pierre about Cami. The lad had yet to get used to the idea of having a father, so how could he be expected to accept the thought of a new mother so soon after the death of his own? But once Pierre met Cami, Vic was certain she would win the boy's heart.

"You'll get to meet Cami soon now, son," Vic ventured. "She's a lovely young woman—high-spirited, beautiful, and she plays the harp like an angel."

Pierre held his stony silence.

"What do you think of New Orleans so far?"

"It stinks!" said Pierre, wrinkling his sun-freckled nose.

Vic sniffed the air and laughed. "So it does! I'm so used to the smell that I don't notice it any longer. Summer's soon over, though. The cool air of autumn will freshen the place."

Vic's heart speeded its pace as they turned into Condé Street. He became aware of a sharp ache in his loins. God, how he'd missed Cami! But soon now . . . *soon!* he told himself. Already, visions of the night to come were sweetening his thoughts. He smiled.

"There it is, Pierre!" Vic cried joyously. "We're home!"

"I don't have a home," the boy muttered under his breath.

Vic refused to allow his son's dour attitude to dampen his own spirits. He was sure that once Pierre settled into his own room with his new family, his temperament would improve.

They rode through the gate into the courtyard. Vic leaped from his horse and raced to the door. Flinging it wide, he called, "Cami? Cami, I'm home, *ma chère!*"

Only silence greeted his cry. But it was more than silence—there was an emptiness about the place. Vic raced down the hall, his heart thundering in his chest. Everything was in order, but nothing was right. He found the rooms empty, Cami's bureau and armoire cleaned out. His heart sank.

Vic did not hear Pierre when the boy came into his bedroom. The man, in his agony, stood staring down at his bed, one hand caressing Cami's pillow.

"Well? Where is she?" Pierre demanded in a surly

tone. "She must not care much about you if she's not even here to welcome you home."

Vic whirled on the boy, his eyes wild and dark. His hand drew back as if he meant to slap his son's face. Then his rage gave way to desolation. He sank to the bed, his anguished face in his hands.

"She's gone," he moaned. "Gone . . ."

The sun had not yet set over the city when Black Vic, still half in shock, answered a sharp knock at his door. He found a Creole gentleman of about his own age, dressed in formal black, his thin face grim.

"M'sieur Victoine Navar?" his visitor asked.

"Yes. How may I be of service?"

The man's expression never changed. His voice remained steely calm. "I come here on behalf of M'sieur Morris Pinard, acting as his second. Owing to your defamation of his female cousin, Mademoiselle Camille Mazaret, M'sieur Pinard requires satisfaction at your earliest opportunity. You, of course, may name the place, time, and choice of weapons."

At first, Vic's mind refused to interpret the words. Surely the man had the wrong residence. A duel? His reputation was such that no one challenged him any longer. His aim was far too sure and deadly. Frowning, Vic forced himself to react.

"Morris Pinard, you say?"

"*Oui!*" the second answered succinctly.

"Could you tell me, sir, where Mademoiselle Mazaret is at this moment? Under her cousin's protection once more?" Of course! Why hadn't he thought of that in the first place? Old Morris had come to

426

New Orleans, found Cami, and dragged her back to Mulgrove.

"She is not," the man replied with a malicious curl of his thin lips. "Mademoiselle has further disgraced herself by taking up residence *alone* at Elysian Fields. Be that as it may, her ruin came at your hands. And for that, you must pay."

Vic's mind was whirling. Cami at her plantation? What could it mean? Why had she left New Orleans and run away from him? Then realization dawned. He had left her, vowing never to return. What other choice did she have? She had no idea that he was now free to make her his wife. He must let her know. He glanced back at the stiff-postured man. But first, he must settle this matter with Pinard. He thought the details through carefully before he answered.

"Tell M'sieur Pinard that I will meet him at dawn, three days hence, beneath *Les Trois Capelines,* the oaks on the Metaire Road." Vic paused, considering his choice of weapons. The sword was his forte, but pistols would end the matter more quickly. "I choose pistols," he answered.

"So be it!" the man replied.

Vic closed the door sharply.

"You're going to fight a duel, mister?" For the first time, Vic heard a note of respect, even awe, in his son's tone.

Vic had no intention of letting Cami know about this senseless matter. He would go to her after it was over and tell her everything. Then, once he had saved enough at his newly acquired position as

427

cotton broker to buy back his plantation, they would wed. At least, that was his plan.

Never did he suspect that Morris Pinard would send word to Cami of the duel. Her cousin's curt missive reached her the day before the scheduled affair of honor. She was in the midst of setting her household to rights, meeting her new servants, renewing acquaintance with those who had served her parents, and, in general, shouldering a man's difficult task with a spunky woman's determination. Everything seemed to be going well until the rider arrived from Mulgrove.

Pushing her sweat-damp hair out of her eyes, Cami sank down on the broad gallery steps to read her cousin's note.

> Mulgrove Plantation
> 3 September 1840

My Dear Cousin Camille,

 You will be pleased, I am sure, to hear that I mean to avenge the wrong done to you by that scoundrel, Navar. We shall meet on the field of honor at the oaks on the Metaire Road tomorrow morning at dawn. After I have done with this blackguard, I strongly suggest that you return to Mulgrove and my protection. Owing to your large dowry, perhaps a suitable husband can yet be found, in spite of your soiled reputation. I will send my carriage for you the moment I return to Mulgrove.

> Your servant,
> Morris Pinard

Cami stared at the note, her mouth agape. She had no idea Vic had returned to New Orleans. Why hadn't Fiona or Vic himself let her know?

She jumped up and ran into the house. Her first thought was to race to the city, find Vic, and stop the duel. Halting in mid-flight, she slumped against the rosewood banister of the stairs.

"That would be useless," she murmured. "Utterly useless!"

She knew enough about Creole ways and Creole gentlemen to understand that once a challenge was issued and accepted, there was no turning back. All she could do was go to *Les Trois Capelines*—those oaks so draped in Spanish moss that they looked like three women in mourning capes—and view the proceedings on that blood-soaked patch of earth where so many noble men had met their deaths.

She thought suddenly of Cousin Beatrice and Lorenna. What would they do if anything happened to Morris Pinard? Surely, Vic would not kill Cousin Morris, only wound him. And that would put an end to this madness.

Determined to be there with Vic, Cami hurried upstairs to change. She would go to New Orleans now to see Vic before the fateful meeting at dawn. She would beg him, for the sake of Beatrice and Lorenna, not to kill Cousin Morris. And while she was there, before the dawn, she would show Vic exactly how much she loved him. Halfway up the stairs, Cami was forced to pause. A wave a dizziness swept over her. This wasn't the first time in the past weeks she had experienced the queasy feeling. She smiled, guessing its cause. Perhaps she would confide her suspicions to Vic this very night.

The next few hours proved long, uncomfortable, and fatiguing for Cami. The swaying of the coach unsettled her stomach. The fall heat wilted her. And her anxiety increased with each passing mile. By the time she arrived at the Condé Street house, long after dark, she felt ill and exhausted. Her knock at the door brought another sharp jolt. A boy, the image of Vic in miniature, opened the door and stood staring at her sullenly.

"M'sieur Navar, please."

"Who wants him?" the boy demanded.

Just then, Vic came into the hall. He paused, froze, then rushed to her, almost knocking the boy out of his way. In the next instant, they were in each other's arms.

"Cami! Cami, my sweet love!" Vic cried. "Oh, God, I was afraid you were gone for good!"

"I went to Elysian Fields, Vic. I had to. I couldn't bear staying in this house without you."

Ignored, Pierre stood by watching with a petulant look on his face as his father kissed this stranger with long, deep intensity. He was still staring at them when Vic broke the prolonged embrace.

"I have so much to tell you, Cami. For starters, may I present my son, Pierre."

"Oh!" Cami cried, smiling down at the boy. "But of course. You look exactly like your father."

Cami bent down to hug the boy, but he shrugged away. Glaring up into her eyes, he said, "Everybody says I favor my mother, not him." He turned his hostile gaze toward Vic.

"Pierre, why don't you go on to bed?" Vic suggested. "It's late, and I need to talk to Mademoiselle Mazaret privately."

Pierre turned without a word and almost ran from them.

"He doesn't like me, Vic. I can tell," Cami said.

"He'll come around, darling. The poor child has had a rough go of it. That's why I didn't want him here when I told you about his mother." Vic paused, gathering his emotions before he could speak. "Cami, Madelaine is dead."

The words fell like a stone into a bottomless well. Cami had no idea what to say. Her joy at hearing that Vic was finally free mingled with guilt that she should feel such elation at news of anyone's death. *Death!* The very thought of it turned her blood cold and her mind back to the reason for her coming.

"Vic, I know about the duel."

"How on earth did you find out?" His face went dark with anger. "I meant to tell you, but only after the fact."

"Cousin Morris sent word. He means to kill you, Vic, then force me to return to Mulgrove to marry someone of his choice."

"The bastard!" Vic raged. Then he took Cami tenderly into his arms. "You needn't worry, my little love. After tomorrow, you'll never have to deal with Morris Pinard again."

"Oh, Vic, you won't kill him? What of my cousins? Morris may not be much, but he's the only man they have to take care of them."

"Don't worry, darling. I plan to fire over his head. Were it up to me, I would call the whole thing off, but . . ."

"I know—the Creole code of honor," Cami sighed.

As they talked, Vic was leading Cami down the

431

hall, toward his bedroom. With every step, his urgency grew. He had ached so for Cami these past lonely weeks—dreamed of the moment when he could once more make love to her. He drew off her cape, her hat, and was working at her bodice by the time they entered the chamber, ready at once to take her to their bed.

But, eager as she was, she stopped him. "Vic, what now?" she asked.

He was kissing her cheeks, her neck, tugging at her gown to get to her breasts. "Now, my little love, I mean to love you within an inch of your life."

She laughed softly and nibbled at his ear. "I know that, and I approve. What will happen after the duel, though? Will we be married right away?"

Vic drew back and stared at her. He shook his head ruefully. "I still can't support you—not in proper style. But soon. I've taken a position on the cotton exchange. I'll invest every picayune and in time I'll be able to ask for your hand."

" 'In time' is too far away," Cami moaned, tearing at his shirt, her own need at a dangerous peak. "I want you now! We'll marry and live at Elysian Fields. I have things running smoothly already."

"Hush!" he told her, kissing her to silence. "I don't want to talk or even to think. I only want to love you, Cami."

With his hands on her breasts, plucking at her erect nipples, Cami conceded defeat, surrendering to desire. Still standing beside the bed, she watched as Vic leaned down, letting his tongue take over his hands' sweet labors at her breasts. Wet fire raged through her as he sucked and licked. It seemed as if all her feelings were centered just over her heart.

Then Vic stepped away. For long moments, he

stood before her, staring at her heaving breasts. The bodice of her gown hung limply over her hips.

"You are more beautiful than I remembered," he whispered. "So beautiful that I thought I would die with wanting you. And now you are here. Are you real, my Cami, or only a vision?"

"I am real enough to burn for you, my darling." Her words were low, throaty, laden with invitation and desire.

Vic reached out and placed his palms on either side of her waist. With one fierce downward motion, he shoved gown and petticoats to the floor. Slowly, savoring every inch of her body, he kissed her until she was almost senseless. She swayed against him.

"Take me, my darling," she moaned. "Take me now!"

Cami never knew when or how they got into bed. Out of the hot dark night, he was suddenly there, poised over her. She felt his tip nudge at her moist, swollen lips, and then came the exquisite sensation she had dreamed of so often. A slow, hot, throbbing slide of flesh into flesh. She was filled to bursting with his love, with his body.

The powerful feeling rose within her so quickly that she tried to hold it at bay, to enjoy it longer. She held her breath and dared not move. But when Vic eased almost out to plunge deeper yet, all was lost. Cami's hips rose to meet his thrust and in the next moment she was lost in a swirl of bright color and passion and love so intense that she had to gasp for breath.

Afterward, they clung to each other, as if time or fate or the very night itself might wrench them apart once more.

"I want to stay this way forever," Cami whispered. "I don't ever want to spend another night out of your arms, my darling. Marry me tomorrow! Please!"

Vic gave her no answer, but she could feel him tense against her.

"What's wrong?" she begged, terror suddenly gripping her.

"I told you before, Cami, I can't live on your charity. You wouldn't want a man who could."

"I only want *you*, Vic. I'll live any way you like."

"It's not just myself I have to think of now, Cami. There's my son. He knows about Golden Oaks. Even if he doesn't remember the place, he expects me to buy it back so we'll have a real home."

"But Elysian Fields *is* a real home, Vic," Cami insisted. "It will be a wonderful place for Pierre to grow up. Why, I'll even take him on expeditions into the swamp to search for Lafitte's treasure. We'll have grand times there, the three of us." She wanted to say, "the *four* of us," but she had a feeling that now was not the time to tell Vic about the child she was carrying, the child she thought of already as their little daughter, Janie.

"Pierre respects me little enough as it is. If I went back on the things I've promised him, he would turn from me completely." Vic rolled away from her. "We'd better get some sleep now. Dawn will come early."

Dawn! Cami had almost forgotten. Before she knew it, they would be on their way to a terrifying appointment with fate. For the first time a black thought crossed her mind.

What if Cousin Morris should kill Vic?

Chapter Twenty

Despite the oppressive heat and humidity the next morning, Cami kept her identity well hidden beneath a heavy black gown, cloak, and veil. Moments after dawn, she sat alone in Vic's closed coach at the edge of *Les Trois Capelines.* The sun had yet to rise high enough to burn away the thick mist that hovered over the dueling field. Straining her eyes to see through veil and fog, she could barely make out the cluster of men—Vic, Cousin Morris, their seconds, the surgeon—as they stood together beneath the oaks, discussing the polite details of the coming bloody battle.

"Pistols for two," she murmured under her breath, "coffee for one." The words sent a shiver through her. Somewhere she had heard these matters of honor described in such a fashion. A grim thought! Hardly as grim, though, as the thought that Morris Pinard might be the only combatant left afterward to drink his cup of coffee.

Again, a shudder ran through her. It was difficult being alone at such a grave moment. She wished suddenly that she had demanded that Pierre be allowed to accompany them. Vic had not wanted either of them here, but Cami had insisted on coming, even if she had to ride bareback all the way. Vic had finally relented after she promised to conceal her identity and remain in the closed carriage. But at Pierre's pleading, Vic had put his boot down firmly, saying to his son, "Dueling is a ridiculous and outdated manner of settling disagreements. You have no reason to feel proud that your father is involved in one. I refuse to let you witness supposedly intelligent men indulging in such bloody insanity. You shall wait for us here, Pierre, until we return around midday."

"And what if you don't return?" the boy had asked petulantly, obviously trying to cover his fear. "What should I do then?"

"I *will* return!" Vic had answered. "You have my word on that, son."

Cami had added her reassurances, hoping to lighten Pierre's glum spirits. Now, as she sat alone, watching her kinsman and the man she loved pace off the steps before turning to fire, she wondered if Pierre might have had a premonition that all was not well.

In the terrible stillness of that morning, Cami heard the counting off of the paces. She saw Vic and Morris Pinard turn to face each other—Vic tall and erect, Cousin Morris short and round, his

436

shoulders slightly stooped. Both men were dressed in formal death-black.

She watched a vulture circle, glide, then come to light on a branch of one of the oaks to watch the proceedings.

"Ready!" came the call. Both men raised their pistols into the air. Then only deafening silence.

"Aim!"

When Cami saw the two shooters point their guns at heart-level, her own heart all but stopped. Silence again. She waited for the dreaded command to fire.

Suddenly, the fog over the field thickened. Or was it a mist over Cami's eyes? A soul-deep chill possessed her. She grew dizzy and weak. Someone was screaming inside her head. Then the sound turned into distinct words. She heard a voice—a woman's voice: "Frank, look out! He's got a gun!"

She glimpsed a strange scene. A man—tall and dark like Vic, a woman with close-cropped brown hair. Behind the pair loomed the unmistakable façade of St. Louis Cathedral, but it seemed much older than the church she knew so well, weathered by time and the elements. A crowd of strange-looking people in peculiar clothing milled about in the gathering twilight. Cami tried to figure out exactly what she was seeing. It made no sense at all.

Suddenly, the man named Frank yelled, "Where the hell is he, Carol? I don't see any gun."

At that instant, Cami's perspective changed. She seemed to be inside the woman named Carol, looking at the scene through her greenish eyes. And what she witnessed sent a chill down her spine. She never saw the gunman's face, only his right arm, his grisly tattoo, and his weapon.

"Frank, there!" Cami cried.

Carol glanced about frantically, then whirled toward Frank. How on earth did they get here? They were in a crowd of tourists in Jackson Square. New Orleans, 1992! But only a moment before, she had been outside the city, sitting in a carriage, watching Frank—no, Vic—under moss-shrouded oaks, a dueling pistol in his hand. Now, suddenly, the time and place had changed—Cami and Vic had changed, too—but the threat of death remained as strong as ever.

"We've been thrown forward again, back into the present," Carol muttered aloud with a sinking feeling. The late afternoon sun flashed once more on the gun barrel. "Frank, look out!"

Everything seemed to happen in slow motion. Frank turned. Carol saw his eyes go wide as he spotted the pistol aimed at his heart. He ducked. She ran toward him. Then a sound like the crack of a whip split the air. Carol watched the bullet tear into Frank's chest, watched the blood spurt from the gaping wound. She knew she was screaming, but she couldn't hear the sound. The only thing she heard was a dull roar inside her head. As she neared Frank, she saw his face register shock. He clutched at his shoulder, staggered, went down.

Carol was beside him then, cradling his head, calling his name.

His lips moved and his eyes flickered open as he stared up at her. "Cami? Carol? What are we doing

438

here?" he whispered between gasps. "Why did we come back?"

Clutching him frantically, Carol moaned, "I don't know, darling. I don't know. But I'm taking us away right now. You'll be okay, Frank, I promise. None of this will have happened once we get back to 1840. Just hang on. Hang on, my love."

Carol closed her eyes and mentally kicked in every psychic power she had ever known. She had to get them out of here. She had to do it *now!*

A short distance away, two cops wrestled the tattooed gunman to the ground. The panicked crowd swirled like a wave around Frank and Carol, threatening to trample them.

"Anybody hit?" yelled a burly, red-faced policeman.

"Yeah, a guy over here," a tourist in a flashy Mardi Gras tee-shirt shouted back. "Frank somebody. I heard his girlfriend holler to warn him just before the shot."

The crowd parted to make way for the husky cop. When the tourist pointed to the spot where Frank had fallen, they found a pool of blood on the cobbles. Nothing else.

The heavy mist cleared, leaving Cami shaken and confused. Where was she? What had happened?

At the very instant that the strange vision faded, a loud shot rang out. Pandemonium broke out on the field—men shouting, cursing, hurrying to and fro beneath the oaks.

Cami stared, unblinking, uncomprehending. "No one gave the command to fire," she told herself with false serenity, sure that the shot was only an echo of the one she had heard during her vision. Yet something told her that someone on the field had fired as well.

"Everything's all right," she murmured, trying to calm herself. "A misfire, that's all it was. They will simply retreat and begin again."

An instant later, she knew otherwise. When the crowd parted only one of the duelists remained standing. The other lay stretched on the ground, the surgeon kneeling over him.

"Vic?" Cami said in a small, uncertain voice. Then his name tore itself from her throat in a high-pitched scream. Cami wrenched the carriage door open and flew across the field. She fell to the wet ground beside Vic's still form and cradled his head in her lap.

"Madame, please!" barked the surgeon. "Give him air. He may be dying."

She stared wildly at the gray-haired physician, her indigo eyes mad with grief. "No!" she shouted. "He is not dying! We came back here so this wouldn't happen." She paused, wondering at her own words. "How can he die when the signal was never given to fire?"

"Pinard stole the advantage by firing before the command," she heard someone say. She didn't turn to see who had spoken. Her eyes remained on Vic's ashen face. His eyes were closed. His breathing was shallow and labored. A gaping wound near his heart oozed blood onto her gown.

As she stared down—silent with shock and grief—her vision again blurred. When her eyes cleared, she was staring into another man's face.

440

He looked much like her own lover, yet his cheek bore no scar. He was dressed in odd clothing—a bright shirt, no coat, and what looked like heavy blue work britches. He wore soft white shoes that were laced and tied. Yet his blood, too, flowed from an identical wound. He stared up at her, his dark eyes glazed with pain. "Carol," he murmured. "Carol, please don't let it end this way."

"I won't, Frank," Cami heard her own voice reassuring the stranger. "We'll go back. We should have stayed. I knew it!"

"Cami?" Vic's eyes flickered open. His voice was faint. He seemed confused. "You looked so different."

"Sh-h-h, my love," Cami cautioned. "You'll be all right. We're both safe now. I promise."

The surgeon frowned at her, admonishing her silently for making promises he couldn't guarantee.

"Can he be moved?" she asked the physician. "If I can take him home, I know I can make him well."

"The shot missed his heart, but only barely," the doctor told her. "He's lost a great deal of blood and he shouldn't be moved, but we have no choice. I need to get him somewhere so I can clean the wound properly, otherwise it will go septic. I've done all I can for him here. At least I've been able to stanch the flow of blood for the time being."

Cami turned to the others who were milling about. Only Morris Pinard stood back, looking properly shamefaced at the gravity of his cowardly deed. She gave him a hard stare. He would pay for shaming himself on the field of honor. From this day on, he would be cast out by Creole society. Taking only a moment's satisfaction in that thought, Cami quickly motioned to the seconds. "Help us get him to the carriage."

The ride back to New Orleans was a horror. Every bounce and bump brought a moan of pain from Vic. By turns, Cami wept and prayed and murmured words of encouragement to her lover. Finally, the carriage rolled into Condé Street.

"Thank God, we made it!" Cami breathed.

For a moment, she wondered what had happened to the other man who was shot—the man named Frank. Then she banished the curious vision from her mind. This was no time for fantasy, she reminded herself sharply. She would have her hands full dealing with painful reality.

September crept toward October in a welter of heat and misery as Cami worked herself to near-exhaustion tending her less-than-cooperative patient. To add to the suffering inside the Condé Street house, another outbreak of yellow fever had the city in panic. Cannons boomed at all hours, and the heat and humidity seemed far worse with the smoke from smudge pots polluting the already fetid air. Cami's morning nausea only added to her discomfort and ill temper. Pierre proved to be the final straw. Feeling neglected by both his father and Cami, the boy took to slipping out of the house at night, roaming the streets with a gang of young toughs. Cami threatened, but there was little she could do to stop him and Pierre knew it.

One particularly scorching morning in late September, Cami woke soaked with sweat and immediately reached for the china chamberpot beneath her bed. After several minutes of retching, she stumbled over to the washstand to bathe her face. Glancing out the window, she saw an officer of the law hauling Pierre up the street by the scruff of his collar. The boy was wriggling, cursing, and spitting.

"What now?" Cami moaned, pulling on her wrapper to meet them at the door.

She opened up to find the tall, grim-faced officer and Pierre with a black eye and a bloody nose.

"Bonjour, madame," the man said coldly.

Cami recognized him immediately. He had brought Pierre home one morning last week after some foolish mischief.

"What now, officer?" she asked, giving Pierre her sternest look.

"It is more serious this time," the policeman said. "He and three others were caught attempting to break into a store in Royal Street. They tried to fight us when we arrived. The older boys—all past offenders—were taken immediately to the calaboose. Knowing this lad's father and M'sieur Navar's present poor state of health, I thought it best to bring the young hellion home. But this is your *last* warning," he said pointedly to Pierre. "Next time, you go with your friends."

"Thank you," Cami said. She took Pierre by the arm and drew him inside. "I assure you, sir, this will not happen again. We are going away this very day."

"Away where?" Pierre growled. "I like New Orleans. I got pals here."

The boy was as bull-headed as his father, Cami fumed irritably.

"Those *pals* are better left behind," she said

firmly. "We are going to my plantation, to Elysian Fields. The fresh air and quiet will do your father good, and I'll have my overseer find so much work for you to do, young man, that you won't have time to get into any more mischief."

"A fine plan, madame," the officer agreed. Then he tipped his hat and left.

Cami sent Pierre off to his room in the charge of Vic's manservant, with orders not to let the boy out of his sight until she had things packed up and ready to go. Then she went to tell Vic the news, dreading his reaction all the while. She had tried before to convince Vic that they would all be better off in the country. But he absolutely refused to go to her plantation—simply because it was hers. Such stubborn male pride she had never seen!

The problem was that Vic was strong enough to argue now, but still too weak for Cami to feel comfortable taking a stand against him. Any upset, she felt, could do him grave harm. But now she must face that risk. With the heat and the illness and Pierre's misbehavior, their only answer was to get out of the city.

When she entered Vic's bedroom, a wave of longing swept through her. This chamber had been the scene of so much happiness, so much love in the past. Not since the night before the duel, however, had Vic held her and loved her. Now she occupied the bedroom down the hall. She had told Vic she would stay there only until he felt well enough to share his bed once more. In Cami's opinion, he was well enough now. Still, he had yet to invite her back.

Vic turned his head when he heard her footsteps. "Who was that at the door?"

444

"A friend of Pierre's, darling." She told herself that she wasn't lying to him, only twisting the truth a bit to save his feelings.

"Where is the boy?" Vic asked. "He hasn't come in to say good morning yet."

"He's in his room, probably sleeping. Vic, there's something I must tell you. And you needn't try to argue with me. I'll hear no further protests on this point. We are going to Elysian Fields today. Your doctor thinks you will recover more quickly in the country, and it will be grand for Pierre. He can begin learning how to run a plantation."

"Cami, how many times must I tell you that I can't live on your charity?"

"It is hardly charity, Vic. I need to get back and make sure everything there is being properly taken care of."

Vic scowled at her. "Then go! What's keeping you?"

"I love you!" she snapped. "That's what's keeping me." She sighed, and made an effort to soften her tone. "Oh, Vic, listen to us. We're at each other's throats night and day. You don't seem to be getting any better and I'm almost ill with fatigue. Pierre is causing trouble . . ."

Vic half-rose, then grimaced with pain. "What kind of trouble? Why haven't I been told of this before?"

Cami wanted to bite her tongue off. She'd blurted the words out without thinking. "Only minor scrapes so far, but he's running with a bad group, darling. Older boys who have been in trouble with the law. We must get him away before it's too late."

"By damn, I'll tend to this . . ."

445

Cami pressed Vic gently back down to his pillows. "You'll do nothing of the sort!" she commanded. "You will stay right there and rest and get well. You *must*, Vic, for all our sakes."

Cami paused, pondering her dilemma. She still hadn't told Vic that she was carrying his child. She'd hoped that the perfect time would arise; however, their days together seemed anything but perfect of late. She looked straight into his eyes, her own brimming with sudden tears. This news could wait no longer.

"There's another reason we must go, Vic. Perhaps the most important reason, at least to me. I'm going to have your child and I'd like the baby to be born at Elysian Fields as I was."

Black Vic's mouth had been open already to argue the point, but her words stopped him cold. His harsh features softened. His own eyes went moist. "A child?" he whispered. "A baby? You're going to have a baby—*mine?*"

Eagerly, Vic reached out to her. Just as eagerly, Cami flew into his arms, letting her tears flow freely. Through her soft little sobs, a laugh erupted. "Whose else might it be?"

Vic cuddled her gently in the curve of his good arm and sought her lips. Cami felt her whole body tingle at his touch, his kiss. Not since before the duel had he exhibited such tenderness. It was as if they had both held their passions in check for so long that, pent up, their longing had built to almost unbearable heights. His tongue stroked hers lazily as his hand groped through wrapper and nightshift to find her breasts. Cami moaned softly into his open mouth when she felt her nipples rise to meet his touch.

446

"Oh, my little love," Vic rasped. "If only I could have you this minute. I ache for you so. Needing you pains me far worse than this hole in my chest."

"We dare not!" Cami warned. "The doctor said you must lie very still for fear of reopening the wound."

Vic sighed and shifted her until his lips touched one erect nipple. He settled with his eyes closed, suckling gently. At the same time, his hand slid under her gown and between her thighs. His slow, loving strokes sent a delicious tremor through Cami.

As her own pleasure built, Cami glanced down at the sheet—now a perfect tent over Vic's lower body. She leaned her head back and closed her eyes, at the same time letting her hand steal under the covers. A moment later, her fingers wrapped his heat in their cool, tender touch. Silence fell in the room. Even as Vic's gentle strokes brought Cami to the heights, her tender caresses pleasured him, soothed him, and, at length, brought Vic his long-craved release. They lay still for a moment afterward, then she leaned down to kiss him as he had kissed her a short time before.

"Rest now, my darling," she whispered, smiling as she rose from the bed. "I must go and make ready for our trip."

Vic's eyes were closed. Cami's patient was sleeping peacefully by the time she tiptoed from the room.

Cami had caught only a glimpse of Carol and Frank. It seemed to her that these phantoms of her mind were simply that. Perhaps her anxiety over the duel had caused them to appear, then disappear almost as quickly. She could never have guessed what Carol had been through—what Carol knew about the things Cami herself would soon be forced to face.

Although it seemed that Carol and Frank vanished effortlessly from Jackson Square on the afternoon of March 4, 1992, the way back to September 30, 1840, was long and treacherous.

As Carol lay over Frank to keep the crowd from crushing him in their panic—willing them both to travel back through time—the woman in the red tignon appeared beside them.

"Choctaw awaits!" she said, then vanished into the crowd.

In that instant, Carol and Frank vanished, too, leaving only a pool of his blood at the site. But they did not go immediately back to the scene of the duel. When Carol opened her eyes, she was in Choctaw's pirogue. Frank lay in the bottom of the boat, deathly pale, gasping for breath.

Would they make it back in time to save him? Carol could only pray that they would.

"Please, we've got to hurry!" she urged Choctaw.

The man's lined face remained impassive. He poled the boat slowly, too slowly.

"You go back to bad times," Choctaw said at length.

"Bad times?" Carol cried. "Frank's dying! Look at him! How much worse could it get?"

Choctaw left the river, following a bayou that snaked through dense swamp.

"Where are you going?" Carol shrieked. "This isn't the way!"

"You know the way?" Choctaw asked. "Me, I

448

don't think so. You got to travel slow, watch the signs, make the right turns. Otherwise, you lost, lady. Lost and *damned!*"

His last words sent a chill through Carol. She stopped trying to reason with him. What good would it do? She'd already loused things up by coming back to the present, by letting the guy with the tattoo shoot Frank. It was all her fault. All of it!

"The guilt, she not yours," Choctaw said, reading her thoughts. "Blame goes back years, generations, to beginning of time. You watch. You listen. You know."

The well-remembered beam of light settled in over a dark spot in the swamp. Again, Carol saw a grand plantation—not Mulgrove—an even finer home. Elysian Fields! Yes, she recognized it now.

She saw a man on the gallery. His left arm was in a sling tied around his neck. Beside him on a table sat a decanter, half-empty. Removing the crystal stopper, he poured himself another drink and tossed it down. His head lolled forward on his chest. His hand dropped and the glass hit the floor and shattered. He was obviously drunk. Carol recognized him suddenly—Black Vic Navar.

Cami came out on the porch. Although she wore a full apron over her gray-blue frock, Carol guessed by the fullness of her face, the high color in her cheeks, and the sparkle of her indigo eyes that Cami was pregnant. She glanced over at Vic, shook her head, then wiped away a tear with the corner of her apron.

"Miz Cami! Come quick, Miz Cami!" A black man in a tattered straw hat came racing around the side of the house.

"What is it, Jem?"

449

"Young Marse Pierre! He done took off to the swamp on that crazy horse, Voodoo. Said he was gone find Lafitte's treasure so he could buy back his papa's plantation for him. I tried to stop him, ma'am, but he got clean away."

"Mother of God!" Cami half-swore, half-prayed. Voodoo had not mellowed with age. Even Cami found him all but impossible to ride nowadays. And the thought of Pierre at the mercy of the wild stallion chilled her blood.

"Gather up some of the men and meet me at the barn," she called. "I'll be right there."

Cami didn't take time to change clothes before she raced to the barn to organize a search party. For once, she was glad Vic had drunk himself into a stupor. Maybe by the time he came around, she'd have Pierre back, safe and sound. Why had she told the boy all those tales about the treasure? If anything happened to him, it was all her fault.

The light in the swamp faded just as Cami and the men set off to search.

Carol roused herself, checked Frank. He was still breathing, just barely. Then she turned on Choctaw.

"Why do you always do this to me? What happened? Is Pierre all right? Why is Vic drinking so much? And Cami, she's pregnant, isn't she? She shouldn't be dashing off into the swamp."

"Think, you!" Choctaw ordered, his dark eyes boring into Carol.

She forced herself to stop and think. And what came to mind sent shivers through her. This was it—the beginning of the end.

"No, it can't end this way!" she cried—furious and frightened and half-crazy with grief.

450

"It can and it will, unless . . ."

"Unless *what*? Tell me, Choctaw!"

He only stared straight ahead and whispered, "You know. Think and you know."

Carol strained to clear the jumble of doubts cluttering her brain. "All right . . . all right," she muttered. "Yes. I do know what's going to happen. Cami's going into that swamp to find Pierre. But she won't be able to save him, will she? The snakebite. Cami's going to die in there—Cami and her unborn child. Pierre, too. All of them. Then there's Black Vic. He's drinking because he can't stand being useless. Until his wound heals, all he can do is let Cami take care of him and Pierre and Elysian Fields. So he drinks to forget, to get away from the mess he's made of his life." Carol stopped suddenly and looked up at Choctaw. "She is pregnant, isn't she?"

He nodded. "Poor little Janie!" he moaned.

Carol's eyes misted as she remembered the small, sad voice. "Yes, poor little Janie. She'll never be born, will she? That's why she keeps calling to me. I have to be there to save her mother . . . to save Janie and give her a chance at life. Otherwise, she'll remain inside her mother—inside that awful mummy from the swamp. I must help them. But how? You take us back, Choctaw! *Now!*"

She glanced up at him, her eyes pleading. He was shaking his head slowly, sadly.

"You can't let this happen!" Carol cried. She felt Frank's pulse. It was weak and uneven. There wasn't much time left. "Not to them and not to us. You take us back now, Choctaw. Right this minute!"

"You think you can change things?" he asked in a mocking tone.

451

"I *know* I can!" Carol insisted, a wild light in her green eyes.

She gripped Frank's hand, holding him tightly. She must not let him slip away. And above all else, when they went back in time, they must go together.

"It's our only hope," she murmured. "Cami and Vic's only hope!"

A bright white light blinded her, then all was blackness.

When next she saw light, it was through Camille Mazaret's indigo eyes.

Chapter Twenty-One

Cami took a deep breath, marveling at the sweet scent of the land—*her* land. She could almost taste the spicy flavor of autumn in the air. October, she thought, was her favorite month at Elysian Fields. She laughed softly. Every month would be her favorite from now on. She glanced over at Vic—so handsome and tall in the saddle—and reached for his hand.

"Are you tired, my darling?" she asked. "We could turn back."

He brought her gloved fingers to his lips, kissed their tips, then smiled. "Tired? The only thing I'm tired of is *resting*. God, I hope I never see another bed!"

"Really?" she asked flirtatiously.

Vic reined his horse closer to hers and leaned

over to give her a long, deep kiss. His dark eyes half-closed, he said in a husky voice, "Yes, really! We don't need a bed, little love. I find the couch in the library quite comfy. The rug by my fireplace as well. And lately I've been eyeing the hammock on the back gallery with no small amount of speculation."

"Oh, you!" Cami cried, feeling her cheeks flush. They had, indeed, made love recently on both the library couch and the bedroom rug. So how was she to know that he was joking about the hammock?

Every day now, Cami could see more improvement in Vic. And with his restored health came a restored appetite as well—for mountains of food and for Cami. It seemed he could never get enough of her these days. Mind you, she wasn't complaining. She'd never been so happy!

As they rode through the oaks toward the river, Cami let her thoughts drift to the months ahead. With the baby due in March, she and Vic had decided to stay on at Elysian Fields for the winter rather than returning to New Orleans for the excitement and whirl of the social season. They would be married in a few days, as soon as the priest Vic had sent for arrived. There was a small parish chapel nearby. It would be less showy than a St. Louis Cathedral wedding, but far more intimate and to their liking.

"We'll honeymoon right here, if that's all right with you, my love." Vic's suggestion had been more than all right with Cami. He'd gone on to explain the rest of his plans. "I still refuse to live on a woman's dole, even if she is my wife. So I figure on sending that lazy overseer of yours packing. I'll take over his duties and run the place as it should be handled."

"But, Vic, that will be so much work for you," she'd protested.

He'd only grinned and said, "Don't worry! I mean to put myself on your payroll, dearest. My portion of the profits will go into a special account in the Bank of New Orleans. In time, I mean to purchase not only Golden Oaks, but the land that lies between our two plantations. By the time Pierre is ready to take over, we'll own the largest sugar-producing holdings in all the area. Our children will be rich, Cami!"

"That will be nice for them," she replied. "I only hope they will also be happy—as happy as we are."

And happy they were. Vic thrived on the country air. As for rascally young Pierre, he was a new person—all eagerness and excitement. He loved the house, the land, the open space. He had grown self-assured in the past month. He rode like the wind, fished like a Cajun, shot like a sharpshooter, and never ceased to amaze and amuse Cami and Vic with his vivid imagination and boundless energy. More than anything else, Pierre loved to sit on the gallery in the evening with Cami and his father and listen to her tell tales of her childhood days. She would always leave Lafitte's treasure for last, until Pierre demanded, "Now, about this pirate and his buried gold, Cami. Exactly where did you say your papa found that chest?"

Cami would oblige the lad, telling the tale over and over until Vic finally refused to listen any longer. He would rise from his chair with a pointed yawn and say, "Time to turn in, don't you think?"

First finishing her story for Pierre, Cami would then follow Vic up to the large, airy room they shared. He would be patiently waiting for her—his dark eyes bright with love. Sometimes they would share a glass of brandy before bedtime. More nights than not, it seemed, they ended the evening with sweet, tender love-making. Their hunger for each other seemed simply insatiable, their passion limitless.

"Looks like we're about to get wet," Vic warned, calling Cami back from her pleasant musings. She glanced up at the sky to see a boiling, purple thunderhead.

"My word, what a cloud!" she cried. "I'll race you back."

Vic caught her reins and, pulling a serious face, shook his head. "Oh no, you won't! No more racing in your condition, my fine lady."

Cami giggled and blushed. She felt more girl than lady these days. When Vic, on occasion, was forced to remind her that she was with child, she always found that reminder both thrilling and embarrassing. To think that she and the awesome, evil-looking Black Vic Navar had done those shocking things Fiona had explained to her in order to put her in this condition! She should have guessed he would wind up seducing her from that first night she laid eyes on him, the night of the ball at Mulgrove.

"How time flies!" she mused aloud. "And how long ago it seems, back to the time before I knew you."

Vic glanced at her, his face serious, a loving light in his hot, dark eyes. "I think I've always known you, Cami. There was never a time when you weren't a part of me and I a part of you."

His words brought tears to her eyes—warm, soft, happy tears.

"Oh, my darling . . ." she whispered, too choked with emotion to say all she longed to tell him. She loved this man so deeply.

A moment later, the threatening cloud overhead opened up. The house was still some distance away so they headed instead for the barn. Seeing no slaves about, Vic leaped down and opened the door for Cami to ride in. By the time they were inside, with the door closed against the storm, they were both soaked to the skin.

Vic reached up to help Cami dismount. She slid into his arms, her gown clinging revealingly to her body. Instead of letting her slip immediately to the ground, Vic held her poised, kissing her in mid-air.

"I like you all slippery and wet," he whispered.

She shivered in his arms. "Well, I don't like it a bit. I'm cold!"

Vic glanced about the barn. Except for a few horses in the stalls, the place was empty. Whoever was supposed to be on duty had doubtless gotten caught somewhere else in the rain.

"Come on," Vic ordered, tugging Cami toward the ladder to the hayloft. "I'll get you warm."

"Vic!" she protested. "Up there?"

"Can you think of a better place?" he asked in a low, seductive voice.

"Oh, honestly!" she answered. "You can't mean that you intend to . . ."

He cut her off with another kiss. "You always said you liked some secret place on a rainy afternoon."

When Cami recalled their first rainy afternoon together in the old nursery upstairs at the Condé Street house, she knew all was lost. She knew and she rejoiced at the thought.

"Come on, woman!" Vic urged. "You're wasting a lot of good rain."

The loft was clean and dry and strewn with sweet hay. Vic found a blanket and made them a bed. Propped against the wall, he pulled off his boots while Cami stood staring at him expectantly. Vic grinned up at her and winked. "Take off your clothes."

Cami glanced about, nervous suddenly. "Undress? You mean, right here—right now."

He chuckled and nodded. "That's what I mean. While me and the horses watch."

"Oh, Lord, Vic! Why did you have to say that?" In spite of her protest and her embarrassment at the thought of the horses all watching her, Cami began to slip out of her wet gown. Moments later, she stood naked and shivering before Vic's admiring eyes.

"Satisfied?" she asked, feigning anger. "Now I'm freezing!"

Quickly, he shucked the rest of his wet things. "Come here," he invited. "I'll warm you."

A moment later, Cami was snuggled in his arms, her damp flesh clinging to his. She wasn't cold any longer.

The rain drummed on and the wind howled, but Cami hardly noticed. Vic held her and kissed her until her whole body was on fire. Then choosing a straw from the hay, he drew light little pictures on

458

her quivering flesh—across her lips, down her chin and neck, then round and round each nipple. When Cami squirmed and whimpered, Vic let the straw travel lower, drawing it over her ribs and down across her slightly rounded belly. At last, Cami could stand his sweet torture no longer. She dashed the straw from his hand and pressed her body to his. Moments later, he was over her, filling her, coaxing her gently but firmly to the heights.

"Ah, I do love the rain," she sighed afterward.

Vic stared into her wide, violet-blue eyes, his own dark with emotion. "And I do love you, my darling," he said.

After pulling on their clothes—clothes that had had plenty of time to dry—Vic and Cami walked hand-in-hand back to the house through the wet grass. The sun was setting.

The air was golden. The storm was over. Or so it seemed . . .

Several days passed before the next ominous clouds gathered over Elysian Fields. There was no rain this time, only a deluge of emotion and terror.

The day began as any other. Cami and Vic rose early, she to see to the running of the house, he to ride out to the cane fields to supervise the workers.

They breakfasted together as the sun was coming up. Over country ham, grits, fluffy eggs, biscuits and orange marmalade, they discussed their schedules for the day. Cami would direct the house servants to air the bedding since winter was fast approaching. Vic thought he'd ride over to the next plantation to look at a mare the owner had for sale. "Voodoo's far too spirited for you to be riding now,

459

Cami. If you insist on staying in the saddle, you need a gentler mount."

Had Cami possessed precognitive powers, that very conversation might have alerted her to the dangers lying ahead. But as it was, she merely kissed Vic goodbye, then went about her early-morning duties.

Not until Vic was long gone and one of the servants was clearing away the breakfast dishes did Cami realize Pierre had not yet come down to eat.

"Have you seen Master Pierre?" Cami asked the girl who was clearing the table. She knew that sometimes he sneaked out early, filling his kerchief with biscuits to eat on the way to his favorite fishing hole.

"No, ma'am, Miz Cami," the young servant answered. "I reckon he's still sleeping."

"Probably so," Cami answered. "Well, keep something warm for him in the kitchen. He'll be down soon, I'm sure."

An hour later, the servants had all the beds stripped except for Pierre's. Since his door was still closed, Cami gave orders not to disturb him. He'd been out late the night before on a 'gator hunt with some of the hands. She smiled to herself, thinking how old Jem had teased Pierre, saying that they planned to take him along to use as 'gator-bait.

Shortly before noon, Cami walked out onto the front gallery for a breath of air. She smoothed her sweaty palms down over the white apron that covered her gray-blue frock. It was hot today for this late in the season.

As she stood staring out over the garden, thinking how beautiful the whole world looked, someone called her name.

460

"Miz Cami! Come quick, Miz Cami!" A black man in a tattered straw hat came racing around the side of the house.

"What is it, Jem?" she called.

"Young Marse Pierre! He done took off to the swamp on that crazy horse, Voodoo. Said he was gone find Lafitte's treasure so he could buy back his papa's plantation for him. I tried to stop him, ma'am, but he got clean away."

"Mother of God!" Cami half-swore, half-prayed. "Gather up some of the men and meet me at the barn," she called. "I'll be right there."

Cami raced toward the barn. She found several of the men already mounted and ready to go when she got there. They had saddled a horse for her as well. She climbed up and motioned them to follow. The search party headed for the swamp.

One of the stable hands, a tall, gaunt slave who was half-African, half-Choctaw Indian, picked up Voodoo's trail.

"Boy went this way, him," the man said.

"You stay in the lead, Choctaw. We'll follow," Cami shouted.

But as they forged deeper into the swamp, following a trail became impossible. Choctaw pointed out bent branches and small broken limbs, but they led in all directions, as likely disturbed by some swamp creature as by Pierre and Voodoo.

The atmosphere in the swamp was close and humid. Mosquitoes droned their eerie songs and plagued the searchers with their stings. Alligators startled Cami's mount twice, almost unseating her. Another time, she nearly fell off when she spied a snake hanging down from a limb.

"Pierre!" she called over and over until her throat was sore and her voice raspy. "Answer me, Pierre!"

She cursed herself a thousand times over for the tales she had told the boy about Lafitte's gold. She had explained to Pierre in detail where her father found the chest. If the boy had managed to stay on Voodoo's back this far, that tiny treasure island had to be where he was headed. Unmindful of the other searchers, Cami plunged deeper and deeper into the swamp. Before she realized what she had done, she was hopelessly lost and alone.

"Pierre!" She kept up her urgent shouts. "Pierre, where are you?"

How long had she been out here? She tried to gauge the time by the position of the sun, but the heavy, moss-laden branches overhead cut off her view. It seemed to be getting dark already. Her whole body ached with fatigue. She was hungry. Her face felt raw and swollen from the bites of mosquitoes, gnats, and yellow flies. Yet she refused to give up.

Finally, she spotted her destination—a small island in the very heart of the swamp.

"He *must* be there," she murmured aloud. If he wasn't, there was little hope that she would find him. And darkness was coming on fast.

Suddenly, she froze. Something was crashing toward her through the tangle of vines to her left. It could be anything—'gator, panther, bear. She held very still, hardly daring to breathe. When a great black head burst into a clearing, she went faint for a moment, then laughed with relief.

"Voodoo, you bastard! You scared the wits out of me!"

The big stallion stepped almost daintily toward her until he was close enough to rub her hip with his soft muzzle.

"Where's Pierre, Voodoo?" she pleaded gently. "We have to find him. Show me where he is. Then we can all go home. This nightmare will be over."

As if he understood every word Voodoo turned and headed back the way he'd come. Cami had followed only a short distance when she spied the boy. He was lying face down in the water, motionless.

With a sharp cry, Cami leaped from her horse and ran to him. Quickly, she turned Pierre over. There was a huge bump on his forehead, but he was still breathing. She pounded his back until he coughed and gagged, sending forth a stream of muddy swamp water.

The moment he came to, Pierre burst out crying and threw his arms around Cami's neck.

"It's all right now, son," she soothed. "You'll be fine. And look, right over there is where my papa found the gold. You really did find it."

Talking evenly, trying to calm the lad, Cami helped him through the water to the small hammock. At least the ground was dry here. They could rest for a while, then, with Voodoo's help, find the way home. Cami herself was hopelessly lost, but she dared not let Pierre know that. He was terrified enough as it was.

The two of them stretched out on a dry patch of sand. Cami began telling Pierre the old Lafitte tales once more, hoping to calm him. Before long, they both drifted off to sleep.

When Cami awoke, the night was the blackest she

had ever seen, and Pierre was no longer by her side. She was cold—shivering. And she was totally alone.

Vic arrived back at the plantation leading the new mare for Cami, only to find that she, his son, and a dozen slaves were off in the swamp somewhere. Lost!

He cursed and stormed, all to no avail. Finally, he formed his own search party, but it was getting late, getting dark. Their time would be limited to barely an hour. Vic decided to take pine knot torches along so they could search all night, if need be.

He kept telling himself as he rode toward the swamp that he would find Cami and Pierre trudging homeward along the way. Surely the two of them weren't lost. They both knew their way around. But when Vic reached the verge of the swamp, his heart sank. Inside that tangle of cypress and oak lay every danger imaginable. He only hoped he wasn't too late already.

Waving his torch over his head, Vic yelled, "Let's find them, boys, and bring them home for a good, hot supper!"

They crashed into the swamp, whooping and calling.

That night was the longest, the blackest, the cruelest of Cami's life. She dared not let herself go back to sleep. She tried to call out to Pierre, but her voice was spent. All she could muster was the barest whisper. All she could do was wait and pray.

After what seemed an eternity, dawn seeped into

464

the swamp. An eerie, pale gray, light slipped through the fog. Cami wept with relief. Now she would find Pierre. Now they would go home.

Her relief was short-lived. When she glanced about, she saw that both horses were gone.

"Oh, no," she moaned. "Oh, God, no!"

She had come miles into the very heart of this wilderness. Without a horse, she would never get out. Panic seized her.

"I'm going to die here," she said matter-of-factly, trying to swallow her fears. It was no use. "No one will ever find me." She glanced about wildly. "This swamp will be my grave." Her hand went suddenly to her belly. She looked down, tears filling her eyes. "Poor little Janie!"

Those tears blinded her to something she should have seen. A swamp rattler lay only a few feet away. Sluggish with the night's chill, the last thing on his mind was attack. Had Cami seen him, she would have remained very still or slowly inched away. As it was, when she heard Pierre's voice call out, "Cami, I found it!" she made a sudden, disastrous move. The rattler coiled, sounded his warning, then struck.

Cami screamed and grabbed her left leg just as Pierre splashed through the water, running back to the island.

"I found it, Cami! Lafitte's treasure!" Then he saw the look on her face and stopped. "Cami?"

"Snake!" she gasped. "Give me your knife."

Even as waves of pain and dizziness washed over her, Cami tended the bite as best she could. But before long she lay fevered and unconscious beside the frightened boy.

"Oh, Cami! Cami, say something," Pierre begged.

Pierre realized finally, in that moment, that perhaps he'd made a mistake by riding Voodoo into the swamp. He vowed that if Cami would only live, he would change his ways.

Black Vic had never liked Voodoo. As the night wore on and the search continued, he came to hate the fiery stallion. Before dawn, he swore to himself that he would destroy the beast at his first opportunity.

But never a gladder sight had greeted Vic's eyes than that huge, devil-black body coming toward him at dawn. He knew how well Cami's father had trained the stallion. At last there was hope, faint though it might be.

"Take me to Cami," Vic said to the horse. "I swear by all that's holy, I'll never hurt a hair in your mane if you find her for me. You'll have carrots, apples, sugar cubes, and as many mares as you can pleasure, old fellow. Just find Cami and Pierre!"

With a look of understanding and sympathy in his great, dewy eyes, Voodoo led the way. An hour later, Vic spotted Pierre on the small island. Cami lay on the ground, fast asleep.

"Papa!" Pierre called, making Vic's heart thud faster. The boy had never called him that before. "Come quick, Papa! Cami's dead!"

The thrill Vic had known a moment before deserted him. An icy hand closed over his heart. Leaping off his horse, he ran through the knee-deep water, then fell down beside Cami, cradling her limp form in his arms. His tears bathed her cold, pale cheeks.

Cami was not dead. But she was as near to death as any mortal could come without actually crossing over. For days she lay in the big bed that she and Vic had shared since coming to Elysian Fields. Vic stayed at her side night and day. He held her hand, he kissed her cold lips, he begged her to open her eyes—to speak to him. Still, she slept on—silent and oblivious—lost in her own world of torment and pain.

Early one morning, a servant knocked at the bedroom door. "Master Vic?" the woman said as quietly as she could.

"Go away!" he growled. "I'll call you if I need you."

"It's the priest, sir," the servant said. "He just come."

For a moment, Vic couldn't think what the woman was talking about. Then he remembered. "The priest, Cami," he whispered. "He's come to marry us."

He watched, unblinking, hoping that his words had gotten through to her. If she loved him as much as he loved her, surely she would wake up now. Surely, she would come back to marry him.

Never a twitch. Never a move.

"Send him away!" Vic roared. The words all but broke his heart.

The servant did not do as her master ordered. Instead, she showed the priest to the dining room and brought him breakfast.

A short time later, the plantation doctor arrived for his daily visit. Vic grudgingly let him enter, then watched as the man felt Cami's pulse, forced her eyelids open to peer at her pupils, poked her and prodded her. At last, he sighed and shook his head.

"I'm afraid there's nothing I can do, M'sieur Navar. I see you've summoned a priest. Wise of you, sir. She can't last much longer."

For a moment, the physician's words didn't register. When they did, Vic had to use all his control to keep from killing the useless doctor.

"The priest is here to marry us, you fool, not administer last rites! Get out!"

Vic fell back into the chair beside the bed, exhausted physically and emotionally. In spite of his determination to watch over Cami, he dozed off. When he woke sometime later, he heard a quiet voice in the room.

"You got to come back, Cami. I told you—I found Lafitte's treasure. Now I can buy Golden Oaks for Papa."

Pierre went silent for a moment. Vic remained still—watching, listening, feeling his heart shatter into tiny pieces when he saw his son take Cami's hand.

"Cami, wherever you are, I hope you can hear me. Me and Papa need you. We need you *bad!* We both love you, Cami. We're a real family with you. Please, come back to us."

When the boy broke down and sobbed, Vic had to bite his lip to keep from weeping, too. After Pierre got control of his emotions, Vic stirred in his chair and yawned loudly, on purpose. He saw Pierre's back stiffen.

"Oh, son, it's you."

"Yes, Papa." Pierre didn't turn, but Vic saw the

boy scrub at his eyes with his fists. "I was just keeping Cami company. She looks real pretty, doesn't she?"

Vic rose and went to stand beside his son. He slipped an arm around the boy's thin shoulders. "She's a beautiful lady—outside and in. We're lucky to have her, aren't we?"

"Yes, Papa." Pierre's voice quivered. He was on the verge of tears again. "I wish she was my mother."

Vic nodded. "She'd make a fine one."

For long moments, father and son stood together in silent communion, their eyes focused on Cami's pale, lovely face.

If only ... if only ... The useless words kept churning inside Vic's head. Then an idea began to dawn. A meaningless, hopeless, outrageous idea.

"You know the priest has come, son," Vic said quietly. "He's going to marry us. So Cami really will be your mother."

Pierre stared up at his father, his face grave. "R-eally? When?"

"How about right now?" Vic asked, forcing a smile that hurt his face and his breaking heart. "Why don't you run down and tell him to come up here?"

Pierre grinned—uncertainly at first. Then the meaning of the wedding caught hold of him. If Cami was about to marry his father, then she couldn't be dying.

"I'll bring him right up," Pierre called, already racing out of the room.

Vic took a few moments alone with the priest to explain his odd request.

"But she must answer," the priest argued. "How will she do that?"

"I'll answer in her behalf," Vic told the man in a no-nonsense tone.

A short time later, Vic and Pierre stood on opposite sides of Cami's bed—the father holding her left hand, the son her right. Harp music drifted up from downstairs. Cami's dark-skinned pupil wasn't very good at the instrument yet, but she did her best for the occasion. Another of the servants had gone out to the garden and quickly cut a bridal bouquet of late-blooming roses. The blood-red flowers lay on the bed beside the unconscious bride.

The priest cleared his throat, then began with a prayer for the salvation of the bride's eternal soul. Vic cast a frown his way. "This is a wedding, not last rites," he warned under his breath.

As the holy man droned on and on with his preamble to the ceremony, Pierre felt something peculiar. He tightened his hold on Cami's hand and glanced toward his father. Vic returned the boy's stare, his own expression grave. Pierre wanted to tell the others, but he knew that it would be impolite to interrupt, especially to interrupt a priest. Still, he was sure he had felt it. Cami had squeezed his hand.

"Do you take this woman to be your wedded wife?" the priest intoned.

"I do!" Vic answered.

Vic glanced quickly down at Cami. He was sure he had felt her fingers move in his when he made his pledge. Her eyes were still closed, her face expressionless. He told himself he was only imagining what he wanted to feel.

"Camille Mazaret, do you take this man to be your lawfully wedded husband?"

Silence greeted the priest's question this time. Intent on his examination of Cami's face, Vic forgot that he was supposed to answer. The priest repeated the question.

"Camille Mazaret, do you take this man, Victoine Navar, to be your lawfully wedded husband?"

Again, silence. They were all staring at Cami—at the tears seeping from the corners of her eyes. No one spoke. No one moved. They stood frozen in time and space—watching, listening. They all saw it at the same instant. Her colorless lips moved slightly.

"Cami," Vic rasped.

Pierre's grin was so wide it nearly split his face.

The priest cleared his throat and repeated his question one more time.

"I do." The words were not even a whisper. They seemed more like the wings of a butterfly brushing a light summer breeze. But they had issued from Cami's own lips.

"She's alive!" Pierre whispered. Then he gave a joyous shout. "My mother's alive!"

Oblivious to the others in the room, Vic knelt beside the bed, cradling Cami in his arms.

"My darling," he whispered, awed. "My precious, darling wife! You've come back to me."

"I was never away," she murmured. "I was there in your heart all the while. I have been there forever. I'll remain yours through all eternity."

A faint pink tint suffused Cami's lips. Vic leaned down, warming them with a tender kiss.

Cami had no idea where she had gone for so

long, but it had been a dark, cold, lonely place. Then the oddest thing had happened. It seemed someone had come to her from faraway to lead her back. *Carol,* she thought, wondering who the woman was.

Now sunlight showered her bed and her husband's arms held her lovingly. The scene was pure rapture in gold. She returned his kiss from the very depths of her soul.

A small, warm hand touched her cheek. Cami's eyes opened. Pierre, his handsome young face grave, stood staring at her.

"I found the treasure, Cami," he said solemnly. "More gold than you ever saw." Pierre paused for a moment, fighting for control. When he spoke again, his clear, young voice was strong and steady. "But the treasure—the real treasure, Cami, is *you!*"

Happy tears brimming in her indigo eyes, Camille Mazaret Navar clasped father and son to her at once. They were a family at last—a loving caring family. Together they would face new hopes, new dreams, new tomorrows.

Epilogue

Newspaper clippings—

New Orleans, March 5, 1992:
MURDERER CONFESSES, SHOOTING VICTIM VANISHES

A bizarre shooting incident took place yesterday in Jackson Square. According to numerous eyewitnesses, the gunman, identified as Orville Percy Jones, 55, an escaped murderer from the Louisiana State Penitentiary, fired into a large crowd of tourists striking one man. Panic ensued. Once officers restored order to the scene, the victim of the shooting had disappeared. Evidence found at the scene indicated that he had been wounded.

An eyewitness, Roger W. Ross of Plano, Texas,

told officers, "I saw the whole thing—the man with the gun and the guy he shot. There was a woman, too. She tried to warn the victim right before he got hit. She called him 'Frank.' I saw him go down. It looked to me like he was shot right through the heart. Then everybody panicked, figuring the shooter was going to keep firing into the crowd. They closed in around the man on the ground and the woman with him so I couldn't see them any longer. When the cops grabbed the gunman, then cleared everybody away, the guy that got shot was gone. I mean, gone like he'd vanished. There was blood on the pavement—lots of it. But not a sign of the fellow named Frank or his lady friend."

Another witness at the scene, Joe Crozat, owner of the nearby Let-The-Good-Times-Roll Café, stated that he recognized the victim as Detective Captain Frank Longpre of the New Orleans Police Department. Crozat identified Longpre's female companion as Carol Marlowe, a visitor from North Carolina.

A call has gone out to area doctors and hospitals in the event that Longpre went somewhere for treatment of his gunshot wound. However, no reports have come in.

The manager of the Hotel Dalpeche, where Longpre and Marlowe were staying, told authorities that he had spoken to the pair earlier in the day as they were leaving the hotel, but he did not see them return. A check of their rooms brought no further information.

Authorities are checking on several leads, but are clearly baffled. Anyone having any information on the whereabouts of Detective Captain Frank Longpre or Carol Marlowe is advised to contact the police department.

The suspect, O. P. Jones, has corroborated eyewitness reports that the victim was Frank Longpre, stating, "Yeah, I shot him. He put me away and I been waiting a long time to get even. Well, I showed him. He's dead, take my word for it."

In a surprising revelation, Jones also confessed to the abduction and murder of Mrs. Frank Longpre, a case that had gone unsolved since May of 1980 when Eileen Longpre disappeared from her home in Metaire. The details of this grisly crime will be printed at a later time.

Jones was arrested at the scene and made a full confession. He was shot and killed by police a short time later when he attempted to escape.

New Orleans, March 5, 1992:
CARNIVAL PRANKSTERS SUSPECTED OF BODY SNATCHING

The county coroner's office reported earlier today that the remains of an unidentified body are missing from the morgue. According to a spokesman for the coroner's office, the corpse, discovered in December of last year, was awaiting positive identification after being pulled from a bayou by a fisherman.

"It was a right strange case," the coroner's spokesman stated. "This wasn't your normal floater. This was the mummified corpse of a woman, and from what we could tell, it'd been in the swamp a long time. Years."

Asked if there were any leads as to what happened to the corpse, the spokesman said, "We figure it was probably just a Carnival prank. You know the crazy things that go on this time of year. Odd, though, how that mummy just vanished into thin air."

New Orleans, April 30, 1841:
Monsieur and Madame Victoine Navar of Elysian Fields and Golden Oaks plantations are pleased to announce the arrival of a daughter, Jane Carol, on the twenty-second of March. Mademoiselle Janie is welcomed, too, by her brother, Pierre. The Navars will receive family and friends at a reception at Golden Oaks on Sunday afternoon next between the hours of one and five.

THE BEST IN CONTEMPORARY SUSPENSE

WHERE'S MOMMY NOW? (366, $4.50)
by Rochelle Majer Krich

Kate Bauers couldn't be a Superwoman any more. Her job, her demanding husband, and her two children were too much to manage on her own. Kate did what she swore she'd never do: let a stranger into her home to care for her children. *Enter Janine.*

Suddenly Kate's world began to fall apart. Her energy and health were slipping away, and the pills her husband gave her and the cocoa Janine gave her made her feel worse. Kate was so sleepy she couldn't concentrate on the little things—like a missing photo, a pair of broken glasses, a nightgown that smelled of a perfume she never wore. Nobody could blame Janine. Everyone loved her. Who could suspect a loving, generous, jewel of a mother's helper?

COME NIGHTFALL (340, $3.95)
by Gary Amo

Kathryn liked her life as a successful prosecuting attorney. She was a perfect professional and never got personally involved with her cases. Until now. As she viewed the bloody devastation at a rape victim's home, Kathryn swore to the victim to put the rapist behind bars. But she faced an agonizing decision: insist her client testify or to allow her to forget the shattering nightmare.

Soon it was too late for decisions: one of the killers was out on bail, and he knew where Kathryn lived. . . .

FAMILY REUNION (375, $3.95)
by Nicholas Sarazen

Investigative reporter Stephanie Kenyon loved her job, her apartment, her career. Then she met a homeless drifter with a story to tell. Suddenly, Stephanie knew more than she should, but she was determined to get this story on the front page. She ignored her editor's misgivings, her lover's concerns, even her own sense of danger, and began to piece together a hideous crime that had been committed twenty years ago.

Then the chilling phone calls began. And the threatening letters were delivered. And the box of red roses . . . dyed black. Stephanie began to fear that she would not live to see her story in print.

BLOCKBUSTER FICTION FROM PINNACLE BOOKS!

THE FINAL VOYAGE OF THE S.S.N. SKATE   (17-157, $3.95)
by Stephen Cassell
The "leper" of the U.S. Pacific Fleet, SSN 578 nuclear attack sub
SKATE, has one final mission to perform—an impossible act of
piracy that will pit the underwater deathtrap and its inexperienced
crew against the combined might of the Soviet Navy's finest!

QUEENS GATE RECKONING   (17-164, $3.95)
by Lewis Purdue
Only a wounded CIA operative and a defecting Soviet ballerina
stand in the way of a vast consortium of treason that speeds toward the hour of mankind's ultimate reckoning! From the best-
selling author of THE LINZ TESTAMENT.

FAREWELL TO RUSSIA   (17-165, $4.50)
by Richard Hugo
A KGB agent must race against time to infiltrate the confines of
U.S. nuclear technology after a terrifying accident threatens to
unleash unmitigated devastation!

THE NICODEMUS CODE   (17-133, $3.95)
by Graham N. Smith and Donna Smith
A two-thousand-year-old parchment has been unearthed, un-
leashing a terrifying conspiracy unlike any the world has previ-
ously known, one that threatens the life of the Pope himself, and
the ultimate destruction of Christianity!

*Available wherever paperbacks are sold, or order direct from the
Publisher. Send cover price plus 50¢ per copy for mailing and
handling to Pinnacle Books, Dept.17-692, 475 Park Avenue
South, New York, N.Y. 10016. Residents of New York, New Jer-
sey and Pennsylvania must include sales tax. DO NOT SEND
CASH.*